Charybdis -444 I

Why that particular gate had worked when countless others had refused to cooperate countless times was beyond him. Some kind of reverse glitch maybe, but he wasn't going to question his luck. When he emerged from the gate he indulged in a brief, ecstatic moment of believing he'd finally made it home.

Home.

Just when had he started thinking of Atlantis as home?

Since first setting foot in it, quite possibly. It had felt right in a way nothing and nowhere else had in a long time. Each expedition member had been allowed to bring one personal item. He'd brought a second-hand copy of Tolstoy's *War And Peace*, which probably said all there was to say about his emotional ties to Earth.

Atlantis had been a new start and a family.

John figured he should have known better than to care. He'd been quite content in that bubble where fate could only be decided by the flip of a unit coin, because he refused to care. His bad for allowing the bubble to pop. Payback was a bitch.

The Atlantis he'd known was gone. In time-honored human tradition they'd got too curious, too cocky, too greedy. The upshot had been wholesale destruction. Not just of Atlantis, and he'd never understood why he had survived. Perhaps it was punishment. He could have stopped it. Rodney McKay, of all people, had urged caution.

STARGATE ATLANTIS™

MIRROR, MIRROR

SABINE C. BAUER

FANDEMONIUM BOOKS

An original publication of Fandemonium Ltd, produced under license from MGM Consumer Products.

Fandemonium Books
PO Box 795A
Surbiton
Surrey KT5 8YB
United Kingdom
Visit our website: www.stargatenovels.com

S T A R G A T E
A T L A N T I S ™

METRO-GOLDWYN-MAYER Presents
STARGATE ATLANTIS™
JOE FLANIGAN TORRI HIGGINSON RACHEL LUTTRELL JASON MOMOA
with PAUL McGILLION as Dr. Carson Beckett and DAVID HEWLETT as Dr. McKay
Executive Producers BRAD WRIGHT & ROBERT C. COOPER
Created by BRAD WRIGHT & ROBERT C. COOPER

ISBN: 978-1-905586-12-7
Printed in the United States of America

To Mom and Dad — because they always said I shoul[d]

CHAPTER ONE

Charybdis +32

Head cocked, the witch sniffed at the pot propped over a hissing, smoky fire. It smelled almost ready, so much so that she felt her stomach rumble. She reached out and groped around the hearth, warily keeping track of what she touched. Yesterday she'd badly burned her hand, which meant that she was getting careless. Carelessness didn't lie in her nature, never had, and she'd do well not to let it encroach now, not if she wanted to retain her independence—or at least that pale mockery she chose to call *independence*. Truth was, she'd starve if it weren't for the alms the villagers brought her; some out of gratitude or in exchange for a potion or ointment, most because they feared her and gladly parted with whatever food they could spare as long as it helped keep her at a comforting distance from the village.

An unthinkable number of years back, she would have sustained herself by hunting, fishing, gathering roots and berries, none of which was possible when you'd lost your sight. She'd schooled herself not to regret it. When all was said and done, it was a fitting punishment for her blindness so long ago. If she had allowed herself to see the danger, then perhaps—

If.

Her old friend, Halling, once had told her that *If* was the sound of bitterness settling in the soul. He'd been right, about this and a great many other things. What had happened, happened, and it had caused great grief. But she still had much to be grateful for. She had survived after all, and out there, in the village and elsewhere, a new generation of children was growing up. A generation who knew the hardships of living the life of the hunted only from their parents' and grandparents' tales. Besides, she still clung to that fading hope—perhaps it was merely a guilt-ridden dream—that she might yet redeem herself by helping to adjust the outcome. It would have to be soon, though. Very soon, for she was growing tired and careless with age, and the day was approaching when she would be beyond helping anyone.

Having continued their slow search, her fingers brushed against something wooden. "There you are." She picked up the spoon. "Always trying to hide from me, aren't you?"

About to stir the pot, she suddenly stiffened, remaining perfectly still. A warrior's instincts never withered, even when her body did. But by some grace her hearing had remained as acute as that of a much younger woman, though it could have been destroyed as easily as her sight.

There it was again, almost hidden under the burble of the small stream that ran through the cave and provided her with fresh water. The soft clatter of a pebble kicked loose and hitting rock. She was about to have a visitor. It meant she would have to be polite and share the soup. Too bad, but custom demanded it. Sitting back on her haunches and ignoring the pain of ragged joints, she continued to listen.

A few moments later, a soft voice called from the entrance of the cave. "Good day, Mother! Is it permitted?"

Even if she hadn't recognized the step, made heavy by pregnancy, the address would have given away her visitor's identity. Nobody else called her *Mother*. It was either *Wise Woman* or *Witch*, depending on whether the speaker felt the desire to be courteous or to whisper his fear behind a raised hand. Prompted by an innate sense of irony, she had long fallen into the habit of referring to herself as the latter. Nobody, herself included, ever used her name anymore. In fact, it had been so long and in such different circumstances, she had almost forgotten the sound of it.

"Come," she replied. "I didn't expect you, Pirna, and"—there was somebody else there, soft steps, buoyant and barely audible—"Halling the Younger."

The boy drew in a sharp hiss of breath.

"Don't be a fool, Halling," admonished his mother. "She can tell who you are by the sound of your footsteps."

"You shouldn't give away my secrets." The old woman chuckled. "I thought I'd frightened him away for good two days ago."

"You were here?" Pirna asked the boy, surprise and anger mixing in her voice.

"Yes." He sounded miserable, a puppy cowering in the knowledge that he'd done wrong. Well, he might have intended to do wrong, but in the end he'd shown the kind of spirit that would have made his grandfather proud.

"Leave him be, Pirna. He took my side against his no-good friends who would have pelted me with stones for a dare." Suddenly wishing she could see the boy, she turned her head in the direction where she knew him to be standing. "Jinto, your father, was just as much trouble at your age. I could tell you stories that—"

"Don't tell him, Mother!" Pirna threw in quickly. "Please. He doesn't need to be encouraged."

"As you wish. I barely remember anyhow," she said. Careless again! Telling the story of how Jinto had run away one night and inadvertently set free an ancient evil would have meant dredging up memories she'd be foolish to revisit. She reached out. "Come, help me up, have some soup with me, and tell me what brings you here. Do you want some herbs to speed the babe on its way?"

"It's a thought, Mother, but it isn't why I came." Pirna's rough, warm hand closed around hers and pulled her to her feet. "And we won't take what little food you have, though I give you thanks. Let's just sit at the table and talk."

Now that she'd been told that this wasn't a social visit or a request for herbs, she could almost smell the acrid anxiety that edged Pirna's voice and tautened her body. This wouldn't be welcome news. Pirna didn't belong to the kind of people who grew nervous over every little thing. Silently cursing the pain in her joints, the witch groped her way onto a stool.

"You should have some soup," she remarked in an attempt to ease Pirna into the conversation. "It's tuttleroot, Charin's recipe. Do you remember Charin, or had she passed on before you came here?"

Uncharacteristically, Pirna ignored her prattle. "It's starting again, Mother," she said tersely. "Halling and I saw it on the beach. It's starting again!"

"*What* is starting again?"

"The Cataclysm! We saw fire falling from the sky!"

Pirna sounded shrill, and the old woman couldn't blame her. For a few moments she battled a surge of dread fierce enough to make her want to moan. At last, common sense prevailed over instinct. The Cataclysm could not repeat itself. She alone among the villagers knew its cause, and the thing that had ripped planets from their course and fomented untold death no longer existed. Its own power had devoured it. The plasmatic burst of light released by its destruction had been the last sight she'd ever seen.

Brightness vaporizes her retinas, and a tiny rational part of her mind snarls that there is no pain now because every last nerve in her body is too stunned to feel it. But the agony will come. It will come, she knows it and is incapable of fearing it. All capacity for fear is funneled into the fracturing of awareness, again and again and again, her very being pulled from itself, bone and muscle split within seconds, each of which lasts eons or more, the fabric of time itself both stretched and scrunched like a fistful of dead leaves in the hand of a giant. At the moment of utmost entropy, when all her presents are irrevocably torn, she has a nightmarish vision of all her futures, and out of all of them only one, only a single one, offers a faint, mocking hope of undoing what has been done.

"Mother?"

The stool jolted forward, creaking over rock, as she started from the memory. She sucked in a deep breath. The air smelled of stale moisture, fungi growing on the walls of the cave, spices and herbs, and the fresh salt Pirna and the boy had brought in with them on their clothing. She clung to that mixture of scents, examined each aroma, and let it anchor her in the here and now again.

"Forgive me, child. I was listening, but you know how old people are; they drift away with their thoughts."

A hand folded over hers, pressing too hard. "You looked terrified," whispered Pirna.

As well she might have, but the girl and her son didn't need to know why. They didn't need to know about any of this. "I did?" she asked lightly. "It probably was a bout of indigestion. That's another thing about growing old, mark my words, girl! You can't eat tuttleroot soup like you used to. Are you sure you won't try any?"

"Don't treat me like a child, Mother! I can see that you're hiding the truth." Ah, she was a smart one, that Pirna. "You think the Cataclysm is coming again and you don't wish to scare us."

"No, I do not think so. And that *is* the truth." A part of it at least, the part that would most concern the villagers.

"But what does the falling fire mean then?"

"Nothing. You have seen shooting stars?"

"I have!" the boy cried, excitement bubbling in his voice. He sounded younger than she'd ever been, and this was the one great good to come out of the terror.

"Signs from the Ancestors?" his mother added.

"If that is what you wish to believe," replied the witch. "They are small pieces of rock from out there among the stars. They fall to the surface, and as they do so, the air sets them alight."

"The air?" Halling's excitement had given way to profound doubt. "But air doesn't burn!"

She smiled. "Rub your palms together. Fast." The dry, swishing sound told her that the boy was doing as instructed. "Do you feel the warmth?"

"Yes." The sound stopped. "But it doesn't set my hands alight. I don't think I could rub hard enough."

"You can't. But the air can. Hard enough to burn rock."

"You learned this in the city of the Ancients?" Pirna asked, her tone soft with awe.

"Yes." It was a lie. Her people had traveled the stars since time immemorial, and so had Pirna's, but nothing could be gained by making her or the boy long for possibilities lost. What lay out there, beyond the blue of the sky, was inaccessible now and had become the stuff of fireside tales, remembered first-hand by few and soon to be believed only by children.

"But shooting stars don't look like what mother and I saw today," the boy said. "And it wasn't nighttime!"

"Ah, but the larger these pieces of rock are, the more brightly they burn. Some of them are large enough to be seen by day."

"But—"

"That will be enough, Halling!" Pirna cut him off. "The Wise Woman has given you your answer. Do you think you're smarter than she?"

Wise Woman! If there ever was an appellation she didn't deserve! If she were wise, none of them would be here. The boy probably *was* smarter than she.

"Let him be, Pirna," she intervened. "He can't help himself. His grandfather was in the habit of doubting. Besides, it can never be wrong to question things. How else would we learn? What were you going to say, young Halling?"

"The falling piece of rock we saw?" mumbled the boy. "It looked as if it didn't want to fall, that's all."

Deep within her uncurled a tendril of hope, tremulous and reluctant. She was loath to let it gain strength, because she dreaded the misery of having to quash it. Every instinct she possessed screamed not to ask, never to ask, simply to forget. Yet not asking would be cowardly, and she'd never been that. A blind fool, yes, but not a coward. And it was possible, wasn't it? After all, neither Pirna nor the boy had ever seen a spacecraft reenter the atmosphere.

As calmly as she knew how, she said, "Do you recall where the piece of rock went?"

"In the end it seemed to give up. It dropped into the sea. If you look from here, uh"—he faltered, realizing that the witch wouldn't be able to look—"it's past the Eastern Shallows, but a long, long way past them."

The tendril of hope shriveled and died, and this time it barely hurt at all anymore. Perhaps because she'd grown too tired to care; perhaps because the idea of a jumper after all these years had been too fantastical from the start. In truth, it could have been anything, a rock or a simple mistake on the boy's part.

"Well, it won't come back from there, I should think." She forced herself to smile. "And you two should get back to the village before darkness falls. Pirna, send the boy to fetch me when your time comes."

"I will, Mother. Thank you."

CHAPTER TWO

Charybdis -4441

"Liar! God damn you! Liar!"

The shrieks reverberated from the ceiling, and the crystal Elizabeth had been trying to jam back into place sailed across the room, struck a wall and burst into a myriad shards. The colorful little hailstorm looked pretty. Cheery. Cheery was good. She reached into the open maintenance hatch, pulled out a second crystal, threw it, shuddering when it sprayed from the wall in tiny fragments.

"Liar!" she screamed again, furiously wiping her face. The sobs gradually, madly, turned to hiccupping laughter.

Her hand found a third crystal, and she threw that, too, and the next and the one after that, until the compartment was empty. Silence fell, thick and oppressive, making her gasp for breath. Silence, that's what was wrong with this place. Destroy the silence, and...

And what?

And nothing.

How long had it been? Weeks? Months? Years? She'd lost track. If she activated the mainframe—always supposing she managed to do the impossible—there'd probably be a calendar and clock somewhere, but the glutinous pace of seconds turning to minutes turning to hours was as much of an abomination as the silence. Perhaps more so, because it was proof, staring her in the face and laughing.

"Liar, liar, pants on fire," she sang tonelessly, kept singing, kept the silence at bay with it.

The empty hatch yawned at her as if it wanted to suck her in. She didn't like it. Didn't like this room, not anymore. She pushed herself up along the wall, listing like a wino on a bender. And she'd better stick to that wall, too. She was barefoot, and the floor was carpeted with glittering shards of glass or crystal.

What had happened here?

Who'd—

Her toes struck a hatch cover. It fell over, hammering noise through the room. Had she taken it off? A gaping hole in the wall, emptiness behind. Nothing left. A soft, keening sound settled around her, until she realized she herself was making it and stopped. Looking back at the inactive chamber across the room, she gave a small, tired shrug. The glass door stood open, promising sleep and oblivion, but, like every cad she'd ever known, it would fail to keep its promise. Certainly now that the crystals had been destroyed.

Not that it mattered one way or the other. The technology was so far beyond her, she'd never had a glimmer of a chance of fixing whatever had gone wrong. She'd tried, doggedly, during the first endless weeks. She'd sat on the floor, staring at what looked like eclectic *objets d'art*, trying to see a similarity to some type of circuitry she might be familiar with and unable to find so much as a trace of damage. She'd swapped crystals randomly, each time hurrying back to the chamber, getting inside, closing the door, waiting. It'd never worked. And at some point—she'd forgotten when exactly—she'd simply given up. Given in. Whatever.

Janus had told her it was safe.

Had he ever even considered this contingency?

"Who cares?" she murmured.

Janus had died more than five thousand years ago. He must have. Somehow she doubted that he'd made the cut for Ascension—he'd been far too much of a loose cannon. Unless he'd simply been the two-faced bastard his name implied, a two-faced bastard to whom the fact that he'd stolen her life was worth a shrug at most. She preferred that. It left room for anger, and anger was the easiest of emotions, one you could keep at boiling point all by yourself. It also was an antidote to the poisonous despair she tumbled into each time she was crazy or desperate enough to contemplate her situation.

As far as she could determine, the stasis system had malfunctioned late in the second cycle. The failsafe had revived her and spewed her out into a nightmare. At first she hadn't known that anything was wrong. Janus had programmed the system to wake her periodically—once every three thousand years—to allow her to rotate the Zero Point Modules that powered the city. She'd done just that, returned to the stasis room, stepped into the chamber, closed the door, waiting to drift off to sleep another three thousand years. Except, it hadn't happened.

Then, slowly, brutally, realization had crept in. She remembered the terror. She was reminded of it first thing in the morning, last thing at night, wherever she went or stood. She was alone in a deserted city beneath the ocean, alone beyond the scope of human comprehension, galaxies and millennia removed from anyone and anything she'd ever known.

Oh, she'd tried to put a positive spin on things at first. There are no problems, just challenges, right? She'd fix it. She'd make it right, somehow. After all, she was Dr. Elizabeth Weir, the President's favorite troubleshooter: Have plan, will negotiate. Have needs, will find food. And she had. She'd found storage rooms with imperishable rations that tasted like cardboard but kept her going. She'd clung to that perverse triumph, not understanding that it was a Pyrrhic victory. Not until she'd finally been forced to admit that her years with the State Department hadn't equipped her to repair advanced alien technology.

Then she'd conceived some foolhardy notion about exploring the city. After all, that was what had brought her here in the first place, wasn't it? She'd drifted around, climbed to the tops of Atlantis's spires, poked into nooks and crannies. She'd discovered rooms of all descriptions and countless strange devices—none of which she could get to work, because she possessed neither the ATA gene that allowed a select few humans to operate Ancient technology, nor the skill and electronic gear needed to access Atlantis's mainframe. In other words, it'd been like being eight years old and gawking through the window of the candy store without a nickel to your name. What it boiled down to was that she would grow old here, with nothing to do and no-one to talk to.

Perhaps it had been this very prospect that had pushed her over the edge. Her mind was slipping, folding in on itself, no longer able to suffer the lack of human contact and stimuli. She knew enough psychology to have expected it, and mostly she welcomed it. There were times when she'd suddenly come to in some remote part of the city, unable to say how she'd gotten there or what she'd been doing. It meant she'd lost an hour or five—more recently it was days—and every hour lost was a precious sixty minutes she didn't have to live in this place.

Like now.

Well, it was one source of interest, she supposed. You never knew where you'd find yourself next. Perhaps she should start a betting pool.

The idea struck her as uproarious, and she slid halfway down the wall again, shaking with hysterics. Then the laughter broke off, as suddenly as it had come. She straightened up, gingerly started moving toward the door, skirting the worst of the shards. She'd have to act now, while she was still capable of doing it. The only thing that had stopped her so far was the hope of somehow still achieving what she'd meant to achieve. Save lives.

Hope springs eternal.

Not if you messed with time itself, apparently. There was no changing the outcome: some four and a half thousand years from now another version of herself would lead the expedition to Atlantis, the city's shields would fail, and everybody would die, including her. She'd just die a little later than the others.

Out in the hallway, lights activated as she went and shut down again behind her. For a while—who knew how long ago now?—she'd spent days wandering up and down the corridors, making lights come on and off, pretending she was arriving home from work and Simon had heard her car and was switching on the lights in the driveway for her. And she'd go inside, and they'd have dinner and a glass of wine by the fireplace, and they'd talk... That game, too, had palled.

The hallway took her to the control center. The enormous room with its sweeping gallery and staircase seemed to belong to a dead person, every item in it shrouded in white dustsheets, as if waiting for a realtor to drop in and sell the place on behalf of the heirs. Every item, that was, except the console that controlled the Stargate. She'd uncovered that one, left it open, because occasionally she needed a glimpse of salvation. Now she hesitantly stepped in front of the console, one finger tracing the edge of a dialing pad.

She'd thought about it, of course. God only knew how often she'd thought about it. Dial Earth, go back… and end up in the middle of Egypt during the Old Kingdom, where people had yet to rise against a Goa'uld called Ra. Sometimes she fantasized about how she really had gone back and had, in fact, been the driving force behind the revolt. Another, less glorious, scenario was the one where she got taken as host and revealed the coordinates for Atlantis to the Goa'uld. Which probably would spell the end of mankind and countless other races across any number of galaxies.

The only real option she had was to randomly dial an address in the Pegasus galaxy. Suicide by Stargate. She didn't fool herself into believing that there was any other likely outcome. The Wraith had won, after all.

End it right here.

The thought of it was tempting beyond words.

Her fingers continued to caress the pads. It'd be so easy, so—

A pad lit up, then a second and a third.

"My God…"

Elizabeth knew she hadn't activated anything. The gate wasn't dialing; it was receiving an incoming wormhole. She took a slow step back from the console, unsure of what to do. Run and hide in the city? But what if it wasn't the Wraith? What if it was someone… human? Her craving for companionship became so strong it left her shaking, sobbing with tears.

No, she couldn't run. She'd wait and see, and never mind the consequences.

The sequence completed, the last chevron locked—the seventh, so the wormhole was coming from a gate within the Pegasus galaxy—and the event horizon burst into life, bathed the room in shimmering blue light and retracted.

"It's Jumper One." Precise, British tones, and Peter Grodin sat at the console, smiling up at her. "About time, too. They were supposed to be back an hour ago."

She spun away, blood thudding in her ears. Peter was dead. He had drowned four and half thousand years from now, like all the others.

"Elizabeth… Grodin was aboard the satellite," said Dr. McKay's grief-stricken, disembodied voice.

Rodney couldn't have spoken. He lay sprawled in front of the gate, unconscious or dead, and morphed into a tall, uniformed man she'd never seen before, flung backward into the gate by a gunshot.

"Will someone tell me what's going on?" she yelled, knowing even then that she had to be hallucinating.

Another, vaguely familiar voice burst into the control center. "Ma'am, Jumper One is lodged in the Stargate. Teyla, Doctor McKay and myself are in the rear compartment with the major. He's in bad shape."

"Lieutenant Ford?" she whispered. "Lieutenant?"

He stood right in front of her, terrifyingly alien, his left eye suffused with blackness. Past him she could see a small ship emerge from the event horizon. It was ungainly, of the same type as the ships stored in the hangar upstairs.

Abruptly the Stargate shut down.

And the silence was back.

Of course.

She was alone.

Gasping for breath, she absently noted that the delusion had been so intense she'd responded physically. Her eyes, bleared by the glare of an imaginary event horizon, squinted in the gloom now. When her vision returned, the ship was still there, slowly rising toward the ceiling and an opening into the hangar. It was piloted by a dead man yet unborn.

CHAPTER THREE

Charybdis +32

"Now!"

Pirna, sweating and bawling and thrashing for the past eighteen hours, focused every fiber of her body and bore down.

"Good girl," the witch praised her. "Again!"

"No!" yelled the midwife. "You will be killing her and the babe!"

Murmurs of consent rose from the other women gathered in the tent. The witch ignored them. She'd fully intended to remain in the background and let the village women do as they'd always done, provided all went well. It hadn't. Several hours into the labor she'd stepped in, unwelcome as her help was to everyone but Pirna. Deft fingers, trained by decades of substituting for an old woman's sight, had felt the breech and pushed and palpated until the babe was turned at last.

"Don't listen to them," she whispered soothingly. "Nobody will be killed, least of all you and your babe. Do it!"

Letting out a deafening scream, Pirna obeyed. Moments later shouting and outraged squeals erupted from the women, suggesting that a man had entered the tent. Most likely Jinto, half mad with worry. The old woman refused to let the breach of tradition distract her. To her mind, a father had every right to witness the birth of his offspring. And he'd arrived just in time. A damp, kicking little life was slipping between her hands and began to squall lustily.

Relieved to the core of her soul, she gave a rusty chuckle. "There! Didn't I tell you, Pirna?"

Then someone manhandled her out of the way. No matter. Let the midwife take over. From here on out the woman could do no harm.

"It is a girl!" hollered Jinto's deep voice. "Pirna, do you hear? It is a girl!"

"I'm not deaf, husband," Pirna replied hoarsely. "And I'm sure the hunters in the mountains heard you, too."

Laughter flooded the tent, warm and easy and good-natured. It drowned out even the little girl's protests at a world so different from what she'd known these past nine moons and more and dispelled the last remnants of the tension that had built among folk expecting the worst. A pair of hands gently grasped the old woman's arm and guided her to sit on a stool. She was grateful for the kindness, realizing for the first time that she must have been up for a day and a night. Slowly, commotion melted into quiet a contentment that tolerated even Jinto's unheard-of presence in the birthing tent.

Before long she heard hushed conversations, some appraising the merits of the child, agreeing that the little one looked strong and healthy and possessed the requisite number of fingers and toes; others reminiscing about how Sirvin's labor had kept the village awake for a full two days when she'd had her twins, or how young Lila, friendly enough but not very bright, had never even known she was with child until the babe had arrived, quite unceremoniously, halfway down to the beach. The surprised mother, who until that moment had been convinced she was suffering from indigestion, had carried her son home in a clam basket.

Underneath the babble, the old woman could make out the soft, greedy gulps of the little girl who had been given to her mother to suckle. All was as it should be. She rolled her head a little, loosening stiff muscles in her neck, and wondered if and when somebody would think to offer her food. They would, eventually, because they expected it would keep the witch favorably inclined. They were right, at least on this occasion. By her count, she hadn't eaten since noontime the day before, and she felt ravenous.

"What will you call her?" one of the women asked.

"We haven't thought on it yet," replied Jinto. "Pirna was sure it would be another boy, so we've got a name for him, but we can't very well call a girl Tallan."

"Speak for yourself," Pirna said over the titters that rose. "I have a name for her, and a very good one. We shall call her Teyla. Provided you give your consent, Mother."

The tent fell utterly silent. Though unable to see, the old woman could feel the stares prickling on her skin. She was startled into speechlessness, a rare thing for her, as nothing much surprised her anymore, but this request had been entirely unforeseen. An honor, to be sure, and what little vanity she had left urged her to give permission. Still…

"I—" she began but never got to finish.

From outside the tent came a yell. "Jinto! Jinto, you are needed!"

The voice belonged to Wex, Jinto's friend from childhood, and it was accompanied by running footsteps. Wex and his men had been out fishing, so he couldn't possibly realize that Jinto had cause to be preoccupied. A moment later and among the resigned giggles of the women, Wex burst into the tent.

"Jinto! Why don't you—" He stopped abruptly. "Oh…"

The witch fancied she could hear him blush.

"So the lad has decided to arrive?" He sounded gruff with embarrassment.

"*He* hasn't," Jinto pointed out. "*She* has. What is it? Can it wait?"

"It can, until I have greeted your daughter."

Upon which Wex broke into such cooing, it would have made him a laughing stock had anyone dared to poke fun at him. Once a burly boy, he'd grown into a bear of a man, much respected and trusted advisor to Jinto who, after his father's passing, had stepped in as leader of his people—although, as he never ceased to remind the old woman, he didn't feel it was his place. She disregarded his protests with the same regularity. Jinto was a caring and capable leader, which was all that mattered.

Now, it seemed, curiosity and concern had gotten the better of him. He knew well enough that his friend didn't get excited over nothing. "So, what is it?" Jinto asked again.

Clearly, Wex didn't consider the matter suitable for all ears. He lowered his voice to a whisper, and much as the old woman strained, she couldn't make out a word.

"You have done well," Jinto said at last and paused briefly. Then, "Will you go with Wex? There is someone in need of your skills."

Not until a strong hand clasped her shoulder, did the witch understand that Jinto was talking to her. In truth, she would have preferred sleep to tending the wounded or sick, but she knew that he wouldn't ask lightly, especially after what she'd done for Pirna and the babe. "Very well. Take my hand, Wex."

"I have been waiting to hear you say that all my life." He gently helped her to her feet.

"Fool!" she groused, biting back a smile. "You can carry my basket for that."

He led her from the birthing tent and, as soon as they were out of earshot, began to explain. "My men discovered him washed up on the beach, and I thought it best if nobody else found out for now. You know how edgy folk are around strangers since the famine. They'll say we have taken in enough refugees and leave him to die."

"At the beach?" she asked. "Where did you bring him?"

"My tent," replied Wex. "It is past the edge of the village and nobody has much cause to come that way. Which probably is for the best."

"I should think so."

For the rest of the way he kept quiet, leaving her to her thoughts, which wasn't an altogether good thing. She had to force herself not to get excited, though excitement would offset her exhaustion at least. Still, it might mean nothing, most likely did. There'd been other occurrences. Rare, it was true, but it lay in the nature of the sea to bring flotsam, including a body now and again, some poor soul washed overboard from another village's boat. In all the years only one of those foundlings had survived to live out his days wild-eyed and crazed by what he'd suffered. For a brief while she'd thought he might be the one, but she wouldn't go down that road again. And yet, on no other occasion had there been flaming things tumbling from the sky only days before…

"We are here," Wex said abruptly, startling her.

She heard a tent flap being thrown back and rushed foot-steps scurrying toward, around, and past her. One of Wex's men ordered to watch the foundling and now dismissed, either by Wex's silent order or by his own misgivings at the sight of the witch. A tug at her arm, and she followed it into the tent. The heat of a roaring fire leaped at her and wrapped her in a blanket of smells; the faint mustiness that seemed inherent to a bachelor's tent, remnants of stew she would no longer feed to a pig, much less to a person, the pungent scent of salt and seaweed—a blessing, given the other aromas—and the stench of a burning that had nothing to do with the fire in the tent. If she hadn't injured her hand the other day, she might not have recognized it so readily.

"He has burn wounds?" She didn't bother to conceal her surprise. Those were hard to come by on a fishing boat.

Wex let out a startled hiss of breath. "By the Ancestors! I hope you aren't wondering *why* people walk in fear of you," he growled. "His hands are burned. How could you possibly have known that?"

"I may be unable to see, but my nose works just fine."

His only reply was another growl. It hung, finely balanced, in the void between amusement and doubt. Then he tugged her on, eased her to a seat at the edge of his cot.

"I have put your basket right by your feet. See what you can do for him," Wex muttered. "He is unconscious and barely alive, and there's nothing much else I can tell you, except that we found a sheet of metal nearby. It seems he was smart enough to use it as a float, but I couldn't say how long he has been in the water."

Too long, likely as not. She nodded absently, no longer listening to Wex. Now it was her fingers she listened to, carefully heeding everything they said. Some of it was obvious, like the fact that the men had either stripped the foundling or he'd lost his clothes in whatever accident had caused him to end up in the sea. Other things were far more subtle, such as the distinction between the blistering caused by sun and saltwater—mild, all things considered, for it was early in the year yet—and the deeper burns that must have been caused by some other agent.

Or the signs of starvation, which this one didn't show. True, he hadn't eaten in some time, and she could feel ribs, sharp and fragile, standing out from taut skin, but she also felt strong, well developed muscles, far from the hollowness that would have told her his body, in a doomed bid to stave off death, had begun to devour itself.

Even so, he was lucky to be alive. He was burning with fever, its heat rising from clammy skin. He had also broken two bones in his left leg, though she couldn't begin to imagine how he might have achieved that by falling from a fishing boat.

Then she realized what she was doing—gathering reasons to hope—and shrank back. This foolishness would have to be stopped and stopped now, and there was one sure way of bringing an end to it. Her hands reached up, found his face and started to explore—to look. Sunken cheeks under a rough beard. A high forehead, plastered with thick, damp hair, evenly arched eyebrows, straight nose, well-formed lips, now chapped and swollen from thirst. He was handsome, no doubt, and yes, much as she'd wanted to deny it, there was indeed a chance, but—curse her blindness!—she had too little to go on. She needed to know the color of his hair and eyes, needed to *see* him...

Her hands drifted from the foundling's face to his neck, chased a thready whisper of a pulse—too shallow and too fast, but that would improve once she got some water into him. And maybe a stimulant, to be—

The tip of her left index finger retraced its path. Low on the neck, just beneath the pulse point, it had noted a spot of unevenness where the skin had thickened. The old woman felt her heart begin to race, fast enough and hard enough to hurt within her chest.

It couldn't be. After all these years, after endless waiting, he couldn't simply come falling from the sky and be brought to her at death's door. Then again, it seemed just the thing the man she'd known would do. But surely Wex would have recognized him, wouldn't he?

"What is that?" she asked Wex, gently turning the foundling's head so the neck was exposed.

"It's a scar. The shape looks familiar. Could be—" He broke off to let out a low whistle. "It looks exactly like the bite of an iratus bug! But if it were that, he'd—"

"Be a dead man," she croaked, nowhere near as dismissively as she'd intended, but still capable of faint satisfaction at not having told an outright lie. A potent mix of elation and terror churned in her mind and soul—not unlike those heightened sensations she recalled from the moments just prior to battle—and it punished a body long since unused to such fierce emotion. For the first time in a life that had lasted too long, she fainted.

She came to steadied by the strong arm of Wex, who must have prevented her from falling off the side of the cot. "Can you hear me?" he barked, voice rasping with concern. "Teyla Emmagan! Talk to me!"

Why was everyone so intent on remembering her name today? Perhaps this was a sign, too.

"I'm fine," she murmured, hating how weak she sounded. *Teyla Emmagan*, indeed! Teyla had been a warrior.

"No, you are not fine!" Relief at hearing her speak made Wex's concern snap into anger. "I shouldn't have brought you here. You must have been up all night! I'll take you back to your cave now."

"No! I cannot leave. He will die."

"He'll just have to take his chances. I would rather have him die than you."

"No! I'm telling you!" She sensed that Wex was not going to yield, but perhaps that was an advantage, because it gave her an excuse. "Alright. Take me back to my cave. But tell your men to bring him, too, quickly and carefully. He will need constant care, and I don't want to have to do it in this reeking tent of yours."

The warmth was a good thing. And he was dry. Surprisingly, he also was still alive. John Sheppard decided to consider the ramifications of this astonishing development at a later date—preferably when his head hurt a little less—and fell asleep again.

The next time he woke, he noticed that it wasn't just his head that hurt. Clearly, survival had come at a price, and there were several things seriously wrong with him.

What the hell had happened?

Being able to remember stuff would help, but the only thing he could recall was feeling unreasonably cold and wet. That, and being carried. A bunch of guys, a very old woman, and... Wex? But there'd been no kids, he was sure of that. Only a bunch of guys and an old woman. A very old woman, in—

"You are awake again. Good."

He'd been right about the old woman at least. He recognized the voice, a gentle, oddly familiar lilt, brittle with age. It had been woven through some really strange nightmares, the only constant in a scarily unstable dreamscape.

A scrawny hand and arm threaded under his neck, raised his head.

"Ow," he said, trying to sound indignant in a polite sort of way. He didn't want to upset the natives just yet.

"Your head hurts because you are dehydrated. Drink this. All of it."

The rim of a cup touched his lips and triggered a vague recollection. He'd been made to ingest several gallons of Drinkthisallofit since arriving here—wherever *here* was. Of course, he could simply open his eyes and find out, but that carried a risk of aggravating the headache.

"Drink!" the old lady ordered again and jogged his head for emphasis.

Ow!

Drinkthisallofit was hot enough to allow only small sips and tasted healthily—in other words, revoltingly—herbal. He had no idea of its precise curative properties (if any) or if Dr. Beckett would approve of them, but refusal wasn't an option. Been there, done that, got yelled at. His eyeballs felt as if they were coated in ground glass, but he forced his lids open anyway. If he had to drink it, he at least wanted to know whether the stuff really was as Day-Glo green as it tasted.

John found himself squinting into some kind of outsize mug without handle—a gourd?—and felt a small stab of disappointment: the liquid was colorless. Strangely enough, his frivolous foray into the world of the living hadn't prompted any reaction from his nurse. He closed his eyes again, took another sip, swallowed, and pulled a face.

"God, this tastes foul," he whispered. If a wet towel could talk, it'd sound like him.

What the hell had happened?

He'd asked that before. Maybe he should try to get—

"I know that, Colonel Sheppard. Drink it anyway."

What he did instead was swallow the wrong way, flying into a coughing fit that wreaked havoc on his head. She'd gotten the rank mixed up, but she knew his name. How? To the best of his knowledge—which, admittedly, didn't amount to much—he hadn't been lucid enough for introductions.

Who was she?

The second time round, opening his eyes wasn't quite as agonizing. Or perhaps he was getting used to it. He blinked, trying to focus, and eventually the blurred shape hovering over him lost its fuzzy edges. And yes, she was old. Ancient—no pun intended. The fingers holding the mug were liver-spotted, thick-jointed and gnarled with arthritis. Snowy, sloppily braided hair tumbled over a bony shoulder, and the face was withered and scored with wrinkles. Her eyes were white, irises barely distinguishable from the sclera. He doubted that it was glaucoma or any age-related disease—if she'd been taking care of him on her own, she was far too deft to have lost her sight recently—but she definitely was blind. And if you looked past the age and the sightless eyes, there was something else... family resemblance? Though why Teyla had never mentioned it was beyond him.

"I think I know your... granddaughter?"

"I guess I must look that old to you." There was nothing amused in her laughter, just irony and a deep sadness, bordering on despair. "I have no granddaughter, Colonel. I *am* Teyla Emmagan, daughter of Tagan."

"I'm flattered about the promotion, but if you were Teyla, you'd know that I never made it past major," he said slowly, getting a hazy idea that it would be pointless. The woman—whoever she was—was easily old enough to suffer some degree of senile dementia.

"*Major* Sheppard?" Straightening up, she cocked her head as if to listen to an inner voice. "I suppose that *was* a possibility," she murmured to herself. "I don't know what I expected. Not to find him this young, for sure. It might even mean that I'm not the original either." Without warning, she burst into laughter again. "To think, all these years I have never even considered… It just goes to show how much we all want to be unique."

Oh yeah.

Nuts.

Of course there also was a better-than-average chance that he was too dazed to follow.

"What the hell happened?" There. He'd finally said it.

"I was hoping you could tell me, Major. All I know is that Wex's men found you on the beach. Although… Were you flying a jumper?"

The jumper.

That explained everything. For the first time in his short but compellingly checkered career, Major John Sheppard had gone in. Well and truly gone in, not just plopped down a tail rotor short of a helicopter. He'd bumped his head, and that *really* did explain everything.

"Maybe you should get Carson, Teyla. I'm feeling a little… weird."

"Dr. Beckett is not here," she said gently. "You are not delusional, Major. Try to remember what happened. It is important."

"Why?"

"Because, if you remember, you will believe what you are seeing. You will believe *me*."

John wasn't entirely sure he wanted to. He had yet to discover a part of his body that didn't hurt, he might be losing his mind, and he desperately wanted to go back to sleep and wake up a few hours later to find that this was one of those scary-weird dreams he'd been having.

"Were you flying a jumper?" she asked again.

Outside, a herd of small, fleecy clouds is racing past the view port, and just for the heck of it, and because he can, he flips the puddle jumper into inverted flight. Nothing wrong with jazzing up a routine coastal survey, is there? Admittedly, with the inertial dampeners being a notch or three beyond state-of-the-art, it's nowhere near as much of a kick as it should be, but it'll do.

"Oh yes, it'll do," *he whispers, grinning like a five-year-old.*

Flying isn't a job. It's a necessity. Something changes when he's flying. Maybe it's about being happy, but he doesn't care to analyze it. Too easy to analyze things to death. Never far behind the elation lurks the memory, mercifully distant now, of the run-up to his abortive court-martial. He's never admitted it out loud, but worse than anything was knowing that he'd lose flight status upon conviction. Sure, there was always crop-dusting, but it would have been a poor substitute for driving a Pave-Low through a war zone. And even that doesn't come close to driving a jumper. Most fun you can have with your clothes on.

He comes out of inverted flight and chases the little ship into a vertical climb, only easing up when he's about to leave the atmosphere and go orbital. Once, just once, he'd like to do that with McKay, just to see what—

The jolt is so violent, he is flung from the pilot's chair and against the navigation console. His first, dizzy thought is that this can't be happening—*inertial dampeners being a notch or three beyond state-of-the-art*—then he helplessly slides into a vortex of images, past, present, future, fanning into endless permutations of the same events.

He stands behind Rodney, fretting, promising himself never to become a flight instructor. Only one of him will not regret that thought later, all others have lost both McKay and Brendan Gaul to a marooned Wraith, and most never live to tell the tale.

He lies in the rear, that goddamn bug stuck to his neck, feeding. Dozens of him don't make it, because their teams can't bring themselves to kill him.

He sits in the pilot seat, more alone than he's ever been in his life, on collision course with a hive ship, with Elizabeth Weir and Radek Zelenka by his side, chased by countless darts, fire and death blossoming all around, again and again and—

He is Ikaros, flying too close to the sun and falling, wings *aflame, torn apart into a myriad selves, falling and burning and—*

The visions shrivel as suffocating heat triggers some internal alarm. It explodes into shrieks—*stall warning?*—and he puts a hand on the console to shove himself to his feet, flinches away, almost screaming, his palm blistered by hot metal. He struggles upright somehow, knows what he'll be seeing even before he looks out the view port: the jumper is in uncontrolled reentry, systems fried, shields failing, a ball of flame hurtling toward the surface. No flying skill in this galaxy or any other could stop the inevitable, and all that's left for him to do is stand and watch and try to ignore the fact that he can barely breathe anymore.

Falling toward a coastline now, a coastline that should be familiar and isn't, in some subtly distorted kind of way. It's been twisted out of shape like one of Dali's clocks by the same thing that's warping everything else around him. Reality has become a cakewalk, and so he latches on to the one immutable fact that leaps out at him. If his trajectory remains stable—and it will, because there's not enough wind-shear to affect the parameters of speed and mass and gravity—he'll come down right on top of a village that's popped up in a place where there's never been a village before. Athosian? Has to be, though it hardly matters. What matters is that there are people, men, women, children, all of them bodies to be.

"Not gonna happen," he croaks. "Not gonna happen."

The mind-ship interface no longer works, he knows that. If it did, the jumper would have responded to his simple desire not to be pulverized on impact. He stumbles into the pilot's seat, briefly flexes his hands. *It'll be a whole new way of becoming part of your ship,* he thinks grimly as his fingers close around the manual controls. The first few seconds are excruciating, then he feels nothing, because the nerves have been burned along with his skin.

Sluggishly, the jumper responds, and coastline and village drift starboard and out of sight. All that's ahead now is open water, and maybe, just maybe... A sudden image forms in his mind, summer camp for inner city kids, a lake in the forest, and

*he's twelve, barefoot at a pebbled shore, learning how to skip
stones. It's all about speed and angle. Shaped like a broken-off
breadstick, the ship has all the superior gliding capacity of a
tank, but at this point he has nothing to lose by trying. He extends
the drive pods, bartering reduced drag for stability, forces up the
nose of the jumper and flattens the path of descent.*

What's the stalling speed of a puddle jumper?

*Million dollar question, and he probably should have found
out before now. At a guess, twice as high as that of Earth's most
famous flying brick, the space shuttle. Abysmal, in other words.
He's right. The moment he's thinking it, the jumper starts shaking, giving him his answer, and he eases the stick forward to let
it pick up speed again.*

*Arms and shoulders cramping with tension, he plays the
game all the way down, fights barely responsive controls to balance air speed and angle of descent, and, at the last possible
moment, fuels what little power the engines have left into the
inertial dampeners to cushion himself from the impact.*

The last thing John remembered clearly was hitting the surface of the water and being tossed through the cabin like the
crash dummy in a road safety commercial advertising the benefit of seat belts. There'd been a crack, audible even over the
noise of the impact, when his lower leg snapped. After that,
things became alternately black, wet, and cold.

"Ow," he growled again.

"You have my thanks for saving the village and my people,"
the old lady said softly. "It was a very brave thing to do."

"You're welcome." Then it occurred to him that, despite
her promises, he'd got no closer to believing the woman really
was Teyla than he'd been five minutes ago. On the upside,
Drinkthisallofit had been taken out of his face. Good. It smelled
as vile as it tasted. "So, how does this—"

"Don't talk so much, Major." A hard old hand sought his
shoulder and gave it a brisk pat. The woman smiled. "I know
I provoked it, asking you to remember, but now let me do the
talking. You wish to hear how any of this proves that I am indeed
the Teyla you knew?"

"You could start by explaining why you're a few decades

older than me all of a sudden."

"Shh. I said *Don't talk so much*. From now on be quiet. You may nod," she added graciously. "These… visions… you experienced after the impact that knocked you off course?"

Obediently, John nodded.

"They were no visions. They were real." She must have felt him move in preparation for protest, and her hand pinned his shoulder to the cot. "Alternate realities, all colliding in a single, focal point in space-time. They were caused by entropy."

"Entropy," parroted John, unable to stop himself. It was too crazy to believe. *She* was crazy. On the other hand, he had felt it. The splintering of his being into uncounted selves.

"A rift in the fabric of space-time. It has been unraveling ever since, threads becoming tangled, tearing, crossing others they should never have touched."

"I know what entropy is… How? What caused it?"

"We caused it." A tear rolled down her withered cheek. "And you cannot begin to understand the destruction it brought."

"*We?*"

"Our team. The Atlantis expedition. I. At a time in the past that should have been your future."

His throat tightened. He couldn't be sure if her… if *Teyla*'s story was true, but one thing was beyond a shadow of a doubt: she believed what she was saying. Every word of it, and one word stood out—*destruction*.

"Teyla?" Reaching for the fingers that still clamped his shoulder, he realized for the first time that his hand was bandaged. "Tell me what happened."

She let out a shuddering breath, seemed to come to a decision. "I will do better. I will show you. This will not be easy for me. Nor for you. Brace yourself."

"For what?" The question was barely out when he knew, sensed her sliding into his mind with the same absolute poise that had always controlled her physical movement. Oh yes, this was Teyla alright. "I thought it only works with Wraith," he whispered. "Last time I looked I didn't have Wraith DNA…"

"But have I had many years to practice. Do not be afraid, Major Sheppard. Leastways not of me."

CHAPTER FOUR

Charybdis ±0

Suppressing a yawn, John stepped from one foot to the other. Sitting on the floor wasn't an option, was it? Nu-huh. Dust showed up real well on black BDUs. Given that Colonel Caldwell had picked up where Everett left off and made it his mission in life to find fault with everything Lieutenant Colonel Sheppard did or thought of doing, staying presentable would mean less grief and static all round. In other words, the lieutenant colonel would just continue to lean against the wall, propping up a P90, babysitting Drs. McKay and Zelenka in a part of town proven to be detrimental to one's health, and waiting for the fun part of the evening to start. Well, it had to happen sometime. He hoped.

"Elizabeth, there's something you need to see," Rodney's voice droned from somewhere inside a console at the center of the room. Though similar in some ways, the device seemed different from the terminals they'd discovered so far. Larger, more rough and ready, more quaint, in the same way a Commodore 64 would look quaint next to an i-Book. "No, next year will be fine!" snapped McKay. "That's why I'm calling you *now*!"

"If it belongs to archive system, there must be holographic interface," Radek Zelenka pointed out for the fifth time. When he was agitated he tended to lose track of his articles.

Or maybe it was exhaustion. The Czech scientist didn't seem to have gotten any sleep since they'd found this lab—if it was a lab—and his habitual unmade-bed-look had received an interesting makeover. John nursed a mental image of a cot where someone had died a slow death that involved a lot of thrashing. Typhoid, maybe. Or malaria… He embellished the picture by making it an epidemic that had struck down the entire family. They'd all died in the same bed.

"*Ahoj*! Are you deaf?" Zelenka hollered at the pair of legs that stuck out from under the console.

The legs gave a startled twitch, which was accompanied by a hollow clunk from inside the device, which was followed by silence. The legs looked limp.

Could be the fun part had just started... John frowned, fractionally worried. It was the silence that got him. Experience had taught him to expect wailing and gnashing of teeth. "Rodney?"

No reply. If possible, the legs looked even limper.

"Could be I was wrong..." John disengaged himself from the wall, grabbed the legs, and pulled.

McKay was surprisingly heavy. Which, come to think of it, would be natural for a guy who believed that seventeen meals a day constituted a healthy diet. Under the skeptical eye of Zelenka, John kept pulling, exposed a midriff—literally; the shirt had ridden up, and his life was now complete—a chest, a neck, and eventually a sullen and perfectly conscious face.

"I'm bleeding," announced McKay, holding up his right forefinger by ways of proof. The microscopic smear of blood on it must have come from the scratch on his forehead. "Severe head trauma, possibly intracranial hemorrhage. We all know what that means, don't we?"

"No," said Zelenka. "Tell us."

"You had to ask for it, didn't you?" John muttered darkly and let go of Rodney's ankles.

"No, but he'll tell us anyway, and he enjoys it more if he's asked."

McKay looked wounded. It cost him a valuable second, during which Elizabeth Weir entered the lab, Teyla and Ronon Dex in her wake, thus preventing a lecture on the consequences of endangering the greatest mind in the known universe.

"What happened?" she asked, staring at Rodney.

"I presume my pupils are fixed and dilated?" he said.

Okay, they were now crossing the pain threshold. John flicked on the flashlight mounted atop his P90 and shone the beam, interrogation-style, directly at his teammate's eyes. McKay yelped and slapped an arm across his face.

"Seem pretty reactive to me," John informed him and turned to the expedition leader. "Looks like this is some old-fashioned archive terminal, though the console doesn't work. Which explains McKay. Inasmuch as McKay can be explained."

From Ronon's end came a soft snort. By his standards, the Satedan looked positively cheerful. McKay's scowl in no way diminished his glee.

"*Old-fashioned*?" Weir raised an inquiring eyebrow. "As in *museum piece*?"

"If those among us who actually know what they're talking about could get a word in edgeways, it'd be much easier to grasp." Evidently Rodney had convinced himself that a brain aneurysm wasn't on the charts for the immediate future and scrambled to his feet. "It's *not* a museum piece. It's more like a... science project."

"A nuclear device?" Teyla asked. She did a great line in deceptively innocent.

"No! Just because I built one, doesn't mean... Never mind." McKay waved his hands as if to chase off a swarm of gnats and focused on Elizabeth as the person most likely to let him finish a thought. "You know about Tesla, right? Turn-of-the-century—the one before last—picturesque equipment, results we still can't reproduce."

"Such as alternating current," Zelenka suggested serenely.

"That's not what I'm talking about, and you know it. What I am trying to say, and I'd be grateful to be spared further inanities, is that this"—McKay stabbed a finger at the console—"was built from the Ancient equivalent of Radio Shack components. Which explains the somewhat crude look. The device itself, however, which by the way is *not* an archive terminal as my esteemed colleague seems determined to believe, is highly sophisticated. As a matter of fact, you could say it's a standalone computer."

"Mac or PC?" John blurted out.

"Cray, if they'd been able to make any headway on quantum computing. This device is at least as powerful as the Atlantis mainframe, and it's not connected to any other system."

"It's also dysfunctional," Zelenka reminded him.

"Was," said Rodney. "*Was*." Going by the look on his face he'd been building up to this ever since was dragged out from under the console. "It was simply a question of reconnecting the power supply and overriding the security features. So now—"

"You're saying it was password protected?" Elizabeth asked with immaculate timing and deflated McKay's *voilà* moment.

"Yes," sighed Rodney. "Are you sure you want me to continue?"

The question dropped into a trough of silence, and John found himself holding his breath. If anyone decided to reply, this could take a very, *very* long time.

"Thank you," McKay said at last and moved in front of the console. "As I was saying, I was able to override the security features, so now—"

"Rodney?" Elizabeth again.

Across the room, Teyla bit back a smile. Ronon was somewhat less subtle.

McKay exploded. "Do you think this is funny? I've spent two days trying to—"

"No, I don't think it's funny." As so often, Weir's calm undercut his outrage. "I'm just not sure if it's wise to activate the computer. You said power had been disconnected. In my admittedly limited experience things don't unplug themselves, so there may be a reason why someone has taken this device offline. And I'd like to remind everybody that, a few doors down from this room, is the bio-physics lab where we found the nanites."

She had a point, and it coincided with John's own concerns, the ones that explained why Colonel Sheppard was pulling scientist-sitting detail. Not that a P90 would have been of any earthly use against the robo-bugs that had infected a third of the expedition a year or so ago. If nothing else, the incident had taught them to beware of accidentally breaking things in this sector of the city. "You're thinking this is mad scientist central?" he asked Elizabeth.

"Until we've found proof to the contrary, it's safer to assume exactly that and to act accordingly. Which means no switching on or opening stuff until we know what it is or does."

"Elizabeth, this is a computer," Rodney declared in the tones of a saint pushed to the brink of his forbearance. "We *know* what computers do."

He had a point, too, and Zelenka seemed to agree. "If Rodney is right, Dr. Weir—"

"Of course I'm right."

"*If* Rodney is right," the Czech repeated, pretending he hadn't heard, "and anything should go wrong, all we need to do is pull the plug again, but—"

"—given that it's unlikely to be running Windows, nothing *will* go wrong," finished McKay.

Feeling Elizabeth's eyes on him, John returned her gaze and shrugged. "If push comes to shove, *I'*ll switch it off," he said, patting the P90.

At last she gave a brisk nod. "Alright. But be careful."

"Naturally."

Looking a lot happier than he had a minute ago, Rodney struck a sequence of keys on the console's control pad. The keys bore Ancient symbols, and John couldn't for the life of him say whether they represented the local version of QWERTY or something more cryptic. What was the Ancients' position on touch-typing, anyway? His ruminations were interrupted by a hologram lighting up above the console. It winked in and out of existence a couple of times—almost as if it'd gone a tad rusty during the past ten millennia—but eventually it stabilized.

Teyla gasped, McKay and Zelenka stared at each other, Elizabeth took a step back. John knew he was standing there with his mouth hanging open, but he couldn't help it.

"This is different," observed Ronon, sounding moderately intrigued.

The hologram looked young, fifteen or sixteen at the most, but that wasn't the issue. It also looked—

"Is this your idea of a joke?" Whirling around, McKay glared at John.

"I wish," he said, vaguely grateful for an excuse to retrieve his lower jaw from the floor. "But I wouldn't know where to start. Besides, my hair would never do *that*!"

Which was true—and annoying. The hologram sported a

mop of sleek black curls instead of a cowlick that vigorously resisted any attempt to get it under control. Otherwise, however...

Zelenka blew out a slow, stunned breath. "Well, I guess now we know where you get the ATA gene, Colonel."

"He may be correct," murmured Teyla. "The likeness is remarkable."

Apparently, the hologram was thinking along the same lines. It blinked, smiled at John, and finally said, "And who might you be?" Even the voice was similar, still adolescent and scratchy, but definitely similar.

"You first."

"I am Ikaros."

"Turn it off!" Zelenka hissed, suddenly white as a sheet. "Rodney, turn it off!"

"No! Please..." It was the heart-wrenching whimper of a child lost in the dark, and no computer program in the world should have sounded like that.

An icy fist clutched John's gut. "Do it, McKay!" he barked.

A split-second too late, as it turned out. Perhaps for the first time in recorded history, Dr. Rodney McKay had done as he was told. The hologram feathered to nothing. An instant before it vanished, John could have sworn he saw tears on the boy's face. His face...

"It's not a boy," he whispered to himself, fingers tight around his gun. "And it damn well isn't me!"

"Anybody care to explain what that was all about?" Elizabeth asked softly.

Hands trembling, Rodney disconnected a diagnostic cable from his laptop. Finally he turned back to them, almost as pale as Zelenka. "A.I."

"What?"

"Artificial intelligence."

"What's so scary about it?" Asking the question, Dex looked even more blasé than usual. Next he'd put his feet on the table. "I thought we'd already seen that with the computer virus on *Daedalus*."

As per Dr. Weir's orders they'd moved the party to the conference room to discuss the implications of their find. "He's got a point, Rodney," she said.

Oh, that's right, Elizabeth! Go on, encourage him!

Rodney McKay hadn't forgotten his and Dex's first encounter, and he wasn't inclined to forgive it anytime soon. At the moment, however, some clarification might be in order, else they'd still be sitting here tomorrow morning. Unacceptable, because a) he was starving, and b) he fully intended to be back in that lab long before tomorrow morning to make sure nobody, but absolutely nobody, laid a hand on that computer.

"Rodney? You did say that virus was artificial intelligence, didn't you?" Weir kept digging.

Why did people insist on quoting him on explanations that weren't quite... accurate? "I, uh, may have got carried away a little at the time," he offered.

"You? Carried way? Never!"

"In the heat of battle." He shot Sheppard a scathing glance. "The malware on the *Daedalus* was sophisticated, and yes, I suppose it had heuristic components in that it was able to learn from our reactions and predict our likely next steps, which of course could also have been an advanced form of fuzzy logic that allowed it to respond according to preprogrammed parameters, not dissimilar—"

"Rodney," Elizabeth interjected. "Your point?"

"I exaggerated, okay? It was impressive, but it lacked one vital defining element of true A.I. Fact of the matter is HAL doesn't exist."

"Hal?" Across the table from him, Teyla looked confused. "You mean Sergeant Walker?"

"Cultural reference, Teyla." Sheppard grinned. "HAL is short for Heuristic Algorithm, and it—he—was a supercomputer running a spaceship in a movie."

"HAL also killed the entire crew of the spaceship," Radek added dolefully. Trust the Slav soul to put a joyous spin on things. "Similar to what the virus on the *Daedalus* tried to do."

"As the good colonel was saying," Rodney cut in, wishing he'd never made the reference in the first place, "it's a movie.

Not real. In *real* life we're decades—possibly centuries—away from developing A.I. Even the Asgard haven't got it, and that should tell us something."

"Why? I mean, why haven't they got it?" asked Sheppard.

"I can only tell you why *we* haven't got it. True artificial intelligence requires consciousness—self-awareness—and the only computer capable of producing it that we know of is the human brain. Now, if you put the storage and processing ability of an average three-pound brain in I.T. terms, you'd be talking random access memory in the order of a couple hundred *tera*bytes. A state-of-the-art computer with this kind of RAM capacity would be the size of a house, and it'd run hot enough to burn itself out in seconds.

"I'm fairly certain that the Asgard, for instance, could get around that quite easily, which brings me to the second issue, and that's—"

"Never mind, Rodney." Apparently Elizabeth wasn't interested in issues. "What makes this computer you found different?"

Squinting at Rodney, Sheppard, who up to now had been poured in his chair, suddenly sat up very straight. "You mentioned quantum computing."

"That *is* what I suspected looking at the configuration of the device, and, if anything, your juvenile look-alike confirmed it."

"Oh, it did, huh? How?"

Rodney wondered if anybody else could hear the edge of distrust in the colonel's voice. The surprise wasn't the fact that it irked, but the fact that it irked so much.

That might take a while.

The echo of that unpleasant memory was drowned out by a voice that insisted to know why Dr. Rodney McKay, of all people, should care whether some glorified flyboy trusted him. Too right! Two years of diligent—no, *faithful*—service in the face of incomprehension and ridicule, and then one mistake and they crucified him. One single mistake! Okay, the mistake had taken out five sixths of a solar system. He was a great man. Great men made great mistakes. So there!

Only, the real problem lay on a different, altogether less cosmic level; all but dismissing the death of one of his scientists, not to mention Zelenka's warnings, he'd gone to John Sheppard and asked for his trust. And the colonel had given it, run interference with Elizabeth Weir, just so that Rodney could satisfy… what? Curiosity? An itch to get a ticket to Stockholm? Perversely, somewhere, in an unacknowledged corner of his psyche, he'd known that having Sheppard's trust meant more than winning the Nobel Prize. And he'd promptly gone and rewarded it by damn near killing the man…

"Rodney?"

"What?" he snapped, then regained his bearings. "Oh. What was the question again?"

"Not sure I can remember that far back." Sheppard shot him an odd look and sighed. "The question was how a hologram that, uh, bears some vague resemblance to me would confirm that the thing in that lab is a quantum computer."

"The, uh, speed of it. The speed," stuttered Rodney, scrambling to recover a train of thought he'd lost somewhere among pointless regrets.

"It didn't strike me as any faster or slower than any other computer here." Elizabeth sounded skeptical.

Et tu, Brute?

At age three he'd explained to his kindergarten teacher how Fibonacci numbers worked. The woman had had the nerve to punish him for lying. This kinda felt the same. And by the way, just because you're paranoid, McKay, doesn't mean they're not out to get you…

Zelenka jumped in the breach. "Rodney is right," he said. "It was the way the hologram responded. For it to react the way it did to Colonel Sheppard, the computer had to perform a vastly complex situational analysis *and* recognize the fact that the colonel is the spitting image of its hologram." He frowned. "Why would an image spit?"

"I think it actually is *spit and image*," Elizabeth offered. "Can we get back to the subject?"

"Ah." Zelenka looked utterly unenlightened and picked up his thread again. "The recognition of oneself, say, in a mirror or as similar to somebody else is an ability exclusive to"—he'd probably been about to say *humans* and remembered the presence of Teyla and Dex—"intelligent, self-aware life. Primates, for instance, can't do it. A child will need approximately two years to learn it. For computers as we know them, it's out of the question. Even assuming they were capable of such a task, it would take considerably longer than it did for the computer in the lab.

"You see, conventional computers work with bits, with each bit holding a one or a zero. The computer transports these ones and zeros to logic gates and back. A quantum computer on the other hand operates with a vector of qubits, which can hold a one, a zero, or, a superposition of these…" Radek petered out, staring at Dex who'd begun to pick his teeth and inspect the booty. He sighed, defeated, and groped for the lowest common denominator. "Fundamentally it means that quantum computing is instantaneous. That's what makes it so attractive. To begin with, it would revolutionize communications. Encryption would become both unnecessary and pointless, because—"

"I think we're getting off track again," Rodney said abruptly.

"I think we're very much *on* track." Trust Sheppard to pick up on a diversion. "I'm starting to get interested. Why would encryption be unnecessary?"

"Because a quantum computer can crack any code in a heartbeat. Plus, in theory, your message is received the instant it's sent." Part of Rodney wanted to hedge, but there really was no point. If he didn't say it, Radek would. "Meaning it's impossible to intercept. If something's got no gap, you can't drive a wedge in it."

"In other words, if we'd had a quantum computer three weeks ago, the Wraith wouldn't have gotten the jump on the *Daedalus*." John Sheppard projected the intimidating enthusiasm of a used car dealer, which was out of character. As a rule he had the military fixation on grabbing hold of every piece of new and improved technology-likely-to-be-turned-into-a-tactical-advantage well under control.

Unfortunately, recent events justified his enthusiasm. The

Wraith had figured out a way to intercept and decrypt Atlantis's communications with Earth and had promptly dispatched two hive ships to the coordinates where *Daedalus* was set to emerge from hyperspace on her last trip to the Pegasus galaxy. What had saved Colonel Caldwell and his crew's collective bacon was sheer fluke. The hive ships' timing had been off by a shake, allowing *Daedalus* to escape back into hyperspace with only minor damage. Of course codes had been changed immediately, which was roughly as effective as sticking a Band-Aid over a leak in the Hoover Dam. If the Wraith had done it once, they could do it again, and the next time the *Daedalus* or whoever else happened to come their way might not be so lucky. If the Atlantis expedition was to safeguard lives and vital supply lines, communications had to be protected. A quantum computer could do just that.

Rodney felt himself shunted into the unenviable position of a pebble trying to slow down an avalanche and slanted a look at Elizabeth Weir who would have the last word on whether or not the possibilities were going to be explored. Here was hoping for reservations about recklessly boosting computer sciences into the twenty-fourth century.

"Alright," Elizabeth said and rose. "Rodney, Radek, look into it and keep me posted."

Damn.

Around the table, the others were getting up to leave. Rodney stayed nailed to his seat, wrestling down an impulse to order everybody back into their chairs. They had no idea of the ramifications, did they? HAL *did* exist. HAL was sitting in a lab down the hall.

When Weir passed, he cleared his throat. "Elizabeth? May I have word, please?"

It brought her up short. "Did I miss something? You've got permission to experiment with that computer to your heart's content."

"That, uh, would be the problem." He got to his feet, partly because he figured it would be polite, partly because having to look up at her had triggered an incoherent memory of his piano teacher, dripping disappointment as she told him his playing was 'adept'. "Maybe we should… take it a little more slowly."

Stupid choice of words!

"Let me get this straight, Rodney. *You* are telling *me* we should hold back on exploring a new piece of technology?" Eventually her amusement faded, and she gave him a hard stare. "Is there anything you neglected to mention just now?"

"No! No… it's just… a hunch."

"A hunch?"

Was there an echo in here?

"It's not the hardware I'm worried about. It's the software. If Ikaros is a true A.I., we're dealing with an entity who can think several orders of magnitude better and faster than any of us. And while I understand and appreciate the possibilities of a breakthrough in quantum computing better than anyone, I also… Well, what if Ikaros does a HAL? Goes nuts? Or power-crazy? Or simply throws a tantrum? We'd be dealing with an unstoppable quantum-driven genius."

"Rodney, we've been dealing with *you* for two years."

Easy, Rodney. Just stay calm. Calm. Breathe… "Very funny. For all we know we might be handing Ikaros the proverbial loaded gun by tampering with that computer."

"Then I suggest you be ready to pull the plug before Ikaros pulls the trigger. But unless and until it comes to that, I'd like you follow up on every option that may improve our operational security."

"Look, Elizabeth, I've got one word for you: Arcturus." That one word just about stuck in his craw. But if humiliating himself was what it took, fine.

Her reaction wasn't what he'd expected, and maybe he should have expected that. The expression on her face softened. "Rodney, after Arcturus I was this close"—her thumb and forefinger pinched an eighth of an inch of air—"to sending you back to Earth. Accompanied by a comprehensive list of reasons why I was sending you back."

He swallowed. "It would have ruined my career."

"Hardly." Elizabeth flashed a brief smile. "But it might have made you think. I'm glad to hear it wasn't necessary. Having said that, I don't want to see you lose your… zeal, for want of a better word. We need it, which, coincidentally, is why you're still here. So, by all means, go ahead and... have fun!" Shooting him another smile, she left.

Fun? Rodney stared after her for a moment. Maybe she was right. Maybe he'd just lost his cool. His gut told him otherwise, but he chose to ignore it. For now.

Heaving a sigh, he packed up his conventional, non-quantum, non-entity-possessed laptop, stepped out into the hallway, and almost collided with Sheppard, who'd parked himself outside the conference room.

"You okay?" he asked.

"Of course I'm okay," snapped Rodney. "Your teenage double may be about to vent us into space, so why wouldn't I be okay?"

CHAPTER FIVE

Charybdis -4441

Why that particular gate had worked when countless others had refused to cooperate countless times was beyond him. Some kind of reverse glitch maybe, but he wasn't going to question his luck. When he emerged from the gate he indulged in a brief, ecstatic moment of believing he'd finally made it home.

Home.

Just when had he started thinking of Atlantis as home?

Since first setting foot in it, quite possibly. It had felt right in a way nothing and nowhere else had in a long time. Each expedition member had been allowed to bring one personal item. He'd brought a second-hand copy of Tolstoy's *War And Peace*, which probably said all there was to say about his emotional ties to Earth.

Atlantis had been a new start and a family.

John figured he should have known better than to care. He'd been quite content in that bubble where fate could only be decided by the flip of a unit coin, because he refused to care. His bad for allowing the bubble to pop. Payback was a bitch.

The Atlantis he'd known was gone. In time-honored human tradition they'd got too curious, too cocky, too greedy. The upshot had been wholesale destruction. Not just of Atlantis, and he'd never understood why he had survived. Perhaps it was punishment. He could have stopped it. Rodney McKay, of all people, had urged caution…

And trips down memory lane never did anyone any good.

The jumper came to a halt, and he could hear the soft hum of the bay doors closing somewhere beneath. John sagged back into the pilot's seat, shut his eyes, and allowed himself two seconds rest. Given the chance he'd sleep a year, but right now that was out of the question. Because this, whatever it was—delusion, chimera, mirage—wasn't Atlantis, and he wasn't home, and he probably wouldn't be alone for long.

Don't fall asleep!

His eyes snapped open, and he launched himself from the seat as if it'd suddenly caught on fire. In the rear compartment he snatched his P90 from a bench, routinely checked that it was loaded, and opened the hatch. The jumper bay was empty, not that he'd expected anything else. Coming in, he'd caught a glimpse of the dust sheets covering most of the control center, and they'd been a dead giveaway. Still, he was convinced he'd seen movement from the corner of his eye, and as long as he couldn't be absolutely sure that it'd been a reflection or something of the sort, he'd be better off assuming that it'd been a Wraith.

No, wait...

The Wraith hadn't made it.

Then again, he shouldn't have either.

"So assume it is a Wraith," he ordered himself and cautiously moved down the ramp, P90 spot-welded to his cheek.

Try as you might, you can't walk noiselessly in combat boots, not on concrete anyway, and his footfalls sounded absurdly loud, highlighting the silence around him. Even if he didn't know full well what had happened, hadn't lived it, this thick hush alone would persuade him that this wasn't his Atlantis. *His* Atlantis had never been quiet, even at night. Too many people, too many people too busy, and it'd been his job to protect them. As far as failures went, his was a doozy.

Again he shoved the thought away. It was in the past. The whole notion of past had become strictly relative, of course, and John was sure Albert Einstein, while unconvinced by quantum physics, would have appreciated the irony. Time itself had flipped out of sequence, and what once was a stable fourth dimension had turned into a fractured, disjointed game of pinball—played on at least five different machines. Apparently he had the doubtful distinction of being the ball.

The door into the hallway door whooshed open, and he froze for a couple of seconds, listening. Not a sound, apart from his own breathing. He hadn't forgotten the blur of motion he'd seen on arrival, but whoever or whatever it was, it didn't lie in wait here. If it didn't come to him, he'd have to go to it, simple as that. He pulled the life-signs detector from his pocket, doubting it would work—in addition to time, Ancient technology too had been thrown out of whack. At least that was his best guess, based on the fascinating places he'd gotten to visit between a temperamental puddle jumper and an all but dysfunctional gate system.

Much to his surprise, the detector seemed to work, and according to it, he'd been right twice over. There was some-body else here, a lone bright blip, erratically straying along the fringes of the control center. Other than that, Atlantis was com-pletely deserted. He felt a chill streak down his back and fought the temptation of just turning around, getting into the jumper, and heading the hell back out. Wherever he ended up next, it had to be better than a dead city, him, and Unknown Life-Sign. Unfortunately, running wasn't his style.

Yeah, and look where it got you!

Frowning, he started down the hallway as quickly as he could, only braking when he got to the stairs.

"Crap!" he whispered.

Of course the Ancients had invested some thought into mak-ing this stairwell the only access from the jumper bay to the city. Any intruder wanting to get in could be picked off com-ing down the stairs. It had never really occurred to him that, one day, he might be the lucky schmo doing the intruding. He checked the life-signs detector again.

The blip hovered indecisively on the gallery of the control center, giving the impression that it hadn't drawn the same stra-tegic conclusion as Lieutenant Colonel John Sheppard. Then again, though its current position didn't offer a clear shot, it was a good place for watching who was coming down from the jumper bay without being seen oneself.

Okay, make it quick and pray the stairs aren't booby trapped.

He took a couple of deep breaths, ducked from cover, and flung himself down the stairs, keeping low all the way down and diving behind a shrouded console as soon as he hit the gallery. None of the nicely executed acrobatics brought a reaction from his invisible friend. So far, so weird. The life-signs detector showed the blip retreating into a corridor. That left two possibilities: either Unknown Life-Sign meant to lure him someplace more to its tactical liking, or it was as spooked as he.

Somehow he leaned toward the second option.

Time to break out the charm.

Slowly he rose from behind the console. "Don't run away! I won't hurt you. I promise!"

The blip resumed its hover. It wasn't coming any closer, but at least it had stopped heading away. Then it screamed. Going by the pitch it had to be a woman, and if he hadn't known any better, he'd swear there were three of her. The smartest course of action probably lay in catching the banshee and shutting her up before he lost his hearing.

As he ran across the gallery part of him took in his surroundings. The DHD—uncovered for some reason—with the mainframe display rearing behind, dark and inactive; what used to be Elizabeth's office; the conference room, all dead and abandoned, as though the expedition had never come here at all. And maybe it hadn't. This bracing thought carried him out into the corridor.

And then he saw her. She stood at the far end of the hallway, as if frozen in terror. Not a Wraith. She wasn't screaming now, and he forced himself to slow to a walk, to raise his hands—if she wanted to kill him, she could have done so already, and aiming a gun at her wasn't designed to put her at ease.

An ankle-length dress that must have been white at some point drooped from a too-skinny body. It was filthy and tattered, perhaps the only item of clothing she had. Her hair, unkempt for weeks or months and puffed into the wild frizz of a bag lady, was shot with gray and touched her shoulders. Somewhere between panic and madness, she stared at him, eyes wide, irises rimmed with white, and John stamped down on an urge to turn and run after all.

"You're dead," she hissed.

"Ditto." He was surprised he could speak at all.

"You're dead." This time it sounded almost plaintive. Without warning, her legs gave, and he barely caught her before she sagged to the floor.

Floor.

Sitting down.

Not a bad idea, considering that his own knees had turned a little wonky, too.

Leaning against a pillar for support, John carefully eased himself and Dr. Elizabeth Weir to the ground. He wondered if this was how it had felt for Ronon to find a handful of Satedans still alive. Then, in a wash of exhaustion, adrenaline and relief cancelled one another out, and his eyes slid shut again.

Charybdis +32

"What are you doing, Major Sheppard?" Teyla had just returned from checking the place where the villagers left their gifts for her and was stowing away a basketful of fruit and tuttleroot. She could hear him shuffle around in the back of the cave but was unable to connect the noise he made to any specific activity. Whatever it was, though, it occasioned a worrying amount of muttering and groaning. "Major?"

"I'm trying to keep your place from flooding," he grunted, words compressed by effort. "That tremor… this morning… dropped a rock… into your… stream and"—the sudden loud clatter was accompanied by splashes and enthusiastic cursing—"Ow! It's out now." And he evidently had overbalanced and taken a dive into the stream.

She chuckled. "I distinctly recall asking you to stay put and rest your leg."

"Teyla, it's been three weeks. If this leg gets any more rest, it'll start to ferment. Or grow fungus. Or whatever things do when they're not used."

How well she remembered it, this broken-winged impatience with a body that wouldn't do his bidding. "I believe the word you're looking for is *heal*, Major."

"Very funny. So, given that the quakes are a regular occurrence, why do you stay here? Aren't you afraid the cave's gonna come down on top of you one day?" He seemed to have recovered the crude crutches Wex had made for him, hoisting himself back to his feet and hobbling toward his cot.

"The cave won't collapse. You'll see why soon enough."

The cot creaked, indicating that he must have sat down. "How about now?"

"Give it time."

"My leg is fine."

"I doubt that, Major Sheppard. And even if it were, your hands surely are far from fine."

The silence that greeted her observation was answer enough. The burns on his hands had been deep and were slow to heal, and using crutches—or rolling boulders, for that matter—had to be painful. But perhaps his urgency had a reason. Perhaps he sensed something she couldn't. Perhaps they had no time.

And perhaps she simply dreaded the thought of having to send him away. She stalled. "How wet did you get? Do you require fresh clothes?"

"No. Thanks. The fire'll dry me out quickly enough."

Teyla sniffed the air, decided that he was being polite. The fire smelled as though it were about to die. She stoked it, put a couple more logs on the hearth. Then she went about squaring away the rest of her alms. Not much this time, but she wasn't complaining. Winter had been hard and the first crops were a long way off yet. The villagers had to use their remaining supplies sparingly, and since most didn't know that she had an extra mouth to feed—most wouldn't approve if they knew—her rations had dwindled, too. She'd make do. And she'd see to it that her charge got fed properly. He'd need his strength for what lay ahead.

"You haven't… shown me what happened next," he said suddenly.

No, she had not. With good reason. The linking of minds had proved more draining on both of them than she had anticipated, quite possibly because he was human, not Wraith. He simply hadn't been well enough to try again. Until now.

"They activated that computer again?" he asked.

"Yes, they did."

"And? McKay and Zelenka worked out quantum communications?"

"No, they did not."

"They *didn't*? Why not?"

"It became of secondary importance when Ikaros made them, as you say, an offer they couldn't refuse. An offer your military leadership couldn't refuse."

He stirred. "Am I right in assuming that this was a bad idea and Ikaros turned out to be my evil twin?"

"A little of both. Although I don't believe Ikaros's intentions were evil." Guided by years of knowing the exact place of each item in her cave, she walked over to the cot, felt his hand on her arm, easing her to sit next to him. She clapped her fingers over his, gently pulled him into the link. "I believe he truly meant to help."

Charybdis ±0

Elizabeth woke with a start, drowsily blinking into black and unable to tell what had woken her. The mystery was solved when her radio gave another squawk.

What in the name of—

"Elizabeth? Elizabeth! Oh, for heaven's sake, you can't be asleep now! Wake up!" the radio chattered into the darkness of her room.

Reaching over to where she'd last seen the bedside table, she limply padded around until her fingers brushed the small radio set. As it turned out, she'd grabbed it the wrong way and poked the stalk mike into her eye while attempting to find her ear. It didn't improve her mood.

"Do you have any idea what time it is?" she barked when she'd finally managed to fiddle the earpiece into place.

"Twenty-three past two. Why?"

"In the *morning*, Rodney!"

"Yes, I am familiar with the twenty-four hour clock. Thank you, Elizabeth. Now that that's cleared up, would it be too much to ask for you to come over to the computer lab? McKay out."

Murder had never struck her as a particularly viable approach to handling interpersonal issues, but she was contemplating it now. The other alternative was simply ignoring Dr. McKay. Which would last for… oh, five minutes, tops, before he radioed her again. That aside, she was too irritated to go back to sleep.

"Alright," she muttered, rolling out of bed. "You got it, Rodney."

Yawning, she donned pants and a t-shirt and raked her fingers through her hair by ways of getting rid of a rare case of pillow-head. She seriously doubted that Rodney's state of mind would permit him to take in any details of her personal grooming.

A few minutes later she burst through the door of the lab. To her surprise, John Sheppard was there, looking like she felt, bleary-eyed and punch-drunk. Evidently, he'd been thrown out of bed as well. The really amazing thing about it was the fact that Rodney was still alive and apparently unharmed.

"About time," he observed, not bothering to look up from his laptop. "What took you so long?"

"No idea," she said, suppressing that recurring urge to throttle him. "This had better be the cure for cancer or, at the very least, a permanent solution to our little Wraith problem."

"Door Number Two," John said sleepily. "According to Zelenka. Sorry 'bout the cancer cure."

"Radek's here, too?"

By way of an answer, John cocked a thumb toward the back of the console. Zelenka was crouched behind it, tinkering with what looked like a holo-laser array. "You know, it would really be a lot easier if we just connected Ikaros to the mainframe," he lobbed across the console at Rodney.

"Oh, absolutely! And then your friend Ikaros takes over each and every system of Atlantis. Which, I can't emphasize enough, is perfectly within the realm of possibility and should have occurred to you before we even started this."

"*Jde mi to na nervy*," Zelenka growled to himself and added a couple of oaths that were new to Elizabeth. She decided against translating.

"He kinda reminds me of Hermiod when he does that," whispered John, gently listing in her direction.

"More hair," she whispered back.

"More clothes."

The air above the console began to stir and flicker, seemed to congeal for a moment, and then vanished into, well, thin air again.

"If that's what you guys drummed me out of bed for, I'm gonna be seriously pissed," John observed casually.

Rodney spared him a withering glance. "Given that some of us haven't been to bed at all, perhaps you should stop obsessing about your beauty sleep."

"Nobody ordered you to—"

"*Je už málem čas!*" A blend of triumph and satisfaction in his voice, Radek popped up from behind the console like a glove puppet. "Try it now!"

This time it wasn't a stir and flicker; a charge of energy sizzled through the air, and Ikaros shimmered to life. "I cannot believe you people ever managed to find Atlantis, let alone get here!" The boy wore black Special Ops BDUs and a frown. "If I'd known that a simple technical task would take this long, I'd have done you a drawing."

"What's with the costume?" Elizabeth asked, baffled.

It brought a huff from Rodney. "For some unfathomable reason, he appears hell-bent on emulating the good Colonel here."

"There's good news, too," Zelenka chimed in. "In all essential things, such as character, social skills, and general affability he takes after Uncle Rodney."

"I'm glad you didn't include intellectual brilliance," said Ikaros, and going by his moue of disdain he meant every word of it.

McKay ignored him, suggesting that this kind of exchange was a regular occurrence, but Elizabeth gave a small hiss. She was beginning to understand why Rodney had reservations about giving Ikaros access to the Atlantis mainframe. Why he had reservations about Ikaros, period. "Is he always like this?"

"I believe you people consider it impolite to refer to someone actually present in the third person," Ikaros pointed out. "If you have any questions, Elizabeth, feel free to address them to me directly."

Elizabeth?

"That's 'Dr. Weir' to you," John snapped, before she could say it herself.

"Why? You call her 'Elizabeth.'"

"You're not me."

"Certain, uh, privileges have to be earned," she explained, trying to defuse the tension, only remotely worried about the fact that she was attempting to pacify a machine. Whether she liked it or not, Rodney's warning still resonated. *Well, what if Ikaros does a HAL? Goes nuts? Or power-crazy? Or simply throws a tantrum?* To all intents and purposes, this machine was a teenager, and it was the wrong time of day for dealing with teenage fits of temper. "For now let's stick with 'Dr. Weir,' alright?"

"Fine, Dr. Weir." The kid smiled at her. "I've got to earn it, yes? How much would you bet on the fact that you'll let me call you 'Elizabeth' as soon as we're finished here?"

Suddenly she had a niggling suspicion that waking her and John Sheppard in the small hours of the morning hadn't been Rodney's idea at all. Could a hologram be bored? "I don't bet," she said curtly—hedging her bets.

Ikaros shot her a knowing grin, as if he'd heard that little wordplay in her mind. It wasn't the insolence that unsettled her, it was the scary intelligence looking out from behind John's eyes. Not that John—the real one—was stupid by any stretch of the imagination, but what she saw in his juvenile doppelganger defied human terms of intelligence. Hardly surprising. She had scoured the Ancient archives for references to Ikaros and had finally found what amounted to a footnote—short but chilling.

The boy—the flesh-and-blood version—had been identified as exceptionally gifted, even by Ancient standards, and the Council had ordered him enrolled in a special study program. He'd out-studied, out-thought, out-smarted his teachers within months and begun to rebel against the dogma handed down by the Council, which he considered to be narrow-minded and restrictive. The only one of his teachers with whom he continued to have any kind of productive relationship was Janus, already chomping at the bit himself. Student and teacher must have fueled one another's defiance and creativity, but when interviewed by the authorities after the fact, Janus claimed that he'd had absolutely no knowledge of Ikaros's project, said that, had he known, he'd have prevented the boy from going through with the experiment at any cost. It might even be true, because what Ikaros had done was outrageous even by Janus's standards.

Having designed and built a computer prototype capable of sustaining artificial intelligence, he'd then proceeded to upload his own mind into the device. However he had done it—documentation was vague on that—the process had caused a massive power surge, crippling Atlantis's systems. By the time the systems were back online and the cause of the problem discovered, it had been too late. The men dispatched to investigate and help if necessary had found Ikaros's lifeless body next to the computer. The device had been disabled and the lab sealed, pending further investigation—which never had happened, because the war against the Wraith had outweighed all other concerns. According to the archival materials, the experiment had failed, Ikaros had been buried, and the Lanteans had mourned the loss of a promising young mind, and that had been that. According to the archival materials.

In actual fact the experiment was anything but a failure, which raised the possibility that the Ancients had been terrified by the notion of a boy genius whose cognitive abilities were vastly enhanced by a computer; terrified enough to lock the room, throw away the key, and forget about the whole thing. The question was whether the Lanteans' apprehension had been justified. Rodney seemed to think so, but—

"Yes, well, sorry about the little delay," he said. "Mastermind here wanted to do his very own PowerPoint presentation, so we had to synchronize external holo-lasers with his and make them interactive."

"I told you that linking me to the mainframe would have

simplified the procedure to no end," Ikaros cut in.

"Yeah, let's not go over that again. Just do your thing. There are people waiting here."

"Your wish is my command." The boy gave a mocking little bow. As he straightened up, he took a deep breath and the adolescent smirk transformed into a shy smile that highlighted his uncanny resemblance to John Sheppard. "First of all," he began earnestly, "let me say how grateful I am to you. Being locked in a box, even a box with some amazing circuitry, for ten thousand years does tend to get a little… tedious. I owe you, and a long time ago my parents informed me that it is wise always to repay one's debts. I'd like to do so now. My friends, I'd like to present Charybdis to you."

"As in *Scylla and*?" John asked.

"I… don't think I'm familiar with that reference." Ikaros gave a small, baffled frown, as though his being unfamiliar with any kind of reference were entirely inconceivable. And perhaps it was. Then he smiled again. "You'll see. Just watch."

A second holo-laser fired up, its image congealing into a solar system whose primary was a red giant in the last stages of expansion. What was left of its planets—three small worlds, none of them sporting any moons—orbited despondently, as though aware of what their future held. The image zoomed in on the innermost planet. It was small and arid, without discernible climate zones other than desert, and seemed devoid of life.

"We've got it registered as M5P 878," Rodney announced to no one in particular.

"When and how did you come up with this bizarre way of naming planets?" asked Ikaros, then obviously decided he'd rather not know the answer, because he carried on. "We call it Mykena Quattuor. The sun is Mykena. As you can see, it'll turn supernova within a relatively short timeframe—I expect another two thousand years at most—but its system is already dying. It was one of the reasons why we chose Mykena Quattuor as the Charybdis site."

"Who's *we*?" John threw in.

"Janus and I. I gather you are aware that Janus's preferred area of research was fourth-dimensional physics. I refined and expanded on some of his theories, and together we devised a method of modifying carefully selected timelines—Charybdis."

The holographic image changed, simulating the view from a jumper, chasing above the surface at about three thousand feet. The destination of the virtual jumper seemed to be a structure that sat in the middle of a vast, desolate plain. It reminded Elizabeth of an enormous geode turned inside out, a crystalline dome that shimmered in the somber red light of Mykena.

"Charybdis," Ikaros repeated, nodding at the structure. "Well, the outer shell that houses the prototype at any rate."

"Which timeline specifically did you think of altering?" asked Radek, ill-concealed fascination bubbling in his voice, specs sliding down his nose unchecked. He looked as though he already knew where this was going and merely asked out of politeness.

"One of the Council's precepts that always hampered Janus was that nothing he did must interfere with our then-current timeline." The expression on the boy's face left no doubt as to just how moronic he considered this notion to be.

Rodney begged to differ. "Forgive me for pointing out the obvious, but it's one way of eliminating the numerous intriguing possibilities posed by the Grandfather Paradox—always assuming one actually believes in it."

"*Grandfather Paradox*?" Ikaros's eyebrows ratcheted up a notch. "I don't quite see what my ancestors should have to do with it."

"The idea is that you go back in time, accidentally kill your grandfather before he had a chance to meet your grandmother, thereby preventing the conception of your father and, by extension, your own, which obviously means you won't be able to go back in time because you never existed in the first place. The whole thing supposedly is a parable for—"

"Wouldn't it be fair to assume that anybody intelligent enough to contrive a means of going back in time would also possess the basic wisdom *not* to kill his grandfather?" The boy sighed. "Your outlook is as limited as the Council's. Of course Janus and I were more than aware of the risks. You may recall that I said *carefully selected timelines*."

"Which timeline were you thinking of?" Elizabeth asked.

Ikaros smiled at her like a teacher rewarding a pupil who'd finally managed to bring up a constructive question. "The one enabling the evolution of the iratus bug."

"Brilliant idea!" John said enthusiastically.

"I wish you wouldn't always make these things personal," complained McKay.

"This one's *intensely* personal, trust me."

"It makes perfect sense!" Radek cut in. "Without the iratus bug, there never would have been Wraith. And nobody is being put at risk by eliminating the bug."

"So what stopped you from going through with this oh-so-brilliant idea, huh?" Apparently, Rodney had decided to sulk.

"The Council!" spat Ikaros. "They argued that, while the Wraith posed a lethal danger, their presence had also influenced the development of my people in unique ways. That to take the Wraith out of the equation might result in Atlantis never having been built." A little more calmly he added, "We also encountered several problems when we ran the simulations."

"In other words, Charybdis doesn't work," Rodney concluded triumphantly.

"Oh, but it will. I have a solution for every one of those issues. That was the whole point of uploading myself into the computer."

CHAPTER SIX

Charybdis +32

He pulled from the link with a jolt, and for an instant Teyla could feel his shock and an unlikely mixture of pity and scorn. Best not to let on. This was difficult enough without his realizing that, as long as they were linked, she could sense his every emotion.

"You're telling me the kid turned himself into a machine to be able to do the math?" he gasped.

"Essentially, yes," she replied, forcing herself to keep her tone light to counteract his distress.

"Was he insane or just insanely ambitious?"

"Perhaps neither, perhaps a little bit of both." All at once, Teyla felt the chill of old bones, rubbed her arms to warm up a little. Like a shooting star rubbed by the air. She smiled at the memory of Halling, rubbing his hands as she'd told him to do. "Most of all, he was a child. Like all children he was eager to prove himself. Too eager."

"Yes. Obviously." Crutches clattered on rock, then the cot creaked and heaved a little under her. He'd risen. "Fire's gone out," he murmured by way of an explanation.

She listened to the familiar noises of kindling being piled, flames fanned, logs beginning to crackle. It seemed odd not to perform the necessary tasks but merely to enjoy their effects, and she admonished herself not to enjoy it too much, because, before long, John Sheppard would be gone and she would have to fend for herself again. For now, however, she relished the warmth that seeped from the hearth and through the cave.

"So we decided to go ahead with it."

Not a question; a statement, and the acoustics told her that he was facing away from her, most likely staring into the fire. The choice of words was interesting: *we.* He'd begun to identify with what had happened, and while part of her profoundly regretted it—this version of John Sheppard had never been involved and deserved no blame—another part was relieved, grateful even. He needed to identify, feel responsible, to be able to accomplish what she would ask him to do.

"Show me! Now!" he commanded.

A long, long time ago she had tried to explain to a Satedan how certain orders were better left ignored. This was not one of those orders. The time for stalling and enjoying the warmth was over. He seemed to sense it more clearly than she.

"Not here." Teyla rose wearily, struggling to overcome a reluctance that wanted to pin her to the cot, inert and safe and warm. "Come."

"Where?"

"Come," she said simply, extending a hand; the gesture as much of an order as his words had been moments before.

More clatter of crutches, footfalls, slow and clumsy, and then he was by her side. "Where?" he asked again.

Her fingers scrabbled through air until they caught a handful of his shirt and held on. "It's well that you cleared the path." She waved at the rock formation where the creek entered the cavern. "We shall have to wade for the first few meters."

Major Sheppard muttered something unintelligible and, no doubt, unflattering and began to hobble toward the far end of the cave. Teyla hung on and let him be her guide. Of course she could have found the passage on her own—she'd done so hundreds of times before, though not for a long while now—but allowing him to lead, to follow him this one last time, felt right. More so than anything had these many years. The thought brought a smile, one she didn't care to bite back.

A heartbeat's hesitation, then he moved again, and a sharp hiss told her that he'd stepped into the stream. "Good job I'm soaked already," he grunted.

The water came up to her shins, and it was bitterly cold. Within seconds she'd lost sensation in her feet and, desperate to retain her balance, clutched his shirt with both fists. Had it always been this chilly, the current this rapid? She couldn't remember, and it didn't matter.

They were approaching the narrowest part of the passage now. Water climbed her legs and broke around her knees as the rocks pinched the stream up and out in a swift gush. The tilt of his body betrayed that he had to lean into the current to keep his balance, and she tried her best to steady him, although her efforts didn't amount to much. Suddenly she chuckled.

He must have heard her even over the rush of the water. "What?"

"You have a proverb, do you not? About the lame leading the blind?"

"Blind leading the blind. From what you've told me it's close enough."

As vehemently as it had begun, the slick pressure against her legs subsided until it was merely a murmur around her ankles. They had passed the narrows. From here on out it would be easier.

"Keep to the left," she said. "There's a ledge along the water."

"I can't see a damn thing! It's pitch dark in—" He cut himself off before she had a chance to interrupt him. "Blind leading the blind, huh?"

"I used to come here on my own. Keep walking, Major."

So he did, but their progress seemed excruciatingly slow. More than once she had to rein in the urge to prod him into a faster pace, to tell him that the darkness was nothing to fear. Long decades of familiarity had turned darkness into a friend. It made them equals again, hampering John Sheppard and giving her an advantage. Not so unlike their sparring sessions in the gym, all those years ago. What he had on her in strength, weight—and now youth—she made up for in skill and experience.

"I notice you still don't practice enough," she said.

"Hilarious," he gasped. "How much further?"

"Wait." She'd only ever been used to timing herself, and the sluggish pace had made her lose track of their location.

As they stuttered to a halt, she let go of his shirt, reached out. Her fingertips grazed rock either side of her. It was enough of a marker, even if she'd missed the fact that the burble of the stream sounded faint and muted, a long way behind them. She sniffed, tasting the air like a deer, finding it less humid. They were far into the maze already, and she'd do well to pay attention from here on out. It didn't matter too much—eventually all tunnels ended up in the same place—but the quicker they got there the better.

"We are close." She squeezed past him, her left hand trailing along the wall so that she wouldn't miss the junction. Still sniffing occasionally, she led the way, noted how the smell began to change, from the dank mustiness of the caves to something unique and familiar and belonging to the past—and perhaps to the future.

A sudden yelp from behind stopped her dead in her tracks. "Are you alright, Major Sheppard?"

"Damn! I mean, yes. I'm fine. You could have warned me about the lights."

"As a matter of fact, no."

"Of course… I'm sorry. I—"

"It's not important." She never had given any thought to lights, though now their presence seemed obvious; the only surprise being that they were functional still. To the best of her knowledge nothing else was. "What can you see?"

"Looks like a rockslide's come through here. For real. Over there's what must have been windows. The dirt pushed right through them. Other than that it seems… intact. The doorway's clear, but I take it you know that already." He sucked in a deep breath. "I thought you said Atlantis had been destroyed?"

"What we knew as Atlantis, yes. It was more than walls and ceilings and technology, was it not?"

"Yes. Yes, it was." For a moment his voice sounded ragged with emotion, then he caught himself, cleared his throat. "Where are we?"

"At the top of the control tower," Teyla replied and winced. "The transporter no longer operates."

"Of course it doesn't."

It was a long, quiet trek, harder on Major Sheppard than on her. Climbing back up the stairs would be a different matter. Then again, there would be no reason to go back once she'd brought him where he needed to be, would there? If he didn't succeed, she doubted she'd have the strength to carry on, hoping for another miracle in the years she had left. And if he did succeed, there'd be nobody to go back for. Jinto, Pirna, Halling, her newborn namesake, the whole village—

"Teyla?" He sounded worried, must have seen her tremble.

"It is nothing." A brisk wave of her hand dismissed it, and she hoped it would be enough to fool him. Not easily fooled, this one. But at least he couldn't see her face.

Finally the stairs wound to an end. She stopped briefly to orient herself, then groped her way into a corridor on her right. The rockslide that damaged the tower had never reached here. This place lay too deep, too safe in the embrace of the earth that had risen while Charybdis threw suns and moons from their path and kneaded the planet's crust like so much dough. There might be other signs of ruin, but, for her, the only indicator of desolation was the silky cushion of dust and cobwebs that caressed her fingertips.

She could see it in her mind as she walked. The wide, diffusely lit hallway, leading to the control center, bustling with people on errands, leaving their shift or starting it. There were smiles and nods, a joke, or a junior officer's wary berth around Rodney McKay. More people, all with familiar faces, in the control center itself, and—

"Teyla! Stop!"

The shout rang of warning, exploded the reminiscence, froze her in place. "What?" she hissed.

"You almost… tripped." Something seemed to constrict his throat, flatten his voice.

Of course. She *had* tripped. Fallen even, the first time she'd come down here. Then she'd gathered herself, shaken her head, patted around, until she found the obstruction. Under threadbare garments it had had desiccated, leathery skin, arms, legs, a face she'd been unable to recognize by touch alone. Like all the others. Their very facelessness had made it easier to forget, and forgetting had been a necessity. Remembering and wondering how they'd died and how long it had taken them would have turned every waking moment into a nightmare. In time she'd learned to navigate the macabre obstacle course in the control center without so much as touching any of them.

Teyla heard the crutches rattle to the ground, a thud, a soft grunt as Major Sheppard maneuvered himself to the floor. He would want to find out. He could. It wasn't *his* nightmare. Not yet.

"Who is it?" she asked softly and against her better judgment. "Can you still recognize them?"

"No." The word was bitten off and spat out, too rash and too quick.

"Don't lie to me, Major Sheppard." She said it gently, so as to take the sting out of the words.

"You don't need to—"

"I do."

"Would you believe me if I said I don't know him?" There was a trace of relief in his tone, and she understood perfectly.

"It is a man?"

"Yes. Tall, powerful, by the looks of what's left, long dark hair—dreadlocks—dark skin. No uniform. Lots of leather... I've never seen him before."

"Ronon," she whispered, surprised by a fierce spike of grief and remorse, still fresh and corrosive, even after all these years.

Ronon had been with the team, with her, when they'd activated Charybdis on Mykena Quattuor. If she had been taken to this place, this time, he might have been, too. But there were countless versions of all of them, so who was to say whether this was the original Ronon? Who was to say whether she really was Teyla Emmagan or merely a mirror for all of Teyla's conciousnesses? Not that it mattered.

She was the prophet, ancient and blind, as it befitted the oracle. "His name was Ronon Dex. The Wraith destroyed his world."

"I liked him." Not even a question, a simple statement of fact. "I mean, I will like him... when I—"

"You understood each other. Trusted each other. He was on our team."

"Oh. I *did* like him." He tugged her arm. "Help me up."

She hauled him to his feet, and a few minutes later they reached the gallery in the control center. There'd been more bodies along the way, she knew, just as there were dead men and women sitting at the workstations here, but John Sheppard had carefully and without comment steered her around them. Now she heard a faint hitch in his breath, instantly knew what he'd seen.

"When I first discovered this place, I guessed what it was, but I couldn't be sure. Not until I found the Stargate." She wished she could see it, too, just one last time. "This is your way out of here."

"It still works?"

"I don't know." She vaguely gestured in the direction of where the dialing console had to be. "The glyphs aren't raised, so I couldn't—"

"Of course." He moved to the console. A couple of swishes—he was dusting it off. Then soft tapping noises as he touched the glyphs. "First planet we ever dialed," he murmured, and she could hear a smile in his voice. "Kinda fitting, don't you think?"

Athos had been her home world, a lifetime ago. Or many. "Are you trying to flatter me?"

"No. It's the only gate address that came to mind."

Her chuckle broke off when the clang of the first engaging chevron echoed through the vast room. The second, the third, one after the other, until the seventh chevron locked and the vortex of the establishing wormhole roared into the control center and collapsed into a hush, punctuated only by the watery lapping of the event horizon.

"Obviously it works," he said. "Now would you care to show me what happened?"

Charybdis ±0

Mykena Quattuor was a pathetic little dust ball, Mars without the canals or the romance, sullenly veering ever closer toward its primary, as if it knew that going out in a blaze of glory would be the one act that might imbue its existence with a modicum

of interest. Well, either that, or it'd go down in the annals of the
Pegasus galaxy as the site of salvation.

According to Boy Wonder it was going to be the latter.

John Sheppard stole a glance over his shoulder at the computer console that sat, securely tied down, in the aft compartment of Jumper One. Ikaros, going walkies at last. The
kid—*kid*?—had begged, wheedled and thrown tantrums, but
the decision to keep him on Atlantis unless his presence on
Mykena Quattuor was absolutely necessary had been unani-
mous. That had been four weeks ago. Since then, Zelenka and
McKay had turned the Charybdis device upside down and
inside out—and made no headway whatsoever. Okay, they'd
agreed that it probably wasn't a bomb and that the lights came
on when you flicked a switch, but that was just about the extent
of it. Enter Ikaros, who'd said the obvious: *I told you so.*

Must be nice to have superior intelligence.

Rodney probably could relate, but John would just as happily settle for flying a jumper. On the horizon beyond the view
port, almost exactly on the dividing line between day and night,
the light of the giant sun hit a glittering protrusion and refracted
in a symphony of reds. Prompted by his thought command, the
jumper opened a channel to the surface.

"Hey, Charybdis? From up here you guys actually look
pretty. Like someone's dropped a mammoth garnet in the desert."

"If that's supposed to be poetic, don't give up the day job."
The radio belched static, which suited Rodney's mood. In the
past week he'd cycled from fractious-even-by-McKay-stan-
dards to completely insufferable. "Otherwise I'd be grateful
if you could postpone any further outbursts of lyricism until
we're finished here, Colonel."

"And a glorious good morning to you, too, Rodney. Ikaros
and I should be with you in ten. Sheppard out."

He made it in nine thirty-seven. When he emerged from the
airlock into the inner structure of the enormous assembly of
man-grown crystals that formed the shell of Charybdis, a foursome of technicians pushed past to unload his cargo from the
jumper.

In their wake McKay leaped out at him like a kiss-a-gram from the birthday cake. "Colonel!"

Fully expecting Rodney to burst into song at the slightest provocation, John pretended not to have seen him and headed for the control chamber. McKay being McKay—in other words, lacking the take-a-hint gene—the dodge didn't work terribly well.

"Colonel! I... uh... I'd like to apologize for being a little crabby lately."

Not on your life. For Rodney to apologize, events of a certain order of magnitude had to occur first. Such as the annihilation of the better part of a solar system. John kept walking.

"Colonel... John!"

Okay, the first name treatment was cause for worry. McKay didn't really do first names, not with him, anyway. In fact, John harbored a sneaking suspicion that Rodney secretly enjoyed using his rank—something about rubbing in how he was mere military, helpless without the guidance of a scientist. Or something. Only, right now the roles seemed to be reversed, which had John putting on the brakes. Despite a distinct sense of déjà vu all over again.

"Rodney."

The dam burst. "Look, I fully realize that I have no right to be asking you this, especially after—"

"Then don't ask, Rodney." Hiding a wince, he turned away. Definitely déjà vu all over again. He'd kept his voice even, pleasant, but only a fool could have missed the edge in it.

Though Rodney was a great many things, fool wasn't one of them. He sounded tired. "We have no full understanding of how Charybdis works, and it's not for want of trying. You're making a mistake."

Oh, for Pete's sake! They had no full understanding of how half the Ancient technology worked, and there they were, using it on a daily basis. John supposed he should be grateful that the whole Arcturus mess had made Rodney approach things a little more gingerly, but enough was enough. "Rodney, we've discussed it. We've discussed it with Earth. We've got our orders, and you're in a minority of one. It's out of my hands."

"Since when are you the type to just follow orders?"

"Since I became convinced that, where it comes to Charybdis, the benefits outweigh the risk." And John was convinced. If that conviction ever wavered, all he had to do was close his eyes. He'd see the face of Colonel Marshall Sumner, growing more ravaged by the second as the Wraith standing over him sucked life itself out of the man. He'd see Sumner's silent plea for that loose cannon Sheppard to shoot him. And if he'd sensed anything about Ikaros, it was that the kid despised the Wraith as much as he did.

The enemy of my enemy is my friend.

Somehow and disconcertingly, Rodney seemed to have read his thoughts. "Just because Ikaros looks like you doesn't mean it *is* you. But I don't suppose that's ever occurred to anybody."

"Very philosophical." A rumble from the airlock announced that the technicians had retrieved Ikaros and came hoisting the computer console down the short corridor. John stepped aside to let them pass and, with a quick glance at their retreating backs, hissed, "Can we get a move on, Rodney? Like I said, we've got our orders. Tests to run, make the Wraith un-happen, save the galaxy, and all that jazz."

Determined to let any further comments and suggestions slide off his back, he followed the technicians into the inner chamber. It was as close as you could get to stepping inside a geode. Diffuse illumination reached up from floor panels and bounced off a myriad crystals to flood the interior of the dome with a dazzling rainbow lightshow. He'd seen it half a dozen times before, but it never lost its impact. Still, a nagging little voice at the back of John's mind inquired if he might be naïvely thinking that nothing so beautiful could possibly cause any harm.

A querying look from Teyla shooed the thought away. Her gaze wandered on, over John's shoulder and to Rodney, who'd entered behind him, and she tilted her head a little, cocked an eyebrow—a *what's up?* gesture. John pretended to miss it, and casually drifted over to her. She and Ronon had parked themselves at the periphery of the room, together with Elizabeth Weir. John frowned. He wished she'd stayed in Atlantis, but the lure of Charybdis had proven strong enough to overcome even her sense of caution.

Meanwhile technicians bustled like ants around the object at the center of the room. If he didn't know any better he'd say this was a gallery and the object an installation: *Hedgehog Revisited*. Unless it was the local version of a disco, with the mother of all glitter balls.

Zelenka clucked over it like momma hen over the chicks, connecting a small *naquada* generator to Ikaros's computer console. Seconds later the A.I. materialized, prompting gasps and furtive glances from everybody who hadn't seen the kid before—about seventy percent of the people in the room.

"Sir?" one brave soul yelped.

"Yes, yes, yes." Rodney seemed to have regained his stride. "Move along now. There's nothing to see here, apart from an unfortunate family resemblance."

"Actually, they should leave now," said Zelenka. "We're just about ready here, and well… with a view to Arcturus we've agreed on essential personnel only."

"Yeah. With a view to that." Rodney glared at him, then turned to the technicians. "Scram." While they filed out the door, he moved up to the seemingly unstructured pile of crystals that formed the core of the Charybdis device and trained a baleful stare on Ikaros. "Now what?"

Ikaros was quiet—a rare event. He gazed around, his shape translucent and shot through with the brilliant prismatic sparks thrown back by the inside of the dome. It made him look like the integral part of Charybdis he professed himself to be. Ronon took a sudden step back, and John had a fair idea of what had startled the Satedan. He was seeing his own mirror image, dehumanized, ghostlike at best—or something entirely more sinister. And not. The kid smiled, radiating a sense of bone-deep satisfaction, of homecoming.

What was the illusion? Humanity or its absence?

John was at a loss for an answer, though one thing he knew for certain: the notion of emotional software spooked the hell out of him. And maybe Rodney was right. He slid a sidelong glance at McKay who was too busy nursing his impatience to notice.

"*Now* what?" he repeated, breaking the spell.

"Oh," said Ikaros to the room at large. "My apologies. I... I have been looking forward to this for a long time. Ten thousand of your years." Still smiling serenely, he turned to McKay. "Now? Now you shall have to overcome your reluctance to giving me access to technology you don't understand and link me to Charybdis."

Too stunned to even splutter, Rodney gasped, "What?"

"You need to link me to Charybdis," Ikaros said again, contriving to sound like a kindergarten teacher. "The simplest way of doing it is to attach one of those funny little connectors of yours"—he nodded at a spare Rodney had clipped to his jacket—"to one of the crystals. How about the green one there?" he suggested brightly.

"Why?" snapped Rodney, bristling with anger and misgivings.

"Because I like green."

Before John could tell them to get on with it, Zelenka took matters into his own hands. "At a guess I'd say it's because Ikaros can do what eluded us in four weeks of testing that thing." He snapped the connector from Rodney's jacket.

"Have any of you gung-ho types got sufficient education in the classics to comprehend what the original Charybdis was?" McKay asked miserably. "Massive maelstrom in the Aegean, sucking everything into—"

"It's a *story*, Rodney," Zelenka soothed. "Besides, there's no open water on Mykena Quattuor."

"I realize that. We're not sitting in a boat, either, and nobody's tied Colonel Sheppard to the mast. We'll probably pay for that oversight."

"Sounds interesting." Ronon looked as if he was mentally practicing knots.

"Don't get too excited," growled John. "As Zelenka pointed out, it's a *story*."

Rodney snatched back the connector lead from his colleague. "Just as long as nobody says I didn't warn you."

"That'll be the last thing anybody says."

"You're wasting my time!" Ikaros seemed ready to jump out of his virtual skin.

"Oh, I'm so sorry. How dare we?" McKay snarled. He jammed the connector into a port at the back of Ikaros's console and attached the other end to the nearest crystal. A pink one. Presumably he meant to make a point. "At the risk of repeating myself: now what?"

That serene smile was back on the kid's face. "Now I merge."

"You—"

"John!" Head cocked, Weir had placed a hand to her headset, listening intently. "Jumper Two. They're relaying a message from Atlantis."

Jumper Two, piloted by Stackhouse, was in geostationary orbit near the Stargate to maintain contact with Atlantis. It was a safety measure in case of an emergency. John felt the fine hairs at the back of his neck stand on end.

"What is it?" he asked.

A second later Elizabeth looked up. "One of the historians. He thinks the material in the archives may have been sanitized. The medical records he dug up indicate that Ikaros suffered a… psychotic break after his parents and sisters were lost in a Wraith culling."

The kid was still smiling, seemingly oblivious to what Elizabeth was saying.

She continued. "It was Janus himself who stopped Charybdis, John. He felt Ikaros was rushing things because he wanted to avenge his parents and younger sisters. I want you to hold off testing Charybdis till further—"

Deceptively gentle, the Ikaros-ghost cut her off. "My motivation for doing this is irrelevant, Dr. Weir, and it doesn't affect the functioning of Charybdis. You can't prevent the inevitable, but I assure you, nobody will be harmed—except the Wraith."

"John?" Her voice sounded shrill and muted at the same time, echoing madly and dragging like treacle.

"Pull the plug, Rodney!"

McKay executed a classy fish dive toward the generator, but even as he was watching him, John knew it was too late. The ephemeral shape of Ikaros brightened into a whirl of colors, blossoming above the core unit of Charybdis, stretching toward the ceiling, expanding to fill the interior of the dome and suffuse them all. Rodney hung suspended mid-flight, horizontally in the air, fingers splayed and reaching for the *naquada* generator. Too late, even if he had been moving, way too late.

"Don't worry!"

Supremely confident the assurance emanated from the center of the mayhem, Ikaros's voice or his own, John couldn't tell as sounds and shapes spiraled out of cohesion. His awareness screamed at the terror of being ripped apart, and he thought he looked at his hands, watched them multiply into a thousand pairs, some liver-spotted and gnarled, others no larger than a baby's tiny digits, every conceivable stage in between, and then those thousands of hands dissolved into a terrible burst of colors that cancelled each other into white light, searing his eyes and rising toward the dissolving apex of the dome and a dizzy vortex of stars, a massive maelstrom, sucking everything into—

CHAPTER SEVEN

Charybdis +32

His breath came short and ragged, and Teyla berated herself for not severing the link sooner. But he had been necessary for him to see. Absolutely necessary... She reached out again, patted down his arm until she found his hand, squeezed it. "Are you alright, Major Sheppard?"

"Yeah. Yeah, I'm fine. Just dandy." He gave a laugh, utterly devoid of humor. "Relatively speaking, that is. I'm not chopped up into God knows how many bits."

"None of us were. I think," she said.

"Oh yeah? Tell that to this... what's his name? Dreadlocks. Rowland?"

"Ronon. I believe the body we found is an alternate version. The alternates who died were not killed by Charybdis directly but by entropic events that occurred later in their respective timelines."

"Such as?"

"I cannot say. But Ikaros was telling the truth up to a point. Charybdis didn't kill us," she asserted again. "We simply became... many."

"No kidding." Then realization struck him. "You're saying that all the originals are still alive?"

"Barring unforeseen events, yes."

"Given the circumstances that's not much of a reassurance." He snorted softly, then whatever amusement he'd momentarily found dissipated. "So why did you show *me* this?"

She had expected the question; the only surprise was that he hadn't asked sooner. "Because you might be able to help."

"Some people might say it's none of my business."

"You're not some people. You're John Sheppard."

"Some people might argue with that," he groused, but he

didn't sound as though he was seriously putting up a fight. There was a pause, then, "What do you need me to do? I'll help out in any way I can. We should be able to set up the villagers with some of the technology from down here, which should make it easier for them to—"

"Nothing like that," she cut him off quickly. "I need you to find Colonel Sheppard—the original."

"Come again?" The question rode on another dry laugh. "How the hell would I do that? It's a big universe out there, Teyla, and it hasn't exactly shrunk since the last time you stepped through the gate."

"Perhaps I've never stepped through the gate." It could even be the truth. Only the original Teyla Emmagan had ever traveled the stars.

"Do you have any idea what the odds are? Even if I'm... if *he* is still alive, and after all I've seen, I'm less sure than you are. It'd make much more sense if—"

"No! Whatever you could do for us here, it wouldn't matter. Not in the long run. Go!" She made a shooing motion with her hands, much like what she'd do to chase off curious village kids. "Go, find Colonel Sheppard."

"How?"

"The same way you found me."

"Oh? Crashing a jumper and damn near killing myself? There's gotta be an easier way."

"You know what I mean. You will find him. Because you have to. Because you're meant to." Teyla couldn't say from where she took that certainty, but it had been with her through all the years that she'd been waiting for him. Perhaps it was a nugget of knowledge embedded in her mind at the split-second Charybdis activated, or perhaps it was merely that minute shred of salvation left in Pandora's Box after all the ills and diseases had escaped; hope. Either way, it did not answer the one question she'd been asking herself again and again, namely whether hope was a good—or simply the most insidious evil of all. "You must find him," she said, surprising herself with the sharpness of her tone.

"You believe he somehow can fix this." A statement, not a

question. He thought this was the fancy of an old woman whose brain had become addled by age, regret, solitude. Doubt rang through his voice clear as a bell. "How do you know?"

"I know how it sounds, and I cannot explain it. I cannot prove it. I just… *know*. And I hope." There was that word again. "Trust me. It's important that you trust me."

"I always have."

"But you don't now." She heard a soft intake of breath in preparation for his answer. Wishing she could see his eyes to tell if his doubts were as deep as she suspected or if she was beginning to convince him, she raised a hand. "No! Listen to me! Searching for the original will make the difference between giving this galaxy a chance—however remote—to heal and sitting back to watch it self-destruct. And perhaps the damage Charybdis caused was not confined to the Pegasus Galaxy. Perhaps—"

"—it affects the entire universe, including Earth." Major Sheppard finished for her. "Yes, that had occurred to me." There was a pause, then the rattle of crutches told her that he was shuffling away from her. "It's changed," he murmured and quickly added, "I don't mean the dead bodies. The city's changed. It feels different, smells different. Tired. More jaded. We didn't mean to wreck it all when we came here, you know? I didn't mean to wake the Wraith. Rodney didn't mean to blow up a solar system. And we sure as hell didn't mean to—"

"—save the Athosians and give them a new home? Or care about everyone you ever encountered?" she shot back. "Children who find a new toy they don't quite understand may well end up accidentally breaking it. Regrettable as this may be, it's also the single most effective method of learning I've ever encountered. And don't forget, I was one of the children, too. Your people are not the only ones at fault."

It was impossible to say if he had listened. He remained quiet for a long time, and she imagined him taking in the sights around him. She'd wondered, often, what this subterranean version of Atlantis might look like, but eventually she'd begun to see it in her mind's eye as it had been—lofty and shining, jewel-like and without death littering every room and hallway. His words just now proved her right, no matter how cowardly such denial might seem. Retaining a clear memory of the beauty of Atlantis was important somehow, as if the very ideal of the city were a far-off beacon that would guide them all home to safety.

And maybe he was seeing past the ruin too and discerned a glimmer of hope, for at last he spoke. "Where would I start looking for him?"

"Within yourself. You're he, he is you, and you're both part of Ikaros. The one thing I *do* know is that there must be some residual effect of Charybdis that links the alternate versions to their originals. I can feel Teyla—every single one of her. Sometimes I…" Oh, this was difficult! She was an old woman; she shouldn't have to do this. Nebulous memories of suspicion and fear leaped out at her like gargoyles. But he'd believed her then, believed *in* her, when everybody else thought she was crazy at best, a traitor at worst. "Sometimes I can feel the others. You. I probably wouldn't be able to if it weren't for the Wraith gene." She shrugged, trying to make light of it. "I'm certain they're still alive."

"I know," he said, surprising her. "Just before I crashed, I felt— There were hundreds of me, thousands maybe. Some of them died. Some were stuck in the same chain of events, but the outcomes always were different. That's what we're looking for, isn't it? A different outcome."

She nodded. "I don't believe Ikaros was deliberately trying to mislead us. He just never expected *this* outcome. Perhaps it was inevitable all along, but it wasn't supposed to happen. That's why we must change it. Things will not improve if we do nothing. On the contrary."

"Entropy."

"Yes. And I don't think we have much time left. The Stargate will take you where you need to be."

"The gate? I don't suppose you have an address to go with this piece of New Age advice?"

"Any address will do."

"Aw, come on! There's got to— Oh my God," he whispered. "The matrices. Of course… The gate system would try to restore the original matrix. It's probably confused as hell by now, but it would try to take me to him, wouldn't it?"

"That would be my assumption, yes." Teyla suddenly felt exhausted, as if drained by the effort of convincing him, making him understand. And perhaps she was. She'd met more stubborn people than him, but she couldn't quite recall when. "There is no guarantee, Major Sheppard," she added softly, because she had to. Fairness demanded it. "We could both be wrong."

"Or we could both be right. It's a fifty-fifty chance. I'll take it." A smile edged his voice. "Besides, as I remember, there wasn't any guarantee we'd survive the trip to Atlantis either." He hobbled back to her. "I guess a jumper would come in handy. Are there any left?"

"Take your pick. Unless they changed parking positions, Jumper One is in the bay. Try not to crash it again."

"Thanks for the vote of confidence." His laughter broke off abruptly. "What about you? What will you do?"

"I'll wait and see what happens," she replied with a cheerfulness that sounded forced even to her own ears.

"And if we succeed?"

Then you and Pirna and Jinto and Halling and the little girl who bears my name, Wex—none of them will have existed. Perhaps not even I.

She didn't say it. She didn't have to. "Go!" she snapped instead. "We're running out of time. So you'd better—"

A loud clatter startled her into speechlessness, and then his arms closed around her and held her tight. "Take care of yourself," he murmured into her hair. "And thanks for everything."

"Go, John," she said again, gently this time. "Good luck."

Without another word he released her, leaving her to feel oddly alone and unprotected. He picked up his crutches, and she listened to him move away, sounds fading, toward the stairs and the jumper bay. She knew he wouldn't look back. It wasn't in his nature.

Teyla Emmagan smiled and carefully groped her way to what had been Dr. Weir's office, to settle in and wait for success and oblivion.

Charybdis -4441

Home?

A life sentence rarely engendered a sense of nostalgia for the cell you were stuck in. Okay, it was more like a planet than a cell, but still… besides, he hadn't been to the mainland for weeks. Elizabeth was terrified that he wouldn't come back. Not without reason.

Funny how being held prisoner could change your feelings about a place.

John upped his pace, pounding up the catwalk as if that could pound the thoughts from his mind. Not thinking seemed to be one of the precious few options he had for staying sane. Though sanity might be overrated, especially when you were buried alive. Above reared one of the transparent domes of Atlantis and above that a couple of gazillions of tons of water. Oh yeah, by the way, Atlantis was still submerged, which only added to his claustrophobia. It had also been a clue the size of a billboard.

Elizabeth was vague about the exact date—then again, she was vague about pretty much everything, except her determination not to let him leave—but to the best of his knowledge 'Now' was a point in time several thousand years before the expedition would arrive. If it arrived at all. That piece of information alone should have been enough to squeeze the life out of him.

Weird thing was, he still was trying to fight it. Weird, because he'd learned early on that accepting the inevitable made it just a little more bearable. After all, he was the guy who'd persuaded himself to *like* a punitive posting to McMurdo. So, what he should be doing was accept the situation for what it was—inevitable, inescapable—crawl into the coziest corner he could find, eat, drink, and… okay, the being merry part might pose a problem, but he still could make up his own ending for *War and Peace*, a total rewrite of the thousand-odd pages he'd never found the time to read, which should keep him busy for the next couple of decades. Instead…

No, John. We're not going to think about what you're doing instead. 'Cos, let's face it, what you're doing makes you every bit as bug-crap crazy as Elizabeth.

Hope?

You haven't got a hope in hell.

You'll die here.

The thought—the one he'd been trying to outrun all along—burst from cover, butt-ugly as any Wraith, reached deep, twisting his gut and taking his breath away.

"No!"

His shout caromed through the immense room, ricocheting from the inside of the dome, until its echoes were whittled away to mere whimpers of defiance. He was on his hands and knees, pole-axed by desolation, staring through the metal grid beneath him at the shadowy floor fifty feet below.

Yes, there always was that, wasn't there?

Something warm and wet struck the back of his hand. Sweat. Had to be.

The floor below beckoned.

Except, if he jumped, he'd take Elizabeth with him, kill her again.

So let's just pretend we skipped that lesson in pilot school and have no idea of the therapeutic properties of gravity, mass, velocity, and impact.

Breathing hard, willing his hands not to shake, he reached for the railing and pulled himself back to his feet. Slowly, stubbornly, he started running again, picking up speed as he went. He'd just run another round and another one after that, until his body hurt badly enough to make him quit thinking.

A little over half an hour later he was close, his mind blank enough to let a memory drift in: *Ronon and he, barreling up the catwalk as though their lives depend on it, and just for once he manages to leave the Satedan standing. Which in and of itself is sweet, but the pissed look on Ronon's face is—*

Gasping for air, his heart thudding madly, John skidded to a halt, and no amount of willpower could keep him from shaking now. Fine hairs on his arms and neck stood on end, as if brushed by silky strands of time that unraveled, fluttered apart, and released him back into the present nightmare.

It hadn't been a memory. It couldn't be, because it never happened. Sure, he'd fantasized about beating Ronon, but Ronon, who'd had at least six inches on John—all of them in the legs, it seemed—had won every single race.

It never happened.

Yet.

"But it's going to," he whispered, unable to say how or where he derived this certainty. "It's going to."

Part of him grasped that he was repeating that same little sentence over and over, hanging on to it as if to a lifeline. It *was* a lifeline. It meant he had a future. It meant that things could be changed, had to be changed, because to the best—or worst—of John's knowledge, Ronon Dex, like everyone else, had been killed by Charybdis. Or it meant that Lieutenant Colonel John Sheppard had finally gone and done it and snapped.

Bug-crap crazy.

If this was crazy, it beat the hell out of sane.

There was only one problem with it…

Yeah, well, he'd have to solve it, wouldn't he?

Still wheezing a little, he eased himself back into a gentle jog and headed for his quarters. In the shower he bashed the problem around some more and finally arrived at the conclusion that there would be no easy or kind way of telling her. Meaning that he'd better get it over with right now.

Ten minutes later he'd pulled on clean clothes, crudely woven from plant fiber and the next best thing to wearing a loofah, and set off in search of Elizabeth. Usually she was easy to find, either hovering near to wherever he was, to make sure he didn't hatch any escape plans, or sometimes, when he managed to elude or plain bore her, in one of a handful of rooms.

This time it was the mess hall—she'd taken to calling it 'the banquet room'—and she'd sure been busy. He stopped in the door for a moment to watch her, trying to keep the familiar tug of guilt and regret at bay. There was little left of the woman he'd known, of his friend, and he'd made her this way. Ultimately, the malfunction of the stasis chamber must have been caused by Charybdis—at the very least, Charybdis had produced the timeline where Elizabeth was condemned to this.

Every so often, without warning or apparent cause, there'd be flashes of who she'd been, of the real Elizabeth. He'd learned to dread those, because the contrast between who she'd been and what she'd become was unbearable, and after five minutes or an hour or however long it lasted, he'd lose her all over again. Lately these small windows of sanity had occurred few and far between. John tried very hard not to be grateful for it.

In fact, if anything, he'd need her to be lucid now, but it didn't look likely. Apparently they were going to celebrate Christmas, for the fifth time in the last little while. She'd dragged out that old dress again, the one he'd first found her in, and was busy garnishing a table with flowers she'd gathered the last time they'd been to the mainland. Though you'd be hard pushed to identify them as flowers now. The shriveled gray corpses were strewn among the crockery, glitter effect provided by what looked like small chunks of broken glass. Very—

"Oh no!" He let go of the doorframe, let that sinking feeling in the pit of his stomach propel him to the table. "Where did you get them, Elizabeth?" he asked, picking up a control crystal and struggling to keep his voice even. Yelling at her wouldn't help.

Head bent, she peered up through her lashes, like a child caught and put on the spot. "I found them," she mumbled, her fingers picking at a desiccated flower.

"Where?"

"On the little ships."

"Are you completely—" God, yes, of course she was out of her mind! And he should have known better than leaving her unsupervised. He'd never thought… Not that it mattered a blind damn just what he'd thought.

"There's lots and lots of them," she said brightly. "We won't miss these few."

No, of course we won't. Not unless we want to fly a jumper. Not unless we want to get out of this sub-oceanic tomb, make that non-memory happen, recover his life, and hers.

John felt his fingers clench, barely kept himself from shaking her. Instead he scooped up the crystals, checked on the chairs and under the table to make sure he had them all, stuffed them into his pockets. Fourteen, in all. That wasn't too bad. If he could get her to tell him exactly where she'd pulled them, he might be able to fix the damage. He grabbed her hand.

"Show me." Teeth grinding, he added, "Please."

"Not now." She frowned, digging her heels in. "We're expecting guests."

Great! Last time it'd been an invisible contingent from the State Department and a Dr. Simon Wallace who seemed to be part of her personal furniture. As far as stultifying evenings went, it'd been a riot. Largely because she'd insisted he carve a turkey that was as undetectable as the guests.

"They… phoned," he heard himself say. "They'll be running half an hour late."

"Oh." She wasn't convinced and let him know it. "Well, I'll need that time to straighten out the mess you've made. Honestly, John! And you could at least go and shave."

He'd love to, if she just told him where she'd hidden his knife. Probably somewhere along with the rest of his weapons—that particular midnight exploit of hers had taught him the value of insomnia. Still, the shaving issue was leverage of a kind. "I'll shave, if you come with me now and show me. We've got plenty of time."

"I don't know…"

"We can get more of these." He held out a crystal on his open palm, smiled. "You said there were lots and lots of them, remember?"

"Really?"

"Really."

Abruptly she set off, dragging him with her, almost at a run. They made it to the jumper bay in record time. The door slid open, and stepping through, taking in what had happened, what she had done, he felt as if he'd slammed into a wall. He let go of her, just stood there, trying to breathe, trying to hang on to that ounce of hope he'd found and feeling it drain away as if someone had pulled a plug.

It was no longer a question of the glass being half empty. More like the glass being broken to bits.

The hangar floor was littered with crystals, a few of them intact, many—too many—of them smashed. On each of the jumpers the hatch stood open, so she must have gotten to all of them. How had she…? Of course. She'd watched him release the hatch a dozen times or more.

"Elizabeth, what did you do?" he whispered.

"I don't like them," she pointed out with a sweeping gesture at the crippled jumpers. "We don't need them anymore. This is prettier." Smiling, she gathered a handful of splinters and let them tinkle to the floor again.

Barely paying attention—it wasn't as though she could add to the wreckage now—he stepped out into the bay, gingerly tiptoeing around glitzy ruin. The tip of his boot struck a shard, slightly bigger this one, and John realized that this crystal was still whole. He picked it up, numb and without really knowing why he bothered, and added it to the small hoard of survivors in his pockets. It was something to do, he supposed. It beat sitting on the floor, howling. Probably.

He found a total of twenty-three good crystals. They'd make a nice wind chime.

Straightening up, John stared at the nearest jumper. Might as well try, he guessed. More pertinently, he had no choice but to try. It wasn't just a question of being able to leave now. Without at least one ship, they'd starve to death—unless he disengaged the ZPMs, got the shield to fail and the city to rise, so they could go fishing on the pier. Until the Wraith dropped by for target practice.

Balancing his stack of crystals, he walked up the ramp.

"We have to go back!" There was a terse edge to Elizabeth's voice. "We have guests, remember?"

"They'll have to wait." He was utterly past caring to play house with her.

"They'll leave if we make them wait."

Excellent! He'd buy a beer for the first one out the goddamn door!

The interior of the jumper was a mess. He could see how she'd done it now: open every single hatch within reach and see what's in there. Aside from the main control junctions, she'd ransacked equipment stores, tool boxes, supply cabinets and strewn their contents over every square inch of flat surface inside the jumper. He harbored no illusions of any of the other jumpers looking any different. Where it came to stuff like this, Elizabeth was nothing if not methodical. The only piece of good news was that she hadn't gotten to the crystal banks that were hidden behind the seats' backrests.

Empty slots yawned from the overhead compartment that housed the drive pod systems. Which crystal went where, or whether any of the crystals he'd salvaged belonged there in the first place, was anybody's guess. Thing about control crystals, they all looked the same to him. Rodney might have made sense of them, but John Sheppard wasn't Rodney McKay. Under normal circumstances he'd have considered it a blessing, but right now it put him at a distinct disadvantage. The one thing he had in abundance, however, was time. He'd just keep going until he got it right. Maybe. John experimentally inserted a crystal into the top left slot. It didn't fit. Well, that was good. If it boiled down to square pegs in round holes, at least it gave him something to go on.

"Don't do that." Elizabeth had been watching from outside the jumper. Now she reluctantly headed up the ramp, muttering to herself. "You're not supposed to fix it. I don't want you to."

Tough. The fifth crystal didn't fit either, but he still had thirty-two to go.

"If you fix it, you'll leave. I don't like that." She was hovering behind his right shoulder, getting agitated, distractedly fingering tools, pieces of equipment.

"Don't touch anything." Schooling his face into an expression intended to telegraph something between calm and serenity, he turned around. "I have to fix it, Elizabeth. And I will have to leave, so I can try to make things right again."

"I don't like that. Things *are* right."

"No. No they're not," he said gently, turning back to the compartment again.

If he'd continued to focus on her, he might have stood a chance. As it was, he only saw blurred motion from the corner of his eye. Whatever it was she'd grabbed from among the clutter—foot-long and shiny metallic—struck his temple. His skull slammed against the bulkhead for a sensational explosion of pain, then things went black. As he tumbled deeper into that velvety, anodyne zone, he thought he heard Elizabeth's voice.

"I'm sorry, John."

Charybdis -908

He lay on his back on a considerably less than comfortable straw pallet and strained to listen into the pitch darkness of the bunkhouse, which accommodated eighteen serfs. Opposite his luxury cot was a tiny casement—unglazed, because these good folks had either lost the wherewithal to provide such minor creature comforts or never had possessed it to begin with. Either way, the communal bedroom was draughty. He'd pointed out the above-average likelihood of this causing some serious health issues, but nobody had seemed interested. He'd promptly caught a persistent head cold.

By now he could identify individual snores. The resonant, metronomic saw and whistle for instance was Sahar, the foreman. The rattle, apnea, and snap belonged to Sahar's wife, Rilla, who was in charge of the pig swill (the one the serfs ate) and lately had been stretching the periods when she didn't breathe to alarming lengths. Probably because the *snap* came out much louder when you were at the brink of anoxia. For variety's sake, the ancient farmhand, Bordan, didn't snore but cough, whereas the maid communicated in delicate honks, like a very small goose—an apt enough description of her character and intellect. These were the highlights, but he also was intimately familiar with everybody else's nightly noises, which attested to the amount of sleep he'd been getting.

The sky past the casement was beginning to gray, and he scrunched his eyes shut and began counting. At seven—five seconds early, actually—the shrill ring of the dawn bell scattered the snores, hoots, honks, and wheezes. They were replaced by moans and grunts as people reluctantly rolled out of bed. He stretched, absently catalogued the daily array of aches—his back and the mattress were incompatible—slipped on his clogs and shuffled for the door.

The morning was overhung by leaden clouds, shedding a misty veil of drizzle fine enough to creep into your pores. He couldn't recall when he'd last seen the sun or felt dry, for that matter. Prayer was held on a muddy rectangle formed by the main farmhouse, a barn, and the bunkhouse. Most serfs had already assembled, and he squeezed in at the back, behind the broad shoulders of a couple of butcher's apprentices that would keep him well out of sight from the front. He preferred it that way, because it saved him the trouble of feigning enthusiasm over the drawn-out incantations in honor of the Ancestors.

"…and protect us from the evils of Ikaros and let us rejoice in practicing simplicity and moderation," Sahar intoned.

"May the Ancestors grant us simplicity," the crowd bleated back.

He joined in mechanically, knowing that someone was bound to notice if he remained silent. As far as he was concerned any more simplicity would set these good folks firmly on the road to wooden clubs and flint arrowheads. That aside, it might be much more conducive to morale if the working population were fed breakfast instead of platitudes. *His* morale definitely would improve.

Around him, the assembly was breaking up, and with a baleful glance at the monochrome sky, he trudged off in the direction of the sties and the restless squealing of the hogs. Ravenous and eager to be let out, they were snapping and jostling each other in the pen, interrupting their shove-fest only to glare at him malevolently. Making sure his feet were well out of harm's way, he climbed up a couple of the rough-hewn planks of the fence and undid the latch. More jostling, as they all vied to be first through the gate.

It wouldn't be so bad if, at least occasionally, he got to enjoy the fruit of his labors, but luxuries such as scrambled eggs and bacon were reserved strictly for the nobility in the city below.

Suddenly he could taste the salty, savory flavor of a rasher of bacon on his tongue, knew without a doubt that that's what it was. His stomach growled in response, dispelling this odd sensory memory of something he couldn't recall ever having eaten in his life. Trying to ignore both his hunger and the vague unsettled feeling the bacon episode had left, he grabbed a sturdy stick that was leaning against the fence—state-of-the-art agricultural technology—and plodded after the hogs uphill and toward the forest.

The soil on the path, saturated from months of rainfalls and churned up by a thousand trotters, stuck to his clogs in heavy clumps, layering itself under the soles, until he felt as if he were walking on platform shoes. The animals had no such problems and briskly trotted toward the shelter of the trees. By the time he caught up with them, they'd reached a small clearing and looked like they were going to settle in for the day. Sadly for them, he had no intention of sitting here till dusk and soaking through and catching his death. Okay, he'd soak through anyway, but he could at least make a bid at staying warm.

He singled out the lead animal and brought the stick down on its bulging hindquarters. At the third wallop the hog got the message, hissed in outrage, and began moving deeper into the forest, drawing the other animals after it. Repeated taps with the stick steered it uphill on a barely visible trail. Driven by something he couldn't or wouldn't clearly define, he kept going, higher and deeper into the forest than he'd ever taken the hogs before.

The trail was all but overgrown, but the footing had improved. There were flagstones, meticulously laid once, though frost and tree roots had cracked them long ago and allowed weeds to sprout through the gaps. Still, the workmanship was beyond anything they'd be capable of now. His curiosity piqued, he walked faster, no longer caring whether or not the hogs kept up.

At last the trail opened out into a glade. Except, no glade he'd ever met came complete with stairs. Broad and sweeping they arced down toward an arena of sorts. Maybe an amphitheater. He'd heard about places like that, but he'd never visited one; the theaters, much like scrambled eggs and bacon, were reserved for the nobility. Either side of the stairway stretched tiers, half swallowed by the forest. Where he imagined the spectators to have sat or stood, centuries-old trees had breached the tiers and branches protruded through what must have been a railing once. At the far end of the arena below, upstage center as it were, rose a large stone ring, wreathed around by creepers and bearded with moss.

Spurred by a bout of inquisitiveness strong enough to startle him—their culture discouraged inquisitiveness—he shouldered his way past some bushes and headed in among the trees. He began scraping the topsoil off the ground and within minutes found the floor beneath. Not stone, not wood—wood would have decayed ages ago—but some smooth, shiny material that somehow struck him as oddly familiar, as oddly familiar as the entire layout of this place. He pushed further into the undergrowth and found what at first glance looked like boulders. They weren't. They were tables, or benches maybe, overgrown to the point of being barely recognizable. Only, he *did* recognize them. He'd seen them before, though when or where he couldn't begin to fathom. There would have been people sitting here, operating devices now forbidden.

And he'd known every single one of them.

He'd *been* one of them.

The impact of the notion sent him reeling back a step, and he tripped and almost fell. As he tried to regain his balance, he trod on a twig. It snapped with a loud crack. Trembling, he spun around, saw the object he'd stumbled over. Not a rock. Not a branch, either. And he was starting to guess what this place was. He shouldn't be here. He should leave. For some reason that wasn't an option, though.

He crouched clumsily and picked up the skull. It was gleaming white and slick with the pervasive moisture, and it was human, like the rest of the bones. He sniffed it, wondering the same instant how he knew to do this, remembering a dark-haired, excitable man with a white coat and a strange accent. Both of which were immaterial now. The skull had no discernible odor at all, which meant its owner had died a long time ago. Among the bleached heap of bones that had once been a ribcage lay a couple of metal plates attached to a chain. Some kind of necklace or other ornament, perhaps. He set down the skull, snatched the necklace and frowned at it. The metal plates were embossed with several lines of writing: A name. Then a long number. Then *AF*. Then *AB neg*. Then *Catholic*.

He should not have been able to read this—or any other writing, for that matter. Literacy was the first evil of Ikaros. Shivering, he stared at the metal plates, knowing with absolute certainty that this should mean something to him. The name should mean something to him.

Sheppard, John.

Colonel.

That wasn't written on the plates, but he knew it was connected.

Colonel Sheppard.

A face floated free from that muddle of memories inside his mind. Young and annoyingly handsome, though the shadow of distrust in the eyes belied both youth and looks.

That might take a while.

He straightened up, stung as a whole slew of images flooded back. That man, that colonel, had been a friend, which was unusual, to say the least. He didn't have the kind of personality that allowed him to make friends, and he knew it. He cultivated it, because he'd realized early on that it kept people at arm's length. And as long as people remained at arm's length they couldn't hurt you, deliberately or otherwise, they couldn't make demands. It simply was easier this way. Sheppard's and his friendship, prickly and at times almost adversarial, had developed despite themselves, but it most certainly had been a friendship. At least until he'd almost killed the man, succeeded in killing another, destroyed whole worlds.

But even then it hadn't been irredeemable. It—

Startled by the sharp snap of another breaking twig, he whirled around, came face to face with a bunch of wet snouts and red, malignant eyes. The hogs had caught up with him, and for a moment he gazed at them uncomprehendingly. How in God's name had he ended up here, with them?

Squealing with excitement, the hogs pushed past him and toward that desolate heap of bones.

"No!"

The fury was beyond anything he'd ever experienced. As

hard as he could and without caring where it hit or how much damage it did, he brought his stick down on snouts, heads, haunches. The lead animal dropped the femur it had snagged and rounded on him with a shriek. A quick series of blows bludgeoned it into retreat, squeaking and snapping. The other animals trotted after it, and at last the herd vanished into the undergrowth.

Panting hard, he dropped the stick, turned back to the remains. His face was wet, he realized, and the rain had nothing to do with it. It was as though his rage had opened the floodgates to make way for every damn painful emotion that wanted to follow. There was a reason why his only permanent attachment had been a cat that preferred his neighbor's company.

John Sheppard, of all people, would have appreciated the irony of it.

Just as well that he wouldn't find out about it now. Nobody would. Why dismantle a carefully cultivated image, right?

He hung those engraved metal plates around his neck, made sure they were hidden under his clothing. Then he carefully gathered the skull. He'd find a safe place, bury it, though he couldn't really have said why, except that just leaving it here seemed wrong and that a burial, however unceremonious, would make him feel better somehow. And this was ironic, too. Dead was dead. He didn't believe in wakes, funerals, and other feel-good rituals. He was a scientist. He was—

Gasping and suddenly oblivious to the pouring rain, he sat back on his heels.

He was a scientist, a physicist.

He was a prodigy, a Nobel prospect.

He also was stranded in the armpit of the universe, herding swine in a Luddite theme park.

Why?

He still had no recollection of what had happened to make him end up in this place, but he'd find out. He owed it to himself. And then he'd get the hell out of here and look for the others. Colonel Sheppard, with that blithe military approach of demanding the impossible, would expect him to—he always had—and somehow this seemed a far better way of honoring the dead than wakes and all the rest of it.

In the mud at his feet glistened a small shard of metal that must have broken off from some piece of the ruined equipment that littered the place. He picked it up, rose, and wandered over to that desk—workstation?—he'd found earlier. Slowly, deliberately, and partly to make sure that he wouldn't forget it again, he began scratching letters into the weather-pitted surface:

Ikaros.

No. That was wrong. What was he thinking?

He scratched it out, started again.

Dr. Meredith Rodney McKay.

CHAPTER EIGHT

Charybdis +32 to Charybdis -4441

The jumper's rear hatch opened, and Major John Sheppard climbed up the ramp, dumped his crutches on a bench in the aft compartment—good riddance—and limped forward to drop into the pilot's seat, feeling whole for the first time in weeks. Who needed two good legs, if you could fly? He gave a small grin, flexed his fingers and closed them around the stick, trying not to think of how it'd felt the last time he'd done that, three weeks ago.

The systems, all nominal, came online without a hitch. Moments later he hovered above the jumper bay door, watched it open on the HUD, and eased the craft down into the control center and in front of the Stargate. Teyla stood near the top of the stairs. He doubted she'd return to the surface. They hadn't talked about it, but he couldn't shake the certainty that she'd remain in Atlantis. It had become her home, too.

His gaze settled on the onboard dialing panel. Rodney probably could have given him the exact number of possible combinations, though after the first million you might as well stop counting. Besides, Rodney wasn't here. For all John knew, some version of Rodney was lying back there among all the other bodies, and he could only hope that the original was still alive. That all the originals were still alive.

If Teyla was right—and John figured that was as likely as just about anything else—then it wouldn't really matter what address he dialed; the gate system would attempt to reassemble the fragmented matrices and take him wherever the original was. Even if she was wrong and it didn't work, at least he wouldn't have to worry about running into the Wraith. The Pegasus galaxy might be dying, but it was one hundred percent Wraith-free. Go, Ikaros!

"Here's to you, Teyla." He punched in the coordinates for Athos again.

Then he held his breath, again taking in the scale of destruction in the control center. Whatever had happened here, the devastation was worse than it had been after the Wraith had laid siege on Atlantis.

One by one the chevrons engaged, and then the event horizon blasted toward him, vaporizing the rest of the debris that had half blocked the gate.

"Okay…"

With a deep breath, he nudged the jumper forward and into the wormhole. The freezing flash of disorientation he'd come to expect as a given of wormhole travel escalated to the power of ten, and a last conscious thought screamed that there had to be a malfunction. Then awareness snapped to black, leaving his panic to explode the second he emerged on the other side. Except, whatever scenario he'd pictured, it wasn't this. He instantly nursed a bizarre mental image of Jumper One being flipped over, shaken around a bit, and spat back out in the direction where it'd come from. Which wasn't how it worked. Wormholes were supposed to be strictly one way. Apparently this one hadn't read the manual.

To the best of his knowledge, he'd managed an all-time first; he'd gated from Atlantis to Atlantis.

But eventually facts percolated through; unless somebody had done a record-breaking cleanup job, this wasn't the Atlantis he had left. It was pristine by comparison. As a matter of fact, the control center almost looked as it had when the expedition first arrived; completely deserted and still, dark, consoles and equipment covered with dustsheets. Also, it definitely had that uncanny, slightly muted underwater feel to it. Above, the hangar doors opened, as if extending an invitation. Fine. For the time being, John shelved an inordinate number of questions and, with practiced ease, maneuvered the craft up into the jumper bay.

"What the hell?"

It wasn't so much finding his accustomed parking space taken up by Jumper One Mark II. It was the décor, if that's what you could call it. Somebody had gutted the jumpers' crystal banks, smashed the crystals, and scattered the remains on the floor. The result looked like an explosion in a glass factory, and it couldn't possibly have been accidental. Whoever had done this must have intended to disable every single jumper in the bay—and they'd succeeded spectacularly.

John felt a nasty little chill slither up his spine, engaged the cloaking device, and nudged his craft into the farthest corner of the hangar, mind racing and tactical instincts kicking in with a vengeance. Bad news: he was completely unarmed. Every shred of gear he'd had lay at the bottom of an other-dimensional version of the Lantean Ocean. Good news: from what he'd seen so far, the rampage had been confined to the jumpers, meaning there was a chance that he could pick up what he needed from the small armory by the hangar door. The trick would be getting there.

Then again, maybe not.

If anyone were actually manning the city, incoming gate traffic should have created a slightly stronger response than it had just now, namely zip. Of course, there always was the possibility that they had set a trap and were lying in wait for him. No way of telling for sure without a life-signs detector. He mechanically reached toward the compartment that should have held the device and came up empty. Somebody had removed it. Meaning that the nearest life-signs detector probably could be found—

"In the armory," he grunted in resignation. "And it's not gonna walk over here."

He pushed himself out of the chair, wincing at a stab of pain. The bones had knitted, but the leg was wrecked all the same. Carson Beckett might have been able to fix it, but not Teyla with the means she'd had at hand. She'd barely managed to save his life. Shuffling into the rear compartment, he scowled at the crutches. Teyla had insisted he keep using them, but unless he found occasion to hit somebody over the head with them, they'd only get in the way. That aside, he was sick to death of the things.

The hatch slid open on the chaos in the bay. All over the floor, crystal shards glittered like freshly fallen snow, and the hangar was quiet enough to sustain the illusion. For long moments he stood on the ramp, listening. The stillness remained unbroken, no furtive shuffles from men in hiding, no soft intakes of breath, no accidental clink of weapons. He was alone.

Which didn't change the fact that the distance to the armory and the exit door seemed like a mile.

Too bad, John. Standing here, wanting a skateboard won't shorten it.

A skateboard would be fun, though.

He gimped off the ramp, flinched at the crunch of crystal under his feet, disproportionately loud in the silence of the room. Behind him the hatch closed, concealing that unsettling hole in reality and, with it, Jumper One. He'd made it almost to the front of the hangar when he spotted it; something had been dragged from one of the jumpers, parting the shards like Moses the Red Sea and laying a trail to the exit. Where the concrete was bare it showed a track of dull brown smears and spots.

Somehow he didn't think it was rust. Jaws clenched, he followed the trail back to that jumper. Inside, lying on the floor among more crystal shards, he discovered a bloodstained wrench. The only thing reassuring about it was the fact that whoever had wielded it must have seen themselves forced to resort to lo-tech weaponry.

See? Should have taken the crutches, John.

The jumper yielded nothing else, so he headed over to the armory. It seemed untouched alright. *Really* untouched.

"Damn!" he whispered.

If the armory was anything to go by, the expedition had never reached Atlantis in this timeline. There should have been guns and rifles and ammo crates—in short, samples of the entire arsenal they'd brought with them to the Pegasus Galaxy. What he found were a couple of racks of spare drones and selected other items of Ancient technology. No weapons. At least none he could readily identify or use. On the upside, atop a shelf at the back of the room sat a dozen life-signs detectors. He grabbed one, mentally crossing his fingers.

A heartbeat later he sighed in relief as the small screen lit up.

It showed two bright dots as the only inhabitants of the entire city. The dots were engaged in an odd, slow-motion choreography of stop and go. The speed—or lack thereof—was deceptive, and it took him a couple of seconds to realize that he was looking at a hunting pattern; Dot B was stalking Dot A, the scene of the chase gradually moving from the control tower to the storage and maintenance structures on the East Pier, which told him that Dot B had to know its way around—there were thousands of places to hide or set up a nice little ambush out there. Either the dots were stone deaf and hadn't heard the klaxons, or they'd decided that their chase was more important than an incoming wormhole and potential company.

John decided to hook up with Dot B. He'd always had a soft spot for the underdog. Besides, a bit of quid pro quo—assistance for information—might help answer the intriguing question of what the hell was going on here. Dot B was headed up toward the generator station at the East Pier. Good thinking. One little dot could wreak a surprising amount of havoc with the systems that were fed through there, even when the city was submerged.

Given the dreamlike pace at which the dots were moving, he'd have a good chance of intercepting Dot B at the station. John cut across the control center to the nearest transporter, which brought him out at a terminal within two hundred yards of the pier. The transporter door slid open on a blur of movement.

The round shattered the touch panel on the cabin wall, missing him by a hair. Instinct or a sixth sense had made him spin out of the way. Without stopping to think he dived out of the cabin—a dead end now that the panel was gone—hit the floor like a sack of cement, rolled over, and scrambled for the cover of a pillar.

So much for the dots ignoring the warning klaxons. Well, one dot anyway.

A second shot went wide, ripping stone shrapnel from the floor behind him. He heard a shout of frustration, thought he recognized the voice, and immediately discarded the notion, because it would have been ludicrous. Unless…

"Elizabeth! Don't shoot! It's me. John!"

The reply was another round, wide by a mile but pretty unambiguous.

He ducked reflexively, frowned. If anything the lousy marksmanship confirmed it. After all, Elizabeth hated guns. Though why she'd feel the need to shoot him remained a mystery. Admittedly he'd managed to piss her off big time on a few occasions, but this—

A third shot tore through the hallway. Light, unsteady footfalls told him she was on the move, closing in. Waiting probably wasn't a good idea. Even she couldn't miss at point blank range.

The footfalls stopped, then she fired again.

Staking his life on the fact that the recoil would mess up her aim even worse, John darted from cover and down the corridor at a hobbling run that made him sweat with pain. But pain wouldn't kill him, whereas Elizabeth just might. At the end of the corridor lay a spacious hall and a maze of rooms off several stories of galleries and metal stairways. It probably had been a storage area, though they'd never actually confirmed it. At any rate, it'd provide much better cover and a chance to lay low and get a fix on Dot B, who seemed to have done the smart thing and dropped below the radar.

His bum leg buckled under him and he almost fell. A quick slam into the wall helped him stay upright, but he couldn't run anymore. The storage hall was sixty feet ahead—it might as well have been sixty light years. Not a chance. Deciding he'd rather face her than be shot in the back, he pushed himself off the wall. Who knew, maybe he could talk some sense into her.

Hands raised, he turned around and instantly realized that talk wouldn't save him. She looked like something that had escaped from a medieval bedlam, wild-eyed, haggard, a Medusa's head of gray hair flaring around a skull-like face. Her arms were outstretched, elbows locked, fingers strangling a 9 mm Beretta. The barrel of the gun wavered unsteadily as she staggered toward him. Each time she forced it back on target with a frown of concentration. Itchy trigger finger didn't begin to describe it.

"Elizabeth—"

"I told you I didn't want you to leave!" she spat.

Since she'd never told him anything of the sort, it was a safe assumption that the original John Sheppard and Dot B were one and the same. "Elizabeth—"

"I don't want to hear it!"

The round struck the wall inches in front of him, smashing a light panel and showering him in a hail of splinters. Blinking furiously, John resisted the impulse to protect his face; if he was to achieve anything, he had to maintain eye contact with her. "Look at me, Elizabeth! Do I—"

"Get down!"

The bellow came from the storage area behind, the voice familiar enough for him to obey without hesitation—after all, if you couldn't trust yourself, whom could you trust? Wondering whether he'd ever get to finish a sentence, he hit the deck, heard something whiz overhead.

The something—a rubber ball?—hit Elizabeth squarely in the chest, toppling her. In falling, she lost her grip on the gun. The weapon sailed along the corridor, clattering to a halt within a few yards of John. He launched himself forward, starting to scrabble for it same time as Elizabeth was recovering. His fingertips just about grazed the barrel. Another half inch and—

"I don't think so!"

A well-placed kick sent the gun spiraling down the corridor and way out of reach. John's alter ego flung himself atop Elizabeth, straddled her. An expert left hook cut off furious screams and flailing by knocking her out cold.

"I hate hitting women," Lieutenant Colonel Sheppard observed to no one in particular. Then he straightened up, flipped her over, and used the simple sling that had converted a piece of rubber into a missile to tie Elizabeth's hands securely behind her back. That done, he turned around. "And who the hell are y—" His jaw dropped.

"Please don't tell me I always look that stupid when I'm surprised."

To find somebody else unable to finish his thought proved

unexpectedly satisfying. John had aimed for a grin, figured he didn't quite make it, and saw what had to be an identical half grimace on the face staring at him. Conversing with one's own mirror image was just a little on the disconcerting side. Though, admittedly, the mirror image looked nearly as bad as he felt, right down to the rough, homespun outfit. Unshaven and filthy and unsteady on his feet now, his reflection was pale as a sheet, his eyes a little unfocused. Together with a scabbed-over gash on his temple, calling to mind the bloodstained wrench in the jumper, it suggested a severe concussion. That aside, food must have been in extremely short supply around this version of Atlantis. John himself looked a tad less than well-fed—an inevitable result of the infamous tuttleroot soup diet—but the original was a hair shy of emaciation. So was Elizabeth, come to think of it.

They continued staring at each other for a moment, then the original—John felt a little inconsequential, like having a star-athlete, four-point-zero-GPA older brother who was reaping all the glory—said, "I'm guessing this is another one of the numerous entertaining side-effects of Charybdis?"

"Oh yes."

"So, who… uh…" The implications were starting to sink in. One of the few things nobody had ever accused him of was being slow on the uptake. Looking less confident than a superior officer should, the Lieutenant Colonel cleared his throat. "Which one of us is—"

"The original?"

"Yeah."

"You are."

"How do you know?"

"You outrank me. Sir." John startled himself by sounding rather more acrimonious than he'd meant to sound and suppressed a wince. Things really didn't get any more idiotic than being jealous of yourself.

"I got lucky," offered John the Elder. "When we managed to return Earthside the brass informed Elizabeth that, while I'd been performing competently, the job of military leader of Atlantis was a colonel's billet. Elizabeth… Elizabeth refused to have Colonel Caldwell foisted on her and insisted they fix the problem the easy way."

John read the guilt and regret in his eyes—*his* eyes—and felt a flash of it churning in his own stomach. Casting a wry look at that hag-like figure muttering and writhing on the floor, he murmured, "You probably saved my life, and if it's any consolation, I very much doubt she's the original. Besides, you seem to have won the grand prize. You're the lucky guy who gets to fix it all."

"Says who?"

"Teyla."

"Teyla is alive?"

"A version of her. She may be your Teyla. At any rate, she assures me that all the originals survived."

It brought a first cautious smile—surprise, relief, and maybe brittle hope. "So, how about I pull rank and debrief you, Major?"

Charybdis +32

After the watery murmur of the event horizon had sucked back in on itself and told her that the wormhole had disengaged, Teyla sat on the stairs leading down to the Stargate for a long time, listening to the silence, conjuring up the many different voices that had once filled Atlantis. Funny how she'd suddenly hear people she hadn't thought of in years, decades even, simply because she'd never known them well enough. Which wasn't their fault, and they didn't deserve to be forgotten. John Sheppard's presence had brought them back to her.

And now she'd lay them to rest. All of them.

They, like this Atlantis, reeked of death, and she'd smelled enough of that.

She rose, stretched stiff limbs, wiggled her toes and pumped her fists to force some circulation back into them. It was the cold. Before now she'd never realized how freezing cold this place was. She wondered if there was a plume of condensation each time she exhaled. Probably. At last, pins and needles bit her fingers and toes, announcing that blood flow was restored, and she cautiously felt her way back up the steps and toward the corridor. For once she didn't navigate the obstacle course of debris and dead on autopilot. She couldn't afford to. She had to find the right body.

There was no telling when exactly she'd come to the decision, though she believed that it must have been brewing in her subconscious for quite some time. When the notion had hatched during her silent vigil just now, it had done so fully formed. She took it as an omen that she was meant to obey the impulse and, after all, it wouldn't make a difference in the end. Not for her, not for the people in the village above.

Trying to persuade herself that none of them had ever been meant to exist didn't help. If she truly believed it, why had she helped to safely deliver her tiny namesake? Why, over the years, had she healed countless injuries, saved lives even? Pirna's, for one, and the thought of what would happened to the woman who had befriended her made her ache.

Had she truly had the right to set Major Sheppard on this course? If he succeeded... If he succeeded, every single person in this galaxy, in an infinite number of galaxies in all the timelines Charybdis had created, would wink out quietly without even knowing and be spared the horror that was inevitable if he failed. Those who had survived the cataclysmic birth of those timelines more than thirty years ago could tell of unimaginable destruction and loss of lives. But as terrible as it had been, what was to come if Major Sheppard failed would be infinitely worse. It had already begun. She could feel it in her bones. Perhaps even the doubts she was having were part of it.

And loitering here, wondering, fishing for reasons not to act, wouldn't improve the outcome. On the contrary. She—everybody—was running out of time. Charybdis was becoming unstable, a by-product of the entropy it had caused. The outward indicators seemed almost accidental; tremors like the one that had caused the rockslide in her cave, the unusual number of storms this past winter, even Pirna's pregnancy at a time when she should no longer have been able to bear a child. Internally, the signs were less inconspicuous; she felt, hour by hour and day by day, the erosion of the barriers between herself and her alternate versions. Holding on to herself and her sanity was getting increasingly difficult, as a myriad other consciousnesses pressed in on her mind like the weight of water onto a crumbling dam. When—not if—the dam burst, they'd all be swept away in a torrent of chaos. She'd seen all her futures, and too many of her alternates were already dying, while the original was about to face grave danger. Teyla couldn't be completely certain, but she became more and more convinced that, if any of the originals died, there would be no righting this.

Reaching out, her fingertips encountered the top of what had to be the city monitoring consoles. There would be a chair ahead, occupied by a dead technician. Another nameless memory, he; in fact, she couldn't even say who'd been on duty the day they all died. She gingerly made her way past the body. Then she was out in the hallway and crept along the wall, toes brushing the floor ahead so she wouldn't trip. At one point she stubbed against something soft, heard a whisper of fabric—somebody's clothes. A crane's step carried her over their owner. After that she encountered no more obstacles all the way to where the corridor opened out into a lounge where she had nearly fallen earlier.

He would be somewhere around here.

Bracing herself against the wall she got down on all fours and began to crawl, moving her hands in slow searching sweeps just above the floor. Suddenly she realized what it reminded her of, and she laughed—they'd played this when they were children; one of them would be blindfolded, the others would hide a treat or toy under a pot, and the blindfolded kid would have to find the pot by batting the ground with a cooking spoon.

Her laughter died abruptly when her fingers caught in a shock of matted hair. Holding her breath, she held on to one of the tresses, examined it carefully. It was a braid or rather, a tightly intertwined strand.

"Greetings, old friend," she whispered. "And I hope you'll forgive me for doing this."

From the pouch attached to her belt, she fished a hunting knife. A gift from her father, it had been hers for as long as she could remember, though it never had seen use such as this.

Respect for the dead was something Athosian children were taught from early childhood, and what she was about to do went against everything Teyla believed in. The knife clutched in her right, she felt with her left: a shoulder, upper arm, forearm covered in threadbare material that was rotting away around the corpse. Dust and the peculiar musty odor of ancient death rose from it and made her sneeze. She found the cuff of the shirt and then the shriveled, leathery skin of a hand. It lay palm up and open, almost relaxed, its fingers curled slightly from dehydration. Clasping the knife even tighter and gritting her teeth, she grabbed one finger, hesitated briefly, and then cut it off, half expecting to hear a sudden scream of pain. There wasn't a sound, of course, apart from a gentle thud when the dead hand fell back to the floor. Only then she realized that, absurdly, she had kept her eyes scrunched shut.

Teyla blew out the breath she'd held, gently patted the body's chest. "Forgive me," she murmured again, stowed the knife and finger safely in the pouch, and returned to the control center.

At the dialing console she stopped, again wondering about the wisdom of this idea. What swayed her in the end was the certainty that she couldn't possibly make things worse. Her hand slid over the smooth surface of the console. In her mind's eye, she tried to picture the order of the glyphs, which was much harder than she'd have liked to admit. After all, she'd looked at it hundreds of times in the past, but all that wanted to materialize now was a confusing jumble of symbols.

Why hadn't she memorized their precise position?

Because she'd never seen the need, it was as stupidly simple as that.

Her fingers traced the layout of the console, struggling to remember. The glyphs weren't raised, as they were on a DHD, and all she felt were the smooth edges of the of the dialing panels. She only needed the one symbol. Only the point of origin, for if she was right, it wouldn't matter which Stargate she dialed, she'd always be taken to the place and timeline where her original was. If she was wrong—well, it wouldn't matter. Not that much, in the grander scheme of things. Her left hand hovered over one panel, and she was almost completely certain that this had to be the one. Nothing left but to try.

With her right, she dialed a random sequence of six symbols, listened to the reassuring noise of engaging chevrons as she went, and then pushed the seventh with her left. The seventh chevron failed to lock. It could mean one of two things. Either she was wrong about the point of origin, or the six coordinates she'd dialed before were not a valid Stargate address. Given the infinite number of possible combinations, the second option was more than likely, and it was unreasonable to expect that she would accidentally hit an address on the first attempt. She'd just have to keep trying, however long it took.

Hours later she felt a little less determined, but she doggedly dialed again. Eventually she was bound to find a viable address. When it happened at last it took several seconds to sink in. She'd pushed the six coordinates, heard the chevrons engage, pushed the point of origin, and moved to dial again so mechanically that she barely noticed the seventh chevron locking. It was the whoosh of the event horizon cascading out toward her that drove it home; she'd found her place to go.

And she'd have to hurry now.

Hand over hand, she guided herself along the console, onto the handrail along the gallery and down the stairs. As she reached the last step and ran out of rail, she hesitated for a moment, then caught the whisper of the event horizon and used it as a beacon to orient herself. Mere steps into that no-man's-land between the stairway and the Stargate she tripped over a piece of metal she'd never considered might be there. She pitched forward without time to brace herself and came down hard on more debris, pinning her right arm under her body. The snap of breaking bone was audible even muffled by her body and clothes.

Old women's bones! Curse them!

For a few seconds she lay there, panting against the agony in her wrist, half tempted to just quit fighting, wait for death, and have it over with. Except, she'd never quit anything in her life. She didn't have it in her. With a furious cry she pushed herself to her knees and carefully tucked the injured hand into her jacket. Then she started crawling forward, scrabbling across rubble and bodies, no longer caring if the departed might feel desecrated. She had to make it before the gate shut down. If she didn't, she knew she wouldn't have the strength to try again. Once she stopped to listen out for the soft gurgle coming from the Stargate, found she was still on track and closer, much closer now.

Without warning the pile of rubble gave under her weight. She curled up as best she could to protect her broken wrist and, in a small avalanche of debris, she tumbled downhill and into the wormhole, which swallowed her shout of triumph.

Charybdis +13

By fall of dusk the town of Iraklia on Paphos III was well and truly decimated. An honest day's work, Ronon thought with a surge of disgust he didn't bother to hide. Nobody cared, because it didn't matter. You could be disgusted all you liked, you'd still do the bidding of the Behemoth. Same as the Commander, who even now was strutting across what had been the town's market square, scratching his nether regions and adjusting his pants before sending a one-eyed glare at a handful of survivors. Bruised and battered and bloodied—likely as not half of them wouldn't live through the night—the townspeople huddled between a detachment of hulking, grinning guards. The Commander hawked up a gob of phlegm, spat at them, and strode on toward a hastily erected tent where he'd take his supper.

A lazy southerly breeze lifted wads of smoke from smoldering houses and still burning piles of corpses. As the smoke rose, it dropped flakes of oily ash, gummy like glue, that stuck to your skin and hair and clothes as a constant reminder of what you'd done that day. It also dropped a blanket of smell, the uniquely terrible stench of roasting flesh that seemed too heavy with sin to be carried off on mere air.

The spoils of war.

Maybe he'd simply chosen wrong, once upon a time.

No, that wasn't fair. Not fair to himself. Not fair to his calling. Not fair to people like John Sheppard and Teyla

Emmagan—or Dr. Weir who had been a warrior of words rather than the sword.

Ronon made a conscious effort to rein in the well of grief the memory had unleashed. The Behemoth would sense it and turn it against him. It always did, exploiting any scrap of emotion its components could offer. Some enjoyed feeding it; Ronon didn't. It wasn't what he'd signed up for.

Maybe it was.

He'd stopped caring by then.

Except, he looked at the wholesale slaughter and devastation around him and found he still cared.

Get beyond it. You haven't got a choice.

A few houses over, a couple of soldiers dragged another townsman—hardly more than a boy, this one—from the blazing ruin that had been his home. He was blackened by smoke, coughing and spluttering, his clothes literally burned off his back, but he was still kicking at the soldiers. Brave but stupid, as the boy should know. This was by no means their first visit to Paphos III, and word tended to get out quickly. After this, Ronon very much doubted that any town on the planet would ever fall behind on its tithe again, no matter how severe the summer drought or how lousy the harvest.

Without apparent reason, the two soldiers changed course, dragging their captive toward him. Ronon knew what was to come as soon as he sensed the will of the Behemoth stirring. After all, he'd asked for it. Their faces expressionless, the men stopped before him and dropped their captive like a sack of garbage. The youngster sagged to his knees, eyes raised and defiantly staring at Ronon. Tears—of fury rather than of pain or fear—had tattooed pale patterns onto soot-stained skin. This one wouldn't beg, which was a relief.

Against his will Ronon's fingers tightened around the hilt of his sword. This must be what it felt like to be possessed by one of those Goa'uld Sheppard and the others had told him about. He didn't even begin to fight it. He'd tried before, countless times, failed countless times. One thing he had learned, though; the quicker he smothered his own volition, the more merciful the victim's death would be. So he pretended to be a spectator, somewhere outside his body, uninvolved and emotionless, there only to judge the neatness of the kill.

It was swift and it was fast, and Ronon spun away as soon as it was done to avoid the accusation staring from dead eyes. The setting sun, dyed crimson by the haze of smoke above the town, caught on the edge of Ronon's blade and triggered an explosion of reds. Struggling to contain his rage, he wiped the blade on his pants and sheathed it. Then, in a back corner of his mind, hopefully safe from the Behemoth's prying, Ronon offered a brief prayer for forgiveness to the youngster and whatever deities the boy might have believed in.

He'd never have thought that, one day, he'd wish for the Wraith back. Much as he'd hated being a runner, at least they'd left his will alone. Had he chosen to do so, he could have killed himself and ended it at any time. He'd willed himself to survive instead. But this was different. The tiny assembly of metal and silicone the Wraith had implanted in his back to track his movements had never been part of him. The Behemoth was, and by his own choice. The fact that he'd been lied to didn't matter. Not to him. Experience should have taught him better.

After the screaming confusion of Charybdis had chewed him up and spat him out, he'd woken on the shores of an Atlantis radically different from anything he'd known. A patrol had found him and brought him before the Ancestors.

Teyla's saintly Ancestors.

Suave and slick, as silky as their robes and wavy locks, and so persuasive you could talk to them for days without getting a single straight answer and never even notice it.

Oh, they'd been kind enough at first. They'd fed him and clothed him and, while they were at it, healed his injuries with gadgetry Dr. Beckett would probably have given his right arm just to clap eyes on. They'd instructed him in Wraith-free Ancient history, and a what a tale of miracles it was; unheard of achievements in culture and science, up to and including near-immortality. Somehow they managed to make you believe you were blessed just by having the privilege of hearing the fairytale.

Only, they left out a few salient details. Or, if they didn't sin by omission, they embellished the facts.

Like the one about how they'd picked up where the Wraith had never had a chance to leave off. Ronon had seen it with animals; if there was no predator—and there was none strong enough or advanced enough to defy the Ancestors—they'd spread like wildfire and wreak havoc on everything and everyone that got in their way. Naturally all was done with the best interest of the Pegasus galaxy at heart. Lesser races had to be put in their place at regular intervals, lest they developed the gall to resent their slavery. So much for this whole ascension and non-interference thing—if these Ancestors here had ever toyed with the idea of ascension, they didn't mention it. They liked their current plane of existence just fine.

Lucky for all the other planes.

Shame he couldn't have ended up on one of those.

Behind him a group of laborers arrived to remove the corpse. They looked all but identical, barrel-chested with short, sturdy legs and long, muscular arms; they communicated in grunts—a marginally functional crew of hominids, bred for menial labor. Watching them at their task worked Ronon's nerves raw. He clenched his fists, unclenched them. Inside his consciousness the Behemoth snarled, then went quiescent, sated and content.

After a thorough assessment of Ronon's health and physical parameters, the Ancestors had determined he was suited to join their army, should he wish to do so. He had wished. It was something he knew, after all, perhaps even companionship and a place to belong. Besides, where else could he have gone? A million miles in the opposite direction might have been a good idea, but at the time nobody had told him that he'd be signing his soul away.

A low infrasonic rumble sent a bone-deep tremor through him, set his teeth on edge, and scattered the pointless what-ifs he'd been wallowing in.

"Hey!" One of the soldiers who'd led the boy to execution slapped Ronon's shoulder. "Wake up! Change of plans." The man pointed upward at a troop transporter.

Rapidly descending through the atmosphere, it slowed only when it seemed to skim the peaks of the mountain range beyond and pushed itself in front of the sinking sun, a massive night-black bulk outlined in blood-red. The vessel came to a halt directly above the town, some sixty feet up, plumes of smoke catching under its glistening belly. No lofty speeches on the subject of crime and retribution from on high this time. Given that the town was all but dead, it would have been a waste of clichés. Instead, three explosive metallic clangs signaled the unbolting of the loading hatch as soon as the vessel had come to a complete standstill.

As the twenty feet wide ramp began reaching for the ground beneath, Ronon sensed the call of the Behemoth, forcing the troops to assemble. He quickly scanned the crowd closing in around him. Only about a thousand men. Half the number that had been brought here. So the rest would be left behind to secure the town and its surroundings. Not that any of this mattered, but he liked to be aware of these things.

The bottom edge of the ramp touched the ground, surprisingly gently, chasing up tiny swirls of dust. Across the square the flap of the tent flew back and the Commander emerged, picking bits of food from his teeth. Knowing what the man had been dining on, Ronon choked back a bout of revulsion and pulled his attention elsewhere.

Just as well, for ahead of him the men had started to fall into formation to move up the ramp, shoulder to shoulder, six to a line. He joined them, grateful to be leaving this place—although he was quite aware of the fact that, wherever they were deployed, it'd only be more of the same. Always would be, but at least he got a chance to switch off in the meantime. His original assignment had been to remain planetside and instill terror in the denizens of the neighboring towns and villages.

"Move out!" bellowed the Commander. Going by the bleariness of his remaining eye—a cat's eye, yellow and cold—he was half drunk.

Ronon's bleak mood darkened further when he realized that the Commander would be joining them. In real terms nothing could be more terrifying than the Behemoth, which made the half-blind bastard pretty much redundant, but Ronon still was careful around him. The man was a sadist, and needlessly inviting grief never did anybody any good.

The line in front started heading up the ramp, and he fell into step. A few minutes later he was inside the familiar dark bowels of the transporter, and a synthetic voice from somewhere above allocated him to A39-D. The man to his left gave a jealous grunt, while Ronon himself stood frozen for a moment, blinking in surprise. He'd realized early on that the allocation of bunks couldn't possibly be random. Probability dictated that, if it were, he should have ended up with the same neighbor at least once in all those years. Instead there'd always been unfamiliar faces in the surrounding bunks. Friendship, even camaraderie, among the men was discouraged, because closeness among the rank and file might encourage mutiny. As long as the soldiers believed they were each on their own, they would protect themselves by obeying absolutely. It made you wonder whether the Ancestors fully trusted the power of the Behemoth.

All of which meant that there was a reason why Ronon Dex had been assigned a prime bunk. Perhaps some perverse punishment for his mildly seditious thoughts earlier. This trip might last just long enough to acquaint him with comfort, and the three-week jaunt immediately following would see him banished to a hole above the latrine.

In the meantime, however, he might as well make the best of it.

His mind made up, Ronon jogged down the corridor leading off to the right. First advantage of A39-D, it was on the lowest deck, closest to the ramp, meaning you could sleep nearly an hour after the guys on the upper decks had their reveille and got ready to move out.

The corridor branched out into several others, and the air lost the modicum of freshness it had had nearer the hatch. But the stench of burning flesh was gone, too, replaced by a subtle aroma of ozone and lubricant that spelled recycled oxygen. His serial number lit up on the wall of a hallway to the left, and Ronon followed the marker down two more corridors. When the glowing number came to a halt and winked out, he knew that the A39-D was better than good. It was the top bunk right at the back of a dead end. There'd be absolutely no traffic past him during the trip.

No longer bothering to hide a grin, Ronon climbed up into the bunk. Overhead gleamed another figure: 7. He acknowledged and grabbed the rations tube that sat on the blanket. McKay had constantly complained about what they'd called MREs, but Ronon would have killed for one of those. The taste might be odd, but at least they had some kind of taste and texture, unlike the perfectly balanced, perfectly flavorless paste contained in the rations tube.

By the time he'd eaten and disposed of the tube, the overhead counter stood at 1. He rolled out of the bunk again and made it to the section's cleansing cubicle just as Number Six's cycle was up. The inside of the cubicle was just large enough to accommodate one man. Carefully filtered radiation dissolved his filthy combat overalls and burned blood and dirt off his skin and hair. Not quite the same luxury as a hot shower, but the troop transporters didn't have the storage capacity to carry anything other than drinking water. The cycle lasted two minutes, at the end of which the cubicle released a fresh set of coveralls. Grateful to have shed the stink of death at least for a little while, Ronon returned to his bunk.

Chasing sleep, he lay on his back and listened to the scuttlebutt drifting from other bunks. Mostly idle gossip, but sometimes you could catch a nugget of real information. Tonight the conversation centered on the nature of the deployment.

"I overheard a communications specialist," one of the voices, a very young one, stated importantly. "We're going back to Atlantis."

It raised a couple of snorts. "Sure. That's why they're in such a hurry."

"They should be." The young voice sounded indignant now. "The guy said someone came through the Stargate."

In the roar of laughter that followed nobody heard the hissing breath Ronon sucked in.

CHAPTER NINE

Charybdis +4

"Streamers," said John's junior twin, something between bafflement and exasperation in his voice, and nosed the jumper clear of the Stargate.

"Pretty!" chirped Elizabeth. It made a change from her trying to shoot people or bash their brains out and generally reenacting Stephen King's *Misery*.

Behind them the wormhole disengaged. In front of them opened the control center—*a* control center—or what was left of it; a clamshell grotto, dappled with sunlight spearing through a shattered ceiling and wreathed in honeysuckle and a whole bunch of other creepers that clung to anything that would hold them. Woven in among them were strips of cloth, dyed in all colors of the rainbow and fluttering in a gentle breeze. They were the only thing that moved beyond the view port; of the people who must have put them up there wasn't a hair in sight.

The jumper glided from the grotto, through a stand of giant cedars, and out onto a sheltered clearing, hovering to a stop right at the edge. If Sheppard Junior's debriefing was anything to go by, this landing was a heck of a lot softer than the one before last. John was still trying to wrap his head around the information and figure out whether or not to believe even half of it. Then again, he found he didn't actually care all that much. Not after having woken up in a locked storeroom with his head hammering and his nose in a plateful of thin air à la mode, which was what Elizabeth had expected him to survive on. On the upside, you puked a lot less on an empty stomach. It had taken hours until he was clearheaded enough to assess his situation and realize that, before long, he'd be too weak to move and claw his way out of there through a ventilation duct. The one thing he'd never anticipated in the days of hide and seek that followed was that he'd end up saving himself. So to speak.

Of course, the entire notion of the doppelganger and having to rescue the galaxy could have been brought on by massive frontal lobe damage, but if that was the case, he'd go with the hallucination. It was preferable to reality.

"You coming... sir?"

A generous dash of irony in his own voice yanked him out of the reverie. Then again, if you couldn't take mockery from yourself, who could you take it from? That aside, it might be a good idea to try and stay focused.

As John shoved himself from his seat, the vertigo struck again and he took a couple of deep breaths. "Coming," he murmured and hoped the process wouldn't entail pitching forward and flat on his face.

The rear compartment did a wild shimmy and snapped to a halt, abruptly enough to make him stumble and reach for a handhold. He grabbed his own arm. So to speak.

"It's alright," his double said. "I've got Elizabeth."

Meaning, *Let's not embarrass one another by mentioning our slightly-worse-than-mint condition.* They could be tactful if necessary.

John gave a grateful nod and gingerly walked down the ramp behind Major Sheppard and whatever version of Dr. Weir this supposedly was. They'd decided to take her through the gate to find the original who, with any kind of luck, might just have a fix on the location of one of the McKays. Because one thing was certain: without Rodney they—*he*—wouldn't stand a snowflake's chance in hell of making Charybdis un-happen. And that, apparently, was the name of the game.

Unfortunately, there was no welcoming committee made up of originals, doubles, or third parties. The clearing was as deserted as the grotto had been, and they'd have to go look for whomever had put up the carnival decorations around the Stargate. A hike was just what he needed, John thought grimly. What both of them needed, he amended with a glance at his twin's awkward limp.

Behind them, the hatch of the jumper closed, and the cloaked

ship vanished from view. Out here the air was warm and pregnant with the scent of flowers and something else... incense?
It smelled good enough to eat. From somewhere among that
green, fragrant screen of plant life drifted birdsong and the rustle of small animals going about their small animal business.
Elizabeth drifted off into the glade and began picking the pink
and purple flowers that grew in abundance.

Peaceful.

John harbored a deep distrust of all things peaceful. They
usually weren't.

He exchanged a quick look with his alter ego who, going
by his frown, was on the same page—surprise!—and checked
the life-signs detector. "There's twenty-odd readings southeast
of our position."

"*How* many?"

"I'm concussed. I could be seeing double."

"If it's all the same to you, I'd rather not rely on that."
Sheppard Junior pulled out the Beretta they'd taken from
Elizabeth; the only weapon they had between them. He hesi-
tated a moment, then held out the gun. "You want it?"

It was tempting, but John shook his head. "Like I said, I
could be seeing double."

"Fair enough. What do you want to do?"

"Sneak in, see what we can see." Which would be a tall order
with Elizabeth in tow, but leaving her behind was out of the
question. John thought for a moment. "It's a surprise, Elizabeth.
We have to be very quiet." She was so wrapped up in her hunt
for flowers that she didn't listen. A shaft of brilliant sunlight
breaking through the branches spun a halo around her head, and
for the first time in what seemed like ages she looked serene.
Despite his reservations against things peaceful, John hated the
idea of shattering that serenity. "Elizabeth? Do you hear?"

As if to prove him right, the sunbeam vanished without
warning, dulling colors and casting the glade into murky shadows that were deepening by the second.

"I don't like this," she murmured, looking up at a sky that
was rapidly turning ink black above the canopy.

She'd barely said it when a bolt of lightning struck the

ground mere yards away from them. Instantly the air was filled with the amp-laden stench of ozone, and a roar of static electricity drowned out Elizabeth's scream. A quick glance at Junior assured John that it also worked wonders for his cowlick. Above, the clouds spun into a giant charcoal swirl; its dark core glowering down at them like a malevolent eye.

It was gut instinct rather than meteorology that made him yell, "Take cover!"

The next bolt exploded where they'd been standing mere seconds ago. A jumble of limbs, they lay in the underbrush at the edge of the forest, and Junior gasped, "Damn, that was close! Call me paranoid, but it feels like somebody's taking pot-shots."

"Just because you're paranoid doesn't mean they're not out to get you," intoned Elizabeth, making the Johns look at each other in surprise.

While they were still staring, something crashed through the canopy and struck the ground near them with a solid crack. A second missile followed, then a third and fourth and tenth, in quick succession and picking up speed, until a whole barrage of fist-sized hailstones shattered branches and chewed up foliage and piled heaps of icy baseballs into the clearing. But louder than the rest of the infernal racket was the constant clang of ice on metal.

"Crap!" Junior hollered over the barrage and pointed in the direction of their cloaked ship. Not so cloaked anymore. There was a squarish, ice-free patch of fern and moss, above which more baseballs were bouncing in midair. Kinda obvious... "We've got to get the jumper out of here."

"Too late!" Tapping the screen, John thrust the life signs detector at his alter ego. "The natives are heading for shelter. Our way."

"Crap!"

Yeah. He'd got it the first time. The best they could hope for was that the abovementioned natives would be too preoccupied with getting out of the storm to pay much attention to any oddities in their front yard.

Dragging Elizabeth with them, they backed deeper into

the trees. As if on cue, the intensity of the hailstorm doubled. Apparently the local weather gods were intent on pounding them into the ground. Huddled against a massive fir, they tried to get as much protection as they could. It wasn't much, though it hardly mattered, because through a gap in the bushes John now watched the first of the natives stagger onto the clearing and toward the grotto.

Above and beyond the rustic fantasy fashions that matched the color scheme of the streamers in the glade, you really couldn't make out all that much. They all ran with shoulders hunched and arms wrapped over some pretty impressive hairstyles to protect their heads. Where faces weren't hidden by jutting elbows, they were obscured by beards as impressive as the coiffs. John had counted seventeen people when, suddenly, Elizabeth slipped from his grasp and shot forward.

He thought he heard her say, "They need me!"—yes, at least as much as they needed a hole in the head—and then she was out in the clearing, grabbing the arm of a woman who promptly stumbled in shock and attempting to haul her off to the grotto. Predictably, the woman started screaming, audible even over the roar of the storm. It drew a threesome of men who tried to pry their companion from Elizabeth. Oblivious to hail and lightning, she hung on like a limpet.

While John swallowed a blue streak, Junior slid him a *Now what?* look.

John shrugged. You had to be as nuts as Elizabeth to expect her to keep their presence to herself for any length of time; she'd try and arrange a dinner party at the earliest opportunity. The best they could do was retrieve her before she hurt somebody, accidentally or otherwise. Patting Junior's shoulder, he pushed himself up—the head-rush was getting worse, he noted—and stepped from cover and out into the clearing. The next thing he heard was a shout, then Junior slammed into him in a ferocious tackle, tearing him to the ground. The lightning struck inches from his head.

"Now we're even," Junior grunted into his ear and proceeded to pull him to his feet. "I suggest we stay under the trees."

"Just what I'd been thinking."

"You okay?" Junior frowned.

"Little dizzy. Thanks."

One of the men who'd been busy peeling Elizabeth off the woman had broken from the group in the clearing and came running toward them, one arm folded over his head, the other waving furiously. "Back!" he shouted. "Go back! Go away! You're upsetting the balance!"

They were *what*?

Pointlessly trying to dodge the hail, the man shambled closer, shoved through the undergrowth, and finally sought shelter under the same tree as they. Not overly tall and a little on the scrawny side, he stood there, panting hard, squinting through fogged-up spectacles barely held together by copious amounts of twine. Thinning hair hung to his shoulders, dripping wet, and his beard was similarly soaked and scraggly.

"*Hair* meets the Exodus," muttered Junior.

Their one-man welcoming committee either hadn't heard him or ignored the remark. "You must leave. You're upsetting the balance, can't you see?" The neo-biblical look might have been misleading, the accent wasn't.

"Radek."

"Zelenka."

They'd spoken in unison, and Zelenka blinked in surprise. "How do you—?" He ripped off his glasses and smeared the condensation around with a dirty sleeve. Then he put them back on and blinked some more before gasping, "Colonel Sheppard!"

"That'd be him." Junior cocked a thumb at John. "I'm Major Sheppard."

"*Hovno!*" Under that beard Zelenka, or whatever version of the above this was, turned white as a sheet.

"That sounded rude," observed Junior.

"It was." In his timeline, John had received some instruction in basic Czech swearwords.

"You shouldn't be here," Zelenka hissed. "You—"

"For God's sake, Radek, don't—"

"I no longer go by that name. After the disaster you caused, we—the survivors—radically changed our lifestyles. And ourselves. I now am Brother Moon."

"Alright. Brother Moon." John resisted an overwhelming urge to roll his eyes, less from diplomatic considerations than because it would aggravate his headache. As chirpily as anyone could in a thundering hailstorm when confronted with Brother Throwback-To-The-Sixties, he asked, "You wouldn't happen to know where Dr. Weir is?"

"That's none of your business. Leave. Haven't you done enough damage?"

"We'll leave as soon as we've spoken to Elizabeth."

"Sister Rainbow doesn't want to speak to you."

"How about we ask Sister Rainbow"—John managed it with only a tiny beat—"ourselves?"

"She doesn't want to—"

Three more men scurried across the clearing now and closed ranks behind Zelenka who drew himself up to his full height and announced, "These people have to leave, Brothers. They don't belong here. If they don't go voluntarily, we shall have to… persuade them."

"*Persuade* us?" Junior arched an eyebrow. "So this pacifism thing isn't part of the playbook, is it?"

John shot him a warning glance. Antagonizing the ashram, for want of a better word, wouldn't get them anywhere. Then again, any further antagonizing seemed impossible. By the looks of it, they were well and truly there already. Unfazed by such petty considerations as chain of command, the Brothers moved in—in a decidedly non-pacifist kind of way. On a good day, he'd have had no problem taking on each of them individually, but all three of them was a bit much. Not to mention the fact that this wasn't a good day by any stretch of the imagination. Junior seemed to have arrived at the same conclusion, looking meekly cooperative all of a sudden.

Clearly uncomfortable with the situation, the tallest of them murmured, "I really regret this, but—" His gaze snapped to somewhere behind John's shoulder, and his eyes went wide. As a matter of fact, his whole demeanor gave an impression of huge relief.

Moments later John realized why. A group of stragglers

came stumbling down a narrow forest trail behind them, lugging along a basket heaped with those pink and purple blossoms they'd rescued from the hail. A gust whipped a handful of flowers from the top, plastered one of them across his nose and mouth, half drowning him in that same siren fragrance he'd noticed stepping off the jumper. Maybe that explained why these folks were rescuing flowers rather than food crops. Soaking wet and windblown, they were herded on by Dr. Elizabeth Weir. Peeling the blossom off his face, he wondered whether she was the original version, prayed that, if so, she was *compos mentis*—though she herself obviously doubted it right now. She'd frozen in her tracks and stood staring from John to Junior and back. Finally she forced herself to take a few steps forward and very carefully touched his arm, then Junior's.

"You're real," she rasped. "You're both… real. And alive… How…" Suddenly she broke into a huge smile. "God, it's good to see you! You must—"

"They must leave!" Zelenka cut in. "I doubt either one of them is who he seems to be, and they're putting us all at risk. It's the doing of Charybdis. We can't trust them, Sister Rainbow."

Sister Rainbow begged to differ. "They're injured, Radek. This isn't how we treat people in need of our help. We'll take them with us, listen to what they've got to say, and take it from there."

Charybdis -908

There it was again! A crackle in the undergrowth, as if a foot had accidentally landed on a dry twig—though the notion of anything *dry* in this place struck him as ridiculous.

Little hairs on his neck stood on end, and Rodney stopped, held his breath, waited.

Nothing. Like the last time and the time before.

Like the last time and the time before, he counted the hogs to make sure that none of them had separated from the herd and was trailing them somewhere in the bushes, which could have accounted for the noise.

A dozen ugly brutes, all present and correct.

And maybe he was just paranoid. In the five weeks since his discovery, he'd returned to the ruins whenever he thought it was safe—in other words, irregularly and only after taking detours so erratic that, more than once, he had gotten himself lost and never even reached the site. Chances were that the sound had simply been a larger than usual splotch of water hurtling from a branch.

Skin all over his body prickling with hyperawareness and nerves, he grabbed his stick a little tighter and started walking again. He could have sworn that he heard another furtive rustle just then but shrugged it off. Hyperawareness and nerves. He was sensitive. He also was running late, and he didn't want to get into trouble again for bringing the hogs back after nightfall. That had happened one too many times lately, and Sahar, no doubt goaded by that nosy zealot of a wife of his, had begun asking some awkward questions.

But sneaking back to the ruins as often as he could had become a necessity. Each time he'd find something else that jogged his memory. He remembered Charybdis now, though the satisfaction of having been right where that was concerned hadn't lasted terribly long. Being right wasn't going to fix his current predicament. Though the technological iconoclasts who were running the planet had never gotten round to trashing the equipment left among the ruins, said equipment had been subjected to what probably amounted to several centuries worth of rain. None of it worked.

Given time and a little bit of ingenuity—and Rodney had a lot of the latter, if he said so himself—he might be able to repair some of it, but whether that would extend to such crucial bits as the dialing console was anybody's guess. That aside, even if he managed to get the gate to work, where would he go? The ruins and remains left little doubt that he was, in fact, on Lantea, trapped in some fourth-dimensional nightmare concocted by Charybdis.

Oh, he'd *so* been right!

"You're overreacting, Rodney. Let's just see what it can do, Rodney. We've got it under control, Rodney," he rapped out angrily.

And no, he had no trouble thinking badly of the dead. After all, they'd taken the easy way out, sat in some cushy Nirvana or paradise or wherever their personal belief structure said they'd go in the Hereafter, and left him stuck *here*. It sure as hell lent a whole new meaning to 'caller in the wilderness.'

The hogs seemed to have recognized some hidden landmark or caught the scent of home; they shifted gear and broke into a bumbling downhill trot. He stumbled after them, slipping and sliding in the perennial mud and never even bothering to side-step the small streams that had decided to make the trail their temporary bed.

Fifteen minutes later he emerged from the edge of the forest. Below and surrounded by water-logged meadows lay the jumble of barns, sheds, stables, bunkhouses, and residences that made up the farm. Above and pressing closer hung the leaden bellies of clouds, pushing up against the mountains and waiting to burst. Somewhere there had to be vast stretches of open water for such ridiculous amounts of rain to develop, but the claustrophobic cocoon of rock and forest and fog all around offered no clues as to where the sea might be.

Down on the farm tiny dots scurried about their tasks, and from what they were doing and where they were going, Rodney estimated that it must be coming up for the evening feed. He'd barely be in time. Way ahead, the first hog obviously scented the swill. It gave an excited squeal. At the sound the dots below behaved as if word had gotten out that the Vandals were coming. They stopped whatever they were doing, briefly peered uphill, and, to a man, scattered and disappeared into the safety of the buildings.

Frowning, Rodney froze in his tracks. The weirdness levels in this place were naturally high, but this was a little on the bizarre side, even by local standards. Maybe it was some kind of holiday he hadn't heard about yet. Shaking his head, he prodded the nearest hog and started walking again. He'd find out soon enough.

He found out as soon as he reached the yard.

They swarmed from sheds and stables and—so he *had* heard something!—down the hillside behind him like some giant cockroach infestation. He remembered the roaches; a local militia he'd first encountered during his brief stay in the city an eternity ago. They were steel-clad and armed with swords and lances and looked purposeful in a less than reassuring way.

Rodney spun around, looking for a bolthole. There was no way out. The yard was enclosed by buildings to make the farm more easily defensible. All the doors were shut and where they weren't shut they spouted armored men. Behind the windows clustered faces, wide-eyed, not with fear as he grasped in a split-second's realization but with anticipation; Rilla, glowing with righteous satisfaction, Sahar next to her, trapped somewhere between shame and fury—ringside spectators, waiting for the bull to be brought down to shouts of *Caramba* (or whatever the appropriate exclamation was) and the rattle of castanets. Rodney had no doubt as to who was starring as the bull.

Throwing down his stick—in a non-confrontational manner, he hoped—he raised his hands. Blood sports offended his esthetic sensibilities, and he'd be damned if he gave them the spectacle they obviously were spoiling for. Besides, he had a remarkably low pain threshold.

"Come on, let's just be—"

The blow struck the back of his knees, made them buckle under him, and Rodney pitched face-down into the stinking gunk that covered the farmyard. So much for striking a conciliatory note... and breathing was a bad idea, too.

His nostrils were blocked, and when reflex kicked in and he gasped for air, he sucked up a mouthful of mud and suddenly remembered that unforgettable occasion when he was forced to fix a problem with the waste disposal system on Atlantis. Same stink. Choking and coughing, he tried to raise his head, an effort made substantially more difficult by the fact that somebody had planted a boot between his shoulder blades. Rough fingers tied his hands behind his back, and then he found himself abruptly hauled to his feet. Raising his face into the perpetual rain, Rodney hoped the downpour would clear off enough sludge to enable him to breathe again.

The roaches closed ranks around him as though they expected him to run. Fat chance of that. He'd never even get past the midden heap. The chief cockroach glared at him from squinty eyes and spat. "Heretic!"

An acidy fist of panic began to pump in his stomach. He was up against the fundamentalist death squad. Every child here had heard the tales, and the stories all had one thing in common: they made medieval witch hunts seem civilized by comparison.

"Look," Rodney began, annoyed to hear that the shivers caused by rain and cold and fear managed to seep into his voice. "I'm not even from here. You're making a huge mis—"

"Silence!" roared Chief Roach. He was worse than Caldwell on a bad day. "Bring him!"

Among gradually more daring jeers from behind the windows, they escorted him into the largest of the barns. It had one thing going for it: in here it wasn't raining.

The center of the barn had been cleared to accommodate a large table, flanked by a couple of smoking braziers. Behind that fetching arrangement stood a large, fur-covered armchair that looked more comfortable than any other piece of furniture Rodney had ever encountered in this place. Then again, so would a bed of nails. Besides, it wasn't the chair that was of interest so much as the personage sitting in it. He was withered and skinny and scraggly-bearded and the dyspeptic aura made him a bureaucrat of some sort.

That was good. Bureaucrats had rules, and they lived to abide by them. Rodney was a physicist, and physics was all about rules. Which meant they had some common ground. So perhaps—

The barely formed, anemic little bubble of hope burst with what Rodney could have sworn was an audible pop. On the table in front of the bureaucrat and illuminated by three oil lamps sat the complete contents of Rodney's secret cache; a jumble of equipment, odds and ends he'd one by one salvaged from the ruins, smuggled back to the farm hidden under his cloak, and stashed away under some loose floorboards in a derelict stable. Among them were a handful of still intact control crystals, a meager selection of rusty tools, a laptop that was dead as a dodo but maybe good for gutting, a spiral notebook and pen he'd used to keep an inventory of his finds and jot down any thoughts, and the potential treasure of treasures, a zero point module that might or might not be depleted. His first order of business had been to try and jury-rig a simple voltmeter to test the ZPM. By the looks of it, that plan had just been deferred indefinitely.

Lances planted on the ground, his guards stood in a semicircle around him and stared at the collection on the table as if it consisted of black candles, goats' heads and all the rest of popular satanic paraphernalia. The bureaucrat, on the other hand, didn't seem to harbor such superstitions. When he finally raised his eyes, he ignored the gadgetry in front of him and gazed through Rodney with the expression of a pious but profoundly saddened basset hound.

Great! A true believer…

"Bring forth the witness," said the bureaucrat. His voice, reedy and dry as old leaves, barely rose above a whisper.

Rodney had to strain to hear him over the incessant drumming of rain on the roof and wondered why he actually made the effort. Somehow it seemed far more sensible to just switch off and pretend this was happening to somebody else.

The witness, so-called, was Rilla, Sahar's wife, not that this came as much of a surprise. She must have had advance notice, because she wore finery usually only dragged out for the indoctrination… pardon him, *prayer* meeting on their half-day of rest. Frilly and in a green that clashed with her complexion, the dress made her look like piece of moldy puff pastry, perfectly matching her intellect. In her and her escort's wake a crowd of serfs thronged into the barn. Apparently the proceedings were public.

Eyes bulging, Rilla took one glance at the official and dropped into an awkward curtsey that made the puff pastry bubble around her. "Master!" she yelped from somewhere amid heaving fabric. "It is such an honor!"

Master?

The honorific was only given to men of Ancient descent. Rodney squinted at the bureaucrat—at best the oil lamps accentuated the gloom, but they certainly didn't brighten things—and noticed the earring the man was wearing. A small red gemstone set in silver made the old boy an Ancient of minor lineage.

"Yes, yes, yes." He sounded supremely bored. "Make your testimony, woman."

Rilla reemerged from the folds of the puff pastry and pointed at Rodney. "This one," she announced, "is a heretic."

"That is why we are here," the bureaucrat informed her. "Tell us what brings you to make this accusation."

"He was late returning with the swine."

"And?"

"Then he was late again, and again."

"That does not make him a heretic."

"It does, too, Master. He was late because he defiled the swine by taking them to a forbidden place."

Explaining that the defilement of swine had been the last thing on Rodney's mind probably wouldn't help.

"The animals' meat is tainted," lamented Rilla. "They will have to be cleansed before you can take partake of them."

Oh please! Since when did ruins carry trichinosis?

"We shall take care of that," the bureaucrat assured her. He seemed remarkably unconcerned by the lethal dangers of tainted hog. "How did you know about this forbidden place?"

"I didn't!" Her air of superiority exploded abruptly, and Rilla looked so terrified that for a moment—okay, a shake at most—Rodney almost felt sorry for her. "I didn't know, Master, and I swear I never set foot in the place. I only found out when I followed *him*!" She was in her element again, and the terror in her voice had been replaced by pure venom. "*He* went into the place and touched things and took them. Perhaps I shouldn't even have looked, but I merely watched to be able to accurately report this sacrilege to you, Master."

"I have no doubt of it," murmured the Master. "Those things he took? Are those the items?" A tremulous sweep of his bony hand indicated the collection on the table.

"Yes, Master." Rilla nodded as if she were trying to give herself whiplash.

It was hard not to do the same thing everybody else did,

namely stare at the table. But Rodney figured that, if he looked, he'd think about what would happen—or, more pertinently, *not* happen—now that they were taking away his one, measly chance of getting out of this place. And if he thought about that, he might just lose it, which wasn't an option. He didn't really rate his odds of talking himself out of this mess, but neither did he intend to give them the satisfaction of seeing him rant and wail. Of course, the road to hell was paved with good intentions…

"You saw him take all of these? How many times did you follow him?"

"Only once, Master." The witness turned crimson, which clashed with the color of the puff pastry. "When I'd realized where he was going, I wouldn't set foot in that accursed place again."

"Of course."

Heartened by the approval, Rilla pointed at the notebook. "I did see him take this."

The bureaucrat's fingers spidered toward the notebook, took it, opened it. Eyes straining in the despondent flicker of the oil lamps, the man studied the contents. There was a subtle shift in his face, as if all those wrinkles suddenly had been snapped into harsher angles. He might well have considered the proceedings farcical so far—not that it would have changed the outcome—but now he was deadly serious. *Deadly* being the operative word. Though he couldn't read it, he clearly was able to identify Rodney's scribblings for what they were: script. Presumably this was the part where things would get ugly.

"Who did this?" The guy's wispy voice had taken on a menacing edge.

The surprise of being addressed directly made Rodney gasp. He inhaled a lungful of oily smoke from the braziers and ended up in a coughing fit that had him choking and wheezing until his eyes watered.

"Answer me!" the official screeched.

The witness gave a panicked little squeal, and the crowd of spectators, who until now had kept up a low-key murmur of opinions and utterances of horror or contempt, tumbled into a cowed hush.

Between two hacks, Rodney squeezed out, "I did."

"Liar! You're a pig herder, boy! You're not even of age yet!"

Oh yes! Rub it in, why don't you? Not enough that he'd ended up marooned in the Dark Ages, no! In causing this almighty temporal mess, Charybdis had seen fit to add a humorous twist by turning him into the Pegasus galaxy's answer to Dougie Howser. Which admittedly had come in handy for purposes of staying under the radar—who, apart from that nosy nemesis, Rilla, paid attention to a teenager?—but right now a little more dignity would have been nice. Because there was only so far you could push a boy genius. "I am a scientist."

The crowd began reciting what had to be the local equivalent of Psalm 23.

The witness reeled back in terror. "Disciple of Ikaros!"

Rodney couldn't help himself. He burst out laughing. Quite hysterically, in point of fact. So much for dignity... Then again, if they thought he was nuts, who cared? Given his situation, a temporary insanity plea probably was as effective a defense as any. "Ikaros was a snotty-nosed wunderkind with delusions of grandeur who couldn't have taught people how to tie their shoelaces." Regaining some of his composure, he added, "I am a physicist." He might as well have told them he was a New Age holistic healing guru. No, actually, that would have made sense to them. "I'm... I'm a scientist."

Uhuh. *And yet it moves.* Rodney figured he now knew how Galileo must have felt before the Holy Inquisition. He could still recant, he supposed. No... Oddly enough, he was less scared than he'd been before, negative pain threshold or no. He had his pride, and he *was* a scientist, not a pig herder, even if—

Someone used Rodney's mouth and Rodney's voice to announce, "I *am* Ikaros."

His immediate impulse was to clamp both hands over his mouth. He hadn't just said that, had he? He couldn't have. So who? Rodney felt a dizzy bout of disorientation and it was all he could do not to scream.

The bureaucrat scowled at him through another stream of

smoke from the braziers. "You may try to pretend to be insane, but you will confess quickly enough, and we shall apprehend your fellow heretics. I had hoped it wouldn't come to this, but alas…"

Insane.

Maybe that's what it was. Maybe he wasn't pretending. Maybe he'd snapped.

The air that filled Rodney's lungs was nowhere near coinciding with his actual need for breath. Lightheaded, with limbs heavy as lead, he focused to squeeze out whomever or whatever seemed to have invaded his mind, hijacked his body. Insanity wasn't an option. His mind was all he had, all he'd ever had.

He saw himself discovering the ruins of Atlantis, saw his hand—*his* hand?—scratch a name onto a worktop.

Ikaros.

No!

Dr. Meredith Rodney McKay.

That's who he was, and he wasn't going nuts!

Oblivious to the silent battle, the bureaucrat heaved himself from the chair and rose to his full height of five foot two and a half. "Men wiser and less patient than I shall question you, and you shall not be able to thwart them. Take him to the city," he snapped at the militiamen.

Rodney barely registered the guards grabbing his arms—*his* arms?—and yanking him in the direction of the door. Either side the crowd parted, silent now, too busy shrinking from him to come up with witticisms like *heretic* or *disciple of Ikaros.* Here and there rose a murmur of disappointment from someone who'd been hoping for a companionable stoning to break up the tedium of the workday.

Outside it was still pouring, and the cold splashes of rain on his face helped him to regain some sense of reality. Maybe it had been the smoke inside the barn. Nothing fresh air couldn't fix, right?

As the guards dragged him across the yard, it suddenly occurred to him that Rilla and all the other interfering fools hadn't found the site where he'd buried Colonel Sheppard's remains. The thought cheered him up to a surprising degree.

CHAPTER 10

Charybdis +13

The steady background hum of the transporter's engines abruptly changed in pitch, telling Ronon that the ship had dropped out of hyperspace. At last. The night had been endless. Ever since that kid a few bunks down had mentioned the possibility of someone activating the Stargate, he been unable to stop his thoughts from churning.

Every child knew that the Stargate system no longer worked. Not reliably, anyway. At regular intervals some genius or other would dial up some gate address or other and vanish never to be seen again. Nobody had ever heard of anyone actually *arriving* through a gate.

Which was precisely the point that had kept him awake.

If someone had arrived, then who? And what did it mean?

Not that he was overestimating his own importance, but there had to be a reason why they wanted *him* there. He could think of one—could but didn't, so as not to alert the Behemoth that kept slinking along the fringes of his mind like a panther, ready to pounce on any morsel Ronon might accidentally toss its way. Naturally, trying not to think of that particular reason was like trying not to think of pink Wraith after someone had expressly forbidden you to do so. The notion recurred again and again, wearing a different face each time, but in the end it always came back to another Charybdis survivor trying to find him.

And maybe this was just his longing for the only companionship he'd known since the Wraith had stuck a transmitter in his back and made him a runner, and he was giving himself away for nothing.

He slapped down the image of salvation and evacuated every thought from his mind, until he was completely focused on his body, regulating his heartbeat and breathing and relaxing one muscle after the other. Beneath his consciousness hovered a sense of the noises around him—men yawning, grunting, stirring in anticipation of the ship's arrival at its destination, wherever that was—and of the Behemoth hissing in annoyance at Ronon's refusal to offer up any information.

About an hour later and without warning, all sounds ceased. The transporter had come to a standstill, and the men momentarily stopped their rustling to listen to the silence. Then new noises erupted; soldiers throwing their gear or themselves off the bunks, slapping of shoulders, last-minute jostling for the latrine, excitement or frustration at having to move out again.

Still keeping his mind a blank, Ronon sat up, swung his legs off the bunk, strapped his sword to his back, and leaped to the ground. The current of soldiers engulfed him, and he let it, figuring that it was safest not to think and simply allow himself to drift. For however long it would last... He had a feeling that his period of grace was expiring fast.

The usual blockage at the top of the ramp, caused by men scrambling to line up for an orderly descent, seemed to be non-existent today. Within minutes he found himself squinting into harsh morning light barely tamped down by the shadows beneath the transporter's belly. When his eyes had adjusted, he saw that they were indeed back on Atlantis.

He could smell it, too. Crime and filth and poverty, seasoned with the heady scent of war. The transporter was stationary above one of the countless military embarkation areas. The area was surrounded by squat, ugly buildings in all shades of gray imaginable; barracks. Windowless, because the soldiers were so feared and hated by the general population that you could always find an eager soul willing to take out a man or two with one of those antiquated firearms people hid in seemingly inexhaustible stashes. Behind the barracks rose the black and silver towers of this city of Atlantis, stranded on dry land and nothing like the Atlantis he remembered. The cold orgy in metal and glass struck him as even more sinister than the eerily organic, half-digested design the Wraith had favored. The buildings loomed over you as if to remind you that you were being watched. Constantly and by unfriendly eyes. It was the same everywhere on the planet.

What set this landing site apart from all the others was the fact that it lay right at the edge of the government district of Atlantis. This was his first time back here since he'd been initiated to the Behemoth. He couldn't say he'd missed the place.

Ahead of him, soldiers filed down the ramp and toward the barracks—past a detachment of armed-to-the-teeth government security troops that had arranged themselves snugly around the Commander. For once in his life he looked distinctly uncomfortable. Ronon bit back a smile, thinking that this almost made the return worth it. His smile died a swift death when he noticed the ST officer's stare on him. The man turned to the Commander, mumbled something. This wasn't good. Couldn't be. Ronon wanted to shrink into the flooring of the ramp.

Instead he stepped onto the stained concrete of the parade ground, eyes front, trying to blend in. It didn't work, of course.

"Hey! You!" barked the Commander.

Never breaking his stride, Ronon turned his head. "Me, Excellency?"

"Yes, you! And you damn well know it! Step over here!"

Grimacing, Ronon fell out and crossed over to the ST unit and his commanding officer.

"Is this the man?" the ST officer asked. "Former Specialist Ronon Dex?"

The surprise just about tripped Ronon. In almost ten years, ever since he'd joined the Behemoth, he hadn't heard his name spoken aloud. Usually it was either *Hey! You!* or his serial number. But more than the simple acoustics of the thing, it proved that his suspicion had been correct. Somehow this was connected to his past, and he had to work hard to keep his elation at bay. So he stood quietly and let the fat, one-eyed bastard do the answering.

"That's him," the Commander grunted. "I'd like him back, though."

"I don't care what you'd like," announced the ST officer. "I've got my orders." He turned to Ronon. "Follow me."

Wordlessly, Ronon did just that. The rest of the security

detail fell in behind him, in case he got any fancy ideas. He was marched past his fellow troops—who ducked their heads, avoiding eye contact at all cost, their whole demeanor yelling *Thank the Ancestors, it's not me!*—and across the parade ground to an open surface glider. The ST officer motioned him to climb aboard, and he was happy to comply. If life had taught him one thing, it was that a wise man didn't question amenities but enjoyed them while they lasted.

Which is precisely what you should have done last night, Dex!

As it turned out, the amenities didn't last for long. The glider never even rose high enough to sneak a look over the barrier wall into the residential slums. After a short hop past the spires of the government administrative complex, it banked steeply, slowed to an almost complete halt with the anti-grav boosters running full-throttle, and settled outside the main entrance of the Defense Command Center.

The STs jumped out and secured the sidewalk, still intent on stopping any escape attempt their charge might make. Overkill, considering that the Behemoth would stop him in his tracks if Ronon so much as thought of trying. That aside, he wanted to find out what the hell was going on before he entertained any notions of running even though, given a choice in the matter, he'd have done his level best to avoid revisiting the DCC.

At the top of a broad set of stairs the entrance to the center loomed like a huge black maw, doors noiselessly sliding open and shut at irregular intervals to gobble up scurrying people who were dwarfed to antlike proportions by this monolith of a building. The primary cause of death among ants was getting stepped on...

The doors opened, gobbled, shut, and he and his escort headed across a cold, marble-glistening lobby and toward a bank of transporters at the far end. The space was so enormous that the echo of their footsteps seemed to come at them from all sides, mingled with the hushed voices of unseen people. Now and again a single word broke the surface of unintelligible murmur like a bubble, out of context and surreal.

Daytime.

Nosebleed.

Gruel.

The transporter lacked the kind of controls Ronon remembered. Instead of a touch schematic it had an opaque screen, flickering with a steady stream of numbers. Coordinates, no doubt, though he couldn't even begin to decipher them. The device was operated from a wristband the ST officer wore. Ronon filed it away for further use; if you wanted to get anywhere in this building—or, more to the point, if you wanted to get *out* of this building—you needed one of those wristbands.

Then the floor seemed to fall out from under him while his stomach leaped for the ceiling, and he silently cursed the engineer who'd decided to skimp on the inertial dampeners. Maybe it had been deliberate, to unsettle the delinquents. In this place down wasn't a good direction. The memory made him clench his teeth, and he felt a thin sheen of sweat cooling on his forehead. The ST officer smiled a razor of a smile, and turned to the door. They'd be there soon, wherever *there* was.

As suddenly as it had begun its descent, the transporter jerked to a stop, its door opening on another lobby, one that was uncomfortably familiar. Ronon pulled his features into a blank mask. Behind that steel door across from the transporter bank someone was screaming; high-pitched agonized yelps, one after another, triggered by each push of the Behemoth into a consciousness. Someone was being initiated. Hooray for them.

"Feeling cold, soldier?" the ST officer asked, ogling the goose-bumps that raced up Ronon's arms.

"No, Excellency. I don't feel anything, Excellency."

The razor smile snapped open to release a throaty laugh, then the officer turned left, past the door that locked in the screams, and down an empty, dimly lit corridor. Ronon stuffed his relief into a small, tightly sealed pocket of his mind.

The end of the corridor was closed off by yet another door, massive enough to protect a treasure vault. In front of it was a checkpoint manned by yet more STs.

One of them scanned the officer's wristband for his orders, then nodded at Ronon. "Is he to enter?"

"That would be the point of bringing him down here," the

officer snapped.

"He'll have to have a probe, then," the ST replied, unperturbed.

"Fine. Just hurry up. They've been waiting long enough in there."

"Hey! You! Place your head there." The ST indicated a metal chin rest.

Ronon did as ordered. Everyone underwent probes on a monthly basis to ensure that their conditioning was fully functional and they hadn't, by some miracle, contrived to outwit the Behemoth.

A mechanical arm swung up from under the chin rest, rose, and the probe telescoped out at him until it touched his left eyeball to look at whatever patterns were forming on his retina now. He'd trained himself years ago not to flinch when it happened, and it wasn't painful, just unpleasant. The unbearable part was knowing that somehow the Behemoth in his mind would be tattling with the probe, telling on him and his behavior. If the computer derived any danger signals from the data transmitted by the probe, the consequences could be… ugly. Of course you never really knew what kind of thought or feeling counted as a danger signal.

Then, quietly and unspectacularly, it was over, the probe retracted, and the ST gave a bored nod, as though he were disappointed that this subject hadn't been plotting a military coup in his spare time. "He can go."

The officer looked mildly surprised but bit back any comment. In front of them the door swung open, a yard-thick bolt-bristling chunk of metal. Beyond lay a cavernous space, white and sterile, and at its center, like a displaced work of art or an object for laboratory study, sat a Stargate. More Security Troops lined the walls, positioned at short intervals, their unblinking focus on the dormant gate, and for a brief moment Ronon wondered what it must be like to pull that detail, standing there for days, weeks, months, knowing that you were pointlessly guarding against an invasion that couldn't happen because the gate system no longer worked.

Then his attention was drawn to a group of three men in

long white robes—Ancestors. Two of them, young and eager, were strangers, but Ronon instantly recognized the oldest of the three, even though he hadn't seen the man in ten years. Maybe the stoop was a little more pronounced, the face a little more lined, the hair a little grayer, but there was no mistaking him—Marcon, junior member of the Defense Council back when they'd first met, now its leader. Marcon had debriefed Ronon after they'd found him washed into the inner harbor of Atlantis, a sodden rag doll, more dead than alive. Marcon had pretended to be a friend. Marcon had told him all the beautiful lies.

Hatred boiled through him like molten steel, white-hot and consuming. Ronon had killed a man for a similar betrayal, and in his memories that man's face became overlaid by Marcon's, making him want to sigh in satisfaction. Then the pain struck. The Behemoth ripped through his head in punishment for the forbidden fantasy, and he gasped, struggling to get his mind and feelings back under control.

If Marcon had noticed, he gave no indication. Instead he dismissed the ST officer with a curt nod and smiled at Ronon. "Ronon Dex! It is good to see you're keeping well, my friend."

As if you care, old man!

The silent outburst brought another bolt of pain, less ferocious this time, and Ronon forced himself into uttering an approximation of a civilized reply. "Greetings, Marcon."

"I'm glad you came," Marcon continued as though Ronon had been given a choice. "We need your expertise. Come."

His arm described a graceful arc, inviting Ronon into an embrace as comrades would, hands clapped on shoulders, on their way to the inn to reminisce about the good times they'd had together. Ronon tasted bile, and something in his face or posture finally must have warned Marcon off. The arm dropped, and Marcon nodded a silent acknowledgement; no more lies, no more pretense. They were master and slave, it was as simple as that.

"Come," he said again, a hint of something other than unctuousness in his tone... respect? Probably not. "I promise you will find this interesting."

The two younger men—Marcon's aides—followed at a polite distance, apparently accepting without question that the Chairman of the Defense Council would take a common soldier into his confidence. Marcon led the way into a narrow corridor that branched off the room where the Stargate was kept and ended in a laboratory. In the middle of the lab sat a large examination chair, its backrest to the corridor, and around the fringes of the room ran an extensive array of computers and diagnostic equipment and synthesizers that would produce anything from drugs to man-made enzymes.

A duo of technicians practically jumped when Marcon strode into the room. Smiling again, he raised a placating hand. "Please, don't let me interrupt your work." After which he proceeded to interrupt their work. "Do you have any further insights?"

One of the technicians spoke up. "There was a broken wrist, which we mended. We also found evidence of recent, spontaneous cell rejuvenation on a massive scale. The only part of the body unaffected is an area of the posterior cortex, which shows an impairment that is resistant to treatment."

Something at the back of someone's brain was broke and couldn't be fixed, Ronon translated silently. It was of vague interest, as he'd never heard of any disease or injury—barring old age and death itself—the Ancestors couldn't heal, but somehow he doubted they'd brought him here because they wanted him to give it a try.

"Are there any similarities to him?" asked Marcon.

To whom?

Marcon's bony finger pointed at a transparent cubicle set into the wall. It was filled with a clear fluid and suspended inside swam a body. The skin was pale, doughy, looked as if it wanted to slough off in places, and parts of the corpse were badly decayed, but there was no mistaking it: McKay.

Ronon drew in a sharp breath, sucking back the nausea that threatened to race up his throat. Inside his mind the Behemoth uncoiled, wakened by this jolt of emotion. Fists balled, he fought for control harder than he'd ever done. After all, what was there to get upset about? It was a corpse, dead and pickled for years, and it no longer had anything to do with the person who'd inhabited it. Ronon's grief for the annoying loudmouth wouldn't change a thing, least of all the fact that his best hope of getting out of this had died with Rodney McKay.

"... their genetic profiles are subtly diverse." The technician's lecture had rolled on as though nothing had happened. "I would assume they're not from the same planet, possibly not even from the same galaxy. The woman's profile closely corresponds to those of various remains we've discovered on a planet called Athos. Except, there is a strand of non-human DNA spliced—"

"What woman?" Ronon started at the sound of his own voice and the sharpness in it; he hadn't meant to say it out loud, let alone invest it with such urgency.

"Ah." Marcon turned to him, the smile back in place, broad enough for Ronon to want to slap it off the man's face. It had been a ploy to get a reaction. "Of course. The woman. Please show him," he added to the technician.

The man activated a control, and the examination chair swiveled around, revealing its occupant. Oddly enough, the first thing that struck Ronon was that she hadn't changed at all, making him keenly aware of his own graying hair and the lines that thirteen years of killing had scored in his face. The clothes were different, not the utilitarian garb of the warrior he was used to seeing her wear, but a rough skirt and blouse, woven from plant fiber and well-worn. Her eyes were closed, and she didn't move.

"What—?"

"She is sedated," the technician answered before Ronon could ask. "The examination would have caused too much discomfort otherwise. She'll wake up in a little while."

"You recognize her." It wasn't a question, and Marcon stared at him intently.

The Behemoth blossomed in Ronon's mind like a poisonous flower, tendrils wrapping around neurons, sapping all resistance from them. "Her name is Teyla Emmagan," he ground out, hating himself.

Finally something had deadened Marcon's smile. "You're lying."

"You know I can't. *Your* lies made sure of it."

"Such venom, my friend. You amaze me. The pain must be quite unbearable."

It was, but Ronon didn't care right now. "I'm telling you the truth."

"Then why, after coming through the Stargate, which by the way nobody has done in recorded history, would she ask for Teyla Emmagan? She also had this on her," added Marcon, holding up something that looked like a shriveled chunk of leather.

"It's a finger." Squinting at it, Ronon felt faintly disgusted. "Mummified, I'd say."

"Quite right." Marcon sounded pleased. "Normally, it wouldn't be remarkable; after all, who knows what kind of bizarre rites her people practice. However, this diligent young man here"—he patted the technician's shoulder—"thought it wise to test the relic. Imagine his surprise—and mine—when it turned out that, apparently, the digit belongs to you."

"Then he made a mistake." By ways of illustration, Ronon wiggled a complete set of ten non-mummified fingers.

"He did not," said Marcon before the technician could vent his indignation. "In fact, he repeated the tests three times, always with the same result. I want to know the meaning of this, that's why you are here. She knows you; she will trust you. When she wakes up, you will question her. Once I am satisfied that she has told you everything, you will deal with her as I see fit."

The Behemoth started laughing.

CHAPTER 11

Charybdis +4

The camps were well and truly divided now, something Elizabeth had been trying to prevent for a long time. Feeling increasingly out of step with everyone else hadn't helped because, much as she tried not to let it show, her sense of alienation had a way of communicating itself to the others. And while she truly believed that their survival depended on the group remaining cohesive, this latest development might well be the wedge that would drive them all apart. Radek had formed convictions that were all but religious in their fervor, and religion appealed to people, shaken and uprooted as they were. So they followed him.

Well, she'd deal with it later. Now she had other priorities, three of whom sat in a corner of the grotto behind her, huddled around a small campfire and looked after by the handful of people who remained in Elizabeth's camp. Outside the unseasonable storm raged on, showing no sign of abating. The crops were destroyed already, and what little they'd managed to store wouldn't last them for a week. Four years of back-breaking labor, cultivating the flower, had been wiped out in minutes by the hail. They were back to square one, worse off perhaps, because of the friction among them.

Elizabeth shivered, pulled the sodden cloak tighter around her, and turned back into the scant protection of the grotto. In the corner across from the Sheppards and that heartbreaking alternate outcome of Janus's proposal, her double, burned another fire, and gathered around that were Radek—Brother Moon—and his followers. They'd been carrying on a hushed debate, but now things had mellowed down. She knew why and, inhaling the sweet scent of the blossoms, was tempted herself, because it would calm her.

The meeting broke up, and several people disappeared into the tunnel—once a corridor—that led to their storage chamber. Presumably they were going to take stock of their supplies. Good point. Elizabeth supposed she should have suggested it straightaway, but with everything else that had happened the oversight was excusable. Besides, she had a pretty good idea of what the tally would be, even without literally counting the beans.

Radek rose, caught her eye, and ambled over to place a hand on her arm and give a sheepish little smile. "I'm sorry, Sis—Elizabeth. I never meant to overstep the line or question your authority. I'm just concerned about all this." He waved toward the opening of the grotto and the storm raging in the darkness beyond. "I—"

"I know, Radek." And she did.

Like all the others, he had no recollection of how they'd ended up here, but ever since Elizabeth, who did remember all too clearly, had made the mistake of telling them, Radek firmly believed that Charybdis lingered and was sentient. The possibility couldn't be discounted, considering that Ikaros had joined with his creation. But if Charybdis was indeed sentient, as Radek argued, then it would attempt to preserve itself and interpret any attempt to reset the four-dimensional structure it had established as threat. One such threat, he insisted, were people skipping from one timeline to another as the Johns and the alternate Elizabeth had done.

"Would you mind if I join you?" he asked.

The question rattled her, because it threw into relief how far they'd drifted apart. "Radek, there is no *my people* and *your people*. We're a community. Of course you're welcome to join."

It brought another sheepish grin. "Merely a figure of speech." He squinted into the darkness. "It's close to dinner time, I guess. Sister Dawn plans to cook vegetable stew. Our... guests... must be hungry, and perhaps they'd like some food and tea. Consider it a peace offering."

Nobody with functional taste buds would mistake Sister Dawn's culinary efforts for anything of the sort, but Elizabeth decided to accept the offer in the spirit in which it was made. Détente. "That's very kind, Radek. Yes, I'm sure they'd like dinner. So would everybody else, I guess. It's been a long day."

"Yes, it has. I'll let her know." He trotted off to where Dawn was scraping out an old drum that had been converted to a cauldron.

As Elizabeth approached her new charges she could feel the heat of the small campfire and was grateful for it. The wood had gotten wet, and the smoke hung like a black, swirling canopy beneath the ceiling of the grotto. Just outside the flickering halo cast by the fire, she stopped for a moment and watched, if only to reaffirm to herself that she had done the right thing by refusing to turn them away. Confused and frightened, her double was in no condition to go anywhere, and John—the pair of him—plain worried her.

So what else was new?

She smiled despite herself, realizing somewhat to her surprise that she'd actually missed worrying about him. But there was worrying and then there was worrying, and with that trite realization her smile died. If they were on Earth—or on *their* Atlantis for that matter—Major Sheppard's leg would bump him off flight status permanently, and as for Colonel Sheppard, he looked ready to pass out. Not for the first time she wished that it had been Carson Beckett rather than Radek who'd ended up marooned in this place with her.

Yes, Elizabeth, and you can go right on wishing until you're blue in the face. It won't change one damn thing.

With that bracing thought she stepped up to the fireside. The Sheppards interrupted their inconspicuous observation of the goings-on over by the other campfire, and Elizabeth's double looked up at her, frowning in bewilderment.

"Do I know you?" she asked.

Seeing yourself lose your faculties was disconcerting, to say the least. Elizabeth swallowed a gasp, pasted on a lopsided grin. "We've met."

Colonel Sheppard cast another glance at the second campfire, then gazed back at her and cocked his head. "Sorry about stirring up trouble, Elizabeth. I take it you've managed to smooth things out a little?"

She crouched, leaned forward, and spread her hands over the flames, soaking in the warmth. "They're afraid," she said softly. "Some of them, including Dr. Zelenka, have invested Charybdis with godlike powers, even if they wouldn't quite put it that way. They believe this storm was caused by Charybdis because it doesn't want you here. It's fighting back."

"It's entropy," Major Sheppard said dryly, massaging his leg. "Though if you want to describe it as the wrath of God, that's probably not too far off."

"How did you find me?"

"We didn't. She did." He nodded at her double and launched into a complex explanation about alternate versions and matrices and originals and how the Stargate tried to put Humpty Dumpty back together again.

Halfway through the lecture Radek came over, carrying a tray with clay mugs on it, steam curling over them. Trying hard not to wobble, he got down to his knees and placed the tray on the ground. Then he ceremoniously handed the mugs to their guests. "You probably can use something hot," he said simply, all perfect host, as though his earlier altercation with them never had happened. "It's tea."

Both Sheppards looked ecstatic, but apparently neither found it constructive to turn down the offer.

The alternate Elizabeth sniffed the brew and beamed. "It smells delightful," she said brightly. "Please, you must let me have the recipe."

With a sudden pang, Elizabeth realized why her double's behavior struck her as so familiar; this version of her had fled back into the safe template of her childhood, impersonating the perfect politician's wife her parents had wanted her to be. No matter if the world came crashing down around you, you weren't to show a wrinkle and the party must go on. Her mother had epitomized the principle all her life, without once admitting to the stultifying boredom of this endless succession of charity dinners and junior leaguers' baby showers. Perhaps she really hadn't been able to notice it...

"You mean to tell us that the gate system *works*?" Radek's

comment was laced with a skepticism that barely avoided being impolite and yanked Elizabeth back into the Here and Now.

Major Sheppard took a careful sip of the tea, evidently decided that it wasn't as bad as it sounded, and said, "It works up to a point. Neither of us"—he nudged his twin—"could have gotten here on our own. It looks as though, if you're an alternate, the system will attempt to hook you up with your original, and that's the only way it works right now."

"So—" Radek slid a glance at Colonel Sheppard who'd wrapped his fingers around the mug of untouched tea. "Drink, Colonel. It's brewed from the blossoms of a local flower, and we observed several curative properties. Among other things it's a pretty good analgesic."

"I'm more worried about the other things," John observed, directing his gaze from the now very happy crowd by the other campfire and back to Elizabeth.

"It's safe, John," she said. "Really. You'll get approximately the same effect you would from a glass of wine, except it's more pleasant and without the risk of a hangover. Fundamentally, all it does is make you relax."

It wasn't the entire truth, and nobody knew it better than she. By the same token, if John turned any paler, he'd start to glow in the dark, and his painful squint suggested a roaring migraine. Right now the benefits of the blossom far outweighed its risks.

"I don't see you drinking any," he said, his voice terse.

"But you see me drinking it," Radek said before Elizabeth could reply, took a spare mug from the tray and drained it. "See? I understand your doubts, and I'm truly sorry to have caused them in the first place, but you must believe me, please. We're really not trying to harm you."

Finally, John took a tentative sip. "Could be worse, I suppose." He drank again.

"So." Looking pleased, Radek resumed his earlier thought. "This would imply that you came here specifically to find Elizabeth? Now that you've found her, what do you want of her?"

"We were hoping you could tell us where Rodney—original or alternate—is." John—the Major this time—finished his tea, gave a droopy-eyed blink, and placed the mug back on the tray. "I like this stuff. You got any more?"

"One's enough for now." Grabbing Radek's wrist, Elizabeth prevented him from getting up to fetch some more. "It can hit you quite hard when you're not used to it. And no, I'm afraid I've got no idea what became of Rodney. He never was here. I don't even know if he's still alive."

Trying to ignore the weight of responsibility and guilt that pressed down on her, she struggled to just keep breathing. There was a lot to be said for madness, Elizabeth thought, looking at her alternate who'd curled up like a kitten and was falling asleep by the fire. If she simply went crazy, she wouldn't have to face the fact that she'd failed on an unimaginable scale. Rodney and everybody else who'd died or gone missing that day—all of them were on her conscience. She could have stopped the activation of Charybdis, but she'd chosen not to believe Rodney. Her gaze wandered to the tray and the mugs, and she craved some of the tea, if only to make her forget for a while.

"Why?" Radek said.

Why what?

"Why do we need to find McKay?" Colonel Sheppard's speech sounded faintly slurred. But the tea couldn't kick in that fast, could it?

Scared all of a sudden, she asked, "John? Are you okay?"

"Yeah. Tea seems to work." He scrubbed his hands over his face as though to wipe away his fatigue. "McKay? I thought that would be ovbi… ov… obvious. We need him to figure out a way of getting us back to Atlantis—*our* Atlantis—and stop Charybdis from ever happening. But if we can't find him, it's up to you, Zelenka. We haven't got much time left."

"Less time than you'd imagine," Radek affirmed gently. His eyes were warm, smiling, but Elizabeth couldn't say whether it was how he felt or whether it was the blossom extract. "Suppose I help you, Colonel—and keep in mind, you no longer can order me to—and by some miracle you succeed. What will happen to us?" He'd gradually raised his voice, and everyone in the grotto was listening now. The happy noises had died down completely.

In a flash, she knew what he was playing at and that he was stone-cold sober for once. His mug must have contained hot water, nothing more. "Radek! Don't do this! We have to—"

"Stick together?" He laughed. "We never have. Because you're different, aren't you? You won't be affected by any of this!" He turned back to the Sheppards. "What will happen to us?"

Major Sheppard blinked heavily, struggling to focus. "You won't ever have existed," he murmured. "You won't—"

"We won't be there any longer. We'll be wiped out!" Arms spread wide, Radek rose like an angry prophet. "You heard him, brothers and sisters. They'd destroy us without thinking twice about it. And Elizabeth here—I won't honor her by using her chosen name—would help them. Because she is one of them, not one of us."

Us and them.

That's what it had boiled down to, what she'd been afraid of all along. In a way Radek had been right: the arrival of the Sheppards and her double had upset a precarious balance, and the resultant upheaval could destroy them all.

Across the fire from her, Colonel Sheppard was struggling to rise, sluggish and uncoordinated, and awkwardly slumped back against his alternate, who began giggling uncontrollably. Elizabeth clenched her fists. "How much did you give them?"

"Enough," Radek said simply. "They won't be able to put up a fight, which is what I hoped for. It's never been my intention to harm them."

"So what are you planning to do with them now?"

"Send them back to where they've come from."

"You heard them, Radek. It won't work unless you go with them. You'd have to leave, which is the last thing you'd want to do, isn't it?" It wasn't exactly a fair move, but Elizabeth no longer cared. Leaving the planet meant not having access to a drug that made this version of Atlantis seem like the happiest place in the universe. Nobody wanted to leave, and the thought of never being able to return would be terrifying. "Besides, how would you dial out? There is no dialing console."

For a brief moment it looked as though she was getting

through. Then Radek shook his head. "Who says they were tell-ing the truth? And I suspect they've got a jumper." He stepped over to the Sheppards, who were all but unconscious by now, and began searching them. Tucked into the waistband of Major Sheppard's pants he found a handgun, which he discarded with a mixture of indifference and disgust. Next he discovered a cloak remote, which was what he'd been looking for all along. "I thought so," he declared and activated the device.

Elizabeth whirled around and strained to see past the dark-ness and pounding hail beyond the grotto. At the far side of the clearing a faint gray outline materialized. Frustration made her grit her teeth. "For all we know, sending them back through the gate could kill them!"

"It's unfortunate but preferable to them killing us. Besides, if they've been telling the truth the gate won't work, will it?"

"Radek—"

"Make sure she doesn't interfere," he said calmly.

When Elizabeth turned back she almost collided with Brother Star, who was built like a linebacker and had the mindset of a Marine. The rest of the group closed in around her; a wall of once familiar faces that somehow had mutated into alien masks risen from a nightmare. And who could blame them? They'd gotten the gist of what Major Sheppard had said: if the effects of Charybdis were reversed, they'd cease to exist.

"Sorry, sister." Somehow Star contrived to sound both apol-ogetic and implacable at the same time.

Then a bright burst of pain exploded at the back of her head and sent her spinning into blackness.

Charybdis -908

Rodney McKay had persuaded himself that the tales of the local inquisition were vastly exaggerated. It'd been the only way of getting any sleep at all. Besides, so far and contrary to the propaganda, nothing seriously detrimental had happened to him. True, his current abode wasn't exactly pleasant, and the exquisite boredom of spending twelve days in an eight by eight subterranean cell defied description, but on the other hand, nobody had strapped him to the rack either. The worst damage he had sustained was a complete set of blisters from when he'd been power-walked down to the city, but even those had pretty much healed by now. Okay, two larger ones showed signs of turning into bunions, but considering the alternative he ought to congratulate himself.

You forgot to whine about the cold and the rats.

Well, yes, there was that.

He was hearing voices. One voice, to be precise. Still refusing to consider insanity, he'd put it down to the stress of the interrogation at first, but now he was more inclined to ascribe it to some form of malnutrition. Had to be. It had gotten worse since they'd thrown him in here without so much as listening to his side of the story. He'd decided to protest his treatment by refusing to eat. Not that it was much of a hardship. So malnutrition had to be it. Lack of potassium? Manganese? Zinc? Some mineral deficiency at any rate, and where was Carson Beckett when you needed him?

You mean the excitable person with the funny accent?

"Shut up!"

God, he needed some decent food! He needed some food, period.

As if on cue, his stomach cramped painfully. In front of a small hatch at the bottom of his cell door sat a wooden bowl, slid in at dawn by the warder. A large, mangy-looking rat was slinking around it, sniffing at its contents, and Rodney stared at it miserably.

Second thoughts about that pointless hunger strike? Personally, I don't care about whether or not you're killing yourself, but I'd take exception to any attempts at killing me. Especially pointlessly.

"Who said it was pointless? Hunger strikes worked for Mahatma Gandhi."

Ma-who?

"Mahatma Gandhi. One of the great— Oh, no, no, no! I am not going to validate a delusion by talking to it."

There was no other choice, he supposed. He had to start eating again.

With sudden determination, Rodney heaved himself off the dank, half-rotten heap of straw that unsuccessfully tried to impersonate a pallet, and shuffled over to the bowl. Giving an aggressive squeal, the rat turned on him. He launched a kick at it, missed, but it sufficed to send the rodent scurrying for a hole in the corner. Inside the bowl sat a fist-size heap of gray gunk that looked like nothing so much as a mix of oatmeal and lard, left standing in a hot, moist climate for at least a day too long.

"Oh God…"

The mere thought of swallowing any of it made him feel nauseated.

It looks like an excellent medium for Clostridium botulinum, E-coli, and salmonella. By the way, don't rats carry Yersinia pestis?

"Who asked you?"

Nobody. I like to give the benefit of my expertise voluntarily.

"I *don't* like. So shut up already!"

He'd been yelling loud enough to give himself a tinnitus. In the slowly settling silence, Rodney got the distinct impression that his invisible playfellow had gone into a sulk. Good. Maybe now he could have some peace and quiet. The gunk beckoned.

Clostridium botulinum, E-coli, salmonella, Y. pestis.

Great. The worst part was, the blabbermouth had a point. There was no way anybody could safely eat this, though Rodney's stomach begged to differ. You could actually hear the growl, and for some reason that provoked a lurid mental image of steak and lobster—plenty of butter for the lobster—baked potatoes and coleslaw. Chocolate brownies for dessert. Definitely chocolate brownies, though lemon meringue pie might be a viable alternative. And coffee. Lots and lots of coffee, with whipped cream on top…

Rodney moaned, buried his face in his hands, and tried to picture the first of Bell's equations for describing quantum states. When the lemon meringue pie inserted itself as a variable, he gave up, sagged back onto the straw and blankly stared at the wall.

You were right the first time, you know?

"About what?"

You don't have a choice. If you eat, you might *die. If you don't eat, you* will *die. In my experience, definite beats possibility every time.*

"Deep. Really deep. Moving, even. Did I tell you to shut up?"

Repeatedly. You don't like me, do you?

"Whatever gave you that idea? I don't even know you."

That's beneath you. Especially in view of the fact that, for a human, you're remarkably intelligent.

"Oh thanks. I still don't know who you are."

Which wasn't entirely true. Rodney had a pretty good idea, but in this instance at least, the possibility outweighed the definite—in other words, as long as he did nothing to verify it, he could pretend this wasn't happening or, more pertinently, hadn't happened. Not again! As if that whole hideous episode with Lieutenant Cadman hadn't been embarrassing enough...

"Why me? Why does it *always* have to be me?"

Wrong place, wrong time.

"Oh, so now it's my fault?"

If you hadn't decided to hop the moment you did, I wouldn't be here.

God, Rodney could almost see the smug little bastard shrug! At least there were no indications of *his* body wanting to do the shrugging... so far. "Hop? I don't hop."

Do, too.

An image surged up from some reservoir of memory that had remained blessedly untapped so far. John Sheppard shouting 'Pull the plug, Rodney!' over sounds that, like all things electromagnetic, were already being distorted in the singularity created by Charybdis. He himself leaping for the naquada generator and straight into that soaring column of light born of the fusion of Charybdis and its creator. Evidently he'd somehow become incorporated into the mix, or the mix had become incorporated in him. Either way it was perfect. Just perfect.

"And why this remarkable reticence up until now? If you don't mind my saying so, it seems a little out of character."

Your amnesia presented a bit of a problem. I didn't want

to risk freaking out you and, by extension, those superstitious country yokels.

"Too kind." Rodney was tempted to bash his head against the wall. Brain damage suddenly seemed a small price for driving out the incubus.

Kindness had nothing to do with it. It just struck me as counterproductive. So I decided to on a more subtle approach.

"I can't tell you how glad I am that you didn't opt for blunt," groaned Rodney. Then something dawned on him, and he sat up straight. "It was you! You led me to the ruins. You got me to salvage the equipment."

He sensed a distinct surge of pride.

The idea was to nudge you into fixing some essential equipment to enable us to go back and repair the damage. It would have worked, too, if you'd been a little more careful about covering your tracks.

Of course! He'd known that someone, somehow would manage to twist this around and blame him. "And what's this *us* business? There is no *us*. As far as I'm concerned it'd be best for everyone involved if you simply disappeared. It's way past your bedtime."

For a long, blissful moment he thought Ikaros might have taken the hint. The stillness in his mind felt comfortable, relaxing as a hot bubble bath. Just as Rodney wanted to slip in deeper, the goddamn kid bounced back.

Look, Dr. McKay, I'm sorry. I was only trying to help.

"That's what you said the last time," Rodney snarled savagely. "Do the world—the universe!—a favor and *stop helping*!"

The stillness descended again, but this time he was under no illusion that it would last. Ikaros seemed incapable of taking no for an answer. True to form, the kid floated back in short order.

I know why you don't like me. I remind you of yourself.

"Oh, please!"

It didn't sound convincing, even to Rodney's own ears, because the kid had a point. Almost from the get-go, he'd seen bits of himself in Ikaros. The smarts, the pushiness, the arrogance—and the solitude underneath. Naturally you couldn't admit to the latter, which was where the arrogance came in. Besides, if you didn't believe in your own superiority, who else would?

"Fine. Okay. So we have certain things in common."

The kid was smirking. Don't ask him how, but Rodney knew it.

"It still doesn't mean I'm going to play along with this."

There's nobody else who could fix this. You were right from the start. Charybdis doesn't work.

And that's what they called 'laying it on with a trowel.' How stupid did Ikaros think he—

Listen to me! I'm telling you Charybdis doesn't work, and don't for a moment think I enjoy making this kind of confession. My best guess is that it has created an infinite number of timelines, all of which will become affected by cascading entropy—if it isn't happening already. I suppose I should have seen it coming, but you know how it is when you're enamored of an idea. You've been there.

Hadn't he just? He would have done anything to follow through with Arcturus—as a matter of fact he *had*, up and including the abuse of people's trust—because he'd absolutely believed in it and in the fact that he was right. Not that this was any of the kid's business.

"Let me see: destruction of the better part of a solar system; destruction of unknown multiples of galaxies, potentially universes. Can you spot the difference?"

Are you familiar with fractals?

Did bears go potty in the forest? And what did fractals have to do with the price of fish?

They're always the same shape no matter what their size. There is no difference, Dr. McKay. You know where I'm coming from, and I need your help. The universe needs your help, if you will.

Oh, that's just great! Roll out the big guns, why don't you?

"Do you see me wearing a red cape?"

What?

"I don't have a great big 'S' emblazoned on my manly chest either. And finally, there's the minor detail that I'm looked up in a cell."

There was a distinct sense of Ikaros shaking his—its?—head, bristling with impatience.

Dr. McKay! Unless I'm completely wrong, which has happened no more than once in the past ten thousand years, Charybdis has become sentient. This means it'll attempt to neutralize everyone who could potentially threaten it.

"Sentient? Charybdis is a program! Granted, it's rather sophisticated, but it's still a piece of software that—"

So am I. A piece of software, I mean. But, as you realized quite astutely from the outset, we're talking about quantum computing here. And that's what makes all the difference. Because, if you whittle it right down to the basics, you're no different from Charybdis or me. You consist of quantum hardware and software. All life does.

Rodney felt himself go very still. Infuriating as it might be, the kid was right. It was entirely possible. For all they knew now, higher consciousness—soul, if you will—ultimately functioned on a quantum level. Charybdis could very well have become sentient. Sentient life made from the very building blocks of the universe, with the capacity to manipulate those building blocks... there was no telling what Charybdis could affect if it wanted to. Anything was possible. Anything at all...

Exactly. The very fact that you—we—are locked up here with some kind of witch trial to look forward to would attest to it. You have to get us out of here and destroy Charybdis, and you have very little time to do it in.

Naturally. Why was it that nobody ever said, 'Rodney, life as you know it is at the brink of destruction and you have five years to work out a solution'? Noooo, it always had to be, 'Rodney, do the impossible. Within the next fifty-eight seconds!'

That's because you work better under pressure.

"How the hell would you know?"

Ikaros didn't answer. Of course there wasn't much to be added.

A way out.

Sure. Nothing easier than that.

After all, the cell was only carved from solid rock, with a narrow, barred slit just below the eight-foot ceiling to admit a measly trickle of daylight. The ensemble was closed off by a nicely crafted hardwood door, reinforced by metal bars. In other words, all it took was small amount of high explosives. Piece of cake.

In the first instance, though, he had to survive to get out. Rodney's gaze wandered to the gruel bowl. The rat had slunk back, and even it seemed to have second thoughts about the bowl's contents. Then again, the brain needed energy to function. He slid off the pallet and angled for the bowl. The rat bared its teeth for show and backed off. There was no cutlery to go with the feast, presumably to frustrate any suicidal tendencies the prisoners might develop—which in a roundabout way suggested that the substance impersonating food wasn't immediately life-threatening. Somewhat reassured, Rodney poked a finger into the bowl and scooped up a small amount of gunk. It drew strings.

Yeah, well, so did macaroni cheese.

Scrunching his eyes shut, he tentatively licked his finger. Bad idea. Prolonged contact with the taste buds definitely was a bad idea. Still not looking at what he was eating, he scooped up some more, gulped it down without daring to chew—for all he knew he might encounter things that moved in there—and emptied the bowl within a couple of minutes. The gourmet meal sat in his stomach like a lump of rubber, but at least the hunger pangs had stopped. On the downside, he still was no further on the genius escape plan. Perhaps if—

For a moment he thought he'd imagined it, but the sound continued, proving that, for the first time in nearly two weeks and not counting the priceless situation with Ikaros, the unexpected was happening. Nobody ever came down here, except the warder who made his round at dawn to leave the fresh—relatively speaking—food bowl and remove the old one, and that would be it for the rest of any given day. Now Rodney heard footfalls—correction: bootfalls—out in the corridor.

At least two sets as far as he could make out, neither of them the indifferent, wooden-clogged shuffle of the warder, and they were coming closer.

A new prisoner?

He listened carefully.

No, the steps were too confident.

Whoever these people were, they were coming to get someone. And that someone would be him. As if to underline the point, the bootfalls came to a halt outside his door, and he thought he heard the metallic clink of keys. He backed into the farthest corner of the cell, for all the good that would do.   .

"Idiot," he muttered, mainly because it distracted him from being scared out of his wits.

You can't afford to be! Keep your head together!

"Don't tell me what I can and can't do! You got me into this—"

The rattle and clank of bolts, then the scrape of a key, and then the door swung open. Rodney broke out in a cold sweat. He was under no illusion that they might have decided to let him go and figured that this was how the strapped-to-the-rack part started.

They were huge, Ronon-sized, and they looked twice as mean.

Raising his hands, Rodney took a tentative step forward. "I'm coming voluntarily. So don't… don't… Just don't. Where are we going, by the way?"

If they'd heard him, they did a good job of hiding it. Or maybe they were mute. Without a word, they flanked him, each wrapping a beefy hand around his biceps, and hauled him through the door, along the corridor, past a dozen other cells and up a narrow flight of stairs.

In a lobby at the top of the stairs, swathed in pompous purple robes, stood the bureaucrat Rodney remembered from his remand hearing—if you could call it that. The man stared at him mournfully. "Your trial is concluded. It has been—"

"What trial?" spluttered Rodney before he could remind himself that, when dangling between two linebackers, silence was golden. "I haven't even had a defense! I should have—"

"Quiet!" the linebackers roared in unison. Not mute after all.

"Why should you have had a defense?" the bureaucrat inquired reasonably. "What you have done is indefensible. Your punishment shall be commensurate with the crime, and it shall be public. Before that you shall be on display for three days, as a warning to others. Take him away."

"Just wait a minute! What about my appeal? There has to be—"

"Quiet!" Unlike their physique, the linebackers' vocabulary needed work.

But nobody listened anyway. His job done, the bureaucrat had turned around and was slouching back to his office. The linebackers, having been given their orders, started dragging him into a humungous hall lined by fluted columns, through a succession of smaller rooms, and finally out onto a small balcony. At last Rodney knew where they were; the northern side of the acropolis. Below spread the vast square of the agora, and he could see the tiny shapes of market traders and shoppers scuttling all over like busy insects, seemingly impervious to the rain. Of course it was raining. What other weather was there in this place?

Mounted on the parapet was a sturdy wooden crane with a basic pulley system, and suspended from that on a hempen rope was an empty cage. Rodney blinked at it, took in the contraption, and succumbed to a queasy shudder when he realized the exact nature of the *display*.

Like automata the linebackers went about their chore. While one of them kept hold of Rodney—who had no intention of flinging himself off the balcony; so what was the point?—the other reeled in the cage and opened a small door whose rusty hinges creaked in protest. Clearly there hadn't been a *display* in quite some time. Which should guarantee him an appreciative audience, Rodney thought bitterly as he was shoved into the cage.

More creaking as the door fell shut behind him. The linebackers didn't bother to lock it. Why should they, when the inmate had nowhere to go? The cage gently lifted off the ground, swung out over the parapet and descended in jerky bounds, each of which made Rodney throttle the life out of the

metal bars he was clutching. After a drop of about thirty yards it
came to a stop at last, swinging and twirling erratically.

A vertical rock wall wobbled past, the northern face of the
hill on which the acropolis sat; then, on the agora below, a swirl
of congregating insects, all staring up and pointing at the display amid shouts of excitement. Having reached maximum
torque, the cage stopped revolving for a blessed moment before
it started on its backward rotation. Rodney groaned. The second
he did, he wished he hadn't because somehow the groan shook
loose that lump of nausea he'd been trying to suppress. Still
holding on to the bars, he slumped to the cage floor in a bone-
less heap and proceeded to rid himself of the gruel he'd forced
down less than an hour earlier.

He only understood what a lousy idea that had been when
his gaze inevitably followed the fall of the gunk, which was
tumbling toward the bottom of a black chasm that seemed to
reach all the way to the bowels of the planet. The memory of
a long-ago trip to Athens, Greece, flashed through Rodney's
mind. He'd taken the mandatory sightseeing tour to the
Acropolis there, and the guide had obligingly pointed out the
Barathron; a deep cleft in the rocks, which the ancient city state
had put to good use by dropping convicted criminals into it for
permanent disposal.

There could be no doubt at all as to what would happen three
days from now. The knowledge that he'd likely die of a heart
attack long before his body hit the ground wasn't quite as comforting as one might have thought.

I think Charybdis is on to us, Ikaros observed helpfully.

"Oh, really?"

CHAPTER 12

Charybdis +13

She was stirring at last, and Ronon half wished she weren't, wished that something had gone wrong, that the technician had made a mistake, and that she'd never wake up. Anything, even death, had to be better than what was to come.

They'd been taken to a chamber behind the laboratory, a small, simple affair all in white that contained a single bed and a chair, and ostensibly they were alone. He knew well enough it was a fallacy. Embedded in those bland walls were photo crystals and audio receivers, and everything they'd do or say would be transmitted elsewhere in the complex, to a much more luxurious room where Marcon and his aides would monitor every word and move. Even without the surveillance equipment he wouldn't have any choice but to do exactly what Marcon had told him to do; the Behemoth was awake, trembling with excitement, waiting for betrayal to commence.

And Ronon would betray, as planned. Marcon wanted to know how Teyla had managed to make the Stargate work, and Marcon would get what he wanted. He always did. Once he had the information, Teyla was expendable. There could be no doubt as to what that meant. Besides, Marcon had as good as ordered it already, and she wouldn't be able to keep herself alive by proving her usefulness as a warrior. According to the technician, she was blind.

Ronon couldn't even begin to imagine what it must be like for her. Horrible frustration at no longer being able to accomplish the simplest tasks, and he wasn't sure he'd have the strength to still go on in her place. But out of the two of them she'd always been the stronger, the one more in control—not that he'd ever admit it.

She sighed, then tensed, telling him that she was awake

and alert to his presence. "Who is there?" Her voice sounded hoarse, sandpapered by the sedative they'd given her. "I need to find a woman called Teyla Emmagan."

"So you've gone looking for yourself now?"

A gasp, then her right hand reached out, groped, searched, until it found his and held on. Hard. "Ronon? You're Ronon!"

He couldn't help it. He smiled. "Good job you can't see me. You might not have recognized me."

"I'm surprised you were able to recognize me. After all, I'm—" Cutting herself off, she let go of his hand, flexed her fingers several times, looking stunned. She bent her knees as though she were testing the joints and at last sat up in one fluid move and touched her face. "Oh… that… that's unexpected," she murmured.

"What is?"

"In the timeline where I've come from I was over seventy years old and afflicted with all the aches and pains you'd expect at that age."

"Timeline?"

"Charybdis… You remember Charybdis?"

"Yeah. Unforgettable." Ronon snorted. "As a matter of fact, until I saw you, I thought everybody else was dead. What about Charybdis?"

But she'd already jumped ahead to another subject. "You remember. Only the originals… You're the original!"

"The original what?"

"It's not possible…" She still wasn't listening. "I shouldn't have been able to find you. I shouldn't have got here. I—" Her face lit up with a spark of realization. "Of course! Your finger!"

He remembered Marcon showing him that ghastly chunk of dead bone and tissue he couldn't recall losing, but how did that matter? She wasn't making sense, probably still dazed from the sedative. The Behemoth hissed, angry and impatient, pushing him to pursue the information it wanted to obtain. "What do you mean by *timeline*?" Ronon ground out.

"Charybdis created them all," Teyla replied distractedly and without making much sense. "And there's an infinite number of versions of us, but only one…"

A flash of agony blotted out what she was saying as the Behemoth demanded to know the identity of *us*. He hadn't meant to groan, but he must have, because the next thing he became aware of were Teyla's hands clamping his shoulders, sightless eyes trained to where she guessed his would be.

"Ronon! Ronon, what's wrong?"

And how was he going to answer that? *I don't want to betray you, but there's this thing burrowing through my mind forcing me to do it anyway*? Hardly, though he wondered how many words he'd actually get out before the Behemoth… Did what? What could it do? Hurt him? Yes, obviously. Kill him? Given the situation, his death would be the best of any number of bad outcomes. Which made things very, very simple.

Suddenly he started laughing through the unholy pain in his head. For once Marcon had overreached himself. He'd manipulated Ronon into a situation where he had nothing left to lose and everything—his honor most of all—to gain. Marcon had made him invulnerable in a way he'd never expected.

"Ronon!"

Teyla sounded scared, and she had every reason to be. This could go terribly wrong. The only advantage they possessed, the one Ronon banked on now, was the fact that she had something Marcon wanted. As long as she didn't tell him anything, she'd be reasonably safe.

"Don't say another word until I tell you," he gasped and grabbed her hand. "Come with me. Quick!"

It was barely an idea, let alone a plan. The only thing he knew for sure right now was that he had to get her out of here. He pulled Teyla off the bed, and she was far too seasoned a warrior to resist or ask questions. She also trusted him implicitly, he realized, queasiness pooling in his stomach at the notion of what he still might do. No promises, no guarantees. He'd only ever pushed back so far against the Behemoth, because there'd never been a reason to endure the consequences of taking it further. Now there was.

Question was how long he'd last… The door, less than five steps away seemed on a telescopic slide into endless distance, its outline shimmering in colors that couldn't possibly exist. Five steps, and the two he'd taken so far had required inhuman effort, all but forcing him to his knees in a sludge of treacly heaviness.

"Ronon!"

"Don't talk!"

His own voice roared in his ears, unbearably loud, the sound distorted and pulsing, filling his skull with its insane pressure, and he could swear he felt the Behemoth move, thrashing about, raking his brain with its claws. The third step loomed like a rock face, impossible to scale, except he no longer believed that, couldn't afford to believe it, and he was going to—

The rock face burst apart in a white-hot explosion of pain, and Ronon fell, helplessly pitching forward onto hands and knees, bringing Teyla down after him, and he was screaming like a thing possessed, howling until the walls of the room bulged outward with the noise.

Without warning, it all stopped, tumbled into the utter silence of a winter morning, brilliant with freshly fallen snow. For what seemed like an eternity he heard nothing, felt nothing, half decided that he was dead. Then he realized that he was panting as though he'd just outrun a whole wing of Wraith darts—if he was panting, he was breathing, and if he was breathing, he was still alive. Even McKay wouldn't be able to dispute the logic of that.

Teyla's hands searched again, found his face and cupped it and withdrew almost as quickly. "You're wet," she whispered, about to lick her finger and determine the nature of the liquid.

"Don't!" Ronon clamped her wrist in an iron grip.

"You're hurting me!"

"Sorry." Taking a deep breath, he eased his hold a little, took stock. Though his head still swam, the pain was gone completely, as if it'd never existed, and there was no presence to constrict his mind or force his will. The hand he was still grasping glistened with blood. He brushed his fingertips across his face and neck, realized that he was bleeding from his nose and ears, and sat back on his haunches in surprise. Couldn't be a stroke; overall he was feeling too good for that. No nausea,

no nothing. It could be a ruse on the part of the Behemoth. Or
it—

"Ronon? It would be helpful if you told me what's going
on."

"Nano-robots. They use them for mind control. Clean your
hands, else you get infected."

He reached over to the bed, ripped off the sheets and wiped
her hands as best he could. They'd have to take care of the
rest as soon as they had access to water and two minutes to
spare. Right now, their clock was ticking way too fast for his
liking—if it hadn't run out already. Marcon had to have realized what was happening and would be on his way down here
with a contingent of STs. The tactically most sensible thing to
do would be to dispatch the guards in the Stargate room, but
Ronon doubted that would happen. The Ancestors' paranoia
wouldn't allow them to leave the gate unattended. In any case,
he and Teyla had to make it to the lab before the STs arrived,
wherever they came from.

"I'm fine, and I'll explain everything, but now we gotta
go. Fast." Pulling Teyla to her feet after him, he headed for
the door—so easy and everyday now—opened it a crack and
carefully checked the hallway outside. Still deserted, which
was good news, and at the end of it gleamed the lights of the
laboratory. "Quiet," he whispered. "Hang on to my shirt."

Her hand wandered to his side, grabbed a fistful of fabric,
and he let go of her and drew his sword. A few more steps
brought them to the entrance of the lab. Teyla glided along
behind him, a noiseless shadow. Cautiously, barely daring to
breathe, Ronon poked his head around the corner. The technician was on his own, no STs in sight, and the lab door leading
out into the second corridor and the room with the Stargate was
closed. Securing that door—the only ingress to the lab from the
side where the most immediate threat would come from—was
the first order of the day.

The lab technician's back was turned, and he seemed completely immersed in his work, dissecting that mysterious surplus
finger and inserting the samples he took into small, transparent
containers. Momentarily Ronon wondered what the man was

hoping to find, then he shook off the thought as pointless, and detached Teyla's hand from his shirt. Grasping her shoulder, he signaled her to stay put, received a brisk nod of acknowledgement. Then he raised his sword and tiptoed forward until the tip of the blade nudged a spot midway between the technician's shoulder blades. The man froze, back stiffened, and dropped the container he'd been in the process of sealing.

"Don't move," Ronon said mildly. "Might make me jumpy and then things could get real messy. Now, I need you to lock the door."

"I can't do that from here," the technician croaked.

"Turn around. Slowly."

Shivering, the look of a cornered rabbit in his eye, the man did as he was told. Sweat beaded on his forehead, his raised palms were damp, and he oozed the acrid smell of fear. "You can't do this," he stammered. "The Behemoth won't let you. It will stop you."

"What if it *wants* me to do it?"

The terror on the technician's face deepened as he obviously contemplated a global malfunction of the Behemoth, causing hundreds of thousands of soldiers to turn against their masters and their masters' property. Ronon grinned. The idea had a lot going for it.

"What's the Behemoth?" Teyla had been listening attentively, but attention hadn't stopped her from getting confused.

"Later," promised Ronon and waved the technician over to the door. "Lock it."

The way his knees wobbled it was nothing short of a miracle that the man could move at all. But move he did. Fingers trembling, he keyed the lock code. From inside the door came the clank of bolts sliding into place.

"Good." Ronon smiled at him, which provoked another shudder. Then he smashed the pommel of his sword into the pad, destroying it. It wasn't going to keep the STs out forever, but hopefully it would slow them down just long enough. "And now you're going to tell me where the hidden exit is."

He wouldn't have thought it possible, but the technician turned yet another shade paler, enough to make Ronon worry that the man was going to faint.

But instead of passing out, the technician pulled himself together, marshaled that ounce of courage he possessed, and stuttered, "Wha...what do you mean? There is no hidden exit. The only door is the one you just ordered me to lock."

"The Behemoth asks you to quit lying to me. It doesn't like lies."

Smiling again, Ronon emphasized the point by placing the tip of his sword against the man's neck, just above the carotid artery. He felt almost as confident as he sounded now, because the technician's startled reaction had already proved that his guess was correct. He'd banked on the Ancestor's obsession with covering all bases, even the unlikely ones. There was no way they'd have only one access route to the Stargate and leave themselves without an escape hatch or a means to ambush the enemy, should such an enemy ever manage to arrive through the gate.

Of course, if Teyla really had solved the problem of making the system work, he'd also just cut off their own easiest escape route, but that was a question of getting your priorities straight; in the short term, staying alive took precedence. They'd find another gate eventually.

"So. The hidden exit. Where is it?" Steel nicked skin, and Ronon watched a trickle of blood run down the technician's neck. The man yelped. "No! Please! It's... There! It's behind there!" He pointed at the bank of computers that ran along one side of the lab.

Ronon couldn't see so much as a crack in the wall to indicate a hidden doorway, but that meant nothing. The Ancestors' technology wasn't as sophisticated as what he'd seen in *his* Atlantis, but it ran a close second. It'd be simple enough for them to cloak the exit. "Open it." Something else occurred him. "And disengage the alarm before you do so."

Another yelp. "How did you—?" The technician flinched from the minute increase in pressure applied to the blade. "Yes! Yes, I'll do it. I... I need to get to that computer, alright? The passage is password controlled."

It made sense. This way you could—

"He's lying." Her head cocked, Teyla seemed to listen to something only she could hear. "He is planning something."

"It that so?"

"No… No!" the man gasped and turned on Teyla, furious all of sudden. "How would you know, woman? What are you? Some kind of witch?"

For reasons best known to herself, Teyla grinned. "Perhaps. But you see, if a person loses one sense, the others sharpen to make up for it. The sound of your voice gave you away. I recommend you practice lying more often. Now, the truth. You don't want me to curse you, do you?"

Taking an involuntary step back, the technician collided with Ronon's chest. Before he could correct his mistake and skip forward again, Ronon had him in a stranglehold and gently reduced his victim's air supply to the minimum requirement. "Alternatively, I could just hurt you. A lot. Which do you prefer?"

"Please…" The whimper barely squeezed past Ronon's chokehold. "She's right. I was lying. Please… here. It's the red button," he croaked, flopping his arm until the sleeve of his robe slipped to reveal a wristband like the one the ST officer had worn.

Sliding a glance at Teyla, Ronon saw her nod. Must be his lucky day. "Take it off. Nice and easy."

Nice and easy no longer was in the guy's vocabulary. With all the signs of panic, he ripped off the device and held it up. "Red button," he stammered again.

Ronon snatched the wristband, spun him around, landed an uppercut on the technician's chin before the man had come to a standstill, dropping him cold. "Right. Let's get the hell out of here." Stepping over the crumpled body, he sheathed his sword, held his breath and pushed the red button, hoping that Teyla had read the man right.

Seemed as though she had.

The wall behind the computer banks twisted out of focus, and for a moment Ronon thought that he'd been wrong, that the Behemoth was reasserting its presence, and braced himself for an onslaught of agony. It never happened. Instead, he watched the whole side of the room burst into a rainbow of colors as the force field, and with it the illusion it had generated, dissolved. Behind lay another hallway, descending into the bowels of the Defense Command Center.

It was wide enough to accommodate the standard marching formation of six men to a line, with a low ceiling that, like the walls, was soundproofed. Inset into the floor at regular intervals were light panels, glowing in a dull red and providing just enough illumination to see where you were going. Best of all, there wasn't a soul waiting in the tunnel.

"Ronon? What's going on?"

For a few seconds there, he'd clean forgotten Teyla's presence. He whirled around guiltily, and as he turned his gaze caught on that huge, gross jar of McKay preserve. Something she'd mentioned earlier popped into his mind. "You said you found me because you had my finger?"

"Yes, but—"

"How?"

"It has your DNA, so the Stargate took me to you. It's something to—"

Ronon no longer listened. Three swift strides brought him in front of the preserve jar. There probably was a release mechanism somewhere, but he didn't have the time to look for it. This would have to be done the old-fashioned way… He drew his sword, aimed at the middle of the glass tube and swung. The impact almost broke his wrist. Not glass, then. Great.

But then there was the faintest of whispers, and he saw a hairline crack running out from where he'd struck the tube. Two more blows finished the job. The tube exploded in a fountain of shards and stench and liquid, drenching him to the skin, and he barely jumped out of the way of the corpse toppling toward him. Gross!

"What are you doing?" Teyla was starting to sound pissed off. Not that he could blame her. "And what's that smell?"

"Whatever they use around here to pickle dead people."

McKay's body lay on the floor like something about to melt, and Ronon fought back the urge to gag—substantially helped by loud banging from the door.

"You in there! Open up!" The STs had arrived.

"If we're going anywhere, now would be a good time!" advised Teyla.

Then a new voice from outside. "Ronon, you don't want to do this!" Marcon yelled through the door, a tremor of fear in his voice. Yes, resistance definitely would scare him. "Surrender! You won't survive it if you don't."

And he wouldn't survive if he did.

He raised his sword one last time, brought it down with barely a glance and snatched whatever body part he'd just sliced off... an ear? If nothing else, it was easy to stow. Fighting that urge to hurl again, he stuffed the ear into his back pocket, wiped his hand, and grabbed Teyla's arm. "Let's go!"

As they bolted through the opening, Ronon activated the wristband again, and the force field reestablished behind them. It wouldn't keep them safe, not by a long shot. As soon as the STs broke down the lab door and realized that the fugitives were gone, Marcon would know and have the tunnel opened. They had maybe ten minutes, if that, to get a comfortable head start. It would have to be enough.

Still holding on to Teyla, he set off at steady jog. "You okay?" he asked as he ran.

"Yes. What kept you in there?"

The embalming fluid dripping from his booty had soaked through Ronon's back pocket. It felt sticky on his skin and made him want to squirm. Never mind. "I got us a ticket to meet the one guy who's able to fix this mess."

CHAPTER 13

Charybdis +4

At some point before the lights went out, Brother Maniac had told John—that would be Lieutenant Colonel Sheppard—that they were living in the Age of Aquarius. Or something. His head disagreed. Capricorn came closer, especially as Capricorn was butting its horns against the inside of his skull. Persistently and with the kind of vengeance that could be achieved only through years of determined malevolence.

He groaned.

In response, somebody removed something warm and wet from his forehead, replaced it with something cold and wet, and said, "Thank God!"

"Elizabeth?" That couldn't be his voice, could it? It sounded like somebody had run it through a veggie grinder. He tried again, with moderate success. "Elizabeth?"

The answer came in stereo. "I'm here, John."

Followed by, "About time."

His voice, with vastly improved smoothness, probably because he hadn't actually said anything.

Then a female solo, "Don't get your hopes up. He is waking up, but it might take a while yet."

John figured he had two options; either assume he was hearing things and leave it at that, or open his eyes and check it out. He knew which option he preferred, but he also had a nasty suspicion that this particular option wasn't really an option. As if to confirm his hunch, there was a low rumble and the ground shook.

"Damn," said his voice—the smooth version. "That's the third in the last hour. We had the same thing happening in my timeline. Teyla thought that Charybdis was causing it."

"I don't like it here. It's dirty," complained one of the

Elizabeths. "And damp."

The other one soothed, "We won't have to stay here much longer. Just until John comes round." In a whisper, obviously not meant for her alter ego to hear, she added, "We've got to get out. It's not safe."

"I know," the smooth voice hissed back.

Okay. Time to take that option, which was easier thought than done. Next to extracting a team of injured Rangers from deep within Taliban territory in Afghanistan, opening his eyes was the trickiest thing he'd ever tried to do. His eyelids weighed a ton, for starters, and he was constantly scrambling for a foothold on that greased slope back into oblivion. The other senses were more accessible.

Wherever he was, it was cold. Clammy. John could feel the ground under his fingertips—rock—and it was moist and covered in something slick, algae or moss or sediment. The place also smelled funny, musty, dank, as though it hadn't seen sunlight in… ever. There was a constant, slow drip-drip-drip coming from his left, and the sound, just like the voices, had that hollow, echo-y quality. Belowground then, a tunnel or a cave.

And they'd just had a seismic tremor. Oh goodie.

"Why the hell didn't you wake me?" he groaned.

"We tried, believe me."

"Should have tried harder, Junior."

There was no reply other than a soft scraping of metal. The next thing John knew was a cascade of ice water exploding in his face. He gasped, spluttered, and finally yanked his eyes open, only to be rewarded by a new attack from the Capricorn as the dim flicker of a torch hit his retinas.

"Oh boy…" Passing out again seemed like a great idea, and he devoutly wished he could afford to. At least his head would stop hurting that way.

"Better?" His alternate was grinning, but right behind the smirk sat a whole heap of worry and impatience.

"No," John grunted, forced himself up from the cloak—whose?—he'd been lying on, and shuffled sideways so he could sit leaning against the rock at least until their present locale quit doing the loop-de-loop around him. Gradually the motion stopped and with it the worst of the nausea. His head still hurt, though.

The vista he'd gained didn't improve matters. They were belowground alright, in a high, narrow rock chamber claustrophobic with stalactites. Several of them—too many for comfort—had broken off during the tremors, their shards littering the floor of the cavern. Two tunnel mouths gaped at opposite ends of the chamber; the lower one was drooling water that rapidly advanced to where they were camping out. Pick an exit... Across from him guttered the torch, which someone had wedged into a crack in the rock. Shivering and smoking, its flame shed just enough light to make out the faces of Junior and the two Elizabeths, all of them ghostly pale under streaks of dirt, their eyes huge and dark. They looked like they'd been down here forever.

"Anybody care to fill me in on what I missed?" John asked. "You can leave out the glaringly obvious, like us getting drugged by Brother Love and his traveling freak show."

"He's scared, John," Elizabeth said. "When you arrived, he—"

"There's scared, and then there's dangerous. Those folks have started a goddamn cult, with Radek as their messiah!" John sucked in a breath, somehow managed to swallow his anger. It wasn't going to achieve anything other than making his headache worse. He squinted at Elizabeth. "What are you doing here?"

"I left the cult, so to speak. Quite some time ago, actually." She gave a wry smile. "When I realized that the flower was addictive, to be precise."

"The tea... You *knew* and you didn't stop us from drinking the stuff?" John figured he would have to revise that not-getting-angry decision, headache or no.

"The dosage you had wasn't enough. Otherwise... Look, you know me better than that, Colonel. I've never frivolously put you in harm's way, and that hasn't changed." Her voice had taken on an edge, but she seemed to notice, eased off. "You'd have to ingest the blossom extract regularly for several days to become addicted. Prepared properly it wouldn't even be strong enough to knock you out like it did. I swear I had no idea of what Radek had planned."

"So how does the addiction show?" asked Junior. "Paranoia and delusions of grandeur?"

"No. You simply won't be able to bring yourself to leave this place."

John blinked. "Good old Homer... the Greek one, not Simpson. It's the original island of the lotus-eaters, isn't it?"

"*The Odyssey...*" She shot him a brief smile. "Your choice of reading matter never ceases to amaze me."

"Actually, we watched the NBC series," Junior threw in.

"Speak for yourself." The absurdity of that only dawned on John when he clocked Junior's grin. He sighed. "So, what happened?"

"This is part of a huge cave system beneath what used to be Atlantis here," Elizabeth explained. "Star and a couple of his men discovered it last year when they were out hunting. One of the men slipped and fell into a sinkhole. After we'd rescued him, we started exploring—the usual, in other words. We were hoping that this might provide us with a refuge in case we ever came under attack, but it turned out that the caves were simply too dangerous. If it's raining hard enough flash floods submerge the tunnels, and they're completely unpredictable." She shrugged. "Well, you can imagine. One of the teams got caught in one of those. Two of the men never made it back. Besides, we couldn't find a second access to the caves. Without a backdoor to get out if you have to, no hiding place is any good."

Staring toward the pitch darkness of the upper tunnel, John asked, "I take it we're not hiding, then?"

"Not exactly," Elizabeth replied grimly. "Radek wanted to get you off-planet as quickly as possible. Once you were out cold he and his people piled you into the jumper and tried to send you back through the gate." Pausing for breath, she shook her head. "It was the weirdest thing I've ever seen. The wormhole engaged, but it wouldn't let the jumper pass through the event horizon. After that they decided the best way to make you disappear was to take you to the sinkhole and lower you down. I tried to prevent it, but Radek had told them it was the only way to appease Charybdis, so the others—"

"Figured they'd abandon common sense and take their chances with a bit of human sacrifice," John finished for her, grimacing. "Nice. Which brings me back to my initial question: what are *you* doing here?"

"Attempting to keep you alive. All three of you were out cold, which could have been a death sentence down here. I insisted on coming with you. Radek didn't seem to mind," she added dryly.

"Crazy. Crazy, but thanks."

"You're welcome."

So, if he recapped correctly, they were trapped underground with no known way out, and if they tried to return to sender they'd likely get tossed right back into the sinkhole by Zelenka and his disciples who were in the throes of some kind of superstitious frenzy. Even the fact that someone had been kind enough to leave them with a torch couldn't dispel John's certainty that in at least one timeline created by Charybdis today had to be Friday the thirteenth. His gaze drifted to the lower tunnel and the water pouring in from there. Was he imagining it, or had the volume increased? Even if it hadn't, their chamber definitely was flooding. At the bottom end of the cave a stalagmite that looked like the Hunchback of Notre Dame stood up to its knees in water. Last time he'd looked, the water had only reached mid-shin.

"Somebody please tell me that *that*'s where we came from." John pointed at the lower tunnel.

Thankfully, Elizabeth nodded. "I don't really know the caves; I've only been down here a couple of times, but considering the hailstorm I decided it was best to keep moving uphill as soon as Major Sheppard and my alternate were awake and able to move."

Good point. "So how did I get here?" asked John.

Both Elizabeths stared at Junior who tried to look innocent. Did he always make such a bad job of it?

"He carried you," the original Elizabeth said.

"Sorry." John winced. He knew the state Junior's leg was in. "Like I said; crazy. Crazy, but thanks."

"Don't mention it. You're at least ten pounds underweight anyway." As if to demonstrate that his leg wasn't an issue, Junior rose and gimped over to a trickle of water gushing from a stalactite to refill the canteen he'd emptied into John's face. "Besides," he added, "Teyla seemed to think we need you."

Teyla's confidence was flattering, but John had no idea how to merit it, given that there were no Rodneys running around on this planet. Worse, given the vagaries of the Stargate system, there obviously was no way of gating elsewhere without an alternate willing to act as a conduit to his or her original's matrix. He doubted that Zelenka would volunteer. In other words, they'd have to do this the old-fashioned way.

"Where's the jumper now?"

"Where you left it. Why?"

"Because we're getting out of here." Clinging to a stalagmite for dear life, John maneuvered himself to a stand. That loop-de-loop thing happened again, and he held on until the rotation of the cave slowed down a little.

"Haven't you been listening, John? There is no exit."

"You said you hadn't *found* one. Elizabeth, stay with me; Junior, you look after her double." With that, John groped his way toward the upper tunnel, hoping he'd be able to stay on course.

Charybdis +13

The wall ahead was real. No matter how often Ronon punched the controls on the wrist unit, the concrete remained solid.

A few minutes ago they'd emerged at a subterranean crossroads from which eight other corridors branched off. He'd had no idea how far they'd come or where exactly beneath the government district they were, and there'd been no time to scratch his head and wonder. So he'd taken nearest turn—and led them straight into a dead end.

Behind him the footfalls and shouts of the STs were approaching far more quickly than he would have liked.

Beside him Teyla's breath came in harsh gasps, as loud as a

bellows to his ears. "What is it?" she rasped.

"Trouble."

He whirled around, stared back into the tunnel where the STs' flashlights slashed crisscross beams over walls and ceiling. Some fifty yards back in the direction where they'd come from gaped a dark opening, a niche or, if he was undeservedly lucky, another corridor.

No luck, deserved or not. It was a niche, just large enough for him and Teyla to flatten themselves into the shadows and quit breathing. Ronon was under no illusion that the STs wouldn't find them in here, but it would buy them a minute or two. A lot could happen in a minute or two. At the very least they'd have time to prepare to die.

Shouts firmed into snatches of words.

"Along there!"

"They're trapped!"

"Careful! At least one of them is armed!"

The STs ran past, still keeping an orderly rank and file despite the excitement of the hunt, until they realized that the cul-de-sac was empty and surged to a halt like a wave breaking on the cliffs. A moment's silence gave way to rumbles of confusion as the men in front turned, searching. The murmurs were stilled by a cultivated baritone drifting along the corridor.

"Well, where are they?"

Ronon recognized it instantly, the siren song of betrayal. Marcon. Marcon was down here.

"They're gone," an ST shouted back.

"They can't be! Are you sure they took this corridor?"

"Yes, Excellency. We're positive."

"Then they must be here. There is no way out." The voice was coming closer, at a measured pace, as though Marcon had all the time in the world. And he had, of course, because he was right. There was no way out. He laughed, softly, mockingly. "Ronon, my friend! You know which quality I've always admired most in you? Your refusal to acknowledge defeat, even when it's staring you in the face. But you had best break the habit, amusing as it is. Give yourself up now, and I promise you the end will be swift—and as painless as I can make it."

Ronon's fist clenched around the grip of the sword. The voice was close, so close. He could picture it easily; burst from cover, with one slice of the blade cut the lying excuse for a man in half, and never mind what happened after. Death and oblivion didn't sound too bad. He would have done it if he'd been alone. But he wasn't alone, and he owed it to Teyla to go down fighting for their escape.

Then the beam of a flashlight made the decision for him. It fingered along the wall, found the niche, found Ronon's chest. At the other end of it, an ST's eyes went wide, his mouth opened, about to shout out his discovery. Ronon wasn't going to wait for it.

He propelled himself out into the corridor the same instant as Marcon came abreast of the niche. The blade snapped across the man's throat, while Ronon's left arm clamped around his chest, pulling him in front of his body like a shield. Startled outcries from a few STs exploded through the tunnel and rolled away into silence.

"Anyone tries to follow us and he is dead," Ronon said and threw a quick glance over his shoulder. "Teyla. Hang on to me."

She slipped from the niche, one hand searching until it caught the fabric of Ronon's sleeve, held tight. Slowly, never losing sight of the STs, Ronon began to back away toward the open end of the corridor, dragging Marcon with him. Gawking and immobile, the STs let them go. He had suspected as much. At least for the time being the Behemoth wouldn't allow them to endanger the chairman of the Defense Council who, ripe with sweat and fear, trembled in Ronon's grip. Suavity had fled Marcon with a vengeance, revealing him for what he was: a coward. Ronon allowed himself to enjoy it just a little.

They reached the main tunnel without incident, turned the corner, lost sight of the STs. "The quickest way to the surface?" he hissed in Marcon's ear. "And don't lie to me."

"You won't get away with this!" Marcon whimpered. "It's only a matter of minutes until the Behemoth orders them to disregard my safety and—"

"I know. So we'd better hurry up." Ronon let the blade bite

a fraction of an inch deeper into Marcon's throat. "Answer my question."

The man groaned. "Continue along here. The third cross corridor to the right leads to a flight of stairs and straight to the surface."

"He's telling the truth," Teyla whispered.

Ronon shot her a look, realizing too late that a gesture she couldn't see would hardly get him an answer. "How do you know?" he asked.

"I can feel it."

Ah. That explained it...

"Keep moving. We haven't got much time." She gave him a gentle shove.

True enough. And Marcon seemed to share their desire to put distance between them and the STs.

The corridor narrowed and began to lead uphill. Promising, but Ronon wasn't going to let his hopes rise just yet. They were buying added lifespan in two-minute increments, was all. He lengthened his stride, forcing Marcon into a jog. Teyla kept pace behind him. The first cross tunnel flashed past, unlit and dusty, burrowing into black, then the second, not much more inviting. Just before they reached the third corridor, the STs shouts caught up with them, driven on by the flicker of flash-lights in the distance. The Behemoth had made up its mind. Marcon yelped, tripped, ran on, stinking with fear now.

Ahead and to their right the third corridor yawned. Barely wider than Ronon's shoulders, the tunnel seemed to predate the rest. It meandered wildly and was showing signs of decay—in places, groundwater was seeping up through cracks in the floor, and the lighting, dim and desultory, looked to be on its last legs. Finally they came up against a spiral staircase that disappeared in pitch darkness after ten steps or so—no way of telling what was lying in wait up there. Then again, it still beat the certainty of what lay behind.

Ronon stopped.

"What?" hissed Teyla.

"Take the lead. There's no lighting up there, and you've got more practice with this than I have."

Chuckling softly she slipped past to take point. "Hold on to me," she ordered Marcon and started up the stairs.

An eternity later—by now Ronon figured they'd probably come out a the top of the Flight Surveillance Tower—she froze. "There's something ahead. A door or some other kind of barrier. Can you sense it?"

Sense it?

Though now that he focused, he thought he could feel something; the air seemed denser, packed more tightly up here. "I guess so. I—"

"Shh!"

He'd heard it almost the same time as she. When he turned around he could just about make out a faint, unsteady graying of the pervasive black; reflected brightness from the flashlights the STs were carrying. "Go!" he hissed.

Some ten or fifteen steps further up, Teyla stopped again. "It's metal," she whispered. "Probably a door. I don't hear anything on the other side."

Another dead end. Maybe. Unless Teyla was right. Unless...

Letting go of Marcon who was nothing but a wheezing bundle of fear now, Ronon pushed past her. His fingertips played over cool steel. No hinges, no lock. He grimaced, then felt for the wrist control he'd taken from the lab technician. The red button was the second from the left in the bottom row, he remembered that. Fumbling across the small keyboard, counting, he thought he'd found it, pushed.

Nothing.

And there would be no time for a second attempt. Below, the bootfalls and shouts of the STs were getting louder rapidly.

Marcon whimpered, suddenly lunged forward and grabbed Ronon's arm. "It's her they want," he hissed. "You understand, Ronon? They want the woman. She's the one who came through the Stargate. All you have to do is give her to them. A push will do. At the very least it'll buy you and me time to escape."

A whole disbelieving whirl of thoughts raced through Ronon's mind and all at once crystallized into realization. Marcon was compromised. He would be the first to die once the STs caught up, and he knew it.

"Good idea," Ronon whispered. "But mine's better."

He rammed a flat palm into Marcon's chest, his rage fueling the force of the punch. The chairman of the Lantean Security Council toppled backward and tumbled down the stairs in an uncontrollable fall. Ronon wished he could have seen it, but hearing the screams wasn't bad.

"What was that?" murmured Teyla.

"He must have slipped."

"Clumsy. Sounds like he's keeping our friends busy, though."

"Yeah."

Broken-necked or still alive, Marcon would, at the very least, block the stairs for a while.

Another minute bought. Ronon tried the wrist control again. This time the steel barrier obligingly did what the wall in the lab had done and dissolved, revealing a vast room. Squinting against a sudden onslaught of brightness, muted and erratic as it was, he blew out a soft sigh of relief.

"We're good to go?" Teyla asked softly.

She'd barely finished speaking when an explosion rocked the building and all but deafened him. Then, after a heartbeat of utter silence and through the ringing in his ears, Ronon heard muffled screams riding on the back of the detonation. The area immediately in front of him was filled with swirling smoke and dust, and he now recognized the significance of that warm, unsteady light that penetrated the gloom: fire. Without another word, he yanked Teyla through the opening, and sealed it behind them.

"Where are we?" Then she must have smelled it. A flicker of panic danced across her face. "Fire," she hissed.

"Yes."

Gradually the haze of dust and smoke left behind by the detonation rose, carried upward by hot air and dissipating, probably through some vent in the ceiling. The room drifted into focus like a stretch of landscape emerging from a bank of fog. It was devastated. Debris littered the floor; pieces of metal, charred and so grotesquely twisted that they offered no clue as to what had been destroyed, chunks of machinery ripped from their fastenings and shattered like toys—and bodies. Most casualties seemed to be civilian, poor bastards living in the slums, pressed into labor here for a wage that barely allowed them to feed their families.

Suddenly a shrill, drawn-out whistle ripped through the air and resolved in a new detonation that shook the ground and nearly knocked him off his feet. Stunned, he realized that the first blast he'd heard couldn't possibly have been the one that had destroyed this facility—if it had been, he and Teyla would be part of the carnage now. Multiple explosions, three at least. It seemed the government district was under attack, either from the homegrown resistance, consolidated at last, or from those outside hostiles the Ancestors had styled into a bugbear.

Either way, the timing was a gift. The STs would have better things to do than chase a couple of fugitives, and he and Teyla could simply disappear in the general mayhem.

"Let's go." He turned to Teyla, started to see her pale as death, sightless eyes fixed on some vision of horror that had to be at least as bad as this. "Teyla! You okay?"

"The Cataclysm," she breathed. "It's come again. Pirna was right."

The what? And who was Pirna?

Fascinating though the answer might be, they didn't have time for this. He clutched her shoulders, shook her. "Teyla, snap out of it! It's just an attack. You've seen dozens of them. We've got to make the best of the confusion, steal a ship, and get away."

She didn't seem to hear him. "That noise. The whistling… In my timeline Charybdis practically destroyed the Pegasus galaxy. Planets were torn from their orbit, stars turned to supernovas, moons fell into their primaries. Almost everywhere it began with devastating meteor showers… it was like living in a war zone…"

"Teyla, I'm sure—"

"I'm telling you, I know that noise! This place has been destroyed, yes?"

"Yes."

"Look up! What do you see?"

Ronon gazed up, if only because he figured it that humoring her was the quickest way to stop this nonsense. Above him the air had cleared, leaving a plain view of the hall's rafters. What he'd presumed to be a vent drawing off smoke was in fact a massive hole in the ceiling, its edges still smoldering. No missile could have done this.

"Perhaps you're right. It doesn't matter."

Not waiting for her reply, he picked her up, slung her over his shoulder. Between the meteors and the STs coming up the stairs, they didn't have a second to lose. Teyla having to navigate the debris would slow them down too much. From outside screams and wailing and the screech of sirens seeped into the hangar. Inside the only sounds were Ronon's footfalls and labored breathing, the occasional clatter when he trod loose a bit of debris, and the rustle of cooling embers. As far as possible he kept to wherever the floor was clear of rubble, racing a zigzag obstacle course for the doors he'd spotted at the far end of the hall.

He was less than five yards out, when he heard shouting behind him. The STs had arrived. The next moment, an energy blast missed him narrowly and slammed into the wall, tearing out chunks of mortar and masonry. No quaint man-to-man weaponry for the STs; their job was to kill efficiently and at a distance. But even they weren't immune to the carnage. After that first blast there was the briefest of ceasefires while the STs struggled with their surprise and shock. Ronon used the respite to fling himself and Teyla across those last few yards, through the door, and out into a huge loading yard.

The sky was ablaze, glowing in a deep, vicious red, offset by low clouds that loomed black where they didn't suddenly bloom with brightness. It looked like sheet lightning until the meteors burst from the clouds, crisscrossing the air with trails of fire and smoke and hurtling toward the ground. It was beautiful, in a horrific kind of way.

Ronon tore himself away from the spectacle. By the dock along the side of the yard a dozen or so freight gliders stood lined up, never to be loaded now. Their hulls were streaked with soot and peppered with dents and small holes; several of them sat dead on the ground, their engines incapacitated. Desperate for cover, Ronon headed for the freighters. The master stevedore, goods list still in hand, lay on the dock; a couple of his men, barely alive, slumped between two gliders, moaning. Just past them, wedged in between the freighters and dwarfed by them, a small private ground glider was parked.

The sight almost made him laugh; never mind cover, they'd got themselves a getaway vehicle. The glider was hovering, which meant its anti-grav drive was still operational. The glider's owner hadn't fared quite so well. He still sat in the pilot's seat, killed by the same meteor fragment that had left a hole in the back of the glider.

Ronon lifted Teyla over the side and dumped her in the passenger seat; then he pulled the dead man from the glider and jumped into the pilot's seat. He released the parking safety, and the small vessel leaped up a few inches and sluggishly nosed forward. The drive was operational alright, but it was running less than smoothly. Then again, right now he'd settle for a mule provided it got them out of there. As if to confirm that thought, shouts and running footsteps announced that the STs had caught up and were fanning out to search for them.

"Hang on!" he said to Teyla, offered a prayer to any deity that would listen, and slammed the throttle all the way forward.

The glider's engine howled in protest, then the vehicle shot out from between the freighters and across the yard, provoking shouts of rage from the STs. A barrage of blasts followed in their wake. Before Ronon could react, the glider's forward speed all but stalled. To make up for it, the vessel shot ten feet straight up into the air. It was like riding an unbroken horse.

White-lipped, Teyla clutched the edge of her seat, but she never said a word. She could hear those energy blasts coming as clearly as Ronon saw them, and probably thought the glider's erratic behavior was due to evasive maneuvering. No point in bursting that bubble.

Teeth clenched, Ronon fiddled with the controls, unsure of whether or not it would help or cause a crash. He could count the occasions on which he'd piloted one of these things on the fingers of one hand. Suddenly the drive stopped its dissatisfied whine, changed pitch to an altogether more reassuring growl, and the glider began to respond to the controls. Ronon forced it into a steep climb, banked and sped for the corner of the building and out of the range of the STs weapons.

As they soared over the roof, the full extent of the devastation leaped into view. Below, the government district and the city stood in flames and what wasn't burning had been pulverized by the barrage. Ronon sucked in a sharp breath. The scene reminded him of nothing so much as the images of Sateda that probe had transmitted back to Atlantis. Amid the ruin, survivors scrambled for the spurious safety of the buildings. By the looks of it, even a bunker wouldn't protect them.

Teyla had heard his gasp. "It's bad," she said. It wasn't a question.

"Worse," he murmured.

And the meteors kept coming. He swung the glider into a sharp turn to avoid one heading directly for them and then set it back on an easterly course toward the fringes of the government district and the military base.

"Where are we going?" This time it was a question.

"To steal a spaceship."

CHAPTER 14

Charybdis +4

The climb had been over slick, jagged rock, complete with
water cascading toward them, and Elizabeth was soaked to
her skin. The hem of her skirt was slapping around her calves,
feeling colder and soggier with every slap.

"Be careful not to get caught up here." Torch in one hand,
Major Sheppard crouched in the narrow cleft at the top of the
incline. "It's a pretty tight squeeze, and the rocks are sharp."

Yeah. Elizabeth's fingers had the cuts to prove it. No need
to remind her.

"Do you want a hand?" he asked.

"No. I'm fine. Just get out of the way there."

Even to her own ears her voice sounded dull, weighed down
by the thousands of tons of mountain above their heads. Which
was not the best of thoughts to hang on to. With a grunt she
pulled herself up another two feet, then another, clamped her
hand over the edge of the drop, wiggled and kicked her way up
into the cleft, crawled through, and finally tumbled out into yet
another rock chamber. She'd long lost any sense of how many
hours they'd been on the move. Somehow time had become
submerged in an endless sea of misery—aches, fatigue, cold,
wetness—together with the quickly fading memory of the last
rest they'd taken.

Same as the sight of daylight for that matter. Her best guess
was that they were no nearer the surface than they had been in
the chamber where John had woken up at last—if indeed they
were even that close. Though several of the passages they'd
come to had led uphill initially, virtually all of them had dipped
sooner or later, and she had a distinct sense of being deeper
inside the mountain than ever before. So far they'd been spared
the flashfloods—perhaps the hail hadn't melted yet?—but on

more than one occasion they'd been wading hip-deep in ice water. Compared to that, the little trickle down the rock wall was hardly worth writing home about.

Elizabeth pushed herself to all fours and rolled sideways into a sit. The others obviously felt the same as she; they sat slumped against the walls, eyes closed, and there seemed to be a tacit agreement that, for the next fifteen years at least, nobody would walk another step. With a sigh that fell just short of contentment, she tucked her legs tighter to her body and wrapped her arms around her knees for warmth. Besides, the chamber really was too small for four people; if she tried to stretch her legs, she'd kick John, though it was questionable whether he'd even notice. He looked half dead, and perhaps, she thought grimly, he actually was. For a while now she'd been worrying whether he'd sustained something worse than a mere concussion; a skull fracture, for instance. Not that there was a damn thing any of them could do about it...

The thought, disheartening as it was, gradually morphed into some kind of warm fluffiness. Vaguely noting that, at some point, she must have shut her eyes, Elizabeth let herself drift toward that happy place. After all, she'd deserved some fluffiness. She'd just—

"Don't fall asleep!" John might be half dead, but he still could rap out an order if he had to. Somehow he'd even managed to hone that edge of command back into his voice.

Elizabeth's eyes shot open, and she squinted at him. "I wasn't going to—"

"Don't fall asleep," he said more gently. "None of us can afford to. We've got to keep moving as long as we've still got light."

He cast a meaningful glance at the torch, which had burned down to a small stub. It was a minor miracle that it had lasted this far, but sooner or later that small stub would be gone, too, and they had nothing on them that was anywhere near dry enough to use as fuel.

"I'm hungry," the alternate Elizabeth offered and added with a surprising pinch of irony, "You promised me a dinner party."

"It got cancelled." Wincing in pain, Major Sheppard massaged his leg. "The hostess was spaced out."

Hungry. Or ravenous more like. For some unfathomable reason, Elizabeth had omitted starvation from her list of selfish little miseries. It should have come right at the top, because she was just about ready to start chewing on her toes.

"Okay. Let's move out." Heavily leaning against the wall, John groped his way back to his feet. He gave a smile that was as fake as a thirty dollar note. "The sooner we get to the surface, the sooner we can go forage."

'Never' sprang to mind… Elizabeth nixed that thought as defeatist. If the Johns could go on in the state they were in, so could she. Hell, even her alternate, who was at least twenty years her senior and decidedly not compos mentis, wasn't complaining. Much. She rose awkwardly, trying to shrink away from her wet clothes. No longer protected, that moderately warm part between her chest and knees was cooling down rapidly, so getting on the move again probably wasn't such a terrible thing.

John had let Major Sheppard take point, followed by Elizabeth's double. "Go on," he said, waiting for her to squeeze past.

"No way." Elizabeth shook her head for emphasis. "We've been through this already. You're not bringing up the rear. I'd like to be in a position to catch you when you pass out."

"Elizabeth—"

"That's an order, John." In the disappearing light from the torch, she saw him stare at her in disbelief and grinned. "Go on, or we'll lose them."

His only answer was a brief, reluctant nod, then he turned and followed the two alternates.

The passage continued to lead uphill. Elizabeth filed it away as a bit of random information, at the same time refusing to get her hopes up. You could be forgiven for thinking the entire tunnel system was like one of those drawings by M.C. Escher, where staircases went up and down simultaneously. Maybe the whole thing was just a giant optical illusion, and—

Yeah, sure. No raving, Elizabeth. Not yet, at any rate.

Up ahead that dim, increasingly reddish glow from the torch in Major Sheppard's hand came to a halt and seemed to be sucked up by something vast and dark beyond comprehension. As soon as she arrived at his side, she understood, and despite cold and hunger and exhaustion the sight left her breathless with awe. They were standing in the middle of a rock cathedral. It was impossible to tell how far beyond the reach of their torch the ceiling vaulted, but somehow the shroud of shadows overhead managed to convey an impression of absolute enormity. Stone pillars soared toward it, organic things without pattern or regularity, their tops lost in darkness. Throughout the entire chamber, the rock showed crystalline inclusions that threw back the meager torchlight and sparkled like diamonds.

"My God, it's beautiful," whispered Elizabeth's alternate. Her voice had lost that grating little-girlish chirp, and she seemed to be back, as though this magnificent space had somehow released her from madness. "It makes you want to pray…"

At that moment the torch leaped into a final flicker and went out at last. Perhaps praying wasn't such a bad idea, Elizabeth thought, gasping with shock. She wasn't afraid of the dark, never had been, but this darkness, native to a place that never had seen sunlight, was different.

It wasn't… dark.

The chamber was glowing. Swirls of brightness wreathed the pillars, up and up, until they dissolved in a shining haze high above her head. They flowed up the walls and meandered across the floor like an unearthly meadow of flowers. Their sheen reminded her of bioluminescence, but that wasn't quite right, was it? This was more brilliant, and the color was subtly different.

"Somebody please tell me it's not just me," murmured John. "We're all seeing this, right?"

"Oh yeah." Major Sheppard dropped the remains of the torch. It struck the floor in a burst of clatter that echoed and amplified through the cathedral's vault until it sounded like an avalanche. "Sorry," he said when the racket had died down.

"Don't do that again!" John ground out, grimacing.

"Don't worry. I'm fresh out of torches." The Major had moved over to a pillar and was picking at the crystals.

"Whatever it is, it looks valuable," he observed at last and dryly added, "We're rich."

Elizabeth had a sudden, delicious vision of scraping a handful of crystals from the walls and hitting the nearest drive-through. Five double cheeseburgers with everything... provided there still were any drive-throughs in existence somewhere in the universe. Then something odd she'd been noticing all along pushed its way into the forefront of her consciousness and the appetizing cheeseburger vision popped like a soap bubble.

"Look!" She pointed at several patches of black nothingness that broke up the luminous display at irregular intervals all around the cathedral.

"Tunnels," John said. "Obviously crystal-free."

"Not all of them," Elizabeth's alternate piped up.

At the far end of the rock cathedral opened an area where the glow receded into the distance, almost as if it were beckoning them to follow.

"Well, I guess that takes the choice out of where we're going."

A little grudgingly, John began to herd them all toward the lit tunnel. Elizabeth understood his reluctance. Maybe it wasn't entirely rational, but she shared his suspicion of things that seemed to be too good to be true. As if to prove her point, the tunnel was wide, downright comfortable, its floor and walls rounded and surprisingly smooth, which definitely made a change from the rough passages and fissures they'd encountered so far.

"It almost looks manmade," she murmured, already fearing it wasn't. The softer rock was ground away around the crystals, leaving them to protrude like tiny nubs and spikes.

"Uhuh." Absently running his hand over the surface, John shot her a sideways glance. It told her that he knew as well as she that they were looking at water erosion. "I'd suggest we keep moving. Fast."

The tunnel sloped gently uphill, which was the good news. The bad news was that half an hour in they encountered the first signs of recent flooding. If she'd seen it on a beach somewhere, she'd have called it a tide pool. In a niche in the wall a patch of limestone had been eddied out by time and water to form a deep, perfectly round bowl. The water inside shimmered lime green, reflecting the sheen of the crystals and stirred by the flitting shapes of blind, unpigmented fish.

As they moved on they found a second pool, then a third, and then the first rivulets came trickling toward them. The rivulets soon merged into creeks; the river was about to pay a return visit. Eventually they were staggering shin deep through chilly water, barely able to feel their feet and fighting for balance.

Major Sheppard, who was setting the pace, finally signaled a halt and turned around. "You think we should go back?"

"And then what?" If John had actually tried to keep his teeth from rattling, he'd failed spectacularly. "Sit in the dark until we starve instead of drown or freeze to death?"

"Maybe we can wait out the flood. What do you think, Elizabeth?"

She'd barely opened her mouth when her alternate took a tentative step forward. "No," said the other Elizabeth. It came out like a croak, and she cleared her throat, preempting any interruption with an impatient shake of the head, as if she knew full well that they wouldn't be inclined to listen to her. "No," she repeated more firmly. "We have to keep going. If we turn back, we'll all die."

The phrasing took Elizabeth aback, reminded her of old tales of mad seers, prophets who went unheard. But, paradoxically, for the first time since she'd met her twin, the older woman's eyes were clear and she seemed perfectly lucid. Elizabeth's decision, when it came, was based on gut instinct alone; not a rational argument in sight, which was wildly out of character. The only explanation she could have given was that she knew herself, and that other woman, insane or not, *was* herself. "We carry on," she said. "She's right."

John blinked. "Come again?"

"You heard me... *us*," she amended with a quick glance at her double. "Keep going."

"Yes." Major Sheppard was looking at Elizabeth's alternate as though he'd never seen her before. "Yes. She's right."

The older Elizabeth smiled at him gratefully. "Thank you."

"Okay." It sounded a little uncertain, as if John basically agreed but didn't quite trust the process that had brought the majority to their decision. "Move out."

A half kilometer or so further into the tunnel, the water ran knee-high and there was a noticeable current now, even though the ground had leveled out for the time being. Too exhausted to waste any energy on talk, they were walking—wading—each wrapped in their own thoughts, the silence broken only by the sloshing of water and ragged breathing. Without warning Major Sheppard stopped again.

"Listen!" he whispered. "You hear that?"

The sound wasn't unlike a train thundering past at night or trees shaking in a November storm—or a waterfall. The distortion of the echo made it impossible to tell how far away it was, but Elizabeth suspected that it was close and that it would be big. And whatever else it might mean for them, getting to that waterfall was a goal now, at least in the short term. Who knew? There might even be a passage to the surface. Together with a herd of flying pigs…

They plodded on and within minutes reached what had to be the summit of the tunnel. After that the ground fell off as rapidly as the roar of the waterfall increased in volume. The current ran uphill now, which explained why it remained moderate. It didn't make the going any easier, though. As the water crept up to their thighs, their hips, waists, and finally to their chests, they linked hands, forming a chain to steady each other.

"How's your leg, Junior?" John asked under his breath.

"Still attached. It's too cold to feel it," grunted Major Sheppard. "How's your head?"

"Still attached. I'm thinking of diving for a while."

Good Lord! As though one of them wasn't bad enough…

Elizabeth grinned despite herself, vaguely relieved that she still could, because most of her body felt frozen solid by now. She'd all but lost sensation below her knees, and the rest wasn't far behind. If they didn't reach a ledge or some other reasonably dry place in short order, they'd die of hypothermia.

At last she saw something other than tunnel walls and crystal-green refractions on the water ahead. The passage opened out into an immense cavern, far larger than the rock cathedral and filled with mist and deafening noise. Beneath the mist sat the surface of a subterranean lake, black as onyx. The opposite shore was invisible, lost in haze and darkness. To their right, some two hundred meters from the tunnel mouth, the waterfall pounded into the lake, a massive moving column, spraying foam and seemingly burning from within.

"What on Earth…?"

"It's either sunset or sunrise," John shouted over the noise. "That thing's coming from topside, and it's conducting light like a fiberglass cable."

There was her passage to the surface, Elizabeth thought grimly. Some local deity—or, if Radek was right, Charybdis itself—must have been listening in on her thoughts and decided to piss her off. That blood red waterfall would be the last thing she'd see. They had nowhere to go, except back—and even that was doubtful now; in the time they'd been standing here, staring, the water had crept at least an inch up her chest. Chances were that, even if they turned back right now, they wouldn't be able to make it to the rock cathedral. The only choices remaining were either to stay here and drown or to swim out into the lake and drown. She guessed that this was the moment when you were supposed to say, *It was an honor serving with you…*

Apparently not.

Without a word—or perhaps she simply hadn't heard it over the roar of the water—John let go of her hand and flung himself out into the lake.

"John!"

It was an irrational impulse—after all, what difference would it make?—or perhaps the determination to survive as long as possible and force the others to do the same. Either way, Elizabeth pushed herself off to go after him. A hand snatched the back of her shirt and pulled her back, pulled her under for a second, and she came up spitting and spluttering to stare at Major Sheppard's face, inches from hers.

"Don't!" he shouted. "It's not what you think! Look!"

She scrabbled to regain the ground under her feet, swiped the water from her eyes, and stared in the direction he was pointing. Some one hundred meters out into the lake, John was clinging to something square and wooden, and swimming back toward them.

"A raft…"

The Major couldn't possibly have heard her, but he read her lips. "Yeah! If he manages to get it here!"

Good point. The lake wasn't a lake at all, it seemed, but a large underground river. Its rapid current was trying to carry him downstream and away from them. He was kicking hard, gradually gaining ground and aiming for the relatively calm waters of a small recess in the rock, a little over ten meters down from where they were standing. Major Sheppard nudged her and her twin toward the recess to meet him.

As John struggled closer, Elizabeth recognized the 'raft'. It was a fence panel, about five by five feet, of the kind they had put up around their experimental rice terrace to keep out animals trying to feed on the young shoots. She figured she knew what had happened. The terrace had been situated on one of the high slopes of the mountain; the east facing slope was ideal, because it caught a lot of rain, but it also lent itself to mudslides. One of those must have destroyed the terrace and carried some of its fencing down into the ravine below and from there into the river, the waterfall, and on into the caves.

Only a few feet out, John got caught in an eddy but managed to snatch the far end of the outcrop that formed a breakwater in front of the tiny bay. Hanging on with one hand, he heaved and kicked himself and the fence panel into the recess. Up close, the raft seemed desperately small. Looking like nothing so much as a very pale drowned rat, John had pulled himself on top and lay there, breathing hard and resting for however many moments he'd be granted.

Not many, she thought. The water kept rising.

She turned around, caught Major Sheppard and her alternate exchanging a glance; some silent communication Elizabeth couldn't quite interpret.

"What are you waiting for?" the Major hollered and prodded her toward the raft. "Get on!"

Elizabeth couldn't say what had tweaked her antennae—perhaps that quiet exchange, perhaps the odd look in Major Sheppard's eyes. In a flash she realized what he was planning, and she'd be damned if she let it happen. "No!" she yelled. "You two first!"

"Look at the raft!" the Major shouted back. "To paraphrase you, Dr. Weir, 'I will not authorize this mission unless I am sure there is at least a remote chance of success.' There isn't. That contraption will never carry all of us. We need to save as many as we can, and that's two."

If we turn back, we'll all die.

The words jumped into Elizabeth's mind unbidden. Her double had known or, at the very least, guessed correctly. Which didn't change the math. Major Sheppard was right. If they all got on the raft, it'd sink. Using it as a flotation device was possible—and completely pointless. Given the water temperature they'd be unable to hold on sooner rather than later, and even if two of them let go, by that point the other two would be too weak to climb onto the raft.

"You go!" She grabbed her double's arm, tried to pull her forward.

With surprising strength the alternate stood her ground. "I didn't agree to Janus's plan to save myself, Elizabeth. Remember? And remember what *he* told us?" She slid a brief glance at the Major. "The originals have to survive to stop Charybdis from happening."

"What if he's wrong?"

"You know he isn't. There's no other option. Go!"

"I can't just let you die!"

Head cocked, Elizabeth's alternate smiled. "Then don't. Survive."

"You're crazy." It was a low blow and a last ditch effort.

"Even crazy people have lucid moments. Don't waste any more time. Go, and don't look back."

Major Sheppard must have seen the fight drain out of her. He grabbed her around the waist and helped her onto the raft. "Remember the *Odyssey*? This is Hades. Your double and I, we're the shadows. Always have been. Just make sure you succeed." He grinned and nodded at John who lay sprawled beside her, out cold. "You'll have to wake him. He shouldn't be sleeping given his condition, but don't bring him round before you're past the point of no return. I don't want to have this argument all over again. I'll leave that in your capable hands."

With that he gave the raft a shove, propelling it out into the river. Elizabeth could feel a sharp tug when the current grabbed hold of it and spun it away from the shore. She realized that she needn't have worried about heeding her double's advice not to look back; the two alternates disappeared from sight almost immediately, hidden by the rocks that protected the recess.

Downriver lay uncertainty and darkness, and the latter at least suited her mood perfectly.

CHAPTER 15

Charybdis +13

"You're kidding, right? The originals have to survive to fix this Charybdis mess? Do you know what the odds of that are?"

"We'll find out just as soon as you find us a Stargate, won't we?"

Teyla realized how irritable this reply sounded as soon as it came out of her mouth, but she couldn't be bothered to soften it or apologize. She knew exactly what the chances were. She'd known long before anybody else, and she'd lived with that knowledge for thirty-two years. So perhaps she was allowed a little irritability. That aside, she was exhausted, her head was pounding, and the hinges of her jaw seemed to have come loose from all the talking she'd done in the past hours. For once Ronon was nothing if not inquisitive. Not that she could blame him. She had nearly as many questions, she supposed.

"I'm sorry," said Ronon, much to her surprise. As a rule he seemed to avoid apologies. "You look beat," he added.

"Thank you. I'm sure you look vibrant."

"I look the way I smell, if that helps."

"Not really." Teyla never even tried to hide her grin. He smelled ripe, and that was putting it very politely. Then again, she probably wasn't far behind—smoke, sweat, fear, and filth.

"Listen." Ronon's hand landed on her arm. "We're in hyperspace now, so this thing can fly itself for a while. By all accounts these transporters have really nice VIP quarters. How about I take you up there so you can clean up and get some rest?"

"That's kind of you. Cleaning up sounds wonderful, but right now I'm too tired to move a muscle. I'd rather stay here."

It was a half truth. The whole truth was that she did not want to be on her own. Or rather, she did not want to be separated from this tangible tie to her past and future now that she'd found it at last—entirely by accident and after having reconciled herself to the fact that she would not see her friends again. Waking up in that laboratory and hearing Ronon's voice had been as much of a shock as the realization that she was the original after all and that—perhaps *because* she was the original—her journey through the Stargate had wiped out any physical trace of the past thirty-two years of her life. It hadn't given her back her sight, but at least she had the strength of youth again. She'd probably need it, too.

"I appreciate the company. You know me. Always happy to catch up with old friends."

"As I recall, the last old friend you caught up with fell down the stairs, and the one before you ran through with your sword. Should I start to worry?"

"Not unless you've sold me out recently."

She smiled a little. "I haven't. At least not as far as I'm aware."

"No," he murmured darkly. "It seems this time I managed to do it all by myself."

The remark dragged a leaden silence in its wake, as though he already regretted having let slip even this much. Teyla knew from experience that waiting him out would be pointless. She'd die of old age first. Under any other circumstances she might have respected his privacy, but the exchange of information implied two-way traffic, and so far she had been the one to do all the talking. He'd tricked her into it quite deftly, his excuse being that he had to fly the ship he'd commandeered.

Teyla herself had only the sketchiest of memories of that particular escapade and the events leading up to it. Having to rely on acoustics alone didn't help to flesh out the picture. That aside, she knew well enough that, for a while there, it had been all she could do to keep pure, stark panic at bay, and she'd missed more than she normally would have. All that had registered was the stench of ozone-laden air and smoke and blood, the ceaseless pounding of explosions as meteors hurtled into what she presumed to be a city, and the sickening, disorienting lurches of the small vessel as it ducked and danced out of the path of destruction. She recalled a dizzy sense of gratitude when the glider had touched down at last, she didn't know where; that and the fact that she'd barely been able to stand when Ronon had plucked her from the passenger seat and placed her back onto firm ground. He'd dragged her along at a dead run then, not caring whether or not she stumbled, trusting that somehow or other she'd be able to keep pace with him.

The chase had ended under a structure large enough to shield her from the hot ash and debris raining from above and singeing her skin and hair. The reprieve, in the manner of all reprieves, hadn't lasted. Shouts of challenge had warned her that either their pursuers had caught up with them again or that someone else was objecting to their presence wherever they were. She remembered an irrational flash of abandonment when Ronon left her side without so much as a word and, seconds after that, the furious clash and clatter of a swordfight, grunts, screams, and the gurgle of death. Then he'd been back by her side, to herd her up a smooth, steep incline at the same relentless pace. Eventually she'd heard a deep hum, felt a tremor, and the roar of the meteor storm had dulled. She'd surmised that he must have closed a hatch—a very large one at that—and as he guided her on through halls and up stairways to the cockpit, she understood that they were aboard a ship as big as, or possibly even bigger than, the *Daedalus*.

There'd been a handful brave souls who'd remained aboard when everyone else had fled, and they'd done their duty and tried to defend the ship. It had been a hopelessly uneven skirmish and a lost cause. Ronon had set upon them with a frenzy she didn't recognize in him, and he hadn't taken any prisoners. The smell of their blood still clung to him now, vying with that of the crew whose bodies lay scattered in the cockpit behind her. They hadn't stood a chance either.

Teyla knew well enough that behind the relaxed exterior, Ronon was a deeply angry man. And with good reason. The Wraith had stolen his home, his liberty, and years of his life. But something had happened to him back on that planet they'd just escaped that had stoked this anger into uncontainable rage.

It was time to find out, she decided.

"What is the Behemoth?" It seemed to her as if a million years had passed since she'd last asked this question. This time, though, she would insist on an answer.

The soft rasp of skin on leather followed by footfalls said that Ronon had risen from the pilot's chair and was headed for the rear of the cockpit. There was a hum, then an odd kind of creak and rustle, and then a symphony of smells that managed to blot out even the stench of blood and made her mouth water.

By the Ancestors, she was famished!

Attempting to figure out when she'd last eaten, Teyla's best estimate amounted to some time before she'd led Major Sheppard through the cave passage and down into the ruins of Atlantis. And that particular meal hadn't exactly been a feast. This on the other hand...

"The command crews have access to food synthesizers," Ronon observed casually. "Luckily you don't need the ATA gene to use them, or we'd be screwed. He set a plate in Teyla's lap. "Eat! But be careful. It's hot."

So it was. In both respects. Either Ronon or the food synthesizer appeared to have a distinct preference for strong spices, but as far as Teyla was concerned this had to be the single most delicious meal she'd ever eaten in her life. Though it wasn't delicious enough to make her miss the obvious. For the moment however she let it slide, too hungry to worry about prying answers from Ronon. Eventually, after having worked her way through a generous second helping, she set down the plate and got ready to ask the same question a third time.

He must have been waiting for it. Or maybe it really had taken him this long to prepare himself for whatever his answer might stir up. In any case, he preempted her. "There were no Wraith in this timeline," he said, making her wonder how or if this was going to lead around to the Behemoth. "Which was the whole point of Charybdis. Except, it turns out the Wraith kept the Ancients in check, provided a counterbalance to all those smarts and technology."

"An outside threat that occupied the Ancestors and prevented them from turning against planets and civilizations who wouldn't stand a chance against a race as advanced as they,"

Teyla guessed, frowning. "You may have a point there."

"I do. In this timeline the Ancients have *become* the Wraith. It's the ultimate tyranny." He stood again, returned to the food processor.

Teyla controlled an urge to follow and shake the story out of him, whatever it was. Clearly he had to set his own pace.

"Didn't know any of that when I woke up here," he said, handing her a glass.

Its contents had a pleasant pungency, and she took a careful sip. Some kind of wine, aged and thick and heavy. She heard him drain his own glass in one great gulp. Somebody on Atlantis had referred to this as 'Dutch courage'. For the first time it occurred to her that the cause for his reticence might be shame.

"The Ancients here are paranoid. So, when they found me, they took me straight to the city," he continued. "They debriefed me. Marcon debriefed me, to be precise."

"The old friend who fell down the stairs?"

"Yeah. Except, he didn't call it debriefing. And he didn't tell me he was working for their intelligence office. That might have made even me think twice," Ronon said bitterly. "Marcon pretended to be my friend. I wanted to belong somewhere, he offered the solution. I was a warrior after all. Why not join their army? Why not join the Behemoth?"

Sipping some more wine, Teyla tried to find a reason why this revelation should have been so difficult to make and failed. "So the Behemoth is their army?"

"That's what I thought too, until I joined." Ronon snorted, somewhere between derision and disgust. "The Ancestors control it and it's designed to stop the soldiers from rising against them, but ultimately the Behemoth is… an entity that's fueled by the basest instincts of every man in that army. It's hedonistic and violent, it's cruel, it's insatiable, and it feeds on pain and fear. It's everything that's worst in a mercenary, magnified a thousand times and given sentience. And it makes you do exactly what it wants you to do. It made me do stuff that—"

"How?" Teyla cut in because she couldn't bear what she was hearing in his voice.

He blew out a breath, and when he continued he sounded vaguely relieved at having been interrupted. "They tell you that you need to be inoculated against a bunch of diseases, but what those shots actually contain is a few zillion nano-robots that will float into your brain and start rewiring it. The process is... unpleasant.

"It gets better," he said when she let slip a small gasp of dismay. "Don't ask me how it works—maybe Beckett could explain it, I can't—but the nano-robots hook you into this entity, the Behemoth. That's what *joining* means; your mind becomes part of this group consciousness. And from that moment on the Behemoth will determine what you do and how you do it and it'll monitor every thought and emotion, and if you step or think or feel out of line you get zapped, 'cos obviously the nano-robots have access to the pain center in your brain. It's perfect."

A bright crash somewhere at the back at of the cockpit made Teyla jump, then she realized that he must have hurled his glass against the wall. "Apparently not so perfect," she observed quietly. "You managed to break away. That's what happened back at the laboratory, wasn't it?"

The movement was barely audible, and its very quietness painted the picture for her. Fast and smooth as a predator he crossed the cockpit, and then she sensed him right in front of her, trapping her. His hands clamped on the armrests of her seat, and she felt the warmth from his body, smelled the wine on his breath.

"Who says I broke away?" he hissed. "Maybe I've been doing what the Behemoth wanted me to do all along. Marcon ordered me to be your Marcon. To squeeze every last bit of information out of you, especially all the details on how you got the Stargate to work. I've done that, haven't I? Now that I've got the information, I'm to 'dispose' of you. I might do that any moment, whether I like it or not. You can't possibly know what I'll do. Nobody can. Even I can't."

"What if you're wrong? What if I *can*?" Teyla threw it at him like a challenge. "What if I told you that there's nothing I can see that is not completely and exclusively Ronon Dex?"

"How would you—" He cut himself off, drew back, some of the tension sloughing off him. "That gene of yours? Telepathy? I thought that only worked with Wraith."

"As I pointed out to Major Sheppard, I've had plenty of time to practice." She wished she could see his eyes. It'd be easier to tell whether or not he believed her. "There is nothing there, Ronon, I swear. Nothing but you."

That presence hovering above her lifted, and a second later she heard Ronon fling himself heavily into the pilot's seat. "When Marcon gave me that order, I knew I couldn't do it," he whispered. "I told myself that, this once, I'd win, even if it killed me. Only, I told myself the same thing more times than I can count. And I let myself fail every time. A few days ago, I beheaded a boy whose only crime was to defend his home… What does that make me, Teyla?"

"It makes you a man who keeps trying against all odds until he succeeds," she replied just as softly. "I don't see anything wrong with that. On the contrary."

"I could have saved that kid if I'd tried harder!"

"No, you couldn't. Some other soldier would have killed him, and you know it." For a moment she struggled with the impulse to touch him, then curbed it—he wouldn't let her. Not now. "There's another consideration," she added, "even if it is a little selfish; if you had succeeded in breaking away sooner, we'd be dead. If what you're telling me about the Ancestors here is true, there is no way you would have been allowed to live. Somebody else would have been ordered to deal with me, and I very much doubt he would have resisted the Behemoth.

"You saved both our lives, Ronon. Personally, I prefer being alive. Besides, on the more altruistic side, the death of either one of us likely would have made Charybdis irreversible."

"You're saying this was fate?" Ronon sounded huffy with disbelief—which was a vast improvement on despondency.

"I am not saying anything." She shrugged. "Except perhaps that lately I've come up against a great many unlikely coincidences."

"No such thing as co—"

A warning klaxon went off, sawing the air until Ronon found

the control that switched it off. She heard soft tapping as his fingers danced over touch pads, and then the static buzz of data scrolling across a holographic screen. No point in even guessing at what he was doing. He'd tell her soon enough; she'd just have to be patient. Always patience. Teyla barely suppressed a snarl. Patience wasn't in her genes.

Her answer came when the whine of the engines dropped in pitch and a barely perceptible shudder traveled through the vessel—they had dropped out of hyperspace.

"This thing is faster than I expected it to be." Ronon was using that absurdly proud tone all men seemed compelled to adopt when speaking of ships. "That was a proximity warning. We're here."

"And where is *here*?"

"Abandoned mining planet. I used to push guard duty here, until the *naquada* ran out. About as exciting as watching grass grow. But it's deserted, and it's got a gate."

Reentry fell somewhat short of routine, and Teyla nursed a sneaking suspicion that Ronon was making up flight path and procedure as he went along. On several occasions the anti-grav boosters broke into protesting howls while vicious bumps and jolts taxed the inertial dampeners to their limits and beyond. At last, and with a final insane lurch, the transporter bounced to a halt and its engines shut down one by one, until only the steady hum of the anti-grav drive remained audible.

"Smooth," she remarked a little weakly, not sure if all relevant pieces were still attached to her body. "Who taught you to fly? Rodney McKay?"

"Hey, I got us down!"

"Yes."

"And we're practically on top of the gate."

"Good." She took *practically* to mean that the gate was still standing.

Twenty minutes later they stepped off the ramp and into a patch of warm evening sunshine that eased the goose bumps off Teyla's skin. In the shadows beneath the transporter's belly the air had been chilly. A steady swish of tree tops in the breeze told her that they had to be in or near a forest. Pine needles rustled under her soles, sent up a cloud of scent at every step, and somewhere above chirped a bird. After the mayhem of the Ancestors' home planet, this struck her as incongruously serene.

"It's beautiful."

Ronon barked a laugh, caught himself and squeezed her hand. "Be glad you can't see it. They strip-mined. Smells a lot better than it looks, I suppose... DHD's right over there. Wait here while I dial. You said it doesn't matter which planet?"

"It doesn't," she replied, wondering which address he'd dial. Sateda? More than likely. She'd dialed Athos.

The serenity she'd felt was shattered by the familiar noises of engaging chevrons and the watery explosion of the event horizon as the wormhole established. It set her heart to pound and reminded her that they were leaving behind the relative safety of the transporter for an unknown destination. The only thing they could be certain of right now was that they wouldn't be able to return from there.

Ronon's hand locked around hers again, and she shook off the thought. After all, she'd taken this journey once already, on her own and without the advantage of youth.

"Ready?" he asked.

"Ready."

Ten level steps took them into the wormhole. There was the familiar cold disorientation of the trip and then that jolt forward as the gate spat them out into icy rain and wind.

"Oh man," groaned Ronon.

"What's wrong?"

"The place, I guess. It's the Atlantis control center but... Whole city's in ruins, got a great big forest growing right through it. And there's no one here."

While he was talking, he dragged her along behind him through puddles and mud. Teyla's mental map of Atlantis said that he was heading straight for the stairs up to the gallery—provided there were any stairs or gallery left. A few seconds later it became obvious that the stairs at least were still intact.

A step or two from the top, she stopped dead in her tracks, sniffed the air, and grimaced. "What in the name of all the gods is that smell?"

A deep inhalation, then Ronon sputtered and gave a quiet laugh. "That's pig shit."

He pulled her up the rest of the way, until she stood ankle deep in the mud and wet soil that covered what must have been the gallery. Overhead, the canopy had to be closed, because she no longer felt the rain—apart from the occasional heavy drop splashing from a branch and landing in her face like a water bomb released by children hiding in the trees.

"Uhuh. Definitely pigs. There's trotter prints. A lot of them," said Ronon. "And not just pigs. Human tracks, heading off into the bushes. Come on."

Slapped by dripping branches, they wedged themselves through a narrow passage in the undergrowth that eventually brought them out in what she supposed to be a small clearing.

"The control consoles," Ronon informed her. "Or what's left of them. Bones," he added, more subdued. "Lots of bones. Looks like the entire team died up here, and a long time ago. If McKay was here, he didn't—"

Squishing noises and rustling as he moved away, and then a soft little whoop and "I don't believe it…"

"What?"

"Did you know that McKay's first name is Meredith?"

"*What*?"

"Somebody carved it into a console, and it's recent."

CHAPTER 16

Charybdis +4

The raft—if you could call it that—slammed into the rock hard enough to split off a plank along one side of the panel. Not that John could see it; the gentle light from the crystal inclusions in the stone now seemed a thing of the distant past. Still, the crack and the creak and the fact that his right lower leg suddenly dangled in the drink were explanation enough—they'd hit a stretch of rapids. In a quick reflex he pulled up his knee and got his foot back on board. This wasn't over by a long shot, and he preferred coming through it without having his shins shredded. On the upside, the collision had startled him awake. He'd fallen asleep again, no telling how long for, despite his efforts to keep his eyelids jammed open. The headache—how was that for a euphemism?—seemed to have ratcheted up yet another notch, and every time he blinked he was seeing a firework of colored sparks.

Elizabeth lay curled up next to him, snoring softly, which explained why he'd been asleep. She'd been watching him for hours, mercilessly prodding him back to wakefulness each time he threatened to nod off, making him talk, sing, recite poetry, whatever it took, but even her reserves had given out at last.

Another impact rattled through the raft and spun it in the opposite direction. It bobbed indecisively for a second, then swung back and tilted into the main current with a lurch. He felt Elizabeth slide away from him, blindly snatched for her and pulled her back in. It woke her, and she shot up with a start.

"Wha... what's going on?"

"Rapids," he murmured, and even that much conversation shook loose a bass line that thrummed through his skull with malicious relish. Good job he couldn't even remember the last time he'd eaten, else things might get a little messy right about now. He was fresh out of bile, too.

"Sorry," she said. "I didn't mean to fall asleep. Anything you want me to do?"

"Hold tight."

In the absence of paddles or any other means of steering the raft it was the best thing they could do. That, and pray that the fence panel was sturdier than it looked, though John didn't hold out much hope on that score.

As if on cue, the raft hit another obstacle, skidded sideways up the rock and twisted back into the water with a splash that doused them both; an ice cold shower coming out of nowhere.

"Christ!" gasped Elizabeth.

John couldn't have put it better. His jaw hurt from clenching it in an attempt to stop the rattle of his teeth. "Hold tight!" he yelped again.

It got submerged in the shock of another impact, another shower, and this time he also felt another plank come loose. He changed his grip, held on to a piece of planking that wasn't moving—yet—and wrapped his free arm around Elizabeth. She was scrabbling and squirming next to him, making it difficult to maintain his grip.

"What are you doing?"

"Hang on!"

He thought he heard a faint tearing noise, and a second one, and then she was cinching something around his waist. "Lifeline," she shouted in his ear, making him wince. "If we go into the water, we mustn't get separated."

Presumably that tearing noise had been a bit of her skirt and the other end of that strip of cloth was tied around her waist. The tearing part raised the question of how long exactly the ashram weave would be able to withstand the rapids. About as long as their bodies, John figured. If they went into the water it didn't matter whether or not they got separated, because they'd be ground to hamburger.

That happy thought got blasted into oblivion by the next crash.

The impact was brutal enough to jolt him half off the raft, and for a couple of excruciating seconds he was hanging up to his waist in churning water. His ankle hit stone, and he bit back a howl, kicked against the rock instead and levered himself back onto the panel just before it snapped out of its momentary standstill and bounced back into the current. This collision had cost them the loosened plank, reducing the width of the raft to maybe three feet, if that.

And then even that didn't matter anymore, because they were airborne.

Spray clogged the air, was sucked into their lungs with every wheezing breath, and John thought he heard himself scream—when he wasn't coughing for his life. The flight couldn't have lasted much longer than a couple of seconds, but it felt like an eternity; wet, cold, bone-rattling endlessness, until they slammed back onto the surface of the river and the fence panel finally disintegrated beneath them.

He was able to catch half a mouthful of air before he went under. That pokey lifeline around his waist pulled him sideways, which meant that Elizabeth was still there, though not for much longer unless he managed to grab hold of her. The current yanked him around a boulder, and another one—like hurtling down the waterslides—and finally pushed him out into calmer waters, allowing him to pull up for a quick snatch of breath.

And a surprise.

For a split-second he was so stunned, he forgot to swim and almost went under again. There was light. Hardly more than a faint, gray twilight, to be sure, but enough to outline the towering cliffs behind him and lend a ghostly white shimmer to the spray of the cascades they'd just shot down. On either side of the river rose ancient trees and high above John's head the last stars fought a losing battle with morning fog and dawn.

They'd made it out of the caves.

They—

"Elizabeth?"

She hadn't surfaced.

Swearing, John pulled at the lifeline, only to find a frayed end that had got snagged on a piece of wood, which must have been the pull he'd noticed. Panic wanted to rise, but he refused to let it, refused to even think about the chances of finding someone in this light in a large pool with a slow but appreciable current and probably one hell of an undertow nearer the cascades. No point thinking about it, because he damn well *was* going to find her.

He took a few deep breaths, then a final, shallower one and dived. Airy froth churned up by the rapids and the cascades rendered the water practically opaque. He could see perhaps two feet, that was it. Fine, so he'd grope. A few strong strokes brought him to the bottom. Pebbles, which was a small mercy; at least he wouldn't have to worry about stirring up silt as well. He pulled himself upstream along the riverbed, one arm extended, patting all around him. Nothing. Finally, with his lungs burning for air, he shot back to the surface. Then he repeated the process, gradually working his way closer to the waterfall.

When he came back up for the third time, he knew this next dive would have to be the last. He was shaking uncontrollably, and the muscles in his legs were beginning to cramp. Wildly determined to make this one count, he dived directly under the cascades—and found her almost immediately, flopping like a rag doll in the undertow, clearly unconscious. Obviously unconscious. There was no alternative as far as John was concerned. He hauled her in, threaded one arm under hers and across her chest and began kicking out of the milling current and toward the surface for all he was worth, which wasn't very much at this stage. Just when he thought he'd never get clear of the undertow, the river suddenly seemed to change its mind, relinquished its grip, and let him and Elizabeth drift toward a shallow bank.

Crawling on all fours, he dragged her limp body up the shore with him, rolled her on her back, searched for a pulse, which was pointless. His fingers were so cold, he couldn't have felt a one-stroke diesel engine. What was obvious, however, was the fact that Elizabeth wasn't breathing. Blue-lipped and drained of blood her face looked as though it belonged to a wax doll—or a corpse.

How long had she been under? Five minutes? Seven?

It was difficult to say, but at least the fact that the water was cold enough to freeze a polar bear's privates would have bought her some extra time. *If* he could get her breathing again, and *if* he managed to warm her up quickly enough afterwards...

Willing his hands to move with a semblance of coordination, he cleared Elizabeth's airway and began CPR. For the briefest of moments he hesitated before starting compressions—if her heart hadn't in fact stopped this might kill her—then he went ahead, because he didn't have a choice. Five compressions, breathe, five compressions, breathe... John blanked out everything, except that steady rhythm.

After a while—minutes that felt like hours—he felt sweat trickling into his eyes and pouring down his back. His hands and shoulders were aching, and she still hadn't stirred.

"Dammit, Elizabeth! Snap out of it! The originals mustn't die, remember?" John kept going with the dogged determination of a man who had run out of all other options.

Without warning, Elizabeth convulsed in a coughing fit, water gushing from her mouth and nose.

"Yes! Good girl!" He rolled her over onto her side, rubbed her back, while she continued to bring up water.

When she wasn't wheezing and choking up fluid, she was shivering violently, and they didn't have a scrap of dry clothing on them. Perfect. Adrenaline and the glow of exertion had worn off, and John was starting to feel cold again, too. He cast a baleful glance skywards. At some point, while he'd been busy breathing for Elizabeth, fat-bellied, lead-gray clouds had begun to push in, blotting out that timid gleam of dawn. A few hesitant flakes of snow were spinning toward him, tiny and innocuous, and promising hell on whatever this planet was called.

"You're the one who did survival training," Elizabeth stuttered between rattling teeth. "This is when you ask, *What have we got? What do we need?*"

"We've got zip and we need a suite at the Hilton. With a Jacuzzi," he said, grinning in spite of himself. "Welcome back."

"No Jacuzzi. Nothing that involves water," she protested weakly, trying to sit up. "My chest hurts."

"You... uh... you'll probably get a whopper of a bruise there," he said a little sheepishly. "It took a few minutes to get you ticking again..."

"I…" She blinked. "You saved my life."

Uh-uh. No speeches and medals, please. If it hadn't been for him, she wouldn't be here. None of them would. After all, he was the genius who'd insisted on trusting Ikaros and ignoring Rodney. John pulled a face. "You heard what Junior said. The originals have to survive."

Elizabeth winced. "You think they…"

She didn't finish, but then she didn't have to. It was the first time the subject of the alternates had cropped up since that heated and utterly futile argument he'd had with her on the raft, several centuries ago or so it seemed. Of course there'd been no way of going back for them, especially since she'd made the right decision to start with. Or rather, Junior and Elizabeth's alternate had, knowing full well what would happen to them.

"They're dead," he said as gently as he could—absurdly, he thought, because there was no way of making this sound pleasant or comforting in any way at all. "Look at the water levels. They must have drowned hours ago."

Her only reply was a bleak little nod. Then another coughing fit shook her, reminding John that certain essentials needed sorting out before he indulged in the luxury of wallowing in regret. He didn't much like the thought of leaving her on her own, but there was little else he could do. Waiting around wouldn't improve things.

"I'll be back as soon as I can," he said, easing her back until she sat reclined against a boulder. "Stay put. I've got to go and get some of those things we need."

She nodded again, tried a parody of a smile. "If you insist on that Jacuzzi, at least bring a bottle of champagne."

"Yes, ma'am." He straightened up, staggered his way through a head rush—no less than he'd expected—and made for the tree line along the top of the small beach.

It was an old growth forest, none of the trees under a hundred and fifty feet high, densely shot through with brush, ferns, and moss and a whole array of other things you could trip over. After some twenty meters of tripping and swatting aside branches John hit a narrow trail. Absence of any kind of spoor suggested that it probably wasn't a game trail but the route the esteemed members of Zelenka's ashram used to go for a swim or to wash their underwear.

Not a good thing.

By the same token, not having to stumble through the undergrowth would speed this business up considerably. He'd just have to be careful. About half a klick along, the path looped around a moss-backed hillock, overgrown with trees, rocks jutting from its flanks. They looked like limestone. Given the geology of the area, there might be a chance of finding shelter up there somewhere; a cave if they were really lucky, though right now he'd happily settle for an overhang.

John dipped back among the trees, sinking ankle-deep into moss and peat as soon as he left the trail. Under normal circumstances the climb would have been child's play. Unfortunately, circumstances were slightly inferior to normal, to say the least. He pulled himself up a ledge, scrabbling over its edge with the grace and agility of a flipped-over beetle. Lying flat on his belly, he spent a moment catching his breath and studying the snowflakes that were melting on his sleeve. They'd become chunkier in the last little while, and there were more of them. Charybdis was well and truly out to get him.

Oh yeah.

The ledge was just a ledge, no beckoning entrance to a warm and cozy cave with piles of marinated mammoth steak stored inside.

"Crap!" he whispered, struggling back to his feet. This time the dizzy spell was bad enough to make him grope for support.

The hill slowly stopped spinning, and as that weird sizzling sound in his ears subsided he heard a noise that had nothing to do with his blood pressure bottoming out. At least he didn't think so... John gingerly sidled closer to the edge, praying that the next bout of dizziness wouldn't make him lose his balance.

"Crap!" he said again, quieter though more emphatically.

He'd heard right. It was footsteps. The trail ran along the hillside directly below the ledge, and on it Brother Star was heading for the river. Swimming was out, considering the weather, so he probably planned on catching his lunch—unless he'd somehow got wind that they'd made it out of the caves and planned on catching someone else entirely... Either way, Elizabeth was down there on her own and in no shape to run and hide.

And given the shape *you*'re in, John, you haven't got an ice cube's chance in hell of winning a wrestling match with that guy!

True, but he *did* have the element of surprise. Plus, Brother Star was lugging along a nice, big, heavy-looking haversack, which should be cumbersome enough to slow him down at least initially. At any rate, doing nothing wasn't an option.

Brother Star—in enviably dry clothes, by the way—was walking at a brisk pace, clearly alone, clearly unconcerned about what lay either side or ahead of him. He did, however, check his six periodically, which struck John as more than a little odd. Ill feelings among the brethren? Or perhaps Brother Star had made off with this fall's dope harvest.

They might get a chance to discuss it later.

If John survived this.

He peered over the edge for one last, measuring glance and snapped back into the cover of a boulder. Flattened against cold stone, he did the math. Roughly an eighteen-foot drop, he guessed, which should give him plenty of momentum. Below, Brother Star was approaching the target area.

John took a last deep breath, pushed himself off the rock face and jumped. The trajectory was just so, slamming him onto Star's shoulders like some deranged, outsize monkey. Star staggered forward under the weight, sent them both tumbling to the ground in a series of a soggy thuds. The first impact of landing on top of the man had detonated a sparkling burst of agony in John's head, half blinding him. Barely able to stay astride his stunned victim and struggling to ignore the pain, he tried to place a left hook, missed by a mile.

The second attempt was even less successful. Meanwhile, Star lay flat on his back, staring up at his attacker with a look of disbelief in his eyes. If anything, that look intensified when John's third attempt barely grazed the man's shoulder.

"At least defend yourself!" John hissed, somewhat insulted

by the fact that apparently he didn't rate a proper fight.

"If I defended myself, you'd be dead," Star said earnestly. "You hit like a girl."

Somehow that took the wind out of John's sails. There also was the minor issue that he had a point. So far Star had saved him a fortune in plastic surgery, and the furtive undertone of amusement in his voice indicated that it probably had little to do with rules about not hitting guests.

Deciding that it might be better for the remains of his dignity not to reduce the man to tears of laughter, John folded and rolled off his not-so-victimized victim. "What are you doing here?" he grunted.

Star sat up and straightened himself out. "I was looking for you. The cascades upriver are the only other exit from the cave system I could think of, so I was hoping you'd somehow make it there. Where're the other one and the Elizabeths?"

"Why?" Though the man didn't present any obvious threat, John was a long way from trusting him. For all he knew this was some elaborate charade designed to capture any potential survivors.

"Colonel, please." Star actually sighed. "I'm trying to help you. True, we all believe that Brother Moon is right. You shouldn't be here, and none of us wants to cease to exist when you do whatever you're going to do to Charybdis. Having said that, there were several of us who didn't agree with just dumping you in the caves. In the end it was a majority decision, though… you see?"

"Oh yeah. Clear as day. Death by democracy."

Star had the decency to wince. "We just… we just want to live."

"So did my and Elizabeth's doubles."

You could see the blood drain from the man's face. "They're…?"

"Yes, they're dead. Happy now? They drowned to give Elizabeth and me a chance to make it out of there."

The words managed to achieve what John's hapless flailing earlier hadn't. Star flinched as though he'd received a knockout blow. "I'm sorry. I truly am. I… I don't know what to say."

Scrambling to regroup, he angled for the haversack he'd lost in their one-sided tussle, fished around inside it, and at last seemed to find what he'd been looking for. "Maybe this'll help to convince you." He held out Junior's Beretta.

John snatched the gun, unsafed it, and trained it on his would-be rescuer.

"Brother Moon explained its purpose to us. You can shoot me if it makes you feel better." Star gave a tired shrug. "I guess I would if I were in your shoes. But there are only three projectiles left."

"Never mind." Feeling like an idiot, John lowered the Beretta. "I think I'll keep that in reserve for the time being."

With a small jerk of the head at the sidearm, the man said, "Sister Dawn isn't too keen on what happened either. She is in a, uh, position of trust and took it while Brother Moon was asleep. And this." More rummaging in the haversack produced the cloak remote for the jumper. "We figured that way you could go someplace safe."

John took the remote, too, weighed it in his hand. "You do realize that we can't leave the planet, don't you, Star? Elizabeth tells me Brother Moon tried to send us through the gate, without much luck. For the gate to work he would have to come with us."

Star looked uncomfortable. "He can't. I… well, I guess Elizabeth explained about the flower."

"The *drug*, you mean."

"Yes, I suppose you could call it that…"

"No doubt about it."

"Where's Elizabeth?" asked Star, obviously figuring that a change of topic was in order and adding, "I won't tell anybody, I swear."

"I left her near the shore. She damn near drowned." Suddenly aware of how long he'd been gone, John shot to his feet and would have keeled over if Star hadn't leaped up and caught him. Dangling from the man's grip, he scrubbed a hand over his face and stopped when he realized that even that much pressure seemed to set his eyeballs ablaze. "I've got to get back. I need to get some firewood. She's hypothermic… cold."

"And so are you." Star carefully leaned John against a tree. "Can I trust you to stay upright on your own for a minute?" When he got no answer, he took a step back, observed that there was no discernible list in either direction, and gathered his haversack. Slinging it over his shoulder, he took hold of John's arm again and said, "Let's go. I've got dry clothes and food in there, and you can get changed once we get that fire going."

"Why are you doing this?" John murmured, unsure of why he was quibbling with anything, except perhaps that dry clothes and food sounded too good to be true.

"I guess because Sister... because Elizabeth believes that that's what we ought to be about."

CHAPTER 17

Charybdis -908

"Do you think it ever stops raining here?" Teyla sounded frazzled.

"You should see it in winter." Ronon grinned.

After realizing that the journey through the gate had had the same rejuvenating effect on him that it'd apparently had on Teyla, the rain couldn't even begin to bother him. What did make him shudder, though, was the litany of complaints they'd be treated to once they found McKay. Then again, he'd gladly listen to it and the inevitable encores, just as long as they did find the scientist. Ronon wanted to go back to *his* Atlantis and hug a few Wraith.

Ahead the trees were gradually thinning out, admitting wads of glum gray light that seemed tired enough to wink out at a moment's notice. It was impossible to tell what time of day it was, though Ronon guessed it had to be mid-afternoon or thereabouts. If they were lucky they had maybe three hours of daylight left, perhaps four, tops. Which meant that they'd better find themselves some shelter, because even Ronon's current tolerance of the weather conditions didn't extend to wanting to spend the night out in the open.

When they reached the edge of the forest he stopped, pulling Teyla in close beside him. Stretching out before them was a vast alpine meadow that sloped down toward a jumble of farm buildings at its bottom. More than likely the home of those pigs and their herder—who might or might not be McKay. Still, instinct warned him against wading in there and asking questions. Two strangers suddenly appearing out of the mountain wilderness were bound to raise suspicion.

Interestingly, there was a lot of non-agricultural commotion happening on the farm. In pairs or small groups people were filtering out through the main gate and onto the road. Further down in the valley more people from other farms and homesteads joined the stream of travelers. It looked like birds gathering for their winter journey south. Ronon had a fairly good idea of what this was all about.

"You know," he murmured to Teyla, "my father had a farm back on Sateda."

"As a matter of fact, I didn't know that. You never told me."

"Yeah, well, I don't think of it much anymore." Which wasn't entirely true. He did think of it, but he refused to hanker after things that were lost. Neither the farm nor his parents had survived the Wraith attacks. "*Farm* sounds too grand, really," Ronon continued. "He farmed maize, made barely enough to feed us. Once a year there'd be a market in the nearest town, everybody would go and the roads into town looked just like this." A boyhood memory of the sheer excitement of trekking to the fair made him smile whether he liked it or not. "Place was full of gossip. If you wanted to hear all the latest news, that was where you went."

"Let's go to the market then." Teyla grinned. "It's been a long time since I've been trading. I'd like to know if I still remember how to do it."

"Hate to break it to you, but you haven't got anything to trade."

"I'll think of something."

After a moment's deliberation, Ronon decided to stay in the cover of the trees and only cut across to the road further down. A lot further down. It forced them into a detour back toward the interior of the forest, but eventually, the trees thinned again and from below he could hear the rattle of wooden clogs on paving stone and the murmur of conversations. Fewer than fifteen feet beneath them ran the road, filled side to side with a throng of people, all bedraggled, all pushing toward town. The forest trail had handed them a shortcut.

He snatched a fistful of Teyla's shirt, skidded down an embankment and onto the road in a small avalanche of mud and pebbles and twigs, and almost knocked into a burly middle-aged man who glared his suspicion from under the brim of a sodden hat. Several others who'd witnessed their entrance looked equally wary, and Ronon congratulated himself on not stopping at that farm. These folks weren't exactly the trusting kind.

Jerking his chin at Teyla, he offered the first harmless sounding excuse that sprang to mind. "Wife's pregnant. Has to go every five minutes."

Teyla pinched him, hard, and it was all he could do to choke back a yelp. "Why don't you shout it out, so everybody can hear about my private business?" she snapped.

"She's moody, too," he muttered with a conspiratorial wink at the burly middle-aged glarer.

The glare softened a little, but the guy still didn't offer anything in the way of chat. Head ducked between his shoulders against the rain that was still hammering down, Ronon took his cue from him and trudged on in silence, furtively scanning the people around him. Local fashions were so eclectic that he and Teyla hardly stood out. Made sense, too. In this climate you wore whatever was handy.

After about an hour, his taciturn companion finally grunted, "Shame." The hand he waved in front of his eyes clarified the rest.

"She was born that way," Ronon lied, shrugging. "Pretty enough, though."

"Aye," grunted the man and slumped back into his reticence.

Which proved that Ronon had given the appropriate answer, even if it earned him another pinch from his 'wife.'

At last the road emerged from the forest, offering a cloud-muffled vista of a broad river valley below. Smack in the middle, clamping the river like a vise, sat a surprisingly large city. Its center and probably the most ancient part was protected by heavy fortifications—well-maintained, as far as he could judge from the distance—and outside those walls stretched a vast sprawl of small houses. Obviously their residents were deemed expendable, else they'd be sheltered within walls as well. The only protection consisted of an earth levee that didn't look like it could hold back a cup of tea. In places the river was licking over the top already, and people were scurrying to pile up sandbags.

As they drew closer, Ronon recognized the squalor. He'd seen it in the slums festering around the government district in the version of Atlantis where he'd been exiled for more than ten years. The reek of poverty—a nauseating perfume of boiled cabbage, trash and raw sewage—bore down on the road, which bisected the suburb. Though built of stone, the houses were tiny and pockmarked by decay. Hunched in doorways that were shuttered only by strips of moldy fabric sat old people, staring in toothless curiosity. Children, wrapped in wet tatters and frozen blue, darted in and out of the throng pushing along the road, pickpocketing where they didn't beg. Above it all, like a lid to keep in the misery, hung a choking layer of brume, struggling up from countless chimneys only to be pushed back into the streets by the rain and the clouds.

The flow of bodies heading along the road had swollen to a flood heavy enough to separate them from their travel companions and carry them off into complete and welcome anonymity. Teyla stayed in character anyway. The picture of the timid, pregnant wife, she huddled tighter against him. "I smell wood smoke and lots of it," she murmured under her breath. "If they originally built those ruins up in the mountains, their heating should be a little more advanced than that."

She was right. And now that she'd mentioned it, Ronon realized that he'd seen no technology that even remotely approached that of the Ancients. Transport was basic to say the least; most people walked, though here and there he spotted men on horseback. Goods shuddered along either on the bent backs of their owners or in rough-hewn carts drawn by oxen. A quick glance through a window proved that artificial lighting was restricted to tapers and torches, cooking was done on open fires. Tools and weapons were just a hair shy of primitive—down one street he discovered a smithy complete with anvil and bellows.

Before he could decide what to make of it, the procession ground to a halt, and people were being nudged into the backs of folks in front. Nobody complained or protested, so this had to be a normal occurrence. As they approached the outer ring of the fortifications at a snail's pace, Ronon understood what was going on; under the soaring arch of the city gate stood a detachment of soldiers, dressed in leather and polished steel. They'd closed off access, conducting some kind of headcount and only letting a trickle of people pass on into the city, though the criteria for admission remained a mystery. For a while it looked as though anyone carrying weapons would be turned away, but then Ronon saw three heavily armed men being waved through the gate and breathed a sigh of relief. The relief didn't last. By the time they'd shuffled their way to within five meters of the guards, he was able to spot the furtive transactions and knew what was happening.

"Crap," he whispered to Teyla. "Looks like we have to bribe the soldiers to get in. Didn't you say you'd think of something to trade?"

"Leave it to me."

Two young men immediately in front of them were sent back, and then it was their turn. The commander of the detachment took in their appearance with a long, slow glance that betrayed a mix of disgust and boredom, decided that no backhanders would be forthcoming here either, and said, "Not you."

"You are making a mistake." Teyla took a step forward, found the man's arm with surprising accuracy, and placed her hand on it.

"I assure you, woman, it's no mistake. So let go of me," the soldier snarled. "Besides"—he raised his voice so the bystanders would hear—"what's the point of a attending an execution if you can't see it, huh?"

The hopefuls waiting behind Ronon and Teyla dutifully broke into chuckles, pandering to the man's doubtful comedic talents to improve their chances. Ronon barely heard it.

Execution?

"That would be my problem." Teyla's voice had taken on a pitch and tone that startled even him. She wasn't talking loudly—nobody could overhear, except he and the watch commander—but her tone had a creepy, unearthly quality that perfectly matched the white irises trained on the soldier as though she could see him after all. "And believe me, it is far less grave than yours will be when your wife learns that you're in the habit of spending your bribes on a whore."

"Witch!" The soldier jumped back as if her touch had burned him. His face had turned chalky, and though he was trying hard not to show his fear in front of his men, he couldn't hide the tremor of his hands. "Witch!" he hissed again. "Go! Go on. And you too! Take her out of here." He spat at Ronon's feet. "But beware, witch! If I see you again, I'll kill you."

"I'll see you first," Teyla whispered. Her smile promised that, should this contingency come to pass, she'd turn him into a toad. Aloud she said, "Thank you so much, soldier. You are very kind."

The man reeled back, terrified. Ronon grabbed Teyla and all but ran through the gate before the soldier could change his mind—or come to his senses.

"How did you know?" asked Ronon as they rushed up a wide, cobbled street trying to put as much distance between themselves and the gate as quickly as possible. "Don't tell me you read his mind!"

"I read his smell." Teyla grinned. "When a guy reeks of cheap perfume like that, there aren't very many options, are there?"

"I wouldn't know. But how could you tell he was married?"

"Baby milk and home cooking." Her grin widened. "It couldn't have been more obvious."

"If you say so." Stifling a laugh, Ronon pulled her around a corner and slowed his pace now that they were safely out of sight from the gate. "What made you think it would work?"

"A society as primitive as this? He was bound to be superstitious."

The rationale struck Ronon as tenuous, but he didn't quibble. Checking out the neighborhood was more important. Compared to the shantytown outside the walls, this was definitely upscale. The streets were lined by palatial houses, fronted with porticos, soaring pillars, and flights of marble stairs leading up to doors of richly decorated bronze. Many stood open despite the weather, offering glimpses of sumptuous interiors, all gleaming gold and shimmering silk. Large, glowing braziers just outside the doors kept out the cold.

Apparently those were an invitation for travelers to gather around and warm up. Each brazier was surrounded by at least three people, wet and disheveled and rubbing their hands over the heat. Ronon filed it away for further use. Dusk was falling now, an unspectacular thickening of the gray light, and unless Teyla managed to scare an innkeeper into offering them free accommodation, they'd be well advised to find themselves one of those braziers.

In the street folks were still bustling, though the throng had thinned out markedly, a combination of admittance policies and the fact that the street was as wide as any square Ronon had ever seen. The sheer number of people made him doubt the wisdom of coming here. How were they supposed to find one man among the teeming masses? He'd expected the reasonable dimensions of a market town, nothing like this. And there was no guarantee that McKay had even made it through the gate... Well, if they didn't find him here, they could always return to the farm and try their luck there.

Ronon shrugged it off and directed his attention back to the street. Pairs of soldiers strutted among the visitors, but they seemed to be routine patrols, keeping the peace rather than looking for a witch and her companion. Deciding that it was as safe as things got around here, he led Teyla back out into the flow of traffic, which was headed uphill toward a cluster of buildings that towered high above the city proper. At a guess, the main event was going to take place up there somewhere.

As though she'd read his mind—a troubling thought—Teyla said, "You were wrong. It's not a market."

"Does it matter?" he asked. "Still people, still gossip."

"I expect it does matter to the person being executed."

"Can't worry about him... or her."

At last they reached the end of the road, as it were. Before them stretched a vast space, dotted with stalls closed up for the night. Ronon figured he'd found his market after all, though on a far grander scale than a farm boy from Sateda could ever have imagined. Three sides of the square were seamed by structures that dwarfed even the palaces further down the street—temples, most likely. The fourth side bordered on a gaping abyss whose bottom was swallowed by the shadows of nightfall. It separated the market from a vertical rock face beyond. Perched at the top of that sat a fortress, which gave the distinct impression that it was watching your every step and disapproving.

"Cozy," grumbled Ronon.

"What is?"

"I'll tell you in a minute. Come on."

Right at the edge of the chasm a clump of people had gathered, and they were craning their necks, staring up at the fortress. Ronon slotted himself and Teyla in between a couple of other spectators and squinted up in the direction they were gazing. Suspended from a battlement of the fortress and barely visible in the gray-in-gray gloom of the rock and a rain-logged evening hung a cage. He could just about make out a figure huddled inside. The condemned, he presumed, and there was little doubt about the form of execution.

"Who'd have thought that there were any of those disciples of Ikaros left?" one of the bystanders mused. "You'd have thought they'd been rooted out good and proper."

Disciples of *Ikaros*?

As Ronon bit back his own gasp, he felt Teyla stiffen and squeezed her hand to stop her from blurting out anything that might blow their cover.

"By all accounts he confessed straightaway," somebody else offered. "Said he was a 'scientist' and sounded right proud of it, too. Been sticking his nose in the forbidden place, they claim."

The information solidified the sinking feeling in the pit of Ronon's stomach. He backed away from the gaggle of rubberneckers and pulled Teyla with him until they were well out of earshot.

"Ronon!" she hissed. "Will you *please* tell me what's going on?"

"They've got McKay." Ronon sent a last despondent look up at the cage. "And day after tomorrow he'll die."

CHAPTER 18

Charybdis +4

Elizabeth couldn't say when the cold and the relentless shaking had stopped, but stopped they had, and for the moment that was pretty much all she cared about.

She was dry, for the first time in a century it seemed. Her chest still hurt, but the ache was bearable as long as she didn't move. A warm, bright flicker nearby punched glowing halo into the darkness around her. A campfire. Night had fallen, and somebody had built a campfire. Deliciously warm.

She rolled onto her side and blinked at the flames and the sparks they sent hurtling into the dark. Without warning a pair of feet appeared between her and the fire. The feet were clad in the rough, chafing leather sandals she'd been wearing, the kind they'd begun making in the village a few months back and—

The village and everyone connected to it was a threat now. Panicked, she tried to sit up, but a firm hand on her shoulder kept her down.

"Easy," somebody said very gently. "Everything's alright. I'm not gonna hurt you."

The voice belonged to Brother Star and he now squatted beside her, looking quite unthreatening, with a bowl with steaming hot, spicy smelling contents in the hand that wasn't pinning her down. But Star had been part of the gang who'd deposited them in the caves in the first place...

"What are you doing here?" she croaked, startled at how hoarse she sounded. Probably from bringing up all that water, though that hardly mattered right now. "Where is Colonel Sheppard?"

Star shifted aside to clear the view and jerked his head at a figure that lay curled up on the opposite side of the fire. "I know he's injured his head and shouldn't be sleeping," said Star. "But he was so exhausted he literally couldn't stand up straight anymore... and that was *before* he tried to take me on in a fight. Keeping him awake probably would have done more damage than this. I'll wake him in a little while. In the meantime, here. Eat."

He handed her the bowl, threaded an arm under her neck, and helped her sit up. Elizabeth figured she probably should ask what had prompted his change of heart, but she was too ravenous to think. Besides, exhaustion or no, John would never have allowed himself to fall asleep if he didn't trust Star. While she wolfed down the stew—fresh fish and potatoes—Star filled her in on what had happened.

"I'm afraid we can't stay here much longer," he said at last. "I told the others I'd go hunting, so they know not to expect me back anytime soon, but it got dark about an hour ago, and if I don't return to the village, they'll come looking for me, which would be—"

"—a bad thing," she finished for him.

"Yes." He nodded vigorously. "Especially with the weather."

Elizabeth didn't need him to explain. The three of them and the campfire were sheltered by the sweeping branches of a giant cedar. Beyond its protection the ground was covered in at least a foot of snow, and more was falling steadily. She hadn't seen a speck of snow since finding herself marooned on this planet. Not to mention the fact that it was early summer. Supposedly. "Charybdis," she said.

More nodding from Star. "I guess you can imagine what Brother Moon will make of it. If they find you alive now..." He didn't finish. He didn't have to. "I really don't like the idea of sneaking you into the village."

"We'll do it fast and dirty," came a groggy voice from the other side of the campfire. "I don't think I could manage slow and clean." John sat up unsteadily and squinted over at Elizabeth. "How're you doing?"

"I should ask you that."

"I'm fine. Headache's toned down some." Going by the Colonel's general appearance, it was a bald-faced lie. The only thing about him that looked fine—or normal at least—was that shock of black hair, which stood up every which way as usual and provided a startling contrast to his waxen face. "I've done some thinking," he announced.

"About what?" asked Star.

"Matrices."

"Ah." Nothing else seemed to be forthcoming from John's end, so Star laid out his plan—such as it was. "I'm hoping that most of them will be asleep by the time we get there," he said. "And those who aren't asleep will be… you know…"

"Stoned," grunted John, tugging at the coarsely woven shirt he was wearing; Star must have brought for him, same as the clothes Elizabeth had found herself in when she woke. She decided it was better for her peace of mind not to explore just how she'd gotten into those.

"Yeah. The only thing we need to watch out for on the way is any search team they might have sent for me. Once we get there…" Star shrugged. "You two make a run for your ship, and I'll keep anyone who minds at bay. From then on out, you'd better listen to Elizabeth, Colonel. She'll be able to direct you to a hiding place at a safe distance from the village."

"Not gonna happen, Star."

The man blinked. "What do you mean?"

"The one thing Elizabeth and I can't afford to do is hole up somewhere and wait till it all gets better, 'cos it won't. Not unless we *make* it better, and that means going through the gate."

"But it—"

"Yes. I know. It doesn't work, and Brother Moon won't be volunteering for the trip." John scrunched his eyes shut, suggesting that even the dim light from the campfire was aggravating his headache. "I told you I've been thinking. More specifically, I've been thinking that we may not need the entire alternate to take us to the original."

"What do you—" Elizabeth cut herself off, suddenly realizing exactly what he meant. "DNA."

"Yeah. So much of the Ancients' technology is gene activated, it only stands to reason. Besides, what else would the gate use to compare matrices?"

Star frowned. "I don't know what this DNA is, but you can have mine anytime."

"It's something contained in hair, skin, teeth, any part of your body. And yours won't do us any good, I'm afraid. Thanks for offering, though. We need that of Brother Moon." Turning to her, John added, "He's the next best thing to Rodney... provided that the original hasn't developed a god complex, too."

"How do you plan to get Radek's DNA?" asked Elizabeth.

"Leave it to me," Star said. "I'll think of a way."

John directed a probing look at him and finally nodded. "Now that that's cleared up, I reckon we should break camp."

There wasn't much to break, and they were ready to go in a matter of minutes. Well, *willing* to go, Elizabeth amended silently, because John was two weeks of solid bed rest away from being ready for anything more taxing than a leisurely stroll on the beach. Which this probably wouldn't be.

Star doused the campfire and in the meager light of a single torch obliterated any sign that there had been more than one person resting here. "Just in case. I'd suggest you two hang back a bit. Keep the torch in sight, but don't follow me too closely."

It was like staggering through the marshes after a will o' the wisp. The flicker of the torchlight weaved in and out among the trees, disappearing completely at times and leaving Elizabeth and John to stumble through the pitch darkness of a moonless, starless night, pregnant with snow. Then it would reappear suddenly, barely visible anymore through the driving snowfall, and they'd run half-blind and at a breakneck speed just to catch up with it a little. Between the errant light and the darkness, the trek was disorienting even for Elizabeth who knew the area well. Still, on the whole she felt as certain as she could be that Star wasn't pulling a fast one but instead was leading them to the village as promised.

As if to confirm that feeling, a more steady glimmer of brightness began to outline trees and bushes and fern fronds. Eventually she could make out the colorful bubbles of tents and the gleam of oil lamps bouncing back brightly from the thick layer of snow. Drifts covered half the village, piled a white mantle over the jumper that still sat where they'd left it at the edge of the forest, and tongues of snow had pushed in under the overhang of the remaining structure that still embraced the Stargate like a band shell. To the left of the gate—safely out of the way, just in case there ever was an incoming wormhole—someone had built a roaring fire, and figures were huddled around it for warmth. In fact, there were far more people than she would have expected up this late, and the debate was heated; even from the distance she could see stiff shoulders and harsh gestures.

Not good.

Despite the obvious tension, the hominess of the gathering around the fireside triggered a sharp pang of regret in Elizabeth. This had been her home and her family for the past three years, and in many ways she'd come to know these people better than many in her own timeline, perhaps because, in spite of the dangers and difficulties the Atlantis expedition posed from day to day, life had been harder here. They'd had to fight for each basic amenity, and it had welded them together as a group.

And perhaps this simpering bout of nostalgia was caused by a combination of cold feet and the remnants of the drug in her system. In her system and all around her; the plant's thick vines were trailing down from branches and snaking through the undergrowth. Out of sheer habit she checked for mature blossoms. What she saw froze her in her tracks; buds, blossoms, tendrils—everything was encased in ice and shimmering like pink and red jewels. Utterly beautiful and utterly useless. Even if the plants survived and even if this unannounced winter stopped eventually, it would be months until the next crop was available. Which more than likely explained the late powwow around the fire by the gate. If she had noticed, they would have, too, and the community would be angry at the very least, panicked into an irrational frenzy at the worst.

This wasn't good at all. If she and John were going to steal back the jumper, it would be safer to wait until things had simmered down a little. To get caught now...

"John, I think we—"

"Shh!" He grabbed her arm and yanked her into a crouch behind some bushes.

It would have been too late anyway. Star had reached the village and several people spotted him simultaneously. They jumped up and toward him, and now their agitation was more than obvious.

"Must be nice to be missed," John whispered.

"That's not it," she hissed back. "I think they've discovered that they'll be going cold turkey once their current store of blossoms is used up."

His gaze traveled in the direction she was pointing. When he clocked the frozen flowers he swore under his breath. "They'll be pissed."

"To say the least."

"What about Star? He's as dependent on the stuff as any of them. Is he going to go through with it?"

She shrugged. "Your guess is as good as mine, John. Given this development, all bets are off. You have no idea what it's like."

"That's where you're wrong, but I'll save the war stories for another day."

Star hadn't stopped for his welcoming committee. He strode through them and made straight for the campfire, which could mean any number of things. Oblivious to the cold that was again seeping under her skin and into her bones, and wishing she could make out what was being said, Elizabeth watched as Radek Zelenka rose in response to whatever piece of information his renegade disciple had flung at him. Then Star spun around and pointed back down the trail. To her it felt as if he were pointing straight at them.

"He flipped." John swore under his breath. "Let's—"

"They're all dead! I saw them! He's been lying to us all along!" roared Star, and that was audible enough. He whirled back at Zelenka to loose a straight right that caught the erstwhile scientist squarely in the jaw.

Yells of shock and outrage went up among the bystanders, and Zelenka reeled back, clutching his face. When he let go, he spat out a mouthful of blood that blossomed in the snow like one of the flowers. Star launched at him again, slipped and pitched into a headlong fall.

"My God, what is he doing?"

"I think he just got us Zelenka's DNA. The hard way." For the first time in days there was something like amusement in John's voice. "I bet you anything that Radek lost at least one tooth."

Over by the fire, Star pushed himself to his knees, his fist closing around that bloody flower in the snow.

"I know what he's up to," John whispered urgently. "In addition to giving us one hell of a diversion. We've got to get to the jumper. Now!"

He hauled Elizabeth to her feet and prodded her on, along the trail for twenty meters or so. Then he veered sideways into the undergrowth, pushing through bushes and ferns and stumbling over roots to make a beeline for the jumper. He pulled out the remote as he ran, activated it, and Elizabeth fully expected to hear an outcry go up as the hatch slid open. The outcry came, but with a split-second's delay she realized that nobody was paying any attention to them or the jumper. Everybody's attention was riveted on the fight breaking out by the fire.

One hell of a diversion.

Pale with rage, Zelenka flew at his attacker who was still down. Star dodged the onslaught, rolled to his feet, hands kneading the fistful of snow he'd grabbed. He let out an inarticulate shout and hurled that rosy snowball as if to release at least some of his anger before swatting aside Zelenka who'd charged again.

With a dull thud, the snowball struck the jumper and slid down the side of the hull. John shot from cover and dived for it, scraped up every speck of pink snow he could see and a whole armful more besides, shoved it all at Elizabeth.

"Don't lose any of it and get in the jumper!"

"What are you—"

"Get in the jumper!"

Finally one of the ringside crowd noticed what else was happening. "Over there! Look!" It was a woman's voice, not that it mattered.

People swung around, dumbstruck, but their surprise wouldn't last. Elizabeth ducked up the ramp and stayed just inside the hatch to see what was going on. Over by the fire things were getting uglier by the second. Shouts of "Traitor!" went up, a chorus led by Radek Zelenka. People had recovered from their initial shock and the mood was turning against Star with a vengeance. The woman who'd shouted was pulling Zelenka out of harm's way, while three of the men, then four launched themselves at Star. The rest came stumbling through the snow and toward the jumper.

The report of a gunshot rent the air and stopped them in their tracks. Even the foursome that had set upon Star ceased their attempts to beat him into a pulp, and for a moment an eerie silence settled over the village.

It was shattered by John's voice. "Don't make me fire again. The next time I will shoot somebody, I promise."

Nobody was stupid enough to doubt him. Nobody moved a muscle.

Then Star, on all fours, blood trickling from a split lip and eyebrow, hollered, "Go! Get out of here!"

"Not without you! Get your ass into the jumper!"

A smile contorted the Star's bruised face. "But I can't. You know I can't. Once you manage to fix this it won't matter anyway, right?"

"Star—"

Zelenka seemed to have woken up to what was happening. "Stop them!" he screamed. "Don't let them leave!"

It galvanized the whole group into action. Those who'd stood staring so far, broke into a sprint, heading straight for the jumper.

"Go!" Star yelled again and was buried under a pile of attackers.

John Sheppard hovered for a moment, indecisive, then he must have realized the odds; he turned around and in a shambling run scrambled for the ramp. "Dial the gate!" he yelled at Elizabeth. "Doesn't matter where!"

Not bothering to acknowledge, she dumped that freely dripping armful of snow into a storage box, raced into the cockpit and dialed—Atlantis. With any kind of luck they would be going home. John came stumbling up the ramp, slapped the door switch, and joined her in the cockpit. The jumper's engines came online before he'd even thrown himself into the pilot's seat, responding to his thoughts. From outside, muted by inches of metal, came furious shouts and the clangor of fists and sticks pounding the hull. She knew that nothing the men outside could do would leave so much as a dent, but it was unsettling all the same, and she shuddered with relief when she felt the jumper leave the ground.

The small vessel turned on the spot like a compass needle searching for north, until its nose pointed at the event horizon that exploded out toward them in a glorious cascade of silver and blue. To the left of it an uneven fight was taking place, and she grasped in a second what the outcome would be.

"Don't look!" John's lips were compressed in a strained white line, he kept his eyes stubbornly on the large, shimmering target that was the event horizon.

Elizabeth's gaze dropped to the storage box she was cradling in her lap. The snow in it was melting into rose-tinted puddles. At the bottom of one of those sat a small white clump. John had been right. Star had managed to get them one of Radek's teeth. Whether it was enough remained to be seen.

John goosed the engines, the jumper shot forward into the wormhole, and four years of Elizabeth's life dissolved into cold nothing and the vague awareness of a rough, rough ride.

CHAPTER 19

Charybdis -908

Teyla drowsily turned over, smacked her elbow against unforgiving stone, and realized that she actually must have fallen asleep at some point. It bore witness to how tired she'd been. The first thing she noticed was that her sleeping place was markedly cooler than it had been when she'd dozed off. At least it was still dry. Ronon had explained about the porticoes and the braziers and found them shelter right by that large market square where they'd ended up the previous evening.

At a guess, the brazier had gone out.

She swiped her hand across the floor until her fingers struck metal, and she cautiously traced the leg of the brazier upwards, prepared to let go as soon as she felt the heat. There was none. A little residual warmth, perhaps, but nothing else. She must have slept for hours. And the space beside her was still deserted.

"Ronon?"

Apart from a sleeper somewhere to her right who shushed her angrily, there was no reply. So he was still gone. She couldn't begin to imagine what he could be doing reconnoitering for so long.

With a soft sigh, she drew up her knees, pulled her cloak tighter around her, and listened to the rain slapping the pavement. It had to be dawn by now, she supposed. Over the steady crackle of raindrops, she could hear the hurried footfalls of a handful of early risers who one by one arrived in the square among quiet calls of morning greetings. Then the rustle and creak and clatter of stalls being opened and readied. Before long the sounds were complemented by smells. At least one of the stalls was a bakery, and the scent of freshly baked bread drove her half crazy with hunger, especially when an early customer had the indecency of walking past, munching on his purchase.

She barely suppressed a moan.

Then she thought of Rodney, which went a considerable way toward curbing her appetite. He wasn't going to eat either, probably hadn't eaten in however long he'd been locked in that cage—and that, by all accounts, was the least of his problems. Ronon had filled her in on the details of what he'd seen and, together with the gossip they'd picked up the previous evening, it didn't paint a pretty picture. They'd spent half the night in hushed conversation, trying to figure out what to do. By all accounts, Rodney McKay was going to be executed at daybreak tomorrow—which left her and Ronon twenty-four hours, or the local equivalent thereof, to save his life.

The attitude of the onlookers in the market had made abundantly clear that any appeal for mercy would be a waste of time. Which meant a prison break, but how did you break someone out of a prison that was in plain sight of hundreds, perhaps thousands of people? They'd bandied about dozens of possibilities, and the later into the night their discussion lasted, the more scurrilous the proposals became, until Ronon at last had decided he would use the cover of darkness to find out as much as he could about the city and the fortress.

The fact that he hadn't returned worried her. Yes, this was a large place, but yesterday's events had shown that its inhabitants were deeply suspicious and that nobody could be trusted. What if Ronon, too, had been captured? Or worse?

Fear tightened her throat, and the attempt to convince herself that he was too experienced to make any careless mistakes failed. Suddenly something was thrust under her chin, and she gasped with apprehension, sucking in a lungful of warm fragrance. Bread.

"Ronon?"

"Sleep well?" he asked casually. "Thought I'd bring breakfast."

"Where have you been?" Fear and relief funneled into a surge of anger, and she wanted to hit him. About to move, her hands twitched against a crunchy, flaky crust of bread, and suddenly anger, too, evaporated. Instead of striking out, she grabbed the roll, tore it apart, inhaled that magical scent of sourdough and flour and spices. It tasted as delicious as it smelled. "Where have you been?" she repeated around a mouthful of bread.

"Sightseeing." In a series of soft thuds he slumped to the ground beside her.

Teyla heard scraping noises she couldn't place, then a new aroma hit her. Spicy, meaty, mouthwatering.

"Careful, it's hot." Ronon placed an earthenware bowl and a wooden spoon in her hands. "They eat soup for breakfast here. Go figure. Smells good, though."

"Do I want to know how you came by the means to buy this?" she asked lazily, not really caring. The soup was every bit as good as the bread and had started a comfortable pool of warmth in her belly.

"Does it matter?"

"Just curious."

"I made a new friend in a tavern last night" he said. "Got drunk as a skunk, and I helped him home. Did him a favor, deserved to be paid."

Teyla grinned. "Obviously. I hope that, otherwise, your friend is in good health?"

"Hung over, maybe. Anyway, we need the money more than he."

"I'd have been happy with just the bread."

"Food was an added bonus," Ronon chomped between two slurps of soup. "Getting out of here will be expensive."

"Oh?"

"After breakfast we should go for a walk," he said and tore into a chunk of bread.

She listened to the crackle of the crust and, above that, the stirrings of their sleeping companion. Evidently the man was awake enough now that Ronon couldn't risk any further discussion. Just as well. The food deserved her full and undivided attention and was gone more quickly than Teyla would have liked. They were ready to go within a few minutes, and Ronon led her out from under the portico and into the persistent rain. Either side of them people hurried up and down the stairs, which suggested that the building that had sheltered them wasn't a temple, as Ronon had assumed, but some kind of administrative office.

The market had well and truly woken up now, and they were shunted along by throngs of shoppers going about their business. Vendors were praising their goods—everything from beauty products to pig's ears—and serious haggling matches were going on all around. At last the tide of people spat them out on the opposite side of the market where, according to Ronon, that huge chasm gaped to swallow Rodney. It was quieter here, except for another clump of spectators staring up at the cage amid curses and mutterings of outrage and disgust, but Ronon steered her around the group and into the shelter of a small parapet at the lower end of the square. He sat down and pulled her onto his lap.

As soon as she came in contact with him, she realized that he must have changed clothes. He was now dressed in a leather shirt and pants, his chest protected by a metal plate of armor, well scratched and uneven with patches of rust.

"Try and look hopelessly in love with me," he said. "It'll explain why we're alone."

"Am I still pregnant?" she asked.

"We're not married yet."

"Glad to hear it. So, where have you been?" Teyla asked for the third time that morning. "And where did you find this outfit?"

"I've been looking for ways to get into the fortress. Turns out there's only one, unless you're one of the guys in those big houses along the street to the city gate."

"You have to be a guard," she guessed.

"Not just any guard, either. You need friends in high places to pull that detail. Lucky for us."

"Why is that lucky?"

"Because my friend of last night had a brother-in-law in the fortress guards."

"*Had*?" She knew what had happened before she heard the answer, didn't like it.

"He… had an accident." Ronon squirmed uncomfortably. "There was no other choice. Anyway, if we get back to Atlantis and put a stop to Charybdis before Ikaros turns it on, it won't matter, will it?"

"You don't know that."

"Is that what you told that friend of yours, Pirna, and her little girl?"

His voice sounded rough with resentment, and she could feel him tense. The mood matched her own anger. He had no right to throw this back at her... As little right as she had to blame him for dealing the best way he could with an impossible situation. And in truth, she didn't believe that he had killed the guard lightly.

"I'm sorry. I'm the last person who should judge. I set all this in motion." She blew out a breath. "So, this uniform will get you into the fortress?"

"Already has."

He told her how he'd snuck into the guardroom last night, hoping to find out about schedules, watch changes, any intelligence that could be exploited. It had been almost too easy. Nobody had challenged him, in fact they'd barely looked past the uniform and the insignia. It was partly indifference, partly excitement about the impending execution. Dozens of men, most of them off-duty, had been milling in and out, heading up to the battlements to take a look at the delinquent in the cage. Ronon had heard guards take bets on how loudly the crook would scream after he was dropped and how long it would take until he disappeared from view.

After spending a good hour in the stuffy, smoke-clogged guardroom, listening to the chitchat, he had accompanied a couple of other men for a trip to the battlements. On the way up, they'd stopped at a small window carved into solid rock. It opened just above the cage and offered an excellent view of the prisoner.

"Did you see Rodney?"

There was no answer.

"Ronon?"

"I heard you... I don't know if McKay's even alive. The cage is exposed and it's colder up there. All I can tell you is that he wasn't moving. But it was dark, and there was no way of making out every little twitch." Ronon tried to sound positive, but the act couldn't have convinced anybody. Eventually he continued. "Good news is that there are no guards up there—nobody could escape from that thing. There's constant traffic, though, with people sneaking up to take a look. Guards would be better, 'cos at least they're predictable…"

As she listened to Ronon describe the arrangements up at the fortress, Teyla's heart sank. How could anybody reach the cage unobserved, let alone get Rodney up to the parapet and safely out of the fortress—especially when they had to act on their own? Even if Ronon somehow managed to smuggle her into the fortress, she'd be more hindrance than help, because everything that needed to be done required sight. Teyla supposed that up until now she'd somehow believed that there would be some loophole magically presenting itself. Crazy, of course, because experience should have taught her that such a thing never happened.

Unless you made your own loophole…

"You'll need a diversion," she said slowly, an idea tugging at the back of her mind.

"A big one. How about an earthquake?"

"Something a little easier. There are all these braziers everywhere, aren't there?"

"Yes."

"You'd have thought people would be more careful around such fire hazards…"

He leaned back a little, mulling it over. "One fire won't be enough," he said at last. "We'd need three or four at once, in the city and the fortress; we'd need incendiary devices, and you won't find any in this place."

"They've got what we need, but we have to start now. Take me back into the market. I'm sure I smelled it there."

"Smelled what?"

"Just take me to the market." Sensing his impatience, she smiled. Served him right if he had to wait a little. Payback for scaring the life out of her this morning. "You'll see."

Muttering under his breath, he eased her off his lap and guided her back among the bustle of the market. The noise and the labyrinthine arrangement of the stalls were disorienting, and she had difficulty remembering where exactly she'd noticed that smell before. After a while she stopped, frustrated.

"This is pointless. I can't find it like that," she growled. "Can we retrace our steps from where we slept last night?"

Wordlessly, he guided her back along the earlier route. The only sign of his annoyance was the force of his grip on her arm. Traffic had increased, so had the chatter, and the main subject of conversation was the upcoming execution. Teyla tried to tune it out as best she could, focusing solely on her sense of smell. Finally, she caught it, faint, almost like a ghost, but it was there, and she pulled Ronon along with her, colliding with shoppers, apologizing, and staying on the scent.

"There!" she said at last.

The stall sat at the fringes of the market, and there were few other shoppers around. Hardly surprising. The wares sold here were less universally demanded than bread and soup.

"Oil?" Ronon murmured a little skeptically.

"Yes," she whispered back. To the vendor she said, "Would you mind if I sniffed your oils? I can't recall the name of what I'm looking for." A lie, but she didn't want to give herself away by using a name the locals wouldn't recognize.

"If you wish," the woman in the stall grunted, almost as skeptical as Ronon, though she had enough business sense to hold out the various ceramic jars for Teyla's convenience.

The oil in the sixth jar had the peculiar musty, almost rancid aroma Teyla had been looking for. She smiled. "That's it."

"That? That's flax oil," the woman said as though she couldn't believe that anyone would be stupid enough to forget the name.

"How much of it have you got?"

"Three skins." Suddenly the vendor sounded hopeful.

"We'll take them all. My husband will pay and carry them."

Ronon spent ten minutes haggling the exorbitant first quote down to a price that was acceptable. After which Teyla demanded to be taken to a stall—any stall—that sold wool or linens or both. An easier job, as there were at least a dozen of those. Finally they returned to their perch by the parapet, armed with the flax oil and three large strings of handspun wool and a bundle of linen.

"Now what?" Ronon asked curiously.

"Wait and see." She tore off a fistful of wool, poured oil on it, wrapped in a strip of linen, and set the little parcel on the paving, making sure that the spot where she put it was protected from the rain. "It'll take a while," she cautioned him, "but we need to time it anyway, if we want the fires to start more or less simultaneously."

It took about half an hour until she could smell it. The aroma of the oil intensified. Within seconds of her noticing, Ronon let out a low whistle.

"It's smoking. How—?"

"Linseed oil. When it dries, it starts a chemical reaction that burns oxygen. Enough of it to ignite."

He laughed softly. "How did you know?"

"Back on Athos our neighbor accidentally burned down his tent. He'd been oiling wooden tool handles and left the rags in a corner…" She grinned at the memory. "What do you think? Will it do?"

"It'll do. Let's go to work."

Wake up! Hey! Wake up. We need to talk!

Wake up? Who on God's green Earth would be able to sleep in this? He hadn't slept since they'd put him up here.

Rodney McKay groaned and tried to contract himself into an even tighter ball. It made no difference. Any body warmth he might have possessed in some distant past had leached out of him an eternity ago. All that was left was another eternity of wet, windblown misery. On the upside, come break of day tomorrow that would be the least of his worries.

"For once in my life, I can see absolutely no point in talking, so if you don't mind, leave me the hell alone. I'm busy." The reply was barely intelligible through the rattle of his teeth. Which didn't really matter, of course, because that brat Ikaros was squatting inside Rodney's head and no doubt snooped on every piddling thought.

I'd never stoop to snooping. Especially on piddling thoughts. We still need to talk.

"What's there to talk about? We'll be dead tomorrow. *Both* of us. End of discussion."

For a while—perhaps half the first day, perhaps even all of it—Rodney had held out hope that something would happen. If for no other reason, then because the kind of demise in store for him seemed to be too ignominious for words. Terminal velocity in just under five seconds, and by the time he reached the bottom of the gorge his body would have picked up enough speed to all but liquefy on impact.

Hope hadn't lasted. Propelled by the relentless cold and rain and hunger, the notion of Colonel Sheppard riding to the rescue at the penultimate nanosecond—the man's timing tended to be unnerving, to say the least—had slipped further and further into the realm of wishful thinking.

Today, all Rodney asked for was that it'd be over soon and that he'd pass out before he hit the ground.

Did anybody ever tell you that this relentless optimism of yours is downright infectious?

"All the time. I'm famous for my bright and positive outlook, especially in desperate situations. Go away!"

Rodney pulled himself closer to the bars and stared down into the late afternoon light that thickened like pea soup above the square. Another exciting day on the market was coming to a close, but he was delighted to see that he was still able to draw a respectable audience. They gathered along the edge of the abyss, necks craned to a degree that would make any chiropractor cringe in dismay, their faces turned up into the rain. He was as certain as he could be that their mouths were hanging open. What the hell did they expect? That he would start waving at them? Or turn somersaults for their entertainment?

Even at night, when the crowd down on the market was invisible, if it was still there—though, if the rain didn't disperse them, he doubted darkness would—there was no shortage of thrill seekers. Any number of guards visited the parapet, and just above him was an opening carved into what looked like solid rock but had to be part of the fortress. Behind it, an endless procession of faces rolled past, jeering and mocking. The thought that those jeers would be the last thing he heard—apart perhaps from the air screeching past him as he fell—was profoundly depressing.

Oh please! Break out the violins! Who said the situation was hopeless?

One thing you had to say for Ikaros; he had a sense of humor. Rodney almost laughed. The only thing stopping him was the thought that his audience might derive the idea that he'd gone nuts. No, wait! He was the guy who couldn't quit talking to himself, because he'd engaged in a Vulcan mind meld with a ten thousand year old standup comedian. Of course they thought he was nuts.

In other words, it didn't matter.

Except, the moment had passed and the laughter must have been washed into the ravine by the rain.

I ask again: who said it was hopeless?

"You're so right. I'm going to break out my Superman cape and fly off into the sunset."

You're mixing archetypes. It's nearly as bad as mixing metaphors. I could help you.

"*Now* you're telling me?"

I'm not sure it'll work.

"You know, I wish you'd said that before switching on Charybdis."

Why would I? With Charybdis I was sure it would *work.*

Rodney groaned and decided it didn't bear answering. Besides, something new was happening below, something he couldn't recall seeing in all his time here. A sliver of light stole across the market, tinting the pavement in pink and golden hues. The rain had stopped for once, and the clouds had broken just enough to admit a shaft of evening sunlight that could have been painted by Dürer or Caspar David Friedrich. Below, the crowd turned, almost simultaneously, a move devised by some larger-than-life choreographer, and raised their faces toward the sun. Like a faint echo at first, a sound that might or might not exist, a chant rose. As more and more voices joined it became more solid, more real.

He couldn't make out the words, but it didn't matter. He didn't care. Like his fan club on the market square below, he closed his eyes, turned his face into the sun, relishing the brightness and the color and the illusion of warmth that it brought.

You realize that this merely confirms their superstitious notions?

"What?" He wished Ikaros would keep quiet and just let him savor those few moments. The rain would resume soon enough.

Oh, don't tell me you missed the fact that they believe this deluge is some kind of divine retribution for your heresy. Now, at the eve of your—excuse me, our— execution the sun comes out for the first time in months. Obviously they take it as a sign the things will look up once we're dead.

"Thanks for reminding me," Rodney snapped. "For a moment there I almost enjoyed what's probably the last pleasant thing to happen in my life. Good job you nipped that in the bud."

As I mentioned earlier, I may be able to help.

"Don't tell me. You're going to knit a hot air balloon?"

You're hilarious.

Coupled with a distinct sense of sulking. For an ineffably glorious three seconds, Rodney thought he might have managed to shut the kid up. But no.

I may be able to make us both ascend. Charybdis has indicated that it would allow us to do that.

Okay. Two disturbing concepts right there. Not for the first time Rodney wished he could stare the kid down at least. He supposed that imagining the act might do the trick, but for now he settled for prioritizing. "Charybdis has done *what*?"

I joined with Charybdis, remember? I know what it wants, because I'm part of it. So are you, seeing as you decided to muscle in on the act. If you were a little less self-absorbed here, you'd sense it too.

"Yes, silly me, preoccupied with my impending demise. Go figure!" It lacked conviction, and Rodney knew it. The notion of Charybdis's awareness—if that's what it was—infesting his mind alongside Ikaros was more than he cared to contemplate.

Charybdis isn't a killer. It just wants the same thing as you—

"Oh really? And again: oh really? Just to cover both counts here."

—and me. It wants to survive. Getting rid of us permanently

would ensure its survival, and I think it may actually have engineered this entire situation.

"You must be so proud of your brainchild!"

In a way, yes.

The little jerk possessed the cheek to actually *feel* proud. With Rodney McKay's personal emotional repertoire, limited as that might be... though pride admittedly came easy...

I didn't expect this to happen. Obviously. I'd also be grateful if you'd actually let me finish a thought. As I was saying, Charybdis wants to survive. Our going back—hypothetically speaking—and preventing me from bringing Charybdis online would kill it. Hence its determination to take you out of the picture. Your amnesia may have been a first attempt.

"Practice makes perfect," said Rodney.

No, it makes sense. Whether you believe it or not, Charybdis was not designed to kill anybody—except Wraith, of course, and those only in a roundabout way—and it would prefer a solution that enables all three of us to survive.

"And how does ascension—" Realizing the answer, Rodney cut himself off. "We wouldn't be allowed to interfere."

Exactly.

The rift in the clouds widened to a pool of gold set in a mass of dark gray murkiness. Painfully bright, the light spilled over the city, refracting from a myriad puddles on rooftops and in the streets. The effect was as dizzying as the potential of Ikaros's—or Charybdis's—proposal. Rodney's vertigo ratcheted up a notch, and it was difficult to tell what had caused it; the giant glitter ball below or the notion of learning everything anyone could possibly want to learn.

That's what ascension meant, wasn't it?

He rolled on his back, stared up at the churning clouds, and tried to steady his breathing. If he ascended, he could go anywhere he liked, see anything he wanted to see... God, there was every chance of actually finding out how quantum mechanics worked and why! He could hover there, exempt from Heisenberg's Uncertainty Principle, and watch it all happen. Or maybe he could make music in a way even someone like Glenn Gould could only ever have dreamed of... Best of all, if he ascended, he'd stay alive. In a manner of speaking. In every manner that truly mattered.

If he ascended, he'd know where his team mates had ended up. He could find them… and look on as they died.

"Ay, there's the rub," he whispered.

What?

"Hamlet."

No interference, no matter what happened. If you interfered, they un-ascended you, though, if Dr. Jackson was anything to go by, the worst thing that could befall Rodney was to end up in pretty much the same situation he was in now: cold, wet, exposed, and with a ripe case of Alzheimer's. Okay, he'd be minus his clothes, too. Given the climate, that might pose a problem…

Of course, in order to avoid that scenario, all he had to do was not to interfere. Everybody in the galaxy might die—would die, provided Charybdis's entropic tendencies continued—but Rodney McKay would live on.

Rodney found that the cost of survival was too high. Even for his strongly developed sense of self-preservation. "No," he said.

Excuse me?

"You heard me."

Are you saying you prefer a pointless death to unlimited opportunities?

"I'm saying I prefer a pointless death to a pointless life."

And it's never occurred to you to consider what I'd prefer, has it?

"Feel free to go on ahead."

I can't. Not without you. We're… linked. It's either both of us or neither. Rodney… Dr. McKay, we'll both die!

The kid was sounding—*sounding*?—panicked. Considering that Ikaros was some ten thousand years old already, Rodney felt the sentiment was slightly on the greedy side. He also, and somewhat to his surprise, felt sorry for the boy. Apparently even an unreasonably long lifespan didn't diminish that teenage conviction that immortality was a God-given right.

"Look, 'interference' is my middle name," he said. "I won't

stand on the sidelines while Charybdis destroys everything we know, especially if all I've got to look forward to afterwards is eternity consisting of you, me, and—supposing you're right—Charybdis in some sort of primordial vacuum. If the thought of spending eternity in that company doesn't scare you off, watching the universe and everyone in it fall apart should."

I don't care! Everybody I've known is long dead anyway!

"But you *did* care! How did it feel, watching the Wraith take your family and being powerless to do anything about it, huh?"

The response was a furious jumble of pain and rage and sorrow that petered out into the mental equivalent of a little boy's whimper. Rodney recalled moments when he himself must have sounded—*sounded?*—exactly like that, and pushed the memories away with a vengeance, hoping against hope that Ikaros hadn't noticed. And maybe he hadn't. The kid was preoccupied with his own grief.

"I'm sorry." Rodney surprised himself again by meaning it.

After what seemed like decades of silence—funny how it bothered him now, seeing that he'd wanted it for so long—Ikaros finally came back.

You're right.

It was all he said, but apparently it was enough.

As though somebody had thrown a switch, that soothing pool of sunlight winked out. Swirling clouds seemed to collide in the sky, their gray thickening to charcoal to black. With a bone-rattling clap of thunder the skies opened again, releasing a deluge that was like nothing Rodney had ever experienced. Cold, hard pellets of rain were hammering down relentlessly, jumping off the floor of the cage, stinging his face and whipping his skin. On the market below, the crowd flew apart, scattering toward the nearest shelter, their screams of terror or dismay scarcely audible over the roar of the rain.

Charybdis is angry.

"Thanks for telling me. I thought it was just mildly irked."

CHAPTER 20

Charybdis -223

"Radek! Leave!" Selena was shouting it out, but she herself wasn't moving from her terminal.

The holographic image that quivered in front of her work station, at the brink of winking out, showed a schematic of the planet's continental plates. Their drift was now visible with the naked eye, not that Radek Zelenka would have needed a computer to demonstrate that fact to him. He briefly tore his attention away from the figures racing across his own holo-screen, escalating rapidly, and projecting a sequence of events nobody would be able to stop now. Even if the planet's scientific facilities weren't being knocked down like houses of cards. Their own laboratory was no exception.

Ceiling tiles dangled at drunken angles, having ripped loose light fixtures and wiring that snaked halfway to a floor strewn with debris and broken equipment. Windows were shattered, with the exception of one pane that stubbornly hung on in defiance of a crack that split it top to bottom. Across the room a whole section of the wall had caved in about two hours ago. Falling masonry had flattened a slew of instruments, including the monitors for their main seismic sensor array, and half buried a young technician, at the very least cracked a few ribs, at the worst caused severe internal injuries. Two others had volunteered to take her to a hospital that was only four blocks away—in other words, the situation there wouldn't be any different from here, but any speculation on the girl's chances of receiving treatment was moot anyway. Her escorts hadn't returned, so Radek couldn't even tell whether the men and their charge had made it to the hospital in the first place. The safest assumption was that they'd lost three more people in addition to the five who had died from carbon monoxide inhalation the previous night.

"Radek! Move!" The project leader still hadn't moved. Knowing her, she probably didn't intend to. It was her lab, her responsibility, and like the proverbial captain, she was going to go down with the sinking ship.

Not as long as he had anything to do with it. "It's too late, Selena! We have to go! And that means you, too! We—"

"Go where?" she shot back. "No matter what the government tells us, there's nowhere safe, and you know it."

He did. In a last ditch effort to appear to be doing *something*, the planetary government, or what was left of it, had ordered everyone who'd survived so far—few enough, the global population had been decimated—to evacuate to high ground by morning. Morning was now. They should be leaving, but it didn't make sense. High ground was no safer than anywhere else; this was a disaster that impartially struck everywhere, robbing people of the titillating comfort of watching the devastation in some remote corner of the planet on their news screens and donating to the nearest relief fund by ways of paying admission to the spectacle. The evacuation merely was an attempt to keep the pervasive panic at bay and offer the survivors a scrap of hope and the chance to die with a glimmer of optimism in their eye.

And maybe it was his job to justify that scrap of hope and that glimmer of optimism.

It wasn't just time-honored disaster tradition that had prompted the council to send people into the hills above the city. The ruins of the old Atlantis were situated in those hills, and among the ruins still stood the Stargate—the only potential means of mass evacuation. Of course the council had been briefed regularly, and they knew as well as Radek or Selena what the chances were. They'd been trying to get the gate to work for as long as Radek had been here. Twenty-six years. The lab had been established within days of his dropping out of the event horizon, in the hopes that they could duplicate what he seemed to have achieved. He'd told them, time and time again, that he didn't know how he'd done it. All he could say for certain was that, one moment he'd been on Mykena

Quattuor, watching Charybdis going active, and the next he'd landed here. On his own. In a timeline that wasn't his. This much at least was definite, because this was Atlantis—at a time when its inhabitants had either not yet reached or somehow lost their technological advantage. Radek had found himself in the bizarre position of knowing more about Ancient technology than the Ancients. He'd been happy to join the research team at the laboratory, not just for the intellectual challenge but also because getting the Stargate to work was his only way home.

These days he no longer remembered when exactly he'd decided to confine his expectations to explaining the seemingly unsolvable puzzle. Nothing they'd tried, none of the bright ideas he and the team had cooked up over the years, had had any effect. Still they'd never stopped trying. What had continued to spur them on was one simple fact, based on the laws of probability; with every failed attempt their chances of succeeding the next time increased. And that was what drove Selena.

As he looked over at her, he noticed for the first time that most of her unruly mop of hair had escaped the chignon at the back of her neck and flared around her face like a gray, curly halo. Her lab coat was rumpled, and fatigue had blotted shadows under her eyes and carved her crow's feet into deep, angry lines.

"You look terrible," he said, smiling.

"Have you looked at yourself lately?"

He hadn't, but he supposed it didn't take too much imagination to get the picture. At least her coat was only rumpled. His was stained with what had to be at least a gallon of coffee. Though that nicely covered those blotches of grease, leftovers from a meal he couldn't even recall eating.

"This last batch of readings looks interesting. It suggests a temporal not a spatial phenomenon," she offered. "I have to stick with it. Maybe—"

"Show me then." He crossed the room and flung himself into a chair next to her.

It wasn't what she'd expected, and it triggered a frown. "Radek, you can't stay here. You're the only one who stands a reasonable chance of making this work."

Still confident, even after all these years of futility.

"That's exactly why I need to stay," he replied. "Even though, personally, I feel you may be overestimating my capabilities. Show me what you've got."

She brought up the latest figures. They had installed sensors all around the gate to measure abnormalities in the energy flux. Each time they'd dialed the readings had been nominal, indicating that there was nothing wrong with the gate itself. Then, over the past ten days or so they'd occasionally registered energy spikes while the Stargate was supposedly dormant. In each instance, the spikes lasted for the average duration of an intragalactic gate journey and they had always shown exactly the same characteristics. If nothing else, it had confirmed Radek's longstanding suspicion that it had to be the system that was faulty. It also suggested that, somehow, the gates remained interconnected even when they weren't active. Unfortunately, fascinating though the observation was, it also remained completely useless unless they could figure out what it meant. If they figured it out in time, they might save the lives of everybody who had fled into the hills.

As if the planet or fate or Charybdis were laughing at the mere thought of this possibility, a new tremor slammed into the lab. Selena's chair toppled, spilling her under the desk, and Radek flung himself over her, partly to protect her, partly to seek cover from the rain of mortar, tiles, fittings, and other junk that burst from the torn ceiling. That sole, steadfast window pane gave in at last and sent a shower of shards sailing across the lab. Everywhere in the building alarms went off, only this time there was nobody left to silence them. The klaxons barely contrived to add to the noise that seemed to turn the air solid.

To Radek it sounded as though the planet itself was groaning—and perhaps it was; for reasons unknown Lantea was expanding, rapidly, straining at the seams, its continents just about ready to pop off the surface of the doomed planet. All scientific analysis of the problem basically read like the diagnosis of a monumental case of gas.

The notion of a planet suffering from indigestion made him chuckle, though neither their current predicament nor the predicted end result were funny in the slightest. Lantea would simply fly apart, and sooner rather than later.

Finally, the shaking stopped but instead of the leaden post-shock silence—so profound that you could hear the dust rustle through the air—now there was the unchecked wailing of the klaxons. Of all the pointless noises...

Beneath him, Selena stirred and gave a groan loud enough to be heard over the racket. "Get off me," she yelped. "I can't breathe!"

"Sorry." He rolled off her, crawled out from under the desk and rose to survey the damage.

The holographic projector had been knocked out this time, obliterating that entirely redundant simulation of the rate at which the planet expanded. Sadly, Radek's glee at finally finding something useless destroyed wasn't meant to last. Selena's computer terminal was dead, too, and the readings, which he'd never had a chance to study properly were gone. Instead of figures, her holo-screen showed a multicolored fizz of static.

"Oh damn!" Selena had climbed to her feet behind him and stared at her ruined terminal. She was bleeding from a cut above her eyebrow, and the crimson trail of blood had painted a stark pattern into the mortar dust that caked her face.

"*K čertu!*" Radek echoed glumly, his voice struggling for audibility under the screech of the alarms.

The chunk of masonry that had destroyed the terminal had also diminished their last chance, however insignificant, to get the gate to work and save all those people who had flooded into the hills like lemmings. And they still kept coming.

Ironically, the only piece of lab equipment still working was a bank of monitor screens that showed constant surveillance images of the Stargate and the area surrounding it, which was fast getting choked with refugees, all terrified, all desperate to escape. A whole throng of people had gathered under the awning that protected the dialing console and some clearly knew enough to be aware of what the device was supposed to be doing. Which was the extent of their knowledge. A dozen hands at once frantically—and randomly—pushed glyphs, while some impatient or frustrated souls kicked at the base of

the console. One of them was attempting to pry open a maintenance hatch. If he succeeded, the mob was bound to pull out the
crystals and destroy the device.

Radek supposed he should get worried or try to contact the
authorities in a vain effort to dispatch someone to stop these
people. But what difference would it make? Selena seemed to
have come to the same conclusion.

"Just look at them," she said tiredly. "Poor devils."

It seemed the authorities were on to the situation without
being alerted, though whether the soldiers were there in any official capacity was anyone's guess. Radek assumed they merely
were fugitives like everybody else—any kind of societal structure had gone out the window weeks ago, even if, mercifully,
the disorder had stopped short of rioting and violence—and
they simply chipped in because they felt it was their duty. They
pushed through the throng, where necessary shoving people
aside physically, and at last plowed their path to the dialing console. In their majority, the people pawing the device stepped
back as soon as they saw the officers approach, but a handful,
including the man attempting to get into the maintenance hatch,
kept prodding, kicking, and poking.

The fight developed almost in slow motion. An officer
stepped in, addressed one of the amateur technicians. The man
ignored him until the officer tugged at his sleeve. On the monitors, mouths opened and faces contorted with silent screams.
When the first fist flew, Selena gasped.

"What is he doing?"

"He is being scared," Radek replied as gently as one could
if contending with klaxons. "When people are scared, they lash
out. Even people as peaceful as you."

By the looks of it, people were very scared. After that initial,
almost reflexive punch, the mêlée spread like ripples in a pond,
but, unlike ripples that would quiet down with time and distance, the situation escalated further and further. Men, women,
children were swept away and pulled under in a maelstrom of
panic.

With a mix of dread and fascination, barely aware of Selena's
sobs, Radek watched the sea of heaving, thrashing bodies, half

thinking that perhaps this was a better way to die; at least they went out fighting. He was so wrapped up in the macabre spectacle that he almost missed it. A chevron had lit up on the outer ring of the Stargate.

"Selena!"

She blinked, stared where he'd stabbed his finger at the screen. "They actually dialed an address!"

"No." Radek's throat had gone dry and that one syllable stuck in his craw. Which might be just as well, because right now that blockage seemed to be the only thing that kept his wildly hammering heart in place. "No. Look again."

"You're saying it's an incoming wormhole?"

"Yes! Look at the console. If they'd managed to dial a valid address, the symbols would be lit."

The dialing pads were dark. The Stargate, on the other hand, showed four glowing chevrons now, with a fifth coming alight just as Radek glimpsed back at it. The crowd had spotted it, too, and they began pushing toward the gate as their way out, like an audience trying to escape from a burning theatre or sports stadium.

"*Žádná!*" he shouted, horrified. "Stay back! For God's sake, get away from there!"

"They can't hear you!"

Of course they couldn't. And even if they could have, they wouldn't have listened. Helpless, Radek looked on as the seventh chevron locked and the event horizon surged into the throng—men, women, children—and vaporized everyone and everything in its path. Selena let out an inarticulate scream and clutched his arm.

The eight foot swath of annihilation had finally brought the crowd to a dead halt. Too late they came to their senses, faces white and slack, all of them so shell-shocked that they barely seemed to be able to take in what was happening when a squat, roughly cylindrical little vessel pushed its way out of the Stargate.

"Oh, my God," whispered Radek. "Oh, my God…"

He hadn't seen a puddle jumper in twenty-six years, but there was no mistaking it. For a moment he simply stood there,

unable to move a muscle, staring like an idiot with his mouth
hanging open. Then he grabbed Selena's arm and yanked her
toward the door.

"Come! Quickly! We've got to get to the gate. Now!

It was as though the events they'd witnessed only moments
ago had sapped the life from her. She let herself be dragged
over and around the rubble that littered the floor and out the
door. Only when they reached the stairwell, she seemed to
wake up from her fugue.

"Where are we going?"

"To the Stargate! I told you!" he snapped impatiently, regret-
ting the outburst almost at once.

"But—"

"I'll explain later, I promise. But now we have to go.
There's no time." He let go of her, patted her shoulder by ways
of encouragement, and started racing down the stairs, trusting
Selena would follow. Her curiosity was reliable enough.

The stairwell was a deathtrap, and in his mad scramble to
the ground floor all he could do was pray that it wouldn't come
crashing down around their ears. Twisted all out of shape, the
banister wobbled dangerously, and pieces of jagged metal stuck
out everywhere. More than once his coat caught on an edge,
and he had to rip himself free again to rush on, skipping broad
holes where steps had broken off and ducking under loose wiring. The air was thick with dust, and every breath he took—far
too many—made his lungs feel as if they were filled with
ground glass.

By the time he reached the ground floor lobby, he was
dizzy with exertion, wheezing for air, but he only stopped long
enough to determine a safe route to the exit. Once a soaring
space illuminated by skylights and designed to convey the lofty
goals of those who worked here—pursuit of knowledge and
universal betterment—the lobby lay in ruins. They'd actually
heard the crash all the way up to the twelfth floor. The ceiling
had caved in and the skylights had turned the floor into a mine-
field of shards. And worse. He quickly decided that it would be
wiser not to examine what lay beneath the glitter of destruction.
There was no telling how many people had been in here when

the lobby collapsed, but those who hadn't made it out in time must have been caught in what amounted to a hailstorm of glass daggers…

"Oh no!" Selena had caught up with him, panting nearly as hard as he, which didn't stop her from repeating it over and over again, like a mantra or a spell that would make it all go away if only she said it often enough. "Oh no… oh no…"

He wrapped an arm around her and pointed to one of the support pillars. It must have survived the tremor that had destroyed the ceiling and come down in a later quake to topple across the lobby like a felled tree. Free of glass, it formed a bridge to the street.

At the third attempt he managed to pull himself on top of it, then reached down to haul Selena after him. Careful to avoid any unnecessary glances to the lobby floor and the dead scattered there, they balanced across the pillar and finally found themselves outside and under a livid, churning sky.

Heat slammed into them like a mallet. Apparently some of the cooling systems inside the building had still been working, or perhaps Radek simply hadn't noticed before and it had taken the sick color of the sky to drive it home. Out in the open, temperatures were scorching. Near-tropical humidity made matters worse, and without so much as a whisper of wind to stir it, the whole stifling stew hung trapped amid the skeletal remains of buildings. In hindsight Radek thought that he shouldn't have been so surprised. It made sense. As the planet expanded, the atmosphere would have to thin proportionately, offering less and less protection from the sun.

The devastation in the street matched that inside the building, except that things were a little less cramped. Directly ahead rose what was left of the monorail station. The rail had buckled between two support struts. A train was jammed at the bottom of the kink, still trying to move forward, its engine whining angrily.

"Hell," Selena muttered. "I paid my public transport dues a year in advance…" She was coming out of her shock and dealing with the situation the only way you could if you wanted to stay sane.

"Serves you right for being a goodie-two-shoes." Radek grinned. "But I wasn't going to suggest we take the train anyway. It's unreliable at the best of times. I was thinking along the lines of purloining a glider."

"*Purloining?*"

"I would have said *borrowing*, but given that there probably won't be any owners around to ask…" He headed for a large parking area at the opposite side of the station.

Not that anyone could have recognized it for what it was. For all the world it looked like a junkyard. Still, Radek counted on finding at least one glider—a fast one preferably—that was still operational. Finding it quickly would be an added bonus.

The one they found—almost immediately, and they could barely believe their luck—was wedged into a makeshift shelter. The roof at the far end of the station had collapsed, forming a lean-to and protecting the three gliders parked beneath from the falling debris that had flattened everything else in the vicinity.

"I'm piloting," Selena said, shoving him out of the way with a meaningful glance.

"I was about to suggest just that."

Back on Earth he'd never even learned to drive, and the two attempts he'd made at piloting gliders had almost resulted in disaster. Selena, on the other hand, could proudly look back on a whole list of citations for reckless speeding, which might not be much safer but, under the circumstances, would be an asset. All he'd have to do was close his eyes. He climbed into the glider, swiped a little mound of dirt from the passenger seat, settled in—and closed his eyes.

Not a moment too soon.

The next thing he knew was his head being slammed into the backrest by a jolt of sudden acceleration, then the glider banked sharply—hopefully *around* an obstacle—and soared off across the parking area and in the general direction of the hills.

CHAPTER 21

Charybdis -908

Ronon peered through a tear in the sackcloth, checked for observers, and smoothly rolled out from under the stall when he saw that the coast was clear. The lump of oil-soaked wool and linen sat on the counter of the stall, nestled among wrapping material and well protected from the rain.

Which was more than could be said for Ronon. He took an experimental step and squirmed at the squelching of water in his boots. If there was one thing he hated... Early in the evening it had looked as though it might clear up, but the respite had lasted all of fifteen minutes. Then the downpour had resumed, more violent than ever, and you couldn't help thinking that it meant to scour this place off the face of the planet.

"How many left?" he asked softly. They'd set a total of fourteen of the makeshift incendiary devices, mostly in taverns, because access was easy and panic was more likely once the fires started. A couple he'd managed to plant in private houses where the backdoors had conveniently stood open.

Silent like a ghost, Teyla shifted from the shadows behind the stall and to his side. "Five more. I think we should place them all in the fortress. That's where—"

The noise reared up suddenly and didn't seem to want to stop—ever. It began as an almighty roar that rolled up the street, wave after wave of it, followed by a screech that ebbed and rose but never quite subsided. And then the screaming started. Ronon had a flash of that miserable shantytown, shoebox houses stuffed with enough people to make their walls bulge outward; dwelling after dwelling, crammed together as tightly as possible, because space was at a premium between the river and the city walls, and in those narrow, winding alleys hundreds and thousands of people, desperate to get out and drowning like rats. He felt sick to his stomach.

"What was that?" gasped Teyla.

"The levees. The levees have broken."

"The houses by the river…"

"Yeah. More of a diversion than we planned," he conceded grimly. "We can't help those poor bastards, so we might as well make use of it."

She nodded wordlessly.

Holding on to Teyla's arm, he led her away from the market and down the wide street they'd first walked up the evening before. It was virtually deserted now; everybody who could move had sought refuge from the torrential rain, and the porticoes were packed with countless prospective thrill-seekers, jostling for the premium places near the braziers and still hoping they'd see an execution the next morning. Some of them, the older, weaker ones or the very young, had given up on the notion of shouldering their way anywhere near that aura of warmth and sat bleakly staring into the rain. Invariably, they goggled with disbelief when they spotted him and Teyla out in the downpour.

Not good. The last thing Ronon wanted was to stand out.

"Play along with me," he whispered to Teyla. "We're drawing too much attention."

"Am I pregnant again?"

"No. This time you're a thief." He grabbed her a little tighter and shoved her in front of him.

"Hey!" she snapped. "That hurts!"

"Should have thought of that before you went snooping around the market!" he barked back. "Move!"

Ducking her head in a convincing kicked dog impression, she did just that. It had the desired effect. In the manner of people the universe over—or so he'd been told—the onlookers under the porticoes averted their eyes and withdrew deeper into sodden cloaks in an effort to become invisible in the eye of the law. Even better, with Teyla as his captive, he had a perfect excuse for reentering the fortress. Ronon snuffed a grin, and kept plodding on down the street, occasionally prodding his 'captive' for show and noting that, if anything, the weather was getting worse. Some two hundred meters on, they reached an intersection and left the main street for a narrower alley that led up to the fortress.

The runoff down the streets had swelled dramatically, and despite the incline they were wading ankle-deep in water that gushed over cobblestones and lapped at walls and steps and sent all kinds of debris swirling around their feet. The footing was treacherous, to say the least. As if trying to match the rising water, the screaming and shouting beyond the walls had risen in volume, too.

"They're trying to get to high ground," Teyla said.

No need to elaborate. High ground was within the city walls, and by the sound of it a whole mob of terrified people was about to storm the gates. As if to confirm Ronon's speculation, a contingent of soldiers came barreling down the alley toward them.

Rushing past, one of them yelled, "Where do you think you're going, man? They need every hand at the gate! The filth is trying to get in!"

"Some already did!" Ronon yelled back, giving Teyla another shove. "Caught her trying to sneak into a house. I'll join you as soon as she's taken care of."

He wasn't sure whether the man had heard him or cared if he had. Essentially the same conversation repeated itself several times over as they climbed on toward the fortress and encountered more and more troops heading for the gate. At this rate there wouldn't be a guard left in the entire building.

Finally, the entrance to the fortress loomed above them like a huge maw, and for just a moment Ronon envied Teyla for not being able to see it. Had it looked this forbidding last night?

As soon as the question popped into his mind, he chased it away. It was a little late to have second thoughts, especially since the sole guard left under the portcullis had spotted them. A bitter wind was sweeping the downpour almost horizontally into the gate, which, if the guy's face was anything to go by, hadn't improved his mood.

"Hey! Slacker! Aren't you going the wrong way?" he barked. "Now isn't the time to piss your pants. They need every man down there."

Ronon recognized the voice and almost did piss his pants. It belonged to none other than their friend from the city gate. Making a show of hunching his shoulders against the weather, Ronon tried to keep his face in the shadows as best he could, lowered his own voice to a ludicrous bass, and once more launched into the tale of how he'd arrested a piece of rabble about to sneak into a house.

The man squinted at Teyla and smirked. "Should have known. Watch yourself around that one, brother. She's trouble." Leaning in to Ronon, he added in a whisper, "She's a witch."

"She won't make trouble once I'm done with her." Ronon did his best to ignore the fact that the guy's breath reeked of bad teeth, booze, and garlic. How Teyla had come up with cheap perfume and home cooking beat him. Today at least the odor was rather more hellish.

"You'd better make it quick then. I don't trust her." The guard laughed, squinted again, and then an idea seemed to take hold. "Hey, make sure you let me know which cell she's in, brother. I could use a bit of warming up once my shift ends."

The temptation to deck the son of a bitch was overwhelming, but Ronon decided that it would be counterproductive. So, he winked at the guy instead. "It's a deal," he promised and nudged Teyla past the guard and through the gate.

They hurried across an interior court, which stood at least two inches under water, and toward the wing to the left of the gate. Ronon couldn't even begin to imagine what the other sections of the buildings might hold. The structure was massive, less from genuine need, he suspected, than to project a sense of power over the city and surrounding countryside.

"Where are we going?" Teyla whispered.

"The guardroom," he replied, trying to inject it with about twice as much optimism as he actually felt. "Should be empty. We'll leave a fire-starter there, then head down to the cells."

"Good. I think." She didn't sound convinced, not that Ronon could blame her.

Despite his own misgivings, he was grateful when they reached the entrance to the building and, for the first time in hours, a place that was dry. The outer door gaped on a long hallway, lit by a handful of torches in wall sconces and the warm glimmer of light spilling through another open door right at its end. The guardroom was deserted as he'd hoped, cups of wine and plates with unfinished meals littering the refectory table that took up half the space in the room.

"Hungry?" asked Ronon, grinning.

"Not particularly."

"You sound nervous."

"I wonder why." She gave a lopsided smile. Then, "Let's hurry. I've got a bad feeling about this. As if something or someone is going to try and stop us."

He knew better than to question Teyla's instincts. They were always on the money, and of course there was that Wraith gene that seemed to allow her to sense stuff above and beyond telepathic contact.

It took them less than half an hour to place the rest of their oil packages. One they deposited in the guardroom itself. From there a second door led off into several large bunkrooms, and they hid the remaining four parcels in those after making sure that the quarters were as deserted as everywhere else. The bedding would provide excellent fuel.

"How long do you reckon?" said Ronon.

"Difficult to gage," she replied. "It's a lot warmer in here than it was back in the market square, so that should speed things up. I would guess about half an hour, but I can't be sure. The ones we planted in the city should go up soon, though."

"That's what I've been thinking." He hadn't forgotten her warning about the need for haste. The fact that the guards, who had been milling around in droves the previous night, were absent was an unforeseen gift. In Ronon's experience you were well advised to take advantage of those as quickly and as thoroughly as you could, because there was no guarantee that they wouldn't be snatched away again. "Let's do it," he murmured. "Weather's only getting worse."

"Excellent point." Teyla gave a brief smile, which was reassuring. He didn't like her being all tense and apprehensive. It was rare enough to be unsettling. "Have you thought about how you'll get Rodney out of that cage?" she asked.

"Yes. I can do it, though McKay won't be happy." An optimistic assessment, but Ronon chose not to share that minor point. He led Teyla through the guardroom and back into the corridor, which ended at an archway spanning a flight of stairs.

Unlit and narrow, the staircase seemed to lead directly to the bowels of the planet. A clammy draft streamed up from below, making the fine hairs on his arms stand on end. Worse than that, he heard footsteps.

"Crap," he whispered.

"Do you want to go back?"

"No. Probably seen us already." He guided her forward, keeping a firm hold on her arm to prevent her from tripping.

Halfway down, they met a couple of guards who came barging up the steps, breathing hard. Ronon grunted a greeting, hoping that they wouldn't recognize the tension in his body as they squeezed past. He needn't have worried. The guards barely acknowledged him and Teyla, rushing on up the stairwell, intent on their errand, whatever it was. Good luck to them.

"They were scared," Teyla offered softly.

Ronon decided against asking how she knew. This whole telepathy thing was making him feel distinctly nervous.

A couple of minutes later they reached the bottom of the stairs and another corridor. Last night he'd learned that this was one of the levels where prisoners were kept, and the implication had been that there were further floors like this; gloomy and dank and devoid of hope, their low-ceilinged hallways seamed by sturdy wooden doors and the cells they locked. Uncharacteristically hesitant, he ambled to a halt outside one of the open cell doors.

"What?" Teyla asked.

"Look, don't take this personally..." Oh damn, just spit it out, Dex! "You should stay here. You can't help me with McKay, and it'll be easier if I know you're someplace safe."

A brief flare of anger danced across her face—or perhaps it had merely been the flicker of a lone torch five meters down the hall. "That's the worst part of it," she murmured. "Believe it or not, I managed to train myself into forgetting it most of the time. But every now and again I come up against something that demonstrates to me how lacking I really am."

"You're not lacking," he said earnestly. "Your skills are different, is all. And we'll need them again, later."

She gave a soft laugh. "I'd never have pegged you for a diplomat, Ronon. To be honest, the idea is a little scary."

"I know." He nudged her into the cell, pulled the door shut and bolted it. "I'll be back as quickly as I can."

And he'd better keep that promise. If he didn't, he had just sealed Teyla's death warrant.

Shoving that thought aside, he started jogging down the corridor until he got to another staircase at the far end. This one spiraled up floor after floor, to the upper cell levels and eventually to the parapet from which McKay's cage was suspended. Ronon wouldn't have to go quite that far. The place he wanted was only two floors up. He sucked in a deep breath and bolted up the stairs, two steps at a time. The temperature was dropping as he climbed, proof that he was getting close.

Tonight there were no rubberneckers—all of them too busy quelling the riot at the gate—and the landing in front of the window was deserted. Carved three feet through solid rock, the sides of the casement glistened wet, and gusts of wind drove in the rain. He shuddered to think what it had to be like out there in the cage. But McKay wouldn't have to stay there much longer.

Ronon took off the cloak that was part of his stolen uniform, drew his sword, and began cutting the heavy fabric lengthwise into strips. Knotted together they'd give him a reasonably strong rope. From what he'd seen yesterday, he wouldn't need much more than six meters, which meant he would use about half the cloak and should have enough left over to provide McKay with some kind of cover. When he was done, he tied one end of the makeshift rope to a hook set high in the wall, secured the other end around his waist, and crawled out to the edge of the window.

Out of inky blackness, a stinging fist of rain smacked his face and ripped his breath away. He couldn't see a single thing—welcome to Teyla's world—and for long moments he worried that the rescue attempt would fail right here. Then, slowly but steadily, his eyes adjusted and he could make out the gray-in-gray outlines of the cage and the man slumped inside it. Slumped in a different position from yesterday, which was good news. At some point in the none-too-distant past McKay had still been able to move under his own steam. It wasn't saying much, and it might have changed by now, but every scrap of hope helped.

Pushed and pummeled by the relentless wind, the cage swayed nervously three meters beneath the lower edge of the window, and about two meters out from the rock face. It'd be a rough landing, and Ronon would have preferred to jump for a more stable target, but he doubted that things would improve anytime soon.

Balancing on the edge, he eased himself into a crouch, took aim one last time, and leaped. For what seemed like an eternity, he hung suspended, body stretched, hands reaching, then he slammed into the cage, sending it into a wild heave and swirl, and felt himself slip almost as soon as he'd made contact. Fingers locked around rain-slick metal bars he held on for dear life.

The cage gave a lurch that catapulted Rodney out of the corner he'd crawled into and slammed him into the bars on the opposite side. One of the cracks he heard was caused by the impact of ribs on metal, and if he'd been in any doubt, the murderous stab of pain that sent a white shower of sparks flitting through his vision would have clinched it. The other crack, quieter and subtly different, remained unidentifiable until the metal bars moved under his weight. In a panicked flash he realized that the latch of the cage door, corroded by the endless rain, must have snapped. Then he began sliding through the opening and out of the cage. Arms flailing, he clawed for a handhold, snatched a bar with one hand. The fingers of his other hand briefly brushed metal, lost their grip and clutched at thin air. The bar he was holding on to, slippery as a piece of soap—God, how long before he lost his grip there, too?—continued to move. The second he dropped free of the cage and into a sea of agony from his broken rib, it dawned on him that what he hung on to was the door of the cage. Somewhere in the back of his mind he also registered that the unnerving noise he was hearing had to be his own screams.

Then something else shouldered its way into his awareness. "Shut up! McKay! Shut up, damn you!"

The voice, grating and impatient, sounded familiar. For a moment he thought it was Ikaros, but the kid wouldn't have been able to come over quite so offensive. The voice was familiar in a different way. When he finally made the connection, the surprise rammed his screams right back into his throat.

He hiccupped. "Ronon?"

Oh please! Not him!

"I'm busy. If you value your continued existence, shut up!" Rodney hissed ferociously. Ikaros's astute observations were the last thing he needed now.

There was no comeback, so apparently the kid had gotten the message. You had to be grateful for small favors.

Blinking water from his eyes, Rodney peered into the darkness below, relieved when he found he couldn't see much further than his toes. By the same token, he knew only too well what the night and the rain were hiding. He'd stared at it for the past three days. As Ronon did whatever he was doing up top, the cage kept moving erratically, and Rodney could feel his fingers slide millimeter by millimeter. The bottom edge of the door was digging into his wrist, his chest was on fire, his hands and feet were numb with cold, and he could have sworn the ball of his shoulder was inexorably sliding from its socket. Another jerk of the cage swung the door wider and made him swivel a quarter of a turn.

"I'm sure whatever you're doing there is a lot of fun," he yelped, "but I'm slipping. So *stop* moving, for God's sake!"

"Just hang on," Ronon's voice came back, accompanied by another jolt.

Then it was a lurch and a jolt, and Rodney whimpered when he felt his grip loosen some more. "I *can't* hang on!"

"Yes, you can. Quit chatting and save your strength."

Strength? What strength?

He hadn't eaten in three days, and his last meal—if you could call it that—had found its way into the abyss. It was a miracle he was even conscious, and never mind metabolizing enough energy to hold on for as long as he already had. The cage began to list to the side where Rodney was dangling, so apparently Ronon had made his way over. Just as that thought took hold, a gust caught the door and drove it back toward the cage, jamming Rodney's wrist in a metal vise.

It's Charybdis! It doesn't—

"Shut up!" he hollered.

"Didn't say anything." The Satedan's voice sounded strained but reassuringly close now. "Listen to me. McKay? Are you listening?"

"Yes!" As if he had a choice! Talk about captive audience…

"Good. I want you to hold on real tight now. I've got to swing the door back out."

"Swing the— Are you insane?"

"I won't be able to reach you unless I'm inside the cage. I can't get inside the cage unless I open the damn door. In order to open the damn door, I have to swing it back. So hang tight!"

As soon as he had a moment, Rodney would get riled up about how Ronon had the nerve to talk to him as if to a retarded kindergartner. For now he scrunched his eyes shut, held his breath, and tried to compute the time it would take for his fingers to slip completely. The result was not encouraging. According to his calculations, he should have fallen already. The cage dipped some more, and the door moved. He gave a soft groan, almost wishing that he *would* fall, because then at least this nightmare would be over.

In response to this upbeat thought, the cage began to shudder and shift in a cadence of jerky movements that culminated in a thud and another major heave as Ronon propelled himself into the cage. It was the last straw. Gravity finally won out over virtually nonexistent friction, Rodney's grasp opened, and he screamed.

In the very same instant an iron fist clamped around his wrist.

"Oh no, you don't!" the Satedan growled through clenched teeth.

No longer having to concentrate on keeping his fingers clenched, Rodney finally managed to look up, for all the good it did him. Between the darkness and the rain stinging his eyes, all he could see was a dark shape lying prone on the bottom of the cage, his head and shoulders sticking through the door.

The shape's free arm extended as far as possible, and Ronon shouted, "Grab my hand!"

"I can't!" Rodney gasped and anticipated the inevitable reply. "I *really* can't. I've broken at least one rib."

It prompted a string of crudeness from above. Then Ronon grunted, "Okay. This'll be unpleasant."

Unpleasant? As opposed to the box of delights Rodney had been through so far?

His mental diatribe was cut off when Ronon's free hand closed around his forearm. Christ almighty, the man was proposing to haul him in hand over fist! And he'd not been lying—except *unpleasant* didn't begin to describe it. There was a brutal yank up. Simultaneously the vise grip around Rodney's wrist released, only to reappear a second later, clamped around his upper arm, by which time he felt that his shoulder would give for sure.

"Help me!" Ronon snarled, strain flattening his voice.

Gritting his teeth, Rodney lifted his free arm and was just about able to reach the bar beside the opening. If he stretched a little farther... His ribcage howled in protest, but suddenly his fingers found purchase, and he held on and pulled for what he was worth. Not overly much, if Ronon's continued growling was anything to go by. Another yank, a fist clutched a handful of shirt at the back of Rodney's neck, and then Ronon started hauling for real.

Kicking and swearing, Rodney slid into the cage, convinced that his broken rib had shifted. Then the obvious struck him. "Now what?"

"You're welcome." Still panting hard, Ronon climbed to his feet, grabbed the crossbar above the door opening, and pulled himself up onto the top of the cage like a gymnast. Once up there, he lay back down on his stomach. "Grab my hands."

As if once hadn't been enough... Rodney suppressed a sigh

and raised his arms, wincing.

"The other way round!" hissed Ronon. "You want me to break your back? Face me!"

Good point. Rodney hated when other people had those. He also hated the notion of having to back right into the door—far too reminiscent of high diving, *high* being the operative word and it made him crane his neck and look down against his better judgment.

"Hurry up!" the Satedan snapped.

Rodney resigned himself and turned, closing his eyes again, partly in expectation of what would happen in his chest once his feet left the ground. Seconds later he noted that his expectation had fallen way short of the actual event. By the time Ronon pulled him up onto the top of the cage, he seriously considered passing out. What stopped him was the fact that their combined weight had put the cage into a steep list. He felt himself sliding again, more rapidly than ever before, and scrambled for a handhold. At last, as though gravity had been thinking about it and made up its mind, his slide slowed to a halt, but Rodney couldn't shake the feeling that it'd start all over again if he so much as took a breath or batted an eyelid. Consequently, for the time being he decided to do neither.

It was enough that Ronon kept dancing around next to him, though whatever kept the Satedan upright on those slick bars had to be nothing short of a miracle—or a prehensile tail, which actually would explain a great many things. One arm hooked around the chain that held the cage, Ronon freed the end of a rope he must have tied to the chain upon his arrival. Then he reached out to Rodney and said, "Stand up."

"What?"

"Stop fretting. I'll hold you."

Yeah. Question was who'd be holding Ronon…

No viable alternative looked to be forthcoming, so Rodney did as he was told. The bars offered as much traction as black ice, his feet were slipping constantly, and he wouldn't have been able to stand if Ronon hadn't steadied him. At last and with all the desperation of a drowning man grabbing a lifebelt, he clutched the chain with both hands and hung on grimly while Ronon slung the end of the rope under his arms and fastened it across Rodney's chest. The rest of the rope spanned the gap between the cage and rock wall and disappeared into a narrow window above, apparently hooked to something inside the fortress.

"Okay," Ronon said. "You're perfectly safe. Now all you've got to do is stand there, hang on to that chain, and take my weight."

"Take your—"

"Not for long. It'll be fine."

With that Ronon grabbed the rope, which, on closer inspection, revealed itself to be a somewhat less than trust-inspiring affair knotted together from strips of cloth. Christ! The old *Let's escape from prison by tying together the bed sheets* trick… Rodney would have groaned, but at that moment the Satedan swung himself free, and a sharp pull squeezed the air from his lungs and served as another reminder that he was probably developing a pneumothorax this very minute.

The rope sagged under Ronon's considerable weight, and for a few moments the Satedan disappeared below the top of the cage. Then, hand over hand, he pulled himself up toward the window. Prehensile tail… In real terms it took less than two minutes of undiluted hell for him to get there, but to Rodney it seemed like a breathless, agony-riddled eternity. When Ronon reached the casement, hauled himself in, and took the tension off the rope, Rodney almost wept with gratitude.

Almost. What stopped him was the inevitable question: How on Earth was he going to get over there? His idea of upper body strength confined itself more or less exclusively to the cerebral. Then he reminded himself that he was harnessed to the end of the rope, for want of a more accurate word, which meant that—

"Let go!" Ronon hissed from above.

"What?"

"Let go of the chain!" This time it was accompanied by a sharp tug.

Oh no, no, no, no. No way was he—

Just do it! How else are we going to get out of here?

His fists unclenched, obeying a volition other than Rodney's own. For a split-second he stood precariously balanced on two bars, then a violent gust shoved the cage sideways and catapulted him into the air. As he fell, he could hear himself scream over the howling of the wind, then, with a brutal yank, he dropped into the harness and found himself swinging toward the rock face. There was no time to bring up his legs for a buffer, and he slammed sideways into unforgiving stone. It felt as though the left half of his body had been pulverized, and Rodney hung there staring into the darkness and trying to concentrate on catching his breath.

The next jolt, considerably gentler, dragged him upward by about two feet. It was followed by another, and another, and he slowly but steadily came level with the top of the cage again, then rose above it. His life was measured in jolts now, he thought dizzily, a whole new unit all of his own, designed to accurately assess sheer panic. Between the cold and the rope strangling his circulation, he could barely feel his arms anymore, which probably was a good thing.

Jolt by jolt the dim halo of light spreading from the window was getting closer and more intense. Now he was almost within reach of the casement. And the rope looked as if it was fraying. Just his kind of luck. Salvation in his sights and—

Ronon reached down, grabbed Rodney's shirt again and heaved him into the casement. For several minutes they both lay there, panting as though they'd run a marathon, then the Satedan pushed himself to his knees.

"Come on," he gasped, trying to flip Rodney on his back. "We've got to—" He'd succeeded, and his eyes had gone wide as saucers. "Holy crap! No wonder you were a lot lighter than I expected. How old are you?"

"What do you mean, 'a lot lighter'? I'll have you know, I—"

"How old?" Not content with obviously having retained his real age, the man had the audacity to smirk.

"Sixteen, at a guess," Rodney snarled, feeling himself blush. "You can stop grinning. It's not like I asked for this. Anyone who tells you they want to be sixteen again because it was the best time of their lives is lying through their teeth."

"Oh, I dunno…" The smirk widened. "I had a pretty good time…"

"I'm surprised you can remember this far back."

"Of course I didn't have boils in my face…"

"Zits! They're called zits!" Rodney hissed savagely. "And you're wondering why the Wraith decimated your home planet!"

"Not really. They're Wraith. It's what they do. Come on." Ronon dragged Rodney from the casement and into a gloomy hallway, where he tried to untie the harness without much success. Between the rain and the pressure applied to them, the knots might as well have been welded tight. Giving a shrug, the Satedan picked up his sword. "Don't move."

"This may be difficult to believe, but moving is the last thing on my mind." Rodney scrunched his eyes shut just to protect his nerves. "I was thinking of a nice warm bed in which I can precisely *not* move and— ah!" He could feel the tip of the sword working under the rope, dangerously close to his left nipple, and struggled not to flinch. "Just… watch it, okay?"

The rope snapped with a soft pop. "You can open your eyes now," Ronon said and handed him a largish piece of fabric that looked like it might have provided the raw material for the rope. "Put his around you and over your head."

The cloak—at least Rodney assumed that's what it had been before Ronon went to town on it—was heavy and stank of sweat and unwashed soldier, but it was only moderately wet, and it was warm. Grateful, Rodney wrapped himself in it and peered at Ronon. "So how are you going to get us out of here?" The moment he asked the question, something else occurred to him. "And where are the others?"

"Teyla's waiting for us downstairs. As for Colonel Sheppard, well, we're hoping you can help us find him. It's kinda urgent, so let's go."

CHAPTER 22

Charybdis -223

"How long do you plan on just sitting here?"
Elizabeth sounded impatient, and John could relate. Still shaken by Star's death and by the slaughter they'd unwittingly caused when the vortex had lunged into the mass of people here, they'd emerged from the gate to find themselves in the middle of a scene that looked deceptively like the one they'd just left. The cast was bigger, though. Much, much bigger, and by the looks of it these good folks had rather more advanced technology at their disposal than the alternate Zelenka's mob. Which might pose a problem if they decided to take a step back and think. Right now they were attacking the jumper with bare fists and sticks, driven by a volatile mix of rage and grief.

"John?"

"We'll stay put and play possum for now. If we try to fly out, we might hurt more people, and there's no guarantee that they won't come after us with real weapons."

"You're right." Sighing, she settled back into the seat. "What do you think they're doing here in the first place?" she asked suddenly.

"Best guess?" He nodded up toward the sky that stretched red and riotous above the frantic mass of bodies outside the jumper. Somehow John didn't think that this was the usual state of atmospheric affairs on this planet—yet another version of Lantea, likely as not. "I'd say they're having some major natural disaster."

"Evacuees?"

"Yeah. Look at the gear they've got on them. Tents back there. Cooking fires. I mean, it could be some kind of citywide jamboree, but somehow I doubt it…"

It was a fact. Many seemed to have brought only the clothes

on their backs, and they looked disheveled and dirty, as if they'd barely escaped with their lives from whatever had happened here. Others, who appeared to have had a little more advance warning, had brought vehicles—ground gliders, from what John could see—piled high with possessions ranging from bedding and cookware to ancestral portraits. So far, and discounting the righteous fury being vented on the jumper, either personal discipline or the authorities around here seemed to have been able to uphold the law, since there were no signs of looting.

"What do you think happened?" Elizabeth sounded tired, making conversation merely to stay awake—or to keep him awake, which probably wasn't a bad idea at all.

He shrugged. "Your guess is as good as mine. Flood, volcanic eruption, storms; hell, war, for all I know. Maybe they've got some kind of weapon that will do this to—"

For the first few seconds he thought his concussion had finally gotten the better of him. Trees, tents, rocks, everything around them began a slow-motion dance, swaying and heaving. Piles of belongings tilted lazily, as if deliberating whether to topple or not, some spilling to the ground, others somehow managing to find the rhythm of that odd motion and staying upright. A low, rolling noise filled the air, reverberated through the jumper, and seeped into his very bones, stirring up the marrow a bit.

Only when the people outside quit their concerted attack on the jumper and froze in their tracks, thunderstruck, wide-eyed, shouts stuck in their throats, John grasped that the phenomenon wasn't some kind of weird delusion. The shaking didn't stop, and suddenly, as if alerted by some silent signal, the crowd began to part, slowly at first but accelerating rapidly, like a wave rolling in to shore. Kicking and flailing, they shoved and jostled and scrambled over each other, trying to get away from whatever was coming. They weren't quite fast enough.

Weaving like a snake, the crack raced toward them at breathtaking speed, ripping the earth, widening into a maw as it went and swallowing everything and everybody that didn't get out of its way—goods, people, a ground glider that had been nosing its way through the crowd and now toppled sideways into the rift, its driver and passenger hanging on desperately.

"Oh my God!" Elizabeth gasped. "John, the gate!"

He'd realized the second she said it, felt fingers of ice running up his spine, hated the sense of utter helplessness. The fault was heading directly for the Stargate, and all they could do was sit there and watch. If they lost the gate, they more than likely lost any chance they'd ever had of making it back to their Atlantis. Then, as abruptly as it had begun to open, the fault stopped within scant feet of reaching the Stargate, leaving an eerie calm in its wake.

Time seemed to stand still, and the only thing moving was the dust that rose in silent coils above the chasm. Then, slowly and inexorably, the wails started and gradually built into a concert of misery. First it was the survivors crammed along the edges of the fissure, then there came other, fainter screams drifting up from below.

"John..." whispered Elizabeth.

"I know." The life-signs detector showed upwards of thirty people trapped in the abyss. And those were only the ones who had survived the fall. Even as John was staring at the detector's small screen, several of the bright blips winked out. "Crap," he muttered. "Hang on!"

The chasm was easily wide enough to fly a jumper in, and John did just that. Pulling up steeply, he turned into a loop, and then forced the nose of the little ship almost straight down, heading for the bottom. Within seconds he realized that he wouldn't get there. The further he descended the closer the walls grew, a gloomy prison of soil and rock—and remnants of a long-buried structure.

"Atlantis," stated Elizabeth.

"Yeah."

It no longer came as a surprise and merely confirmed his earlier assumption that they'd come straight back to an other-timely version of the planet they knew.

At just over sixty meters down he was beginning to run out of space to maneuver in and slowed the jumper to a virtual stop. Hovering, he rechecked the life-signs detector. There should be two victims just ahead. Several others showed below his current position, and his throat tightened at the sight. There might be time to pick up ropes and helpers crazy enough to abseil from the jumper, but right now it made more sense to try and rescue those people who were lucky enough to be within easy reach. In the long run more lives would be saved that way.

"Get ready to open the hatch," he said to Elizabeth, who gave a sharp nod and hurried aft.

Squinting into the gloom, John eased the jumper forward. He didn't spot the victims until he was almost on top of them. Caked in dirt and unmoving, they could have been part of the earth, and it was impossible to tell whether they were male or female, though one of them definitely was a child. They lay slumped on a narrow ledge, with nothing beneath them but darkness.

And then there was movement; a pair of eyes snapped open, seemingly staring straight at him with a mixture of hope and terror. He swiveled the jumper around until it hovered at a right angle to the wall, with mere inches to spare at bow and stern, and carefully backed up until he nudged the rock just below the ledge.

"Now!" Peering over his shoulder, he watched as Elizabeth opened the rear hatch, admitting a small avalanche of dirt, torn-off roots, and pebbles into the jumper. "You need a hand?"

"No!" She didn't look back, but there was a smile in her voice. "I think we'll be fine."

The rescuees were mother and child, and they'd gotten lucky. When the ground had opened beneath them, they'd slipped rather than fallen, bouncing from ledge to ledge and root to root until that outcrop had finally stopped their slide. Between them they had all of two broken bones; all other damage—a comprehensive assortment of scrapes and bruises and plain shock—was relatively minor. John and Elizabeth plucked twelve more people off the fault walls, all in similar condition; the worst injury being what looked like a skull fracture. It made John wince in sympathy.

Some forty meters east and a little further down from their current position—it was going to be a very snug fit—the ground glider John had watched drop into the chasm was wedged between the walls. According to the life-signs detector both people aboard were still alive, and they were going to be the last victims he'd be able to pick up on this run. The approach was tricky, but he just about managed to ease the jumper into line with the bow of the glider.

From what he'd seen before maneuvering into place, the glider's windshield was broken, and the pilot lay slumped over the dashboard, bleeding from a head wound. The passenger was curled up in the foot well, and John thought he'd seen a twitch of movement—though, admittedly, it might have been a reflection. Neither of them looked as though they'd be able to make it over into the jumper under their own steam.

He was about to go aft and help Elizabeth when the alarms went off. She'd opened the hatch, and practically at the same moment an air quality warning flashed up on the viewport display, quickly changing from amber to red; the carbon monoxide levels were high and climbing. In a minute they'd be off the scale altogether. Simultaneously the life-signs further down in the fault were winking out in rapid succession. Each dying light felt like a personal blow to John, but there was no time to indulge his sense of failure. They had to get out of here.

"Hurry up!" he yelled, stumbling into the rear of the jumper.

His passengers still were too shell-shocked to respond to the situation, and Elizabeth was struggling on her own to pull the first of the glider victims—the pilot—into the jumper.

"Hey! You!" John hollered at a man who was staring holes into the floor.

The guy's head came up, and he gave John a dull glance as if to say *Who? Me?*

Might as well assume he'd said it. "Yes, you! Come and lend a hand, will you?"

For a moment the man continued to stare uncomprehendingly, then a shudder went through him and he blinked and rose and joined John. Together they first relieved Elizabeth of the pilot, whom they left in the care of a couple of other rescuees, then they started hauling the last victim aboard—the passenger. He was as hopelessly mud-caked as everybody else and out cold, and despite his slight build he felt heavy as sin. Dragging him free of the foot well, across the hood of the glider, and into Jumper One seemed to take ages, and John no longer needed a display to tell him that the air quality had reached an all-time low.

Every breath tasted of metal, and the more air he tried to suck in the less oxygen reached his lungs. Rainbow-colored stars sparked before his eyes, his headache had assumed a whole new dimension of intolerable, and he was feeling dizzy—not really advisable when trying to pilot an aircraft. The air scrubbers were working overtime, but the carbon monoxide, pushed up from somewhere below and filling the fault, could freely flood the jumper as long as the hatch was open. Without the scrubbers, they'd already be unconscious and dying, and John knew it.

As soon as they were safely aboard, Elizabeth slapped the hatch controls, and the door slipped shut with a pneumatic hiss. Then she came staggering toward him, blue-lipped with cyanosis. John barely caught her before she fell, half carried her back to the cockpit, and dropped into the right-hand seat. Her hands were shaking, and she was breathing in rapid, shallow gasps. "I'm good," she panted. "I'm good."

"Easy," he said, startled at the rough sound of his own voice. "It'll get better in a second, and you don't want to hyperventilate."

Wrestling down the instinct to yank at the controls and race to the surface—a recipe for disaster, given the state he was in—he coaxed the jumper into a gentle climb. After a couple of minutes he felt a little less lightheaded, his vision cleared, and the relentless hammering in his skull let up by a notch or two. In the rear, the frantic yelps for air simmered down and gave way to whispers of conversation and soft moaning from the injured.

"We'll have to be more careful when we go back down," Elisabeth murmured.

"We won't. Go back down, I mean."

"But—"

Wordlessly, John pointed at the life-signs detector that rested on the center console. Its screen was completely dark now. Elizabeth turned a shade paler and closed her eyes.

At last the edge of the chasm crawled into view, and John felt more grateful than he'd ever expected to be at the sight of a sickening red sky. There was no risk of injuring anyone now; scared of the fault ripping open even further, the majority of people had peeled well back from the edges of the abyss. Their mood had changed completely, bowing to the contingencies forced upon them by this new disaster. They had established cordons of men who held back anyone curious or crazy enough to try and sneak a peek into the rift. In the cleared area between the crowd and the edges of the fault they'd improvised first aid stations to take care of those victims who'd landed within reach of the surface and had been recovered from there.

John brought the jumper alongside the largest of the first aid posts. The men and women manning it, presumably physicians and nurses who'd been among the evacuees—*Is there a doctor aboard?*—stopped what they were doing and backed up a few steps when the hatch opened. Then the first of the walking wounded staggered from the jumper, supporting each other, and the medical staff relaxed visibly. A few daring souls watching from behind the cordon broke into cheers that spread through the crowd and proliferated into a round of applause. It definitely beat the earlier scenario.

By the looks of it, the medics had performed way more than their fair share of triage lately. They went about their job quietly and efficiently, and though it seemed unlikely that they'd even met each other before today, they fell into the odd choreography of emergency treatment with practiced ease. Within minutes of the jumper's arrival every person who had been aboard was receiving medical care.

Elizabeth had helped offload a couple of the wounded and disappeared to talk to whomever, which was fine by John. Let her handle the meet-and-greet for once; diplomacy was her job, after all. Blowing out a long breath, he leaned back in the pilot's seat and tried to relax and somehow bring his headache under control. Failing that, he'd at least have a few minutes in which to groan without anyone listening while he tried to figure out where to go from here. They'd have to start asking round and see if anyone knew a Dr. Radek Zelenka. At least there was no shortage of people to ask, and now they had a goodwill—

Okay, half a minute. He heard the footfalls first.

"John!"

He levered his eyes open and awkwardly turned to see Elizabeth heading up the ramp. "Yeah?"

"I've talked to one of the doctors here. She's agreed to check you out."

"I'm fine," he growled. "We don't have time to—"

"We don't have time not to." She had that ornery look that she usually only wore in her office. "You're the only one who can fly this jumper, so consider it an order, Colonel."

"Yes, ma'am." He supposed he could have argued, but it would have taken too much energy. Instead he managed to inject his reply with a degree of reluctance that left no doubt as to his real feelings. Unfortunately she knew him too well to even acknowledge it, so he'd just have to get up and play along, wouldn't he? Suppressing the last of those groans, he pushed himself from the seat and attempted a jaunty stroll to the rear of the jumper. Apparently the act fell a little short of being convincing.

"Fine, my a... foot." Elizabeth marched him down the ramp like a prisoner.

They headed for a hastily erected tent behind the actual triage area. If you could call it a tent. Basically it was four posts in the ground, holding up a tarp that in turn sheltered a handful of pallets, all of which were occupied. Among the patients here were the last two people they'd rescued. The woman who'd piloted the glider was still unconscious, but her passenger seemed to be fighting fit again, though still not much cleaner than when they'd pulled him from the foot well.

A guy after John's own heart, he was swatting away the ministrations of a nurse. "I don't care! I need to see the person who was flying the jumper!"

"The *what*?" asked the nurse, her face a picture of confusion.

Gateship she probably would have understood, John thought wryly and sent a silent apology to Lieutenant Ford, wherever he might be. He grinned. For starters this was a break he hadn't dared to hope for, and his and Elizabeth's job had just become considerably easier. That aside, it might get him out of being prodded by alien doctors, however qualified.

"The jumper," John said, smiling at the nurse. "The ship out there. Dr. Zelenka, I presume?"

Radek twisted around. "Colonel Sheppard!" Then his eyes grew even wider. "Dr. Weir! Thank God, I've found you!"

There probably was very little real benefit in debating the issue of who had found whom. John let it slide. "Good to see you too. You haven't… uh… founded a cult by any chance?"

"A *cult?*" Zelenka's expression mirrored that of the nurse a few seconds earlier. He seemed older, a good twenty years, if the lines in his face were anything to go by. And his hair was shorter, though he still managed to sustain that unkempt look. Otherwise, and discounting copious amounts of dirt, he looked himself, no wavy beard, no fanatical gleam in his eye, most of all no indication of protracted drug use.

"Give over, John." Elizabeth stepped beside him, and she, too, was smiling with relief. "Hello, Radek. We need to talk."

Charybdis -908

"Move, move, move!" Ronon felt a little like a cow herder, except the current situation wasn't exactly bucolic.

A hand wrapped around one arm of either, he had Teyla to his right, McKay to his left, and was bullying them up the stairs toward the guardroom at a run. Teyla wasn't the problem—she could have gone twice as fast, Ronon suspected—McKay was. Now that the adrenaline and the first buzz of the escape had worn off, the guy was seriously flagging. And, much to his dismay, Ronon couldn't even blame him; after three days in that cage, with hardly any sleep, no food, and plenty of exposure, it was a miracle Rodney was even conscious, and never mind his running a stair-a-thon. In consequence, Ronon considered himself honor-bound to bully as subtly as he knew how.

Of course, *subtly* didn't really work with McKay, who ground to a dead halt, sniffed the air, and yelped, "What is that?"

"Smoke," Teyla said pleasantly.

"They probably haven't made this discovery on Athos yet, but on Earth we've known for quite a while that where there's smoke, there's fire. Common sense suggests to run *away* from fire, not *toward* it."

"We're running *past* it," Ronon snapped, nipping the debate in the bud. "It's the only way out, so keep going."

Without waiting for the comeback, he yanked McKay another couple of steps up. McKay did have a point, of course, but there was little Ronon could do about it, except hope that the fire hadn't spread into the hallway—though, given the pace they were going at, chances were that the entire fortress would have burned down by the time they made it up there.

And he really, *really* shouldn't have thought that!

The smoke was getting thicker by the second, and if it was this bad down here, he didn't really want to imagine what the hallway would be like. The good news was that they were all still drenched from the downpour, which might just save them now. He ran faster, forcing Rodney to keep pace with him.

"It worked," Teyla whispered.

"Too well," he grunted back.

"What worked?" gasped McKay.

"Stop wasting your breath and run."

Finally they stumbled out into the hallway by the guardroom and into a wall of smoke. Black and all but impenetrable, it seemed to fill the corridor like a living thing, breathing malevolence. He pulled the collar of his shirt over his face and made sure that the others had similar makeshift masks—not that they'd be much good in the long run.

Then again, all they had to do was make it to the door, wasn't it?

Eyes streaming, Ronon squinted into the roiling smoke and realized that this might be taller order than he'd anticipated. From somewhere to his right came the whip-crack roar of flames, and he figured that they had to be near the guardroom door, meaning that they needed to carry straight on. That theory was refuted when he took two steps forward and hit a wall. For a second or two, blind panic constricted his throat, and it was all he could do not to start flailing and screaming like a madman. Then a hand caught his wrist and held on tight.

"It requires some practice," Teyla croaked, a hint of amusement coloring her smoke-roughened voice. "I've got Rodney, too. Come with me."

As soon as she started tugging him along, Ronon's disorientation increased. It wasn't the direction he would have taken, about ninety degrees to his intended course and followed in short order by a sharp right turn. Attempting to draw a mental map, he arrived at the conclusion that they inadvertently must have ended up in the guardroom itself and shuddered despite the stifling heat. If it weren't for Teyla, he might have killed them all.

Trying not to breathe and scrunching his eyes shut against the biting smoke, Ronon staggered along. Within minutes he tripped down a couple of steps into a sudden onslaught of cold air and driving rain, and he silently vowed never to complain about the local weather again.

They stumbled away from the building, coughing and choking and turning their faces up into the downpour to let it rinse off soot and grime. Behind them a series of window panes exploded in the heat, peppering them with shards and sending flames streaming into the night like banners. Across the courtyard people who'd run from other wings of the fortress were milling around in confusion, shouting for guards, servants, anyone they deemed qualified to fight the blaze. Someone spotted the bedraggled threesome fleeing the guard wing and pointed excitedly.

Several men broke from the group, led by a short, elderly guy whose pinched looks reminded Ronon of a prune. His robes—a pompous affair of silk and fur hardly suited to the weather—trailed in the ever rising lake that flooded the courtyard and forced him into a forward list as if he were fighting not to be yanked back by them.

"Oh no…" McKay seemed to contemplate an immediate return to the burning guard wing.

"What?" hissed Ronon.

"I know that guy. Worse, he knows me. He presided at my trial, so-called. I have to—"

"Stay put!" Ronon flung an arm around teenage Rodney's scrawny shoulder and pulled him close. With his other hand, he grabbed Teyla's arm. Happy families. "Let me pass!" he roared, breaking into a run, straight toward the overdressed prune, and doing his best to look as wild-eyed as the rest of the gathering in the courtyard. "My wife and son! I need to get them to safety!"

For a moment the man just gaped at them. When it finally sunk in that Ronon wasn't about to change course, he jumped back a couple of steps, bony hands helplessly waving in the air as if to flag up his outrage. "Your wife and son? Why did you bring them?" he asked incongruously, perhaps in an attempt to reestablish some kind of authority. "Women and children are not allowed here!"

A fountain of laughter bubbled up his throat, nearly choking Ronon, but instead of giving in to it, he grabbed his charges tighter and charged past the man and toward the archway and the portcullis.

"Stop them!" the prune squealed at no one in particular. His shrieks caused a brief stir among the other bureaucrats in the courtyard; then they seemed to decide that the fire in the fortress was a more immediate concern and ignored their colleague.

Ronon had the portcullis in his sights, those squeaked-out orders were sliding off his back together with the rain, and for a precious second or two he felt something akin to relief. The rumble of bootfalls echoing from the archway convinced him of the error of his ways. A detachment of guards came thundering into the courtyard and gave McKay's friend a second wind.

"Apprehend these people!" the guy shouted again, this time with considerably more authority. Apparently he had regained his composure.

"You're hurting me!" Teyla hissed softly, and Ronon realized that he was clenching his fists in an effort not to succumb to instinct and freeze.

He let go of both her and McKay, wanting his hands free to be able to draw his sword. Whatever else happened, Ronon Dex wasn't going to go down without a fight. Besides, from what he'd seen of the soldiers here, he probably had a better-than-average chance of taking out the entire detachment single-handedly. He hoped. And—

The guards galloped past him, Teyla, and McKay as though they'd never heard the prune's order. And maybe they hadn't. As they passed, Ronon could all but smell their fear. Something had happened, and he had a pretty good idea of—

"Sirs!" the leader of the detachment yelled. "They've broken down the gate. The city gate has fallen!"

Yep.

The timing couldn't have been better. A furtive glance over his shoulder told Ronon that even the prune had forgotten they so much as existed. He bustled his charges into the shadows beneath the archway and through to the portcullis. The sole guard, Teyla's friend, was still on duty, but Ronon was in no mood to enter into negotiations over why he was bringing his 'captive' back out again, together with an escaped prisoner. Without so much as waiting for the surprised man to open his mouth, he landed a solid right hook on the tip of the guard's chin, knocking him out cold.

"That felt good!" Grunting happily, Ronon watched as the guard crumpled into an ungainly heap at his feet. "Been meaning to do that since I first met the guy."

"Glad to see those charm school classes are finally paying off," muttered McKay.

"If you can talk, you can run. Let's go!" Ronon grabbed Teyla's arm again and began guiding her down the lane at a brisk jog.

Here and there the rain-laden darkness above the rooftops had turned an ugly, pumping red; burning houses where he and Teyla had left their fire-starters. The noise was obvious now, or maybe he just hadn't been paying attention while they were still inside the fortress—screams of panic as people tried to get away from or extinguish the fires in the heart of the city and, from the direction of the gate, shouts and the metal-clad sounds of fighting.

Ronon winced at the thought of them having to push their way toward the gate against the onrush of an angry mob, but you didn't look a gift horse in the mouth. Besides—

"What in God's name have you started here?" McKay panted from behind, more than a little apprehension in his voice. "A palace revolution?"

"We didn't start it. Much."

The shouts were getting louder and below, where the lane joined the city's main thoroughfare, the speckled glitter of torches swung around the corner and surged up the road like a swarm of pissed-off fireflies. And the torches kept coming, a rising tide of lights and noise, sweeping their way. Ronon tried to weigh the risk of being spotted and potentially killed against his increasing sense of urgency when it came to stopping Charybdis. It was no contest, really. Death would delay them indefinitely.

A little further down the road gaped a dark alleyway, once closed off from the lane by a wooden gate that had half torn from its hinges and now creaked and clattered in the storm. He ducked in, pulling the others after him, and wedged the gate shut behind them.

The alley was cramped with items discarded from the houses on either side, heaps of trash harboring things that squealed and swished and scurried through the darkness. They stank, too. Or maybe that was the garbage. Ronon found he no longer cared. Somehow this unplanned stop and the semblance of safety provided by the rickety gate had shaken loose a mountain of fatigue, piled up since he forgot when—when, if ever, had he last slept?—and now hurtling down on him in an avalanche of exhaustion. All he wanted to do was obey that overwhelming urge to sit and rest, slide down the gate and slump into a puddle, heedless of the wet and cold. A pair of shivering shadows, McKay and Teyla had already done just that, finding a wall and an old crate respectively to lean against.

Out in the street the clanging of weapons and the shouts from throats roared hoarse closed in and wrapped him in a blanket of threat.

"Kill them!"

"Drive out the Ancients!"

"Torch the city!"

"Kill them all!"

Torchlight leaped through between the rickety planks of the gate, streaked unsteadily over his companions' faces—McKay's lips were moving; he seemed to be caught up in a spirited discussion with himself—and chased rodents back to their burrows amid squeaks of outrage. The throng outside, filling the street to bursting point, pushed and bumped against the gate again and again. Sooner or later the tired wood and metal would give. So much for safety.

"We can't stay here," Ronon whispered. Ignoring their mutters of protest, he pulled Teyla and McKay to their feet again, flinched when one of them, in rising, knocked over a stack of garbage that came clattering around their feet. "Quiet!"

For a couple of seconds they all froze, but the stampede outside the gate continued unchanged. If anyone had heard the noise, they probably were too busy to investigate. More likely, though, the mob was deafened by its own racket. For now.

He guided Teyla's hand to grab an end of Rodney's shirt and pulled a reluctant McKay in behind himself. "Make sure he keeps moving!" he snapped at Teyla.

Then he set off at a staggering run, dodging trash and rodents tumbling in his path, barely daring to hope that this wouldn't be a dead end.

It wasn't.

Closed off by a similarly wonky affair as the gate they'd encountered first, the far end was a mere two hundred yards or so down the alley, and it led out onto an apparently deserted side street, so quiet you'd think this was a night like any other. Ronon held back on a sigh of relief until he'd checked and double-checked and found this first impression confirmed.

"Have you given any thought to where we go from here?" Teyla demanded.

He swallowed a sharp reply. She was right. She was right… He'd been thinking like a runner, as always, tackling each problem as it came along because all that mattered was surviving this second right now; only when you'd managed that you could start worrying about the next and the one after that and so on. Teyla was thinking like a leader of people, as always, wanting the larger picture to determine means of long-term survival.

"We get out of the city, try to cross the river, and head for the Stargate," he said at last.

"And what then, Ronon?" she asked. "What then?"

"We—" He cut himself off, suddenly seeing what she was driving at. They had no DNA sample to guide them to another original, and unless McKay could figure out a way of making the Stargate work regardless... "We're stuck," he croaked.

Charybdis -223

"In other words, we're stuck." John Sheppard short-circuited the debate among the scientists by jumping to the inevitable conclusion. "We're stuck," he repeated with a finality that made Elizabeth shiver.

The faces around her settled into varying permutations of glum, and she very much doubted that hers looked any more cheerful. The woman who'd been with Radek and flown the glider sagged a little further into herself and absently stroked a bandage that covered a deep cut on her forehead. Two younger men who at some point had materialized from the crowd—apparently they'd been trying to get a colleague to the hospital earlier in the day—glanced at each other and, by mutual consent, seemed to suppress a shrug or sigh.

Once all the injured had been seen to and the physicians relinquished their claim, Radek and his friend, Selena, had requisitioned one of the triage tents. Together they'd moved it a good ways up the slope and improvised a field lab from six folding chairs, several laptops donated by concerned citizens, and a bagful of data crystals, which the two latecomers had volunteered to retrieve from the wrecked glider. It wasn't much to look at, but, as Radek had pointed out repeatedly, the processing power, while not exactly up to the standards they were used to from Atlantis, beat anything Earth could have rustled up at short notice. Elizabeth figured he was trying to reassure himself with the assertion.

Because, so far, the superior processing power had failed to get him or anybody else anywhere.

"I wouldn't exactly call it *stuck*," Selena retorted, sounding more than a little miffed. "It's not like this is some primitive planet. Radek is quite happy here, aren't you?"

"Of course I am."

The confirmation seemed to come as a relief to Selena, and Elizabeth began to suspect that Selena and Radek might be a little more than just colleagues. And why not? He'd been stranded here for decades. Compared to that she herself had been lucky. The vagaries of temporal flux that had arisen in the wake of Charybdis had exiled her for a mere four years. She shuddered.

"See?" said Selena, satisfied. "This may not be your home, but it isn't a bad place. And staying here doesn't mean you'll have to give up all hope. Who knows? You may spend less time here than you think, because, naturally, we'll continue our research into the failure of the Stargate system."

"When?" John hurled the question at her as if it were a missile. "In the next, oh, three days? Have you taken a look outside lately? The entropy created by Charybdis is wrecking this galaxy one planet at a time, and guess what? This one's next in line."

"We only have your word for it that it's entropy or that it's even caused by this… Charybdis," Selena shot back. "And, by your own admission, you got it from some old hag who brews herbal teas for a living. Very sound scientific method, I must say."

"Selena!" Radek interceded. "You mustn't underestimate…"

It was the third time within the past two hours that the debate had arrived at this juncture, and Elizabeth didn't think she could take yet another rerun without starting to scream or throw things. She tuned out the voices and quietly slipped from the tent into what should have been dusk over this version of Atlantis.

Except, you couldn't tell unless you had a watch and knew

the time of day. The sky remained unchanged... No, that wasn't true, was it? The sky still was the same stomach-churning stew of reds, but, if anything, it had gotten worse, shot through with cankers of black, menacing and malignant, that belched great forks of heat lightning. A hot, violent wind had risen, chasing leaves, torn-off twigs, and small debris up the mountain before it. She squinted against the dust it whipped into her eyes, thinking that, maybe, the gale at least was a good thing. It might just help disperse the carbon monoxide that had pooled in and around the rift in the earth.

The area was deserted now. As soon as the doctors had confirmed what had killed most of the people trapped in the chasm, a ragtag crew of police, firefighters, and soldiers, together with select volunteers, had cleared a wide strip of ground either side of the fault and declared it off-limits until further notice. Tamed by terror, the crowd had complied with the kind of listless docility she recalled seeing in the refugees from every war or disaster zone she'd ever visited. It was as if, after losing wherever they called home, any further evacuation merely served to numb them a little bit more, make them a little bit more indifferent to whatever misery would befall them next.

They'd struck their camps, inasmuch as they'd had them, or else simply shouldered their belongings and trudged uphill to where they were supposedly safe and settled again. The mountainside was dotted with their campfires, small and struggling to survive in the wind, vanes of smoke slanted sharply. Elizabeth fancied she could feel their stares on her, some hostile, most expectant, hoping that, somehow, the strangers would work a miracle, open the Stargate, and lead them all to salvation. Part of her wanted to yell at them to stop staring and accept the inevitable.

Just as she had to accept it.

She had failed. John Sheppard, for once, had failed. That whole madcap scheme of somehow going back and making it all unhappen had failed. As a child she'd learned the hard way that, if you broke things because you were thoughtless or careless or both, you couldn't just turn the clock back and fix them, no matter how badly you wanted to. Somewhere along the line she'd allowed herself to forget that lesson, and back then it had only been a canary that hadn't withstood a week of *I'll feed it tomorrow*. This time it was a galaxy, a universe perhaps, and, on a less abstract level, all those people huddled around their choking little fires and their hope.

Elizabeth wanted to scream.

Instead, she whirled around to head back into the tent and almost collided with Radek. "It's getting a little stuffy and circular in there, isn't it?" His smile crinkled unfamiliar lines around his eyes. He was an old man. The realization forced another shudder from her, but if he'd noticed he didn't let on. "Don't let Selena get to you. She can be rather reluctant when it comes to wrapping her head around new ideas. But she's a good scientist. One of the best." A little proprietary pride there.

She returned his smile. "I think anybody would have a hard time wrapping their head around this mess."

"Yes." He fell silent and, just as Elizabeth had done earlier, gazed out at the blistered sky, the Stargate, and up at the refugees' new campsites. Finally he looked back at her. "Suppose we find a way and succeed in reversing Charybdis, what will happen to all these people here?"

And how will you react when I tell you the truth? Like the other Radek in that other timeline?

Stifling a gasp, Elizabeth searched for a palatable answer. It took too long.

"I thought so," Radek murmured. "Selena suspects it, too, which is another reason for her reluctance."

"And what about you, Radek?" she asked carefully, not sure if she wanted to hear his reply.

"You mean will I react as… vehemently as my alter ego?"

This time the gasp tore loose. "Colonel Sheppard told you?"

Radek nodded. "He seemed unusually careful in talking to me. I confronted him. I agree that there was no point in keeping it a secret. That… man… he wasn't me, Dr. Weir."

He could have fooled her, had fooled her, in fact, which was none of this Radek's fault.

"Never mind," she said. "It was a difficult situation for all involved."

"That is one way of putting it…" His eyebrows arched in wry amusement, then he sobered as his gaze wandered back to the evacuees. "I suppose some scientists would argue they're not real. They felt real enough to me for the past thirty years or so. They're good people, you know? The universe will be poorer for their never having existed…" Radek sighed and segued to a seemingly unconnected train of thought. "Approximately a month ago our meteorologists discovered signs that the planet's atmosphere was breaking down at an exponential rate. They were working on finding a way of reversing the deterioration when all the rest of this started. The quakes destroyed most research facilities on the planet, which was when the government decided that evacuation was the only option. Except, they ran out of suitable ships inside a day, with eighty-five percent of the population still stranded here." He turned around to face her. "I guess what I'm saying is that, whatever happens, these people will cease to exist, and that disappearing in a flash is a kinder way to go than slowly suffocating in a toxic atmosphere."

Breathing felt difficult enough even now, though Elizabeth wasn't sure if this was due to objective facts or the oppressive menace suggested by that sickly sky. Even that sliver of hope implicit in Zelenka's words did nothing to improve things. "How long?" she asked.

"If it's going at the rate the meteorologists projected, we've got two days. Perhaps less."

The sliver of hope imploded. "Two *days*?"

"Perhaps less."

She hated herself for asking, but it slipped out anyway. "What can you possibly achieve in two days that you couldn't in thirty years?"

Radek smiled a little. "More than you think maybe. Something happened when you and Colonel Sheppard came through the gate. It gave me an idea."

CHAPTER 23

Charybdis -908

They were wading through bodies or so it seemed, but for all that the city was incongruously quiet now. That runaway train of fury had thundered its way up to the fortress to wreak whatever havoc it meant to wreak up there—or maybe to simply burst into flames, from its own rage or from the blaze that tore through the buildings perched on the hilltop. The fire was plainly visible now, and the water-logged night was lit up by a crimson halo that refracted in the raindrops like a shower of blood.

Very poetic, Rodney. The shower of blood was one of the Plagues of Egypt, if I understand your bizarre mythology correctly. Who is Egypt?

"Not who. What," Rodney replied tiredly. "It's a country. Now shut up."

"Excuse me?" Right ahead of him, Teyla turned around, forcing him to stop. Her head was cocked, face lifted his way, blind eyes gazing just past his.

It was disconcerting. Was she trying to keep up appearances or was it old habit? And just when and how had she lost her sight anyway? He'd never found time to ask.

Maybe it's a topic for a nice fireside chat, Ikaros suggested acidly. *Always provided that big brute out front'll ever let us rest, of course.*

This time Rodney remembered not to voice his answer. That *was* habit, for sure. Speaking out loud. Like normal people would. People who didn't have adolescent prodigies stuck in their heads. Why him, dammit?

I said 'Shut up!' Rodney hissed silently. *And I can't see why you would need a rest. You're not the one doing the walking. Not to mention the acrobatics or the climbing over heaps of corpses.*

The latter wasn't a hyperbole. Or at least not much of one. You didn't have to be a genius to tell that the battle for the city gate had been vicious. Brutal and primitive, just like the weapons used.

When they'd finally reached the gate, the fighting had been over and the passage under the archway littered with bodies; some of them peasants or dwellers of the shantytown, but mostly guards—killed by whatever means the panicked multitudes had found handy. Though well past the gate now, Rodney thought he could still smell the sweet, coppery stink of death. It clung to the rags he was wearing, to his hair, his skin, and it made him gag.

"Rodney?" Teyla renewed her badgering.

"Fine. Fine. Why can't I just think out loud like everybody else, huh? And why wouldn't I be fine? I mean, look at it!" he added, pointing at the vista ahead, realizing too late that she wouldn't be able to see what he meant. He flushed with embarrassment, grateful that she couldn't see that either. Another habit, pointing. He couldn't help it. It was normal. When you were trying to show people something, you pointed, right?

God, she probably thought he was cracked.

Maybe they should just switch topics. Talk about something harmless. Recipes. Hair care, maybe.

Ahead, in the middle of what was left of the street, their intrepid leader, Ronon, had ground to a halt, arms stiff, fists balled as if he were trying to contain... what? Fear? Outrage? Despair? Any of the above was appropriate given the sight, brilliantly illuminated by the conflagrations that were spreading all over the city.

Past Ronon stretched a seemingly endless expanse of black, churning water, still lapping higher with every passing moment. Most of the shantytown was gone, washed away and drowned as though it had never existed. Racing too swiftly, the flood hadn't even left any token debris bobbing on the surface to mark the place where a few thousand people had lived and, in their majority, died.

Ronon spun around, stared at them, and for the first time

since he'd met the man—upside down, as it happened, Rodney being strung up by his ankles—Rodney McKay saw something like defeat in his eyes.

"We've got to find a way of crossing the river," Ronon said, not sounding as if he remotely believed in the likelihood of such a contingency.

For once Rodney agreed, with the sentiment if not with the half-baked notion of paddling across... *that*. They'd simply have to wait. The Stargate didn't work anyway, so what did a few days matter? Surely the rain would stop eventually and the water levels would fall to something less life-threatening, wouldn't they?

Don't be an ass, Rodney! You know exactly what's going on. Or at least you sense it if you don't believe what I've been telling you for days now. Charybdis is doing this, and it won't stop. Not until we're all dead. Until you're dead. You're the key.

"What key?" he yelped, not caring who heard him. Who'd died and made him the Ringbearer, anyway? "Look, keys are things I lose. They have this habit of getting away from me, so I don't think it's a good idea at all to—"

"Rodney." Teyla's hand clasped his shoulder, oddly reassuring, as if she were anchoring him somehow. "Rodney, let us talk to Ikaros."

So much for reassurance.

"Are you crazy?" The Satedan slugger seemed to feel the same way. That was twice inside five minutes. A little disconcerting, if you asked Rodney, but nobody did.

"Ikaros is here," Teyla observed casually. "He is with Rodney."

"Figures. Always thought McKay was possessed." Ronon took a few steps forward, and peered over Rodney's shoulder at Teyla. "If I break his neck, I'll kill that bastard Ikaros?" He sounded altogether too hopeful.

"Ronon!" murmured Teyla. "This isn't helping. We need to find out what Ikaros knows."

Muttering something crude, Ronon backed off, clearing the view of the river. Rodney could have done without the reminder and stared dismally at a large, dark shape, twisting and bucking and groaning as eddies and undertow spiraled it downstream. The shivering gleam of the fires in the city and on the fortress painted unsteady red highlights on weather-grayed wood. It was a barn, or half of one, long emptied of its inhabitants and spinning sluggishly downriver. Rodney tried to make sure there weren't any decomposing cows floating past and suddenly felt himself drift out of control.

"I'll oblige in a second," Ikaros said brightly, using Rodney's voice, using Rodney's arm to point at the barn. "I think right now we should try to catch the boat. The next one might be a while in coming."

"What?" Ronon turned back to the swollen river, understood instantly. "Move it!"

Teyla followed blindly—to coin a phrase—spurred by complete faith in Ronon, if not the presence she'd sensed inside of Rodney. The water seized her like a vise, brutally cold, as cold as the stream in her cave, she thought, gasping, and wondered in some distant corner of her awareness how many thousand years ago or from now that might have been or would be. What she could feel of her body was numb and clumsy and wanted to shrink into a nutshell just to escape from the breathtaking cold. She couldn't say whether her hands and feet were moving, maybe they did, maybe they didn't, she ordered them to keep kicking, paddling, she knew that much. But it wasn't enough. Soaked with water, her clothes were too heavy. Shaking, panting, flailing, she coaxed her fingers to reach for her throat, unclasp her cloak.

They slipped, then an eddy grabbed her, pulled her under, whipped her into a helpless spin. She thrashed against the tow, no longer knowing which way was up, water burning in her lungs, fabric heavy as lead throttling her, her arms and legs aching with the effort, slowing. Slowing. An insidious voice in her mind whispered that there was no point in struggling, that letting go would be so much kinder, simpler. She listened to the siren song, conceding its rightness, relishing the ease of it, allowed herself to sink, and—

If she screamed, she'd breathe in water, which would seal

her fate, so she channeled her fury into renewed motion. She was Teyla Emmagan, she was a warrior, and she would not go out like this. Not like some unwanted whelp tossed into a pond to drown and knowing no better than to give in. When the time came she would go out fighting, but now wasn't the time. She hadn't decreed it yet.

Forcing frozen limbs back into motion, she kicked and clawed away from the maelstrom, not sure whether she was heading up or down, but away at least, away. It had been up. Coughing and choking, she broke the surface and burst into sore-throated laughter when an oxygen-starved starburst of sparks showered through black nothing. Of all the things to see...

The wisp of amusement flew apart like the sparks when realization struck. The black nothing was still there, behind that starburst, and the current had spun her round and round and head over heel. She had no idea where the others were, where she needed to go or how to orient herself.

Stay afloat.

She'd be washed up somewhere, take things from there.

Stay afloat.

Stay—

Something snatched her cloak, hard, and her first reaction was panic and the instinct to tear free. If she'd gotten snagged on a piece of debris, the river could drag her wherever it—

"For God's sake, don't fight me! I've got you!" Rodney. "I've got you," he wheezed again, reeled her in on her cloak as if she were a catch of fish, and pressed her against a scrawny sixteen-year-old chest. "Contrary to the behavioral tendencies of my current age group I'm not trying to cop a feel," he spluttered. "So bear with me."

It punctured her panic like nothing else could have. She half imagined she could feel a hot flush of embarrassment rising from his skin—imaginary or not, the warmth was welcome—and smiled, oddly convinced by a sense of safety. With strong, stubborn kicks and strokes, Rodney steered them in a direction she probably wouldn't have taken on her own, but then, on her own she'd likely have swum in circles. Suddenly she heard a different sound over the roar of the river; the groan of timber joints pulled and pushed by the current to within an inch of breaking. She also heard what sounded like rushed footfalls, then a thump and the dry splintering of wood, and a string of curses.

"Watch where you're stepping!" Rodney yelled, making her ears ring.

Scrabbling noises, accompanied by cussing, and then Ronon shouted, "Teyla! Reach up!"

She flung up an arm, gasped as calloused fingers snapped around her wrist and pulled, threatening to tear her shoulder from its socket. A splintery wooden edge dug into her belly—eaves?—and she found purchase there with her free hand and pushed herself up, anything to ease the strain on her arm. Shingles under her fingertips, rain slick and mossy, but enough were cracked or missing to hold on. Between Ronon's and her efforts, she rolled out of the water and up onto the roof at last and lay there panting, struggling to control the shivers that all but shook her bone from bone.

The roof heaved under her, dipped a fraction, as Ronon leaned further over the edge to haul in Rodney. She didn't stir, merely listened to the now familiar scrabbling, a curse or two, Rodney's groans, a couple of heavy thuds that marked success. The two men had slumped onto the shingles, and for a while all she heard were their harsh breaths, her own coughing, the creak of strained wood, and the ferocious bellow of the river.

Finally, the coughs eased to occasional hiccups, her lungs hurt a little less, and Teyla was able to draw enough breath to speak. "Thank you, Rodney."

"You're welcome. Feel free to mention my conspicuous heroism whenever you see fit." There was a pause during which he spluttered up what sounded like a pint of water. "I don't suppose anybody had the foresight to bring a thermos with hot soup? Something hearty. Chicken noodle, maybe. I haven't exactly been stuffing myself lately, so if you want to ensure my continued functioning, you'd better—"

"McKay!" Ronon's deep voice cut through the diatribe like a knife. "You were going to explain Ikaros."

"Nothing I'd rather do."

Eavesdropping was childish and frowned-upon, but Teyla couldn't help it. She sensed reluctance, resentment, fear too, and a stirring of the presence inside Rodney as it slowly, embarrassed almost, rose to the surface. No doubt in her mind that this was, in fact, Ikaros. It bled all the awkwardness and anger of a teenager, and this one was angrier than most, and for good reason probably. A lot of the anger was directed at itself, not that it would ever admit that.

"Rodney was right in trying to stop me," it said. "Unfortunately the way he went about it was more than usually asinine."

As it spoke with Rodney's voice, she saw the images unfolding in its mind. Those last moments on Mykena Quattuor, Ikaros joining with his creation in a column of swirling light, and Rodney sailing through air and into that light in an attempt to prevent what had been inevitable already. She also felt the merging of entities, Ikaros and Rodney, both terrified by what was happening to them, and a third...

"Charybdis is *with* you?" she croaked, vaguely registering that she sounded almost as terrified as Rodney and Ikaros had felt. As well she might. If it was true, then nothing either Rodney or Ikaros told them could be trusted, because the one trait that marked the Charybdis entity was an all-consuming will to survive, no matter what the cost.

"Yes," said Ikaros. "And it's getting stronger. It's attempting to... stop us from resetting events."

Ikaros didn't say *kill us*, but that was what it—he—had meant.

Ronon didn't quite stifle a growl. "You mean you *knew* that thing was sentient when you let it loose?"

"I didn't *know*!"

"But you suspected." The silence that followed proclaimed that Ronon had stumbled upon the truth. "McKay was right. We should have fried your circuits."

"Can you repeat that?" This was Rodney rather than Ikaros.

"We should have fried—"

"No. The other bit. The part where you said *McKay was right*."

"Fine. You were right. Does it make a difference?"

"It might, the next time."

"If we don't reach the Stargate and get off this planet, there won't *be* a next time."

Ominously, there was no reply.

Teyla scraped a handful of rain off her face, absently thinking that this didn't make a difference either, given how soaked they were. "Rodney?"

When he finally spoke, he sounded beaten, and it wasn't just the crushing exhaustion they all suffered. "Get off this planet? That's your master plan?" He gave a sour laugh. "I suppose it struck you as the least stupid out of a staggering number of piss-poor options, but where exactly do you think we'll be going?" Some shuffling indicated that he must have sat up. "Assuming that the ZPM I found is still functional *and* that I'll be able to reconnect the dialing console, you do realize that we'll never get *off* the planet, don't you? All the gate will do is flip us into a different timeline, which, judging by our combined experiences, will probably be worse than this.

"Of course we can then repeat the process and visit other timelines *ad infinitum*." Rodney sighed. "Ikaros has a theory. In the simplest of terms, Charybdis has enabled the Stargate system to let an infinite number of CTCs intersect with a Cauchy surface. There's—"

"Can't trust anything Ikaros says," Ronon cut in. "Even if I understood it."

He was right, and Teyla's own instinct was not to trust either of them, but the notion that they'd been bounced through time rather than space made some sense at least. "What is that, CTCs?" she asked.

"Closed timelike curves." There was impatience swinging in Rodney's voice. "In a CTC time bends back on itself. Think rollercoaster—" He stopped himself, his frown audible. "On second thought, *don't* think rollercoaster. I don't really want to have to clear that up as well. Time runs in a loop, endlessly. Which, coincidentally, would explain—"

"Why you're sixteen and I was over seventy in my time-line," she finished for him. "Our ages are all over the place, but using the Stargate readjusts them."

"Yes. Thank you. That never would have occurred to me," he snarled. "So, as I was saying, trying to activate the gate won't get us anywhere."

"Got us here in time to save your neck," Ronon observed dryly. "And Teyla found me. Gate works just fine if you've got the DNA of the person you want to hook up with."

"You had *my* DNA? How? Not that I'm nosy or anything…" His tone shifted abruptly. Ikaros resurfaced with a snort. "DNA? That's a bit pedestrian, though the general idea has some merit. In actual fact it's the unique combination of quantum states characterizing an individual that the gate system recognizes. A similar concept, I grant you, but— For God's sake!" Rodney again. "Does it matter? I want to know how they came by *my*… quantum states."

A shuffling noise indicated that Ronon was moving. He shuffled some more, then there was a yelp of disgust from Rodney, and Ronon said, "Thumbs up for perception."

She understood then and a small, desperate urge to laugh did battle with revulsion and won, hands down, when she conceived the mental image. He must have still kept the alternate Rodney's pickled ear in his pocket, forgotten until this moment.

"*That* is revolting!" yelped Rodney, followed by a breath of relief. Apparently someone—either he himself or Ronon—had tossed the offending body part into the river. "Where did you get it?"

"Don't worry. He didn't scream."

"Didn't *scream*?"

"He was dead."

"You might try sounding a little less amused!"

"I might," Ronon conceded, sounding unrepentant.

His words half drowned in the labored groan of tearing wood. An eddy had grabbed the roof and yanked it into a violent series of jounces. A bone-rattling impact, and a few moments of utter stillness. Then the joints burst, shrieking in protest, and their precarious raft shot forward again.

"Whatever you do, don't move!" bellowed Ronon. "And hold tight!"

Needlessly. Lying motionless, barely daring to breathe, Teyla held on for dear life, feeling the list of the structure, feeling that it wanted to capsize and would if they so much as shifted a millimeter.

"Hold tight!" Ronon yelled again.

The warning came a scant heartbeat before the second impact, this one brutal enough to break her grip and hurl her off the roof. Tumbling through thin air, she instinctively curled into a ball, arms wrapped around her head to protect her neck and skull, and braced herself for another bath in freezing water. Instead she struck unforgiving rock and began sliding through dense undergrowth back towards the river. Dazed, she clutched for a handhold. Thorns and brambles ripped through her fingers, tearing skin. She tightened her grip, oblivious to the pain, and finally eased to a standstill. For what seemed like an eternity she simply lay there, winded, while the rain hammered down on her.

Little by little the roaring in her ears ceased, and she heard shouts. Ronon, calling her name, again and again.

"I'm here! Ronon! Here!"

From above came the crackle and snap of breaking branches, and a small avalanche of pebbles and soil trodden loose peppered her face. He found her wrists, clenched his fists around them, and pulled her to her feet and up the cliff.

"Where is Rodney?" she croaked.

"Right here. Not doing so good, though." Ronon eased her to the ground, muttering. "At least we're on the right side of the river. Probably by accident. I swear Charybdis is out to get us."

"Charybdis is out to *kill* us," wheezed Rodney. "Or me at least." He started coughing, a horrible, gurgling hack that seemed to get worse by the second.

"Crap! " growled Ronon. "You're coughing up blood, McKay."

CHAPTER 24

Charybdis -223

Whatever it was the local physician had given him, it kept his headache within tolerable proportions. Or maybe he simply was getting better, though looking back on the last few days—or millennia, who knew?—John Sheppard wasn't willing to bet on the latter. If they ever returned to their Atlantis, Dr. Beckett would have a field day.

The local doc, confronted with several dozen victims from the rift, had been as sanguine about treating John as John had been about being treated, and so, by tacit agreement, the therapy had boiled down to the universal *Take an aspirin and call me in the morning*. Which was fine by both of them, except John was less than confident that there actually would be a morning.

"It's getting worse," said Zelenka. He was riding shotgun, staring through the jumper's viewport and at the travesty that pretended to be a sky.

Worse was an understatement, if John had ever heard one. The atmospheric color scheme had changed to a moldy ochre streaked with black, successfully suggesting something not even remotely breathable. That was one thing. The other, and presumably the one that had grabbed Zelenka's attention, was a large bird of prey straight ahead. The raptor, an eagle or near enough, flapped drunkenly, clearly straining to maintain altitude. Suddenly it went limp and plummeted in a mess of splayed wings and swirling feathers.

"This isn't good," murmured Zelenka. "Not good at all."

"Funny you should say that…" John grunted, glumly watching a second bird drop just a little off to the east from where the first had died of an atmosphere turning to poison. "How long do you think we've got?"

"Difficult to say." Zelenka leaned back into his seat. "I'm

guessing it depends on tissue saturation, which in turn would be dependent on body weight. That bird had what? Thirteen pounds? Fourteen?"

"Sounds about right."

"The average weight of a person is a little over ten times that. You're good at mathematics. You figure it out." Another sigh. "The little ones will go first. Soon."

"Then we'll just have to hurry up, won't we?" John tried to inject it with as much optimism as he could muster, which wasn't a hell of a lot.

Zelenka didn't dignify it with an answer, which John took as a request to goose the jumper into a speed that pushed its safety margins, particularly considering that the pilot's vision got a bit blurry every now and again. Obviously aspirin didn't fix that. Well known fact.

As the jumper leaped forward, the two technicians in the rear compartment stirred nervously and steadied various items of equipment they considered breakable and/or indispensable. John adjusted the inertial dampeners a fraction, to make sure that they'd get their booty up to the mountain camp in one piece. Whether it'd do any good there was a different question.

The previous evening's powwow had ended without a consensus, unless you counted an agreement to disagree. Zelenka's girlfriend, Selena, still insisted on finding a way of scrubbing the planet's entire atmosphere, while Radek, perhaps for not entirely altruistic reasons, was just as adamant about getting the gate to work. It put a certain strain on the relationship to say the least, especially when Zelenka had shanghaied their two technicians to retrieve a bunch of equipment from the city.

If you could still call it a city. John had seen a fair share of destruction, but never on that scale, except maybe in a movie. As a matter of fact, he'd doubted they'd find anything useable. Surprisingly, the building that housed the lab had been relatively intact if all but inaccessible the conventional way. That problem, however, had been one of the easier ones to solve; Zelenka had directed him to the right floor, and John had put the jumper into a hover outside a huge shattered window. The whole salvage operation had taken less than three hours to accomplish.

Now they had a pile of electronic gadgetry John couldn't readily identify, but the fact that the two geeks had gone into paroxysms of delight over it probably was cause for cautious optimism. They also had not one, but two ZPMs, which, as Rodney had never tired of pointing out, was A Very Good Thing.

Of course, it also could turn out to be the equivalent of owning an oil refinery but no car to drive...

Ahead the foothills sloped up into ochre twilight; you'd never have guessed that it was midmorning. In the evacuee camp a timid collection of campfires seemed to dim at the same rate as the people around them ran out of air to breathe. And maybe that impression wasn't entirely subjective—fires needed oxygen to burn.

Clenching his jaws, John reduced the jumper's speed, and banked into a gentle curve for the approach to the solitary tent some two hundred meters below the main camp. Security forces had set up a perimeter, and along it a handful of gray-faced people still stood staring, either to catch a glimpse of the strangers who'd come through the gate or to gawk at that great big hole in the ground that had opened up the day before. From the air the fault looked like a vicious gash, as if someone had attacked the earth with a giant broken-off beer bottle. At its top end the Stargate perched like an undecided suicide on a rooftop. And here was hoping that between them they'd manage to talk it down... so to speak and always provided they were left with enough air to talk or do anything.

The onlookers had spotted the approach of the jumper and were pointing, expectation and hope rolling off them in waves. Their shouts alerted Elizabeth and Selena, who came running down from the main camp where they'd been assisting the evacuees and generally trying to keep people calm. Even from up here John could tell that the exertion left them panting for breath. He winced.

"It's happening too fast."

"We have time," Zelenka assured him quietly. "Not much, but we still have time."

John set the jumper down within a few feet of the tent—no use hauling the equipment any further than they absolutely had to. The rear hatch slid open, letting a thick metallic smell pervade the interior. He'd first noticed it in the city, but this was far more intense. A moment later his lungs felt as if they were squeezed in a vise.

"You were saying?" he murmured.

Zelenka had gone pale with shock. "I didn't think it was that bad yet."

"Yeah, well. I guess we ought to hurry up."

"Dr. Zelenka?" one of the geeks said from the back.

Radek turned around. "What?"

"Perhaps it's advisable to set up in here. It would save time, and I understand that the ship has a device that allows it to improve the air quality."

The man had a point, though John couldn't help suspecting that there was a pinch of self-preservation involved as well. He exchanged a quick look with Zelenka, who shook his head. "We have to have access to both the Stargate and the dialing console. Besides, I don't think those people up there would take it quietly if they saw us holing up inside the jumper."

Zelenka had a point, too. They could all do without another run on the ship, which was virtually guaranteed to happen the moment the evacuees so much as suspected that they were trying to barricade themselves.

Not happy but willing to bow to reason—for now—the geeks gave identical dejected nods and began to unload.

Half an hour later, the computers were up and running and connected to the mysterious gadgetry, and Zelenka sat hunched over a keyboard, a still cranky Selena hovering by his shoulder. If John had correctly understood the tirade she'd launched at Radek as soon as she'd entered the tent, she now was pissed that they'd defied her bleak predictions and returned from the city alive. The geeks scurried, obeying murmured orders, pulling wires, and calibrating things.

John was itching for some way to make himself useful, if only to take his mind off the deepening nightmare outside, but there was no more flying or commanding or general soldiering to be done. He had to hand over the reins, and if he was perfectly honest about it, the loss of control bothered him as much anything else.

"How long will it take?" Elizabeth had appeared by his side like a ghost. Dark smudges under her eyes made her look tired and wan, and he couldn't say if it was fatigue or the lack of oxygen. Probably both. Her breath came in short, shallow bursts.

"No idea." He went for a smile. "Considering that Radek's been working on this for the past three decades, I figure he's due for a breakthrough... oh, within the next ten minutes or so."

"Let's hope you're right." Her answering smile was as unconvincing as his own must have been. "The doctors up in the camp have set up oxygen stations. They're limiting supplies to the elderly and the children, but it's still not going to last long."

The little ones will go first. Soon.

He stared at Zelenka's back, willing the scientist to work faster. As if in response, Radek looked up at one of the geeks, nodded wordlessly. The man—John had been told his name and promptly forgotten it, because there were only so many details his head could process right now—pushed past them out of the tent and toward the dialing console that stood a couple dozen meters up the slope. The crowd along the perimeter stirred, murmuring and expectant. The Stargate, shrouded in unnatural gloom, seemed to share their expectation.

A little hesitant at first, the technician dialed an address, and there were more murmurs as the chevrons lit up one by one. The wormhole established alright, but the event horizon oozed outward sluggishly; a large ferocious animal objecting to being awakened. An off-color animal.

"What in God's name is that?" Elizabeth whispered.

"*Propánakrále!*" yelped Zelenka, and John assumed that, whatever it meant, it echoed his own and Elizabeth's reactions.

Viscous black and orange swirls pumped through what should have been a clear blue, watery surface, as if they were trying to mirror the sickly colors of the sky. The whole arrangement conveyed the distinct impression that it was damaging to a person's health. If the gate had looked like this when Dr. Jackson first opened it, nobody in their right mind would have gone through, no matter how intriguing the prospect of intergalactic travel.

"What *is* this, Radek?" Elizabeth asked again.

"It's…" The syllable seemed to get stuck somehow, and he cleared his throat and tried again. "It must be Charybdis. It's entropic effects are beginning to disrupt the space time continuum. I never thought it would progress this quickly." His fingers danced over the keyboard, chasing graphs and figures across the monitor screen. At last the images froze. "There! You see, recent data had made me suspect that something was causing the Stargate system to operate through time rather than space. This shows that it's definitely happening. Every time you dial coordinates, you will reach a different timeline, not a different location."

"But that's…" Elizabeth shook her head. "Radek, God knows I'm no scientist, but that seems to be a huge leap to me. We're talking about *time* travel here, and even the Ancients"—she shot a quick glance at Selena and amended—"I mean *our* Ancients, weren't able to get a handle on that. The machine they built never worked properly."

"You're right." Zelenka's sudden enthusiasm suggested that, at least for the moment, he'd clean forgotten about the mess they were in. Lucky man. "And I even think the Ancients' tampering accelerated the spread of the disease that apparently killed them all. Basically they must have caused a similar problem to what we're looking at here; entropy, only on a vastly reduced scale."

Weir tried again. "But—"

"On a quantum level," said Zelenka, answering her initial question, "time is immaterial. Everything happens instantaneously. You might say that dimensions as we define them don't exist. At the very least they don't matter. So it's not a big leap at all between space and time—or between the Stargate as a means of intergalactic travel and the Stargate as a time machine. What I can't explain is why the wormhole did transport you when it won't transport other travelers. It could be some kind of safeguard against the Grandfather Paradox, in which case it may be possible to circumvent it, although—"

It started as a soft growl, gradually overlaid with a brighter rattle as the tent, the equipment, the world at large began to shake. The term *death knell* leaped into John's mind, and he couldn't shake it off again. Selena's shout broke through the noise.

"Shut it down! Radek! Disengage the wormhole! Look!" She was staring, horror-struck, at a different monitor, the one that showed a breakdown of the atmospheric composition. There were spikes and troughs, denoting elements, and some of those spikes—no idea what they stood for; chemistry wasn't John's thing—were climbing unchecked even as they looked. "It's the Stargate! The Stargate is poisoning the atmosphere."

It sure looked like it, though in actual fact it probably was more complicated than that. If John had understood Zelenka's theory correctly, then there was a chance that any activation of the gate would speed up the entropy—just like the fault had opened up almost immediately after he and Elizabeth had arrived here. In plain English that meant the Stargate made stuff worse.

Obviously Zelenka agreed. His hand slammed down on a small peripheral switch, and that orange and black obscenity collapsed in on itself. The relentless climb of the spikes on the monitor slowed to a crawl. Not so the tremors. Once stirred, the earth would keep going until it was finished, John supposed. Except—

He was already running before anyone else had recovered from their shock. Shouts of surprise slid off his back like water, and he leaped out of the way of the geek who approached the tent on a collision course with him. The rear hatch of the jumper still stood open, which was a small blessing. A few seconds saved right there. He slapped the hatch release racing past, barely hearing the hum of the closing door as he flung himself into the pilot's seat. Coming to life at a mere thought, the small ship lifted off, and turned its nose toward the gate.

Along the edges of his vision streaked the people at the perimeter, hands clapped over open mouths in that universal gesture of frightened astonishment and incomprehension, but John's attention was riveted on the gate itself and the bizarre dance it had begun. At first it had been a mere shudder, but now the large metal ring was hopping and shaking itself into a full-blown rumba, working loose from its fastenings and slowly tilting forward.

. It could have keeled backward just as easily, but of course *that* would have meant things were actually going in their favor. Duh!

John gave an angry little grunt. This would be interesting, to say the least. How much did a Stargate weigh? He was sure that the exact tonnage could be found in some manual or other, or that somebody must have mentioned it in the course of those endless briefings prior to the departure of the Atlantis expedition, but right now nothing sprang to mind. So it probably was as good a time as any to find out how powerful the upward thrust on those jumpers really was... and he'd better find out while he still had some leverage to speak of.

Careful to avoid putting unnecessary pressure on a chevron and potentially damaging the mechanism, he nosed the bow of the jumper against the upper curve of the gate. For a fraction of a second he achieved a precarious balance; the Stargate steadied and ceased its wobble, then it started to lean on the jumper, weighing it down, making its hull groan and forcing its bow downward.

"Son of a..." John hissed between clenched teeth, resisting the temptation of just stepping on the gas and knocking the damn thing the other way.

Instead he opened the throttle a fraction at a time, trying not to think of what lay below and what his chances of survival would be if the jumper took a nosedive and ended up at the bottom of the ravine with a Stargate on top. The engines shrieked with the strain, and a battery of warnings lit up the HUD like a Christmas tree. John felt sweat pouring down his neck and back—the ultimate in absurd, as it wasn't him doing any of the lifting. Then, agonizingly slowly, the Stargate reversed its motion, still pressing down heavily, but rising and, at least for the moment, safe despite the quake rattling on around it.

Eventually a faint, final tremor rumbled its last, and John risked relaxing cramped shoulders and various other parts of his anatomy. Other than almost toppling the Stargate, the quake seemed to have done very little damage. Their lab tent was still standing, so was the awning over the dialing console. Along the safety perimeter, people who'd dived to the ground rose, dusted themselves off sheepishly. In the evacuee camp above folks were dousing minor conflagrations and beginning an equally minor cleanup.

So far, so good.

Just as he was about to let out a sigh of relief, two things occurred to him: a) he and the jumper were stuck here for the duration, and b) in the unlikely event that anybody should take it into their heads to dial out, he and the jumper were toast.

Charybdis -908

"How is he doing?" Teyla asked between gasps.

"Same as before," replied Ronon without losing his stride—such as it was.

The trek up from the river valley back to the farmlands and beyond to the ruins of Atlantis had proved a gold-plated nightmare. He'd carried Rodney all the way, counting his blessings; Charybdis could have seen fit to turn McKay into a morbidly obese middle-aged slob instead of a scrawny teenager. That aside, he was still alive. Heavy as lead, his body relaxed in unconsciousness, but alive. Ronon had carried enough corpses to be able to tell the difference.

Day had broken a while ago, diffidently and without adding much in the way of light, and it was still raining. In other words, they were still wet as drowned rats, but at least they were warm now, muscles burning from the exertion. They'd seen hardly anybody on the road; a handful of youngsters driving cattle and an old man on an ox-drawn cart. Each time they'd ducked into the bushes by the roadside and waited until the traffic was out of sight; precaution as much as necessary rest.

For the past hour or so, ever since they'd passed the last farm in the valley, there'd been no further encounters. Ronon was picking his way carefully, trying to spare McKay any unnecessary jolts or, worse, a fall. The footing was treacherous, slippery with mud and uneven with roots and rocks, but at least they were somewhat sheltered from the rain and, more importantly, from any prying eyes. Other than their own harsh breathing, the only sounds now were the soft tap-tap of raindrops sliding from branches, the occasional crack of a branch trodden on, and here and there the rustle of a small animal scurrying through the undergrowth.

Eventually, the trees ahead were beginning to thin out and the sullen light drifting through the canopy was getting a little brighter.

"We're almost there," he said.

If Teyla had heard him, she gave no indication. Or maybe she simply refused to buy into this show of assurance. Fact of the matter was, he had no idea what to do once they reached the ruins. According to McKay, the power supply to the dialing console had been interrupted somehow. Then again, when he discovered the ruins his memory hadn't been firing on all cylinders, so there always was the faint possibility that he simply didn't know what he was talking about.

On that bracing thought, Ronon stumbled from under the shelter of the trees and out into the clearing around the ruins to be greeted by a gush of rain. By now he'd given up even on blinking it from his eyes. It just was. Next time he'd get himself stuck in a desert.

In front of him the ruins rose silently, shrouded in moss and vines. Water cascaded down the steps toward the gate and pooled on the tiles, deep enough to hatch trout. Past the bushes and trees that crowded the gallery he caught glimpses of overgrown, decrepit consoles and, scattered around those, bleached bones. The place seemed undisturbed, and it didn't look as if anyone had been here since his and Teyla's arrival two days ago. He'd half expected a bunch of zealots camping out here to ambush any heretic daredevils who might come sightseeing, but apparently the zealots had headed into town along with everybody else.

Ronon dropped to his knees and eased McKay off his shoulders as carefully as he could. Teyla staggered to a halt behind him, head cocked, like a doe scenting the air. "It's safe," she said at last, allaying his lingering worry. "There's nobody else here."

Good. Thank the elements for small favors!

"We have to wake him up somehow," he said.

"I know. Let me…"

Without being able to explain why, he rose and stepped back. It wasn't really a privacy thing, because all Teyla did was cradle McKay's head in her hands, massaging it gently and uttering a litany of half inaudible murmurs. Ronon thought of the guard at the city gate and figured the guy—if he was still alive—would be hollering *witchcraft* again right about now.

"It's nothing of the sort," Teyla replied softly. "I'm simply stimulating certain pressure points."

He could do with some stimulation, too, Ronon admitted silently. There'd been plenty of occasions during his years as a runner when exhaustion and soreness had become a permanent state of affairs, but this was in a league of its own.

Whatever Teyla was doing, it worked. McKay gave a protesting groan and opened his eyes, blinked, groaned again. Clothes plastered to his body, he looked painfully thin, and his face was pale enough to make his skin appear translucent, a sure sign that the bleeding hadn't stopped. If he didn't get medical help soon… Ronon swallowed a curse.

"Don't move, Rodney!" ordered Teyla. "And stay with us."

The response was a grunt, then McKay closed his eyes again. More massaging.

"Rodney! Stay with us!"

"Gah-hmpf," said McKay. Presumably it wasn't an endorsement of her idea. But at least his eyes were focused now, staring up at the cloud-laden sky, squinting away rain. "Where are we?" he croaked at last.

"At the Stargate." Ronon crouched beside him. Fingers fumbling with cold, he pulled the dog tags from under Rodney's sodden shirt. "You need to tell me where you found these."

"Huh?"

"The dog tags? Which heap of bones did you take them

STARGATE ATLANTIS: MIRROR, MIRROR

from?"

Another groan, and McKay turned his head, trying to catch a glimpse of the jumbled remains over by the consoles. "God… How should I know? The hogs got in there… Pick one."

Teyla's eyebrows shot up. "Hogs?"

Ronon squashed that line of conversation before it had a chance to get off the ground. "Not good enough, Rodney. We need to find Colonel Sheppard. That means *you* need to find the bones belonging to these dog tags."

Evidently, McKay didn't enjoy the prospect. "No."

"You have to. So get up and—"

"No, I don't. *You* have to dig a little. I buried the skull over by that tree," he gasped, flapping his hand at a large conifer.

In the grander scheme of things that qualified as excellent news. Ronon grinned. "McKay, you *are* a genius."

Tiredness temporarily forgotten, he climbed to his feet and scrambled to the tree Rodney had indicated. Sure enough, nestled between two gnarled roots was a patch of recently disturbed soil. He dug with his bare hands, and it was easy enough, what with the rain and the earth already having been loosened. Within minutes he returned to Teyla and McKay, holding the skull like a trophy.

McKay stared at it drowsily. "I knew him well, Horatio. He was a fellow of infinite jest…"

"What?"

"Literature. You wouldn't know it."

That urge to string the man upside down from a tree returned, but Ronon resisted it. Just. You had to look on the bright side. Supposedly this was an indicator that McKay was himself and reasonably functional. "You're sure that's the skull that went with the dog tags?" Ronon snarled.

"Yes. I'm sure." McKay glared daggers at him. "Can you see any other buried skulls? No. Didn't think so."

"Just checking."

"Just wasting time," McKay retorted. "Help me up."

"I don't think that's a good idea, Rodney," Teyla cautioned.

"I *know* it's not a good idea. But the console doesn't work, and unless Chewbacca here is proposing to dial in manually,

I need to…" Woozily, he pushed himself to a sit, frowned at the greenery, chattering to himself. "I know there is one… Question is, where did I see it?"

"See what?" growled Ronon.

"Help me up!"

That was only half the job, as they found out soon enough. McKay's legs clearly had developed a will of their own, and he could barely stand, let alone walk on his own. Held upright by Ronon, he waddled through the mud, staggered through the undergrowth, dragged himself around the remnants of desks and equipment. Meanwhile the cascade down the stairs turned into a mucky waterfall, flooding the area around the gate. If they didn't hurry up, they'd have to swim into the wormhole, and Ronon never wanted to swim again for as long as he lived.

Suddenly McKay stopped in his tracks and seemed to almost collapse with relief. "Thank God!" he wheezed. "There it is!"

Half buried in the mud stuck a roughly cylindrical object, the free end looking like a metal ball. Dull and dead and caked with dirt as it was, Ronon might have overlooked it, but, given McKay's obsession with energy sources of any kind, he probably could smell the things at a distance.

"Okay. I know where it goes. Stay put." Ronon eased McKay back to the ground, propping him against the nearest console.

The *naquada* generator seemed to be cemented into the soil, and its weight didn't help. It took some hefty pulling and twisting, but at last the mud gave up its prize, and the generator slid free with a slurp. The hole it left behind instantly filled with water. Obeying a half-baked notion that these gadgets were supposed to be clean, Ronon wiped his sleeve over it, succeeding only in evenly distributing the dirt. If this thing still worked, he'd spend the rest of his life—however short—proclaiming the existence of miracles.

He shot a brief, doubtful glance at McKay, saw that the scientist either had passed out again or was about to, and shrugged. Never mind. He'd now got his bearings around what was left of the control center and knew where to find the dialing console. Grunting and swearing, fingers slipping on wet, mud-slick metal, he dragged the generator alongside the console and sat back on his haunches, swiping rain from his face. The power, provided there was any, wouldn't just amble over into the console, so he'd better find some kind of wiring—or at least a conductor other than water.

Rodney forced a bleary squint at the scene in front of him. Dex crouched by the *naquada* generator, a collection of metal objects in varying states of preservation spread out around him; everything from rusty thumbtacks to blackened strips of aluminum foil. It took Rodney a couple of seconds to make sense of it. The thinking behind this arrangement was surprisingly astute, which, of course, he couldn't admit, so a snide remark would be in order. Except, nothing sprang to mind. Nothing, apart from blood-red swirls of pain and nausea that started spinning every time he so much as contemplated moving. And, of course, he couldn't admit that either. If he did, Teyla would descend on him with the canteen and make him drink some more—increase hydration to counteract the fact that he was slowly but surely bleeding to death; he'd grasped the concept and also knew that eighty percent of it was wishful thinking. Besides, if he drank any more, he'd probably burst like a melon. Or pee his pants.

The aluminum foil might work, even if it only had flexibility to recommend it. He'd have given anything for a couple of decent connectors. He'd have given anything for Dex and Teyla *not* expecting him to work yet another miracle.

And he could wish till the cows came home. Nothing was going to happen until he made it happen. Business as usual, in other words. In the first instance he had to cover the astronomic distance between the erstwhile control desk he was leaning against and the dialing console. Should be fun…

Fingers slipping in freezing mud, he tried to push himself off the ground and failed dismally. He couldn't even sit up straight.

"Help me," he croaked, upsetting the sawdust that seemed to have taken up residence in his alveoli. It provoked a coughing fit, and the sawdust congealed to merrily whirling saw blades. Something warm—*warm*, now there was a change—trickled down his chin. He swiped at it, and the back of his hand came away smeared with a mixture of filth and blood, in what likely enough was an incipient violation of McKay's First Law of Self-Preservation: Do Not Die.

The Satedan had deigned to make his way over, stared, and refrained from commenting for once. Instead he hauled Rodney to the dialing console and the paraphernalia gathered there. It was pitiful. The generator casing was badly corroded, contacts and switches dull and packed with dirt. There was no way of telling just how long the device had been rotting in this place, but its design was based on the prototype developed by Sam Carter and that had been a lot sturdier than it needed to be. So, despite the sorry state it was in, the generator should still work, as long as the core was intact... theoretically.

From there his mind naturally segued back to Sam Carter, a shock of blond hair, that dazzling smile, and those amazing—

Wow! Ikaros produced the mental equivalent of a wolf whistle.

Of all the precocious little... "Stay out of that corner of my head," Rodney hissed. "That's private!"

Sorry.

Yeah. Right. Rodney could practically see the smirk.

Gritting his teeth, he concentrated on the generator. Cold hands and fingers numb from blood loss didn't make for a great deal of precision, but he managed to pry off the lid of a maintenance access. It revealed a relatively dry, relatively pristine interior. On visual inspection—and visual inspection would have to be sufficient, God help them!—the vacuum container that held the *naquada* seemed to be tight, so there was no obvious reason why the core shouldn't be intact. One of the nice things about *naquada* was that it had no half-life, at least none that he had been able to measure.

While all of that was surprisingly encouraging, the generator controls were a different story. He felt a little chill crawl down his neck... or maybe it had been a drop of rain...

"Well?" asked Dex.

"Not really." Of all the patently asinine questions...

Rodney fumbled for the aluminum foil and needed three

attempts to snatch a strip and four to get a hold on a second. His fingers just didn't work properly, and the blood-starved tingle was driving him mad. Muttering to himself, he twisted the thin bands of metal into two approximately foot-long threads and managed to fashion a crude point on one end. He really, really hated MacGyver physics. This would probably burn out inside a minute. Then again, with any kind of luck—ha!—a minute was all they needed. Still muttering, he scraped the crud of centuries from the generator's power outlet as best he could, shoved the pointed end of the aluminum strips in there, and packed some mud around it to hold it place, hopefully for longer than five seconds.

That done, he awkwardly shifted to turn his attention to the dialing console. Catching any air at all was getting more difficult by the second. There no longer seemed to be any room inside his chest. The notion terrified him, and he focused on the console purely for the sake of not having to think about drowning in his own blood.

When he popped the lid of the maintenance hatch, a small torrent of water shot toward him. As far as starts went, it wasn't exactly promising, but it wasn't an outright disaster either. Like all Ancient equipment, the technology of the dialing console was crystal-based and therefore largely immune to moisture. He'd only once come across a problem caused by condensation on the crystals, which wasn't relevant here. The real hitch was that he had to reroute the power supply. Power to the console would have been piped in from one of the ZPMs in Atlantis's generator rooms, with the wiring—in the manner of all wiring—running inside the walls and under the floors. He had to find the main power cable, strip it, attach some more aluminum foil to it, and all of that preferably without getting enough rainwater inside the console to short circuit the entire array.

"I need a knife," he wheezed. "Have you got a knife?"

Dex pressed something into his hand. "Will that do?"

"To debone a mastodon? Possibly."

It was roughly the size of a cutlass, but it would have to do, Rodney supposed. Besides, given the steady deterioration of his motor skills, it was doubtful that he could have kept hold of anything more delicate. As carefully as he could—not very, in other words—he reached inside the console, scraped the insulation off the power cable, and wrapped another aluminum pigtail around the blank wiring. Then he extracted himself from the hatch.

Ikaros screeched into his awareness. *You'll overload the console!*

"Tell me something I don't know! In the highly unlikely event that you've got a better idea, let's hear it."

The kid remained conspicuously quiet.

"I thought so."

Eyes narrow with suspicion, the Satedan stared at him. "I take it your invisible friend has objections."

"My invisible friend was a mathematical prodigy by the name of Charlotte Luisa. Sadly she disappeared just prior to my sixth birthday. We had some of the most stimulating conversations I—"

"McKay!"

Well, it had been worth a try. Rodney should have known that Dex wouldn't be sidetracked. "We have one chance at this... if that."

"*If that?*"

"Yes. *If that.* My bad. Next time people refuse to listen to me, remind me to pack all equipment necessary to fix the entire control center."

He sucked in an exasperated breath, or tried to, and was rewarded by a scythe of pain slicing through his chest. If he talked any more, he wouldn't be around to watch the outcome of the experiment. And if he dragged his heels any longer, he wouldn't be around either. Rodney twisted the aluminum strips together to form a connection between the generator and the console. It'd burn out. Of course it'd burn out... not that he had an alternative.

Gritting his teeth, he slid a glance over at Teyla, who crouched in the meager shelter of a tree, babysitting what supposedly was John Sheppard's skull, then looked up at Ronon. "We'll probably have to run. Fast."

"Figures." One corner of Dex's mouth quirked upward into

half a grin. "Need a hand?"

Muttering something akin to a prayer, Rodney activated the *naquada* generator, then nodded and reached up. Dex pulled him to a shaky stand. At Rodney's feet the generator was beginning to hum, which was one bit of good news at least. Part of him had dreaded to hear nothing but silence and the hammering of rain on the metal casing. The hum quickly thickened to a whine, angry and off-pitch, the homey noise of a *naquada* generator building up an uncontrolled charge.

"Is it supposed to sound like that?" asked Dex.

"Under the circumstances, yes."

For a split-second the generator was bathed in a liquid, turquoise glow, then the surge slammed through breakers and switches, melting circuitry and leaping along the makeshift aluminum connector into the dialing console. Ronon gave a startled shout and jumped back, but Rodney barely noticed. The next stage was essentially simple. In a moment they'd either have lift-off for the entire console or he'd be able to dial.

The surface of the console lit up.

Hands shaking, he began to tap in the dialing sequence for the first planet that shot through his mind, glyph after glyph, mentally yelling at himself to do it faster. With each touch the glassy surface felt hotter and then, between Triangulum and Canis Minor, blue energy discharges started to sizzle along the rivulets of water that ran around and across the glyphs. By the time he finished, the console was vibrating, which was vaguely interesting, but Rodney's attention remained glued to the Stargate.

At least until Dex yanked him away from the dialing console. "Let's go! That thing looks like it's gonna blow any second!"

A heartbeat later it did just that. Rodney was tossed back by the blast, arms flung across his face to ward off shrapnel, and the next thing he knew was being dragged down the stairs toward the gate, legs buckling under him, his chest feeling as if someone had poured liquid fire into it. His ears filled with the thrum of his own pulse and, above that, the outraged hiss of hot, twisted metal struck by the hammer of rain, Ronon's harsh gasps just above his ear, the lighter counterpoint of Teyla's panting breath somewhere on Ronon's other side, and feet that seemed to belong to someone else slapping the ankle-deep water at the bottom of the stairs.

Ahead, inside the Stargate, the wormhole engaged, and the event horizon surged outward as if to greet them. Then it settled back into the ring.

"What the…?" Dex had skidded to an abrupt halt, bringing them to a stop with him.

Instead of a cool, scintillating blue, the event horizon leered at them dark crimson, reminding Rodney of nothing so much as a pool of burgundy—or blood. Either way the prospect of stepping into it was less than enticing.

"What is it?" whispered Teyla.

"The wormhole…" Dex cleared his throat, hedging for words. "Looks… different. Red. McKay?"

Oh, that's right! Just leave it to good old Rodney to explain the mysteries of the universe at the drop of a hat. And never mind that he's at death's door. In more ways than one, by the looks of it…

Go! Ikaros yelled. *You have to go now!*

"I'm not going to—"

If you don't go, it's over! Charybdis will win!

Doubts and scenarios tumbled through his mind, hot and fuzzy like socks in the dryer, but it always boiled down to the same thing: there was no other option. In a few seconds the wormhole, sickly or not, would shut down and slam the door in their faces for good.

"I know," he rasped. "I know. Ikaros says go, and for once I agree with him. We don't have a choice."

Dex lobbed him a double take, nicely executed. "You sure?"

"No! Who do you think I am? God? Go anyway!"

"You'd better be right about this…" With this resounding vote of confidence, the Satedan hauled and pushed them toward the gate and into that menacing sea of red.

Instead of that short, sharp shock followed by oblivion, Rodney had a sense of melting and being pulled in all directions in a slow-motion, alien-tech rendition of some medieval torture rack. He thought he heard screams—Ronon, Teyla, perhaps Ikaros, perhaps himself—and bubbling through the screams came a single word burned into his mind in neon letters: *redshift*. He thought he was staring at it, puzzled in that moment before it all made sense, and then, blessedly, consciousness winked out.

CHAPTER 25

Charybdis -223

Elizabeth Weir dragged the back of her hand across her fore-head, wiping off sweat for what felt like the hundredth time in the past hour. If she had any sense, she'd give up trying to figure out whether it was the claustrophobic lack of fresh air, or the oppressive colors of the sky, or factually rising temperatures, or a combination of all of the above. Fact of the matter was, knowing the reasons wouldn't stop her clothes from sticking to limbs leaden with fatigue and hypoxia. Fact of the matter also was that, as long as she managed to ponder such trivia, she wouldn't be contemplating the current state of affairs and cursing her own inability to change it.

"Bring it down! Carefully!" Radek Zelenka stood by the dialing console, waving his arms like a conductor.

His symphony orchestra consisted of two ground gliders and a handful of volunteers engaged in constructing a sturdy timber frame to stabilize the Stargate, which was still resting precariously on the bow of Jumper One. Behind the viewport Elizabeth could make out John Sheppard's face, a pale speck in the darkness of the cockpit. He would be flying the jumper manually, she suspected, compensating with minute movements of the stick for the tremors that still rocked the ground at irregular intervals and preventing the gate—and himself—from toppling into the rift.

Ever since she'd watched him steer the jumper between the fault and the falling gate she'd been torn between anger and admiration. Anger still had the upper hand. It had been a quintessential Sheppard move, utterly reckless and without any regard for consequences other than the glaringly obvious. Yes, he'd saved the gate—for now at least—but chances were he'd been saving nothing but a completely useless piece of technology. They had no DNA 'key' that would allow them to leave, not to mention that any activation of the gate would only precipitate the death of the planet. In other words, he was putting his life and the only jumper they had at risk for what currently was a great big ring of dangerous waste.

Right now Elizabeth would have given a great deal for a radio and the chance to read Colonel Sheppard the riot act. Again.

And maybe that, too, was merely a way of distracting herself.

"Slowly! Hold it there!" Radek shouted. "No! Right there."

The difference between *there* and *right there* probably was less than an inch. Elizabeth bit back a smile. This was the Radek Zelenka she remembered, an improbable mixture of quietly meticulous and excitable.

Suspended from the glider he'd been guiding in hung a giant 'A' that would form the still missing side of the support frame. Its legs gently touched the ground, bobbed a little, scaring up a cloud of dust, slid into pre-dug holes and settled. Two of the volunteers began to shovel dirt into the holes, tramping down on the soil to compact it around the legs of the frame. It struck her as an absurdly primitive way of salvaging something as advanced as the Stargate, but Radek had assured her it would hold. Probably. For a while at least, certainly long enough to get Sheppard and his jumper out from under the crushing pressure of the gate.

More volunteers were clambering up the frame now, bolting gravity clamps to the top of the contraption, seemingly indifferent to the bizarre contrast between the rough and ready timber frame and the high-tech devices that were supposed to hold the Stargate. Whatever worked… There were no other viable options, at least none that didn't involve threading stuff through the rings—which would be useless the second the gate was activated; the vortex of an establishing wormhole instantly vaporized everything it touched.

The leader of the volunteers directed a glance at Radek, received a brisk nod and a thumbs up. "It looks good! We'll calibrate as soon as—"

"Radek! What in the name of sanity are you doing?" Selena had shot from the tent, somewhere between concerned and furious, hollering at the top of her lungs.

Afterwards, Elizabeth wouldn't be able to say if it was Selena who'd alerted her or the familiar blue glow that glinted from the outer ring of the gate as the first of the chevrons came to life. She felt herself go numb with shock and vaguely registered that some of the noise she heard were her own screams.

"It wasn't us! We didn't dial out!" Radek yelled at Selena, then spun around, wide-eyed, to shout at the volunteers. "Get down! Get down now!" He whirled back. "Selena! The clamps! Activate the clamps!"

The third chevron locked and lit up on the Stargate, and the woman simply stood there like a doe in the headlights. Suddenly, with a shudder that racked her entire body, Selena snapped from her trance, wheeled around and disappeared into the tent. Within moments, red indicator lights flared up on the clamps and the whine of the jumper's overworked engines dropped in pitch by a couple of notes. Elizabeth risked sucking in a breath, if only because it stopped her from chewing her nails. Five chevrons.

"For God's sake, Colonel, get out of there! That's an order!" Even as she shouted it, she knew he couldn't hear her. Or, if by some acoustic accident he had heard, would later claim he hadn't. If there was a *later*…

Jumper One began backing away from the gate, a fraction of an inch at a time, until Elizabeth wanted to climb up there and push. The clamps held, but the wooden construction groaned under the strain, as did the men hanging on to the ropes that had yet to be fastened to poles driven into the slope and intended to counterbalance the weight of the Stargate. By the time the sixth chevron lit up, you could actually see clear space between the bow of the jumper and the gate, but the ship was still well within reach of the vortex. Now it just hovered, as if holding its breath. Everybody was, it seemed, watching and waiting to see whether the Stargate would stand. And then the seventh chevron locked.

The jumper shot up and sideways. With a hair's breadth to

spare, the vortex exploded past the small ship and sent it dancing in the backwash of the engaging wormhole—until John got it back under control, pulled it into a steep loop, and brought it around, backing toward the gate in the wake of the retracting event horizon.

"What is he doing?" murmured Elizabeth to no one in particular.

"I guess he's trying to catch whatever comes out of *that*." Radek had joined her and was staring at the event horizon in dismay. "It's getting worse," he whispered.

That was one way of putting it. For Elizabeth's money, the event horizon looked terrifying, a deep, joyless red, as if the wormhole were sucking the lifeblood out of everything living and breathing in the universe. And if Charybdis acted as they suspected it would, this notion wasn't far off the mark at all. She fought off a shiver, watched crimson reflections play across the hull of the jumper. The rear hatch gaped open, a black void punched into shocking red.

"It's taking too long already. I don't think there's anyone coming through," said Radek.

He probably was right. Maybe someone, somewhere, in the same kind of desperate quandary as they, had attempted to escape destruction and dialed this address, but without a 'key' nobody would be able to travel. And for all she knew, she and John Sheppard and now Radek were the only ones aware of—

A trio of figures tumbled from the wormhole and into the jumper, slack and floppy-limbed like puppets cut from their strings.

John could tell from the various impacts that his newly acquired passengers were unconscious at the very least. A quick glance over his shoulder confirmed it. A tangled heap of three people, none of them stirring. Not that it surprised him. The really amazing part was that they still looked recognizably human after coming through that garish red mess. Which disengaged as he was looking, and good riddance to it. The thought of having to go through *that* in the increasingly unlikely event that they managed to persuade the Stargate to take them anywhere was enough to pitch his stomach into a queasy roll.

"Welcome aboard, folks. Buckle in and enjoy the ride," he muttered. "Even though I doubt it's gonna be half as interesting as what you just did."

Hatch closing, he peeled away from the gate at last and steered the jumper into a gentle landing alongside the tent. When he tried to let go of the stick, he realized that his fingers were curled into a claw, joints frozen around an ergonomically uncomfortable piece of plastic, and he had to make a conscious effort to straighten them. Getting up out of the seat was even less fun. For a moment there his vision blurred to black and he had to grope for support. Eventually the cockpit got bored with spinning, though his head showed no intention to follow that shining example and stop hammering. He'd have to wheedle a couple more of those nice Tylenol-type things out of the medics just as soon as he got a second. For now, though...

John staggered aft and into a wall of stench, a potent combination of sweat, filth, blood and a bunch of components he didn't want to contemplate. Dead fish? Whoever his passengers were, they'd either had a really exciting time lately or their religion forbad the use of soap and water.

Apparently it also forbad motion. None of them had moved as far as he could tell. Suppressing a curse and doing his best to ignore the smell, he crouched beside that pile of bodies. Their clothes were soaking wet and there was a puddle forming on the floor of the aft compartment. Obviously at least water was familiar then. Grimacing, he eased the topmost body of the heap. The weight made it a woman and on closer inspection the curves were obvious. He turned her over, wiped matted, muddy hair off her face... and sucked in a gasp that was somewhere between shock and pure disbelief. Dirt-streaked as they were, Teyla's features might have been unrecognizable, but she'd been on his team virtually from the day he arrived in the Pegasus galaxy. Teyla was a part of home. She also was... his fingers reached for her neck, found a pulse, weak but steady. She was alive.

While he was still checking her for injuries, the person at the bottom of the heap groaned, a deep rumble, familiar in its grumpiness. "Get off me!"

What was left of the heap started heaving, allocated sets of limbs to their rightful owners, and then someone tall and broad and unimaginably grubby sat up, dreadlocks dripping water. Ronon's eyes snapped as wide as saucers when he saw John, and he broke into one of those rare smiles. Not that feral baring of teeth that suggested whoever was around should go and mess with somebody their size, but a genuine smile. "Don't take this the wrong way, Sheppard," he growled, "but right now I want to hug you."

John grinned. "As long as you take a shower first."

"Just show me where." A little stiffly Ronon scrambled to his feet, stretched, did a quick, habitual scan of his surroundings and relaxed when he recognized the jumper. "Can't believe we finally caught a break," he mumbled. "'Bout time, too."

"How did you—?"

Before John could finish, Ronon pointed at the skull lying next to Teyla. "Yours. I'm guessing you twigged on to that whole business with the 'keys'?"

"Yeah. Except, we ran out of body parts."

"*We?*"

"I've got Dr. Weir and Zelenka. The only one missing is—"

"McKay!" Ronon dropped to his knees and rolled that last sprawled form on its back.

Under the mudpack Rodney's face was ashen, drained of blood. The dirt stood out starkly from pale skin, and the shallow breaths he drew raised a soft wet whistle.

John suppressed a curse. "What happened?"

"What *didn't* happen?" snarled the Satedan. "He's cracked at least one rib, probably punctured his lung. The trip through that thing the wormhole turned into didn't help…" He flicked a glance at the overhead storage lockers. "You got any medical supplies left?"

"I can do better than that," John said. "We've hooked up with the locals, and they've got some pretty decent doctors here."

"Good."

Ronon's reply was overlaid by the hum of the rear hatch

opening on Zelenka and Elizabeth Weir. The worried look on their faces changed to the same incredulous surprise John reckoned he'd worn a couple of minutes ago.

"Look what I found," he flashed them a quick grin.

"My God," whispered Elizabeth. "Are they okay?"

"They're a bit dented and they don't smell very good. Teyla's still out, Ronon's strictly unpresentable, but other than that…" He turned serious. "Rodney needs medical help right now."

Somebody had carried her. Somebody familiar, and her first reaction of anger at being taken for helpless had come up against a memory of that bone-crushing trip through the wormhole and faded to nothing again. Teyla hadn't been able to see what Rodney and Ronon had seen in the Stargate, but she'd gathered that something was wrong. Rodney had said there was no choice, that they'd surely die if they stayed. He'd been right, and she'd known it even then… but they'd come very, very close to not surviving. She'd felt the rage of Charybdis, white-hot rage at their stubborn refusal to let it run its course, and she'd felt eons of time folded into nanoseconds, different versions, different lives, all of them trying to pull her apart. It had been nearly as bad as those endless moments after Charybdis had roared into existence.

Now, as she slowly drifted toward consciousness a second time—to remain there, she promised herself—things didn't seem so bad at all. On the contrary. For the first time in what seemed like forever she was warm. Too warm, as a matter of fact, though that thought struck her as sacrilegious. She wasn't complaining. She was dry. She was warm. Not so long ago that had been all she wanted. At least in the short term…

Teyla smiled.

"Teyla?"

This voice didn't belong here, shouldn't be here. *Couldn't* be here. Her smile crumpled into a frown. Maybe that terrible travesty of a wormhole trip had damaged her mind. It was possible, surely, and that meant—

"Teyla, it's alright. You're safe now."

Perhaps. But she was also quite mad, apparently. However,

it might be best to simply play along. "Dr. Weir?"

"Welcome back." There was a smile in the voice now, and a hand clasped Teyla's. "How are you feeling?"

"Hungry." Which was the truth. She was famished and only vaguely recalled when she'd last eaten... The bread and soup Ronon had brought her? When had that been? The morning before they freed Rodney. "Rodney is hurt," she stammered, aching with shame for forgetting about a team mate, however briefly. "He needs—"

"Rodney's doing alright." Elizabeth Weir's soothing voice cut through her anxiety. "He's holding his own. It was touch and go for a while, and the doctors had to remove a lot of fluid from his chest, but he's resting comfortably now. And Ronon's fine, too," Dr Weir added, anticipating Teyla's question.

Yes. She could hear him now, arguing with someone. Teyla smiled, listened some more. There were quite a few people here, and a number of strange voices. A woman, two men; they, too, were arguing with a third man, older, by the sound of him, but familiar all the same. She should— "Dr. Zelenka!"

It sparked a soft laugh. "Yes. He's here, too," Dr. Weir confirmed.

"Hey, Teyla." A whole new voice, very close, very familiar.

"And so is Colonel Sheppard," announced Dr. Weir.

He had to be crouching by the bed or cot Teyla was lying on, and suddenly there was another hand on her shoulder. Alive and real. She'd barely dared to believe it. Somewhere, in the darkest corner of her mind, she'd feared that the skull that had brought them here had been his, that the real John Sheppard was dead. Provided that this one *was* the real one.

"We..." She cleared her throat. "You're not the one I met... before. He was Major Sheppard... He found you, didn't he?"

"Yes." It sounded charged, thick with grief and anger and guilt.

She shouldn't ask, there was too much sadness there, sadness she didn't need, but she couldn't help it, felt a duty to know. "What happened to him?"

"Junior saved our lives," he replied curtly.

And paid a high price for it. The thought cut like a knife, but she was not given any chance to mourn him now or remember his bravery or acknowledge that, in every way that mattered, he'd been as real as the man sitting by her side now. She sensed it coming a split-second before the ground started to heave, just as an animal would. Except, what she sensed wasn't the earth preparing to strike, it was the scorn of Charybdis and its determination to destroy them so that it could survive.

The tremor built, and as the jolts grew in violence the sounds all around Teyla seemed to climb over each other into a cacophony of noise. The clatter of equipment shaking and falling, the far-off wails of panicked people, closer by yells of frustration or warning, and the electronic screams of life-support machinery.

"Rodney!" Dr. Weir let go of her hand, scrambled away.

"The Stargate!" That was Zelenka.

His outcry provoked a stampede of stumbling feet and then answering calls of "It's holding! The frame is holding" — whatever that might mean.

"I don't care!" An unfamiliar voice, a woman's, full of fear and resentment. "Let it go! It's killing us all!"

"No!" Zelenka again. "You're wrong, Selena! We mustn't lose the gate."

The air seemed to get thinner by the second, and Teyla was struggling for breath. But more terrifying than that or the quake or the noise and confusion all around her was the unshakable certainty that they were about to run out of time. Charybdis was winning. Chaos and entropy were winning.

She tried to sit up, found herself pushed back down onto the cot by strong hands. "Stay put," Colonel Sheppard ordered. "It'll be over in a minute. Everything's fine."

"No, it isn't, Colonel!" Teyla couldn't remember ever shouting at him, but she did so now. "We must leave! We must leave immediately!"

Radek Zelenka had always been of the opinion that the most serious disease his esteemed colleague, Dr. McKay, suffered from was chronic hypochondria. This time it was different. The reunited members of the Atlantis team had gathered around Rodney's cot to stare down at his haggard face and wait. It reminded Radek of nothing so much as being eight years old again and forced to participate in his grandmother's wake. The lifeless, ancient death mask had scared the living daylights out of him, and he'd had nightmares for weeks. Much as he would now, no doubt.

His tension was threatening to build into a headache, and it wasn't improved by Selena who hovered in the background, silent now but still disapproving. More disapproving than she'd ever been. He'd had to fight her every step of the way, to expend manpower to salvage the Stargate, to get medical help, to spend precious oxygen on keeping Rodney alive. Determined to protect her own people, she'd drawn the line between *them* and *us*, and Radek was *them* now and it hurt. They'd been together for most of their adult lives, they'd worked together, lived together, loved each other, and all of that had suddenly turned into a thing of the past, didn't count anymore. Selena had made it quite clear that he had only himself to blame. He'd made his choice and, as far as she was concerned, he'd chosen wrong.

Now she spared him a baleful look and slipped out of the tent. He felt relief when she left, and that hurt, too. Gritting his teeth, he forced his attention back on Rodney.

All the physicians who'd been rounded up to take care of the new arrivals had returned to their duties with the evacuees. All but one. He sat on a rickety stool, his gaze glued to the bank of small monitors that recorded Rodney's vital signs, such as they were, and he obviously was dismayed by something—or everything—he saw. McKay was hanging on by his fingernails.

"I've never seen anything like it," the healer mumbled and pointed at the EEC screen. "It's almost as if there's two of him, and whatever the other one is, it's keeping him alive."

"It's Ikaros," Teyla said softly. "Ikaros is still there."

"What?" Dr. Weir and Colonel Sheppard snapped in unison, and Ronon launched into a choppy explanation. Evidently Rodney himself had been none too specific about the state of affairs.

"So the bottom line is that we need him to get us back, but we can't trust him, because the guy who got us into this mess in the first place might be sitting inside his head, running the show?" Sheppard asked. "Great. Just great."

"We *can* trust him." Teyla had sat up on her cot next to Rodney's and tilted her face in the direction of Colonel Sheppard as if searching for his gaze.

"Teyla, you have no way of knowing that," Dr. Weir replied reasonably. "Ikaros lied to us before, and—"

"Wake him up," Colonel Sheppard snapped at the physician, adding a slightly sheepish, "Please."

"I can't do that. He's—"

"Please," echoed Teyla. "We can't wait."

Her earlier warning seemed to resonate through the tent. *We must leave! We must leave immediately!* Radek was inclined to agree. The quake that had rocked the hillside half an hour ago had been more vicious than any that had come before, and the air quality had taken another turn for the worse since the activation of the gate.

The physician was an elderly man, not used to having his authority questioned, let alone overridden. With an indignant grunt he picked up a couple of nerve stimulators and slowly guided them from Rodney's forehead down the entire length of his body. "I will not be held responsible for any consequences," he growled at last, setting the devices aside. "He is waking up now."

"Nobody will hold you responsible," Dr. Weir said gently. "If we had a choice, we wouldn't have asked you to do this. Thank you."

The reply was another grunt.

Radek supposed he should have anticipated it, because he'd witnessed the effects of the stimulator before. It still was startling. A shudder that set the cot to rattle racked Rodney's body, then his eyes snapped open and he dumbly blinked at the canvas ceiling above.

"Hng," he said. Which could have meant anything, but knowing McKay it probably translated as a none too polite request for coffee and carbohydrates.

"Who are you?" asked John Sheppard.

With something of an effort, Rodney focused on him.

"Huh?"

"Who are you?"

"My God, it actually worked," said McKay, and that grimace might have been a smile. "Nice to see you, Colonel. Is my acne that bad?"

It clearly was the last reply Colonel Sheppard had expected. "Come again? Your *what*?"

Ronon grinned. "Don't worry, McKay. You look your age again. No boils."

"Zits!"

"Do I want to know?" Sheppard asked darkly.

"No," said Rodney and Ronon, at the same moment, offered, "He was sixteen in his timeline."

"Like Ikaros," Dr. Weir whispered, frowning.

"Which brings me back to the original question," said the Colonel, who must have been thinking along the same lines. "Who are you?"

"Dr. Rodney McKay of Earth and various other benighted places." With a pained sigh, Rodney settled back into the pillow. "I love it when people are being willfully obtuse…" He opened one eye and peered at Sheppard. "Who in God's name did you think I was? Your teenage look-alike? Admittedly he's making a nuisance of himself, but he generally asks my permission before taking over."

"Generally." While he sounded less than convinced, Sheppard seemed willing to accept Rodney's assertion, at least for the time being. "Look, we're a bit pressed for time here. We need to get back before Charybdis slams the door on us for good. Any suggestions?"

"Don't bother," came a voice from the entrance. "You're not leaving."

Radek spun around, found himself face to face with Selena. Behind her he could see at least twelve more people, including the technicians, grim determination showing in their eyes.

"We have discussed it, and we will not allow you to activate the Stargate again," she said.

Oh, wonderful. You'd think he might have earned himself

a timeline not populated by Luddite zealots, but obviously that was too much to ask for... The issue was academic, of course, because he was fresh out of suggestions to offer to John Sheppard or anyone else. Unless they brought him at least one new double or the double's remains, Rodney had no idea of how to persuade the Stargate to work. And, going by that less than joyous last trip, he wasn't even sure he wanted to try.

"We cannot." The woman looked as obdurate as flint. "As a matter of fact, we've decided to destroy it."

Ha! What did he say? Luddite zealots!

"Selena." Zelenka risked a step forward. "Selena, there is no other way. You must—"

"You've made your feelings quite clear, Radek. And you've made your choice. Let's spare us all the repetition."

Zelenka seemed to crumple and that scarily old face of his crinkled into a stricken expression, beyond hopelessness or hurt. Dear God, the woman was... what? His lover? Ew... a little mature for that.

Who's the zealot now? She's his wife. What did you expect him to do? Live like a monk for thirty years just because he was dumped here?

"Who asked you?" Rodney inquired under his breath.

"Please, Selena?" Elizabeth's features were set in that conciliatory diplomatic mode Rodney hardly ever saw directed at himself. "Please, you have to believe that we never meant to—"

The old woman cut her off mercilessly. "We know you didn't mean us any harm. Not at first. But now you do. You"—she stabbed a finger at Weir—"you seek to protect your people. You consider it your duty. Well, it's my duty too. I will protect *my* people by any means necessary. If that entails sacrificing five... *six*"—a glare at Zelenka—"in order to save the population of an entire planet, so be it."

You couldn't dispute the math. So much for diplomacy...

"*Zatracený!*" Radek seemed to have arrived at the same conclusion. When he lapsed into his mother tongue he usually was impatient or pissed or both. "The planet is *dying*, Selena! You're sacrificing a galaxy, possibly a universe, to save a corpse!"

"That's your theory! A *theory*!"

"It's not a theory. It's a fact."

Rodney heard his own voice say it, felt his mouth form the words, and thoroughly resented the sensation. If he'd been able to, he'd have screamed. *Son of a bitch!*

I'm sorry, Ikaros offered, feeling at least somewhat guilty. *I believe you have a saying: desperate times call for desperate measures.*

"How would you know?" snapped Selena. "You've spent even less time here than the rest of them!"

"I know because I'm the one responsible. I *caused* this. I caused you to exist."

"Ikaros!" John Sheppard looked furious, as well he might. "Rodney said—"

"Yes. I heard him, and I apologize for this. But you have to trust me."

"I'd rather trust Rodney around the latest untried Ancient super-gun," hissed Sheppard.

A little uncalled-for, if you asked Rodney, but nobody did and even if they had he couldn't have answered.

"Bring him back, Ikaros!"

"In a moment. I promise, I—"

"Who are you, Ikaros or Rodney or whatever your name is? And what gives you the right to take our lives?" Selena moved another step forward, and the mob she'd roused was thronging in behind her, smelling of murder. Some of them were armed, all of them were outraged. If the tension rose another notch you could forget about cutting it with a knife. It would shred the canvas walls and roof of the tent.

"She's right!" one of the men behind Selena shouted. "He's already admitted to causing this, so I say we punish him accordingly."

Yep, here we go. Rodney had a nasty sense of déjà vu all over again and began to wonder where they'd stashed their cage. Why couldn't the kid just keep his big mouth shut?

As I said, I'll oblige you in a minute. If you want to get back, you have to let me do this. Now stop distracting me! Ikaros snapped.

Aloud he said, "You can punish me. You can kill me. But in
doing so, you'll merely harm an innocent man. What's more,
you'll rob yourselves of any chance to set this right. And if you
don't set it right, you will indeed destroy an entire galaxy."

The response consisted of grumbles, low and menacing and
disbelieving, and they closed in another foot or so.

Ikaros tried a new tack. Intrepid little twerp... "I'm of
your blood, from the same roots as you, we're of the same
people"—that raised a few eyebrows—"and I did what I did
out of the same desire that drives you now; I wanted to *save* my
people. I also wanted revenge. So much so that I failed to look
beyond the obvious."

His audience was listening now. So was the Atlantis team.
So was Rodney, when it came to that.

"For as long as we could remember, my people—*your* people—had a powerful enemy," Ikaros continued. "The Wraith.
Beings no longer human that stole men and women and children and fed on their life force. One day they stole my family,
and that day I promised myself that, as soon as I was able to,
I would destroy them. So I studied and learned, as fast and as
much as I could, and I built a device capable of altering history itself, of eradicating the Wraith and every trace of their
existence throughout the millennia, because, in the version of
history I created, the Wraith never had evolved.

"I thought it was a safe plan, you see? How couldn't it be?
All I'd done was take the Wraith out of the equation. I didn't
think it would affect the rest of history. But of course it did.
Because the Wraith were part of our history, yours and mine.
The Wraith were the whetstone that honed our instinct to survive, our thirst for learning, our skill at defending ourselves
and, ultimately, our determination to be *better* than they.

"My friends here"—one by one Ikaros indicated Weir,
Sheppard, Teyla, Ronon, and Zelenka—"and I each have experienced versions of time where that whetstone never existed.
Where our people slipped from memory without a trace. Or
turned into a scourge worse than the Wraith, because there was
no force to impede them. Or drugged themselves into inanity.
Or became so terrified of knowledge that they would destroy

anyone who desired to learn. Is that what you wish for our people?" He looked straight at Selena.

Fists clenched, chin raised, she returned his stare. "Even if what you're saying is true, we did not become any of those. Have you seen us mistreat or harm people? Or shun learning? You would be dead right now if we didn't honor science!"

"But you have not developed either! You are frozen the way you were hundreds of years ago. When did you last discover anything new—other than what he showed you?" Ikaros nodded at Radek. "Well?"

Selena sucked in a sharp breath, fished for words. Eventually she retorted, "We were content. We had what we needed and left well enough alone."

"Meaning you were regressing. Because that is what happens when you're standing still while time moves on around you. Your complacency made you obsolete." The words hung there for all concerned to get riled, then Ikaros carried on, now without the sting in his tone. "Your people, *our* people, were meant to develop, Selena. Beyond anything you can possibly imagine. Wiser, more powerful, without fear of death. But it will never happen, will never *have happened*, unless we're allowed to go back and set things right."

"Develop in what way?" She was trying to scoff, but there was a groundswell of doubt and curiosity in her voice that hadn't been there before.

"I could tell you and you wouldn't comprehend it, so I'll show you."

Show her?

Oh no, wait a min—

Rodney felt an odd tug inside of him, something separating, gradually and carefully, a loosening of his being. With it, pain came flooding back like a torrent, and he realized for the first time the full extent to which Ikaros had sustained him. The radiance began above his chest, slowly stretching into bands of brightness. A long time ago he'd seen the security footage from the infirmary back at the SGC. The same type of lightshow had accompanied Dr. Jackson's ascension, and it was worth noting that there hadn't even been left a body behind. Granted, he'd

somehow recovered his mortal coil a year or so later, but the
man's powers of resurrection would put a cat to shame, and
Rodney McKay was confident that his own skills on that score
weren't even remotely in the same league.

Hey! What about me? he screamed somewhere in his mind.

Don't worry. Ikaros's answer felt faraway and growing
fainter by the second. *You won't die. Much…*

What's that supposed to—

And then there was black.

Mingled in with the first shock there were two things that
vied for John's attention; that tentacled glory of light rising
from Rodney's still body, so similar to the luminescence that
had heralded Charybdis's activation, and the frenetic wails and
chimes of the life support monitors.

"My God," whispered Elizabeth. "He's ascending!"

"No!" Teyla sat bolt upright on her cot. "It's Ikaros.
Whatever is happening, it's Ikaros."

"I can tell you what's happening! The son of a bitch is leaving McKay behind!" If there had been a time in his life when
John had felt more helplessly angry, he couldn't recall it. How
did you beat common decency into a life form that looked like
a Day-Glo squid? "He's leaving Rodney to die…"

"No, he isn't," she countered. "He couldn't. Everything he
said was true. And I can still feel Rodney. Rodney isn't dead."

As if to confirm her words, the monitor alarms subsided. A
leaden silence dropped over the jumble of upturned or ruined
equipment the quake had left in the tent. It was broken only by
hushed breathing. Nobody seemed able or willing to speak as
that sinuous glow abandoned its hover above Rodney's chest
and smoothly, almost nonchalantly, approached Selena. Her
eyes went wide and she instinctively backed up a step or two,
into the chest of the technician behind her. It galvanized the
man into action. Pure terror etched into his face he attempted to
shoo off the… thing as you would a fly.

Don't be afraid. I won't harm her or anybody else.

John heard the words in his mind as clearly as if they'd been
spoken, and he obviously wasn't the only one. Selena's knight in

shining armor dropped his arms and reverted to open-mouthed stupor. Selena herself braced her shoulders, took a deep breath and walked straight into… whatever it was.

This time he heard laughter.

It's still me, Colonel Sheppard. I'm still Ikaros. And no offense, but I find thing just a little insulting.

The golden luminescence wrapped itself around Selena, sheathing her in light. Radek let out a stifled shout, but someone—Ronon?—stopped him in his tracks. A heartbeat later it became apparent that there was no need to protect Selena. She stood motionless, on her face a look of rapt wonder that rightfully belonged to a child who'd just encountered Santa Claus and all his reindeer in the flesh.

He had no concept of how long it lasted, but eventually the glow released Selena, swam free and began to elongate as if reaching for the ground. It grew denser, more substantial, assumed appendages that looked conspicuously like arms and legs, dimming at the same time. Then, in the blink of an eye, it winked out and in its place stood Ikaros, still in the BDU he'd worn when John had last seen him, a lifetime ago. The kid possessed the audacity to wink at him.

As if waking from a trance, Selena took a deep breath, cheeks flushed, eyes shining. "He was right," she whispered. "I couldn't possibly have imagined it…" She must have intended to say something else, but was brought up short by Ikaros in his more human manifestation. Her gaze wandered from him to John and back, and at last she gasped, "He is your… son?"

"More like my great-great-grandfather."

"Uncle, actually." Ikaros grinned, then turned surprisingly serious. "Much as I'd love to discuss the family tree, I'm afraid we don't have the time for it. And it doesn't really matter, does it?"

"No, it doesn't." She smiled at him, then turned to Zelenka. "Radek, my apologies for being so… intransigent."

"You always were, you know… a little." Zelenka's voice sounded rough, compressed by a wealth of emotions he was trying to choke back. "I'll miss you."

She gently touched a hand to his cheek. "Me too. And you'll

have a lot more time to do it in than I. I don't envy you."

"Why don't you come with—"

"You know I can't. It would upset everything you're trying to restore." She glanced over at John. "You must leave now. Quickly."

The technician who had tried to defend her was the first to realize what she was talking about, and his face went rigid with fear and outrage. "Selena! What are you doing? You said—"

"I know what I said. I was wrong. And I will not rob our people of their future."

The man clenched his fists. "You are robbing us of our future! *We* are your people! Those children—*children*!—in the camp up there are our people!"

"I *know*!" Her face was wet with tears, and John felt as if someone had punched him in the gut. Maybe these people, these children, weren't supposed to exist, but they were here, right now, weren't they? As far as collateral damage went, it was carnage, pure and simple. Selena shook her head. "You and I, the children, we're unimportant. This is so much bigger than any of us. Believe me, I've seen it. I've—"

The ground bucked, bucked again, and started to roll, sluggish like a large animal waking. Tent poles swayed drunkenly, and the EEC monitor crashed from its stand, scaring the doctor off his stool and knocking over other equipment.

"Go!" yelled Ikaros. "We have to go! Now!"

He was right. They had a minimal window while the folks behind Selena were still disoriented, but once they got over their fright it could get ugly. Exchanging a look with Ronon, who clearly had the same idea, John lurched over to the cot, ripped away blankets and IV lines, and slung Rodney's limp body over his shoulders in a fireman's lift. As he rose, the exertion left stars blossoming on his retinas and his head felt as if it were about to explode, thundering in time with the shocks of the earthquake. Chronic Charybdisitis?

Across the tent, Radek ushered Elizabeth toward the exit, bellowing at the people who obstructed it, ordering them to move. A few of them actually obeyed, but the majority was waking from their initial shock and started to think straight, which meant they weren't about to let the Atlantis team leave without at least a hefty argument—for which they had no time. Another tremor jolted the ground and this one at least working their favor. Top-heavy with Rodney's weight on his shoulders, John barely could keep to his feet. But at the entrance people toppled like bowling pins, arms flailing and legs kicking.

"Colonel! Run!" Sword drawn and Teyla tucked in safely behind him, Ronon was ready to discourage anyone who harbored any notions of getting up prematurely or otherwise preventing their departure.

Climbing over sprawled bodies and twitching limbs, John staggered from the tent and out under a hideous bruise of a sky. In the evacuee camp up the slope a multitude of conflagrations had broken out, cooking fires, kicked over either by the tremors or panicked people, spilled flames on everything in their way. A sweating wind carried screams toward him. He clenched his teeth and forced himself to ignore it all, to focus exclusively on the jumper just a few steps ahead.

The hatch gaped, Radek and Elizabeth already aboard and waiting atop the ramp, helping hands outstretched, waiting to relieve him of his burden. As they eased Rodney off his shoulders and onto one of the benches, Ronon and Teyla came sprinting up the ramp at full tilt.

"Go!" hollered Ronon, slapping the pad to close the hatch.

Past him, John could see the men by the tent regaining their feet. Selena stood in the entrance, talking, cajoling, her words falling on deaf ears as everyone began to run for the jumper. Under the guidance of one of the technicians a few enterprising souls peeled off from the mob and made for the Stargate. Which could be a problem...

"Been there, done that, hated it the first time," John murmured unhappily and headed for the cockpit.

"Where is Ikaros?" Elizabeth asked as he pushed past her.

"Riding shotgun," announced a voice from the front. The kid had materialized in the co-pilot's seat. Clearly ascension had its perks. It saved you a hell of a lot of footwork.

A new tremor struck, shoving John sideways into the chair. He initiated the dialing sequence before his butt even hit the seat, then eased the jumper off the ground and out over the widening rift toward the Stargate. Through the viewport he saw the first of the wrecking crew arrive at the gate. They immediately set about unfastening the ropes that stabilized the frame. For now the quake would keep them from climbing up and deactivating the gravity clamps, but it wouldn't last forever.

On the Stargate the fifth chevron lit up.

"Come on, come on, come on," he whispered.

"Didn't you say you needed a 'key' for the gate to work?" Zelenka had joined them in the cockpit, apparently with the express purpose of asking pertinent questions.

And he had a point, damn the man!

Pretending that sinking feeling in the pit of his stomach didn't exist, John slid a glance to his right. "Ikaros?"

The kid kicked up an eyebrow and gave another one of those insolent teenage grins. "You've got a 'key'," he said as if it were the most obvious thing in the world. "You've got me."

"Well, here's hoping you fit."

Outside, the seventh chevron locked. Then two things happened.

The red and black nastiness that masqueraded as the event horizon soared toward them and retracted into something singularly uninviting.

And Radek shouted, "*Do prdele!*"

John couldn't have agreed more. Either the quake or the wrecking crew had succeeded; the gate had worked loose from its moorings. For a second it teetered on a forward lean as if contemplating what to do next, then gravity won. John's reaction was pure reflex and never wasted a thought on the potential consequences, manifold and ugly. He dipped the jumper into a sharp dive, angled straight into the trajectory of the gate, and watched, heart hammering madly, as that red and black vision of hell rushed toward them and filled the screen.

If nothing else he'd found a whole new way of—

CHAPTER 26

Charybdis ±0

There was one thing to be said for the ride, Elizabeth thought once she could think again. It was over as quickly as it had started, though the exact duration was anybody's guess. She must have blacked out at some point, because she had no recollection of being thrown from her crouch beside Rodney and slamming into the bulkhead where she was lying now, butt over eyeballs. Squirming to get her feet where they rightfully belonged—in other words, *below* her head—she shoved herself up to a sitting position, took stock.

The jumper's aft compartment was illuminated by emergency lights, their dull reddish glow suggesting that whatever was affecting the wormhole had taken up residence in their ship. Which probably wasn't the best notion to harbor right now…

The engines sounded odd—there was an expert technical description—and from the cockpit came a string of profanity, punctuated by *Come on!* and *Hurry up, Radek!*, which in turn suggested that the emergency lights were on for a legitimate reason rather than some kind of entropic infestation.

Rodney had been strapped down at the last moment before they hit the event horizon—or rather, the event horizon hit them—and was still safely on the bench, still unconscious, but still breathing. Just. Ronon was kneeling by his side, watching over him like a hawk.

Back at the hatch, Teyla was struggling upright, her face eerily blank in the red light that shone pink in opaque irises. Elizabeth swallowed a curse. Like everybody else she'd secretly hoped that the return to their own timeline would restore Teyla's sight. Obviously she'd been wrong and, appallingly, this was the lesser of two evils. The alternative—that this *wasn't* their timeline—didn't bear thinking about.

She climbed to her feet and groped her way into the cockpit, doing a double-take when she saw Radek. He, at least, had reverted to how he was supposed to look, if slightly more disheveled than normal, even by his standards. His attention, like John's, was focused on the system status display projected on the HUD, and he acknowledged her only with a brief look.

"Charybdis created a temporal distortion within the wormhole," he offered unhappily. "Its tidal forces as good as drained our fuel cells."

The explanation probably was as close to plain English as he could make it, but Elizabeth still only got the gist; they had a problem. So what else was new? "Where are we?" she asked. "Other than in space, that is."

They'd come through an orbital gate, that much was obvious—and a great deal more promising than yet another permutation of the ruins of Atlantis.

By ways of an answer John coaxed the jumper into a gentle turn. Past the display, the Stargate and the pin-prick brilliance of countless stars swung out of sight and were replaced by a small orange planet veiled in a dust-laden atmosphere.

She sucked in a sharp breath. "Is that—"

"Mykena Quattuor," John said. "Welcome back."

Directly ahead were two other jumpers, one in a geostationary orbit and the second one streaking toward the surface of the small planet.

"I'm guessing that's Stackhouse. And... me. With Ikaros," he murmured with a sidelong glance at the boy who was still sitting in the co-pilot's seat. "That's why it worked, isn't it? Why the gate brought us back? Your original is here."

Ikaros nodded. "Part of it anyway, but my program imprint in the quantum computer obviously was enough. And before you ask, no, I didn't know that, but there was no point in telling you. We had no choice, and hearing the probability of success just would have made you despondent and depressed."

Elizabeth resisted an urge to groan. It was too late anyhow. As Jumper One dipped into a pursuit course, hurtling after its double, she braced herself against the backrest of John's chair. He'd opened a com channel and tried to hail... himself. If you thought about it long enough, it gave you a migraine.

"You... *he* can't hear you. He's your future self," Ikaros said simply. "The timelines are still out of synch. They won't converge until Charybdis is neutralized."

"Great," snarled John. "And how do we do that?"

"With Rodney's help of course."

It was evident that no further information would be forthcoming, and John wisely directed his attention on the task of managing reentry in a damaged jumper. "Hold on," he warned. "This is going to be bumpy."

Bumpy was the least of it. As they entered the atmosphere, buffeted by rock-hard air, the interior of the ship turned into a sauna. And then some. Hot air seared her lungs with every breath Elizabeth took, parched her throat, while her clothes stuck to her skin, gluey with sweat. Dawn blended into dusk, day into night. Clouds streamed past, tore into tatters or obscured the view for seconds on end. Each time they cleared, the surface had leaped closer. Mountains rose at an alarming rate, valleys deepened. They shot out over an immense desert plain, and the temperature inside the cockpit began to drop at last. The ground seemed close enough to touch all of a sudden, racing below the ship in a blur, and then the glittering crystal dome of Charybdis's outer shell popped over the horizon, growing so rapidly that Elizabeth felt sure they'd collide with it.

They didn't.

Instead they struck the ground with a bone-rattling jolt, leaped into the air again for a new bump that segued into a succession of gradually slowing hops. Finally the ship ground to a standstill. In front of them the Charybdis dome gleamed serenely like a jewel.

There was a long moment of absolute silence, shattered by Ronon's roar. "Were you trying to kill us?"

Hands shaking, John let go of the controls. He turned around, pale as death, and attempted a grin. "Ladies and gentlemen, Captain Kangaroo and his crew hope you had a pleasant flight. Please make sure to take all your belongings with you when you disembark."

Radek gave a funny little noise that could have been anything from a pained chuckle to a stifled sob. "Don't tell me. That's why you christened it 'jumper'," he said faintly.

"Hey, you know what they say—any landing you can walk away from is a good one."

"Except I'm not sure I *can* walk!"

"We have to go!" Absolute urgency in his voice, Ikaros pushed himself from the seat. "There's very little time left."

"Yes," said John, sounding like getting up was the last thing he wanted to do. "Radek's only joking."

"That's what you think," the Czech grumbled.

Ikaros either hadn't heard or was ignoring him. Groping along the walls to steady himself, he stumbled into the aft compartment, where Ronon was still clucking over Rodney who hadn't moved. In a corner of her mind that seemed inured to everything that was going on, Elizabeth drew a small spark of amusement from the thought of how embarrassed the Satedan would be when Rodney found out.

"I shall have to borrow him again," Ikaros said. "Only for a little while."

"What? Borrow whom?"

By ways of an answer, Ikaros dissolved into that luminous cloud once more, slowly spun above Rodney for a moment, then wrapped him into a golden glow before vanishing as though he'd seeped through McKay's pores.

Moments later Rodney groaned, stirred, blinked and finally opened his eyes. "What did I miss?"

"Don't ask," growled Ronon.

"Oh good." He blew out a sigh, careful and shallow; an indication that his chest still wasn't much better. Then he pushed himself up, which in itself was a sign that things were off somehow. Rodney McKay had several strengths; heroism in the face of discomfort wasn't one of them. "We have to go."

Evidently John begged to differ. "Don't be an idiot, McKay! You're not going anywhere."

"Colonel, I'd love to argue with you till we're both blue in the face, but right now Ikaros and I have to get to Charybdis."

"Ikaros *and* you?"

"Like he said, he borrowed me." Rodney actually managed

to stand up, wobbled, and almost knocked into Ronon before steadying himself. "Their timeline—the one we're chasing, the one where Charybdis is about to be activated—is showing signs of entropy already. It's getting erratic. Which means that, unless we cut the debate and act now, we'll… both overtake them and be too late, at which point Charybdis will probably gain permanency, because the only people who could conceivably fix this—in other words, us—have managed to miss the fulcrum event. All of which roughly translates as *No time for blah-blah. Run. Run. Run.*"

John had barely set foot outside the jumper and felt the arid wind sweep sand in his eyes, when he realized the implications of it all. Mykena Quattuor turned into the temporal equivalent of a cakewalk. One second he and Ronon were dragging Rodney and his passenger across the dunes and toward the Charybdis dome, the next everything around them seemed to liquefy and then congeal again.

A foursome of technicians pushed past to unload his cargo from the jumper.

In their wake McKay leaped out at him like a kiss-a-gram from the birthday cake. "Colonel!"

Fully expecting Rodney to burst into song at the slightest provocation, John pretended not to have seen him and headed for the control chamber. McKay being McKay—in other words, lacking the take-a-hint gene—the dodge didn't work terribly well.

"Colonel! I… uh… I'd like to apologize for being a little crabby lately."

Not on your life. For Rodney to apologize, events of a certain order of magnitude had to occur first. Such as the annihilation of the better part of a solar system. John kept walking.

"Colonel… John!"

Someone was yelling in his ear, driving spikes of pain through his head. But he hadn't had a headache then, had he? "I'm sorry, Rodney," he rasped. "You were right. You—"

"Colonel Sheppard!"

For a moment the quicksand that was time in this place

let go of him, spat him out just outside the airlock, dizzy and disoriented and staring at the haggard face of Rodney McKay who, coincidentally, looked like death warmed over.

"Don't buy into it!" The voices of four McKays dopplered all around him. "It's past! It doesn't matter!"

Yeah. Right. Easy for the Rodneys to say… Through the tilting world and whirling images around him, John tried to focus on something, anything that looked like it might be stable or linear or in any way reassuring. He found nothing, nothing at—

A hand closed around his, small, strong, calloused, providing a focal point. "Trust me," Teyla said. "It can't distract me."

He thought he must have nodded, shouted, "Hold on to each other!"

Never knowing whether anyone had heard him, he saw himself age beyond comprehension or reckoning and float, a heartbeat later, thumb-sucking and barely formed in an amniotic sac—*2001*, it's a movie, Teyla—and through it all followed the tenuous tug of Teyla's hand, until at last past and future splintered apart and left him standing inside the crystal-studded central chamber of Charybdis.

John had an odd sense of overlapping with another, fainter version of himself, not quite matching, edges a little blurred and fuzzy but growing more defined with every breath he took, and he realized that they must have made it just in time—the second they completely coalesced with their alternate selves here in the chamber would be the defining moment. Not a moment even, but that imaginary, infinitely brief space between moments, just before they all made their mistakes and history would quite literally repeat itself.

It *was* repeating itself.

The merging imminent, that shimmering holographic vision of Ikaros hung above the crystal assembly of Charybdis's core, smiling down at Elizabeth. "My motivation for doing this is irrelevant, Dr. Weir, and it doesn't affect the functioning of Charybdis. You can't prevent the inevitable, but I assure you, nobody will be harmed—except the Wraith."

Elizabeth was turning to him, panic written all over her face, about to shout his name, and John, feeling himself slot into unity with his other self, prayed that this was the beat that he'd missed before. "Rodney! Pull the plug! Now!"

McKay executed a classy fish dive toward the generator, and even as he was watching him, a horrible conviction slammed into John—he was late, again, after all that. The ephemeral shape of Ikaros brightened into a whirl of colors, blossoming above the core unit of Charybdis, stretching toward the ceiling, expanding to fill the interior of the dome and suffuse them all. Rodney hung suspended mid-flight, horizontally in the air, fingers splayed and—

His motionless body began to shed an unearthly golden light. It feathered out into glowing coils, wrapped around the rainbow whorl that was the union of Charybdis and the Ikaros program, snaked through it like a weaver's shuttle though the warp, in living, pulsing threads of gold, compacted the destructive iridescence—it reminded John of nothing so much as a kid kneading the mother of all snowballs—and hurled it back into the core of Charybdis.

In the end it was utterly and oddly unspectacular. The radiance of the crystal core dimmed and winked out, and the dullness spread outward like ripples in a pond to climb the walls of the dome. The being Ikaros had become hovered serenely where his holographic counterfeit had risen only seconds ago. Two of those luminous octopus arms gently lowered Rodney to the ground.

He will be alright, a disembodied voice assured them. *I've healed him.*

Personally, John thought Ikaros might have done that a little sooner.

I couldn't. I wasn't complete before.

Ah. It made sense in a weird sort of way. Not all of him had found its way into Rodney the first time round… only the matching personality traits. John grinned, stared up at that uncanny lightshow. "So you're fully ascended now?"

Somehow the Day-Glo squid managed to throw out a nod.

"Correct me if I'm wrong, and I'm not complaining or anything, but if you're ascended, aren't you supposed *not* to interfere?"

The air rippled with silent laughter.

Rectifying interference could be defined as un-interference, don't you think... nephew? Besides, now it will have been me who has written that rule, so I suppose I rate a little wiggle room.

John didn't even try to wrap his head around the sequence of tenses and its implications. He'd had enough of temporal paradoxes to last him a lifetime. And then some.

You should go now. The crystal lattices are disintegrating, and the dome won't be stable for much longer. I'll see you around.

"Is that a threat?"

Another ripple of laughter, and Ikaros rose toward the apex of the dome, bled through the ceiling. For a moment John could still see a shimmer of brightness shining through the walls, then that was gone, too. The crystal structure dimmed, dullness spreading like a blight.

"Should have put the kid over my knee while I had a chance," growled Ronon. He stood leaning against the wall, arms crossed in front of his chest, his face haggard with fatigue, but he was smiling.

"For once in my life I agree with you." Rodney climbed to his feet and cautiously poked at the remnants of the Charybdis core. "It's dead. He wrecked it. And you probably can scrap that *naquada* generator, too. I'll just have to—"

"Rodney!" Elizabeth and Radek shouted in unison.

Across the chamber, past the brewing argument, Teyla looked at him, her eyes back to their rich, dark brown. Charybdis had never happened, and she had never been blinded by it. She smiled at him. "Maybe we should go home, Colonel..."

Home.

There was a thought.

"Yes. Let's go home."

EPILOGUE

"Congratulations." Carson Beckett flicked off his penlight and pointed at an eye chart on the infirmary wall. "You also read the really wee bits in the bottom line over there, so I'd say twenty-twenty vision. Better than that. Whatever it was that affected your eyes, Teyla, it's cleared up completely."

"Thank you, Dr. Beckett."

"You're welcome." He cocked his head, looked at her quizzingly for a moment.

She knew her thanks had sounded a lot less self-contained than her usual self, but then, no eye exam could measure the vibrancy of color, the richness of texture, the warmth of the smiles she saw. And it couldn't measure what it meant. Nor could she adequately explain it.

Somehow Dr. Beckett seemed to grasp the gist of it though. "Never mind." He grinned. "Go on. Get out of here. You can go check on Colonel Sheppard. If he's hopping around like a yoyo send him right back to me."

"I will." She returned his grin, slid off the gurney she'd been sitting on, and headed out into the corridor.

It was busy at midmorning, people bustling along, on errands or changing shifts, some on their way to the mess for a break, others returning from there. Voices, brisk footfalls, laughter, and a sense of purpose—life. She'd spent a lot of time in the corridors and common areas lately, more than usual, because she needed to soak in this buzz. It went a long way toward dispelling the lingering memories of these same hallways filled with silence, ancient dust, and the staleness of death.

Without consciously intending to, from sheer habit perhaps, she ended up in the control center. At least she could make good on her promise to Dr. Beckett. Not entirely surprisingly, Colonel Sheppard was there, perched on the desk in Dr. Weir's office. He'd been released from the infirmary only the previous day, after a week of strict bed rest to tend a severe concussion. Toward the end of it he'd almost wept with boredom.

"… so Rodney got nowhere?" he asked.

Dr. Weir shook her head. "Apart from managing to repair the *naquada* generator he found nothing. Which left him more than usually frustrated… and frustrating." She gave a pained grin, then discovered Teyla hovering in the door. "Oh. Hi. Come in. What did Dr. Beckett say?"

"I am fine."

Colonel Sheppard perked up. "Does that mean we can take up our sparring sessions again?"

As invited, Teyla took a couple of steps into the office and cocked an eyebrow at him. "Since, in your case, that would qualify as hopping around like a yoyo, I would be required to send you back to the infirmary."

"I sense a lack of due respect. What do you think, Elizabeth?"

Stifling a grin, Dr. Weir tapped a sheaf of printouts sitting on her desk. "I think you both should have a look at this."

The look in Colonel Sheppard's eyes said that he'd just estimated the height of the stack of paper as too high. "Reading's contraindicated for concussion. Can you give us the *Reader's Digest* version?"

"I can." Weir's grin broke free, indicating that she knew exactly what he was playing at. "But you still should take a look at it. I guarantee you'll find it fascinating. More fascinating than *War and Peace*." She settled back in her chair, steepled her fingers under her chin, and the grin disappeared. "I've asked the historians to do some further digging into Ikaros. What they came up with… differs a little from their original research. It seems Ikaros was the one who introduced the Ancients to the possibility of ascension."

The Colonel let out a low whistle. "He *taught* them?"

"Yes. And there was no suggestion of that previously. It looks like we've changed history after all. The ramifications—"

Would go unexplored for the moment.

The klaxons sounded, announcing an incoming wormhole

and cutting her off mid-sentence. Weir shot out from behind the desk. "It's probably Sergeant Stackhouse," she said, heading for the door. "He and his team were on a trade mission to Delana. They're back early…"

Teyla and Colonel Sheppard followed her out into the control center and watched the routine procedure unfold. Black-clad soldiers took position on the stairs and the gallery, weapons trained on the Stargate, ready to defend Atlantis should the need arise. This time it didn't.

The wormhole had barely established when Sergeant Stackhouse tore from the event horizon, leading a group of about thirty people, all of them looking as bedraggled and singed around the edges as he. "Get Beckett down here!" he hollered up to the gallery. "My men are bringing through a couple of wounded."

"What happened, Sergeant?" Dr. Weir was hurrying down the stairs, Colonel Sheppard and Teyla in her wake.

"Meteor storm. They got clobbered bad. The team and I couldn't even make it to the village. These folks"—a sweep of his arm indicated the refugees—"had hunkered down near the gate. We basically took them and ran. They need our help, ma'am."

Dr. Weir sighed. "Sergeant, we—"

Obeying an impulse Teyla didn't dare to explain, her fingers gripped Weir's arm. "My people will take them in, Dr. Weir."

She took a step forward to face the leader of the refugees, a grizzled man, haggard with fear and fatigue, at his side a skinny girl of about six or seven years of age. At Teyla's approach the child looked up, eyes wide in a grubby face.

"I'm Pirna," she said, smiling. "What's your name?"

ABOUT THE AUTHOR

Originally from Germany, Sabine C. Bauer holds a Ph.D. in English Literature from the University of Birmingham and trained at Bristol Old Vic Theatre School. She subsequently worked as a stage director and producer in the UK and United States, and in 1999 started writing Stargate SG-1 fan fiction.

Her first novel, *STARGATE SG-1: Trial By Fire* (released in 2004), was the first Stargate novel published by Fandemonium. Since then she has written a second STARGATE SG-1 novel, *Survival of the Fittest*, and edited several others, as well as contributing two short stories, 'Juju' and 'Genealogy,' to the *Stargate Magazine*. Her short story 'Tesla's Slippers' was included in the science fiction anthology Journeys of the Mind.

In 2005 Sabine emigrated to Canada, now lives on the British Columbian coast with a mastiff and a motorcycle, and is working on an original novel.

STARGATE

SG·1™

STARGATE ATLANTIS™

**Original novels based on
the hit TV shows,
STARGATE SG-1 and
STARGATE ATLANTIS**

AVAILABLE NOW

**For more information, visit
www.stargatenovels.com**

SNEAK PREVIEW

STARGATE ATLANTIS: ANGELUS

by Peter Evans

Horrors often start off small.

A suggestion of a footfall outside the bedroom door, late and close to sleep, and the careful testing of a handle. The far-off sheen of ice on a night-time road. A tickle behind the eye. Little things, caresses at the edge of consciousness, too subtle to fear. It is only when these horrors have been given time to grow and fester that they become known for what they are.

The handle turns, and the door swings inwards.

The ice is an oil-sheened slickness under tires that no longer grip.

The tickle grows into a grinding headache, resistant to drugs, resistant to prayer, steadily building day on day...

So it was with the horror that took Atlantis. It began small, almost too small to see, but it was only awaiting it's chance to metastasize. Despite later recriminations, no-one could have foreseen it. Even Colonel Abraham Ellis couldn't, though the horror began with him.

He never saw it coming. It was too far away, at the end of a tunnel made from swirling blue light.

The tunnel was an illusion, Ellis knew; some weird artifact of the hyperdrive engines. He had no idea why the strange, super-compressed universe his ship was flying through should appear the way it did, no more than he could explain the careening sense of headlong motion he had experienced the few times he had been through a Stargate. In fact, while he knew the specifications and capabilities of his ship down to the last kilo of thrust,

Ellis could claim no real knowledge of how the hyperdrives even worked, let alone how Apollo appeared to be lit blue and silver by a light that probably shouldn't be there.

The mystery didn't bother him. As long as the drives did their job, flinging the great ship between the suns at untold multiples of lightspeed, he was quite content to let them get on with it. Let fuller minds than his ponder the true nature of the light flooding his bridge. The Asgard had, in all likelihood, taken its secret with them to their collective grave.

No, what was really bugging Ellis was the unmistakable, and quite ridiculous feeling that Apollo was falling.

He closed his eyes momentarily, settled back in the command throne, took a long breath. All the familiar sensations were still there – the faint vibration of the deck through the soles of his boots, the cool metal edges of the throne arms, the click and chatter of the systems surrounding him. Somebody walked across the bridge behind him, and he heard their footfalls on the deck. But with his eyes closed and his senses grounded, the falling sensation wasn't there at all.

He opened his eyes. Through the wide forward viewport, between the weblike support braces, the hyperspace tunnel soared and shone. And once again, Ellis was dropping down into a pit of blue light.

"Dammit," he muttered, very quietly.

Major Meyers glanced up from the weapons console, one eyebrow raised. "Sir?"

In response, he just nodded curtly at her panel. Meyers' attention hastily returned to the firing solution she'd been working on.

She hadn't looked up at the viewport, Ellis noticed. In fact, she'd tilted her head, almost unconsciously, as if to avoid looking at it.

Did she feel it as well?

Ellis had heard of the phenomenon, but he'd always dismissed it up until now. Something that civilians might experience, perhaps, or the kind of mess-hall backtalk that went around when the ship was on a long haul and the usual bitching about drills and shore leave was wearing thin. As far as he was aware, there wasn't even a name for it.

Just a feeling that some people had, when looking too hard and too long at the hyperspace tunnel effect, that it either tilted up towards the heavens or dipped right down to the depths of Hell.

Ellis shook himself, angry at his own weakness, and got up. It was nothing, just a failure of perspective, a trick of the eye. Nothing that should be on his mind now, not when he was flying his ship into the middle of a war. "ETA?"

"Seventeen minutes," Kyle Deacon reported from the helm.

"Good. Meyers, get me the bomb bay. No..." He frowned. "Second thoughts, I'll head down there myself. Give McKay a scare."

"Yessir. I'll call you before we break out."

He walked past her console to get to the hatchway, and as he did, leaned down and tipped his head towards the viewport. "What do you think?" he breathed. "Up or down?"

"Down sir," she replied, eyes fixed steadily on her readouts. "Definitely down."

Out in the lightless gulfs of space, two great powers coiled around each other like monstrous serpents. And, like monsters, they fought and tore.

A week before, Ellis had watched the blood of the two serpents spread across Colonel Carter's starmap in a series of vivid splashes: a brilliant, icy blue for the Wraith, a gory scarlet for the Asurans. Each splash, Carter had told him, was the site of a known engagement. Between these battle markers lay the serpents themselves, twisting wildly through each other in three dimensions – an approximation of the two powers' battle lines.

The whole map, in fact, was an approximation, and therein lay the danger of it. "Most of this information is days old," Carter had told him, pointing vaguely at a cluster of splashes. "At best we find out about one of these engagements a few hours after it's over and done. Really, we've got no idea exactly where the fighting is going on."

Ellis had peered closely at the map, a gnawing feeling of worry under his sternum. Carter had scaled the display to take in dozens of star systems, and already half of them were enveloped by the serpents and their terrible wounds. "Is there anything you can be certain of?"

"Just this." Carter had touched a control, and a small green dot had blinked into life in the centre of the display.

"Let me guess." Ellis straightened up. "Atlantis."

Carter nodded. "Trying to get a true picture of events over these kinds of distances is hard. Information travelling at C or below means that simultaneity is bunk – you can't tell if two things are happening at the same time because in relativistic terms there's no such thing as the same time. And information above C, like gate or hyperspace travel, plays havoc with event ordering."

"So we're screwed." Ellis rubbed his chin, still glaring at the map. "We can't get a true picture of what's going on, and what we don't know could kill us."

"Yeah," Carter said grimly. "If the Wraith find out where Atlantis is, they'll swarm us. If the Replicators find out, they'll do worse. The city's long range sensors are great at picking up moving objects, but as for what those objects are doing... Right now I feel like a kid caught up in a bar fight, hiding under the table. I can hear pool cues on heads, but I don't dare stick my own head out to see where the danger is."

Ellis had been in a few bar fights in his time, although he had normally been wielding the cue. "But McKay says he's got a plan?"

"Hasn't he always?" Carter had smiled at him, briefly. "He's gone all retro on us. A series of early-warning sensors, dropped into these systems here..." She touched another key and a chain of yellow dots flared into life and started pulsing. The map turned around on itself, stars swimming past each other as the galaxy rotated about the Atlantis marker, and Ellis could see how the yellow dots were spread evenly around it; close to, but never quite touching, the two serpents. "The sensors are stealthy – scanner absorbent, mostly passive... They spread out to form VLAs, then communicate with their relays through narrow-beam communications lasers. That's old technology, but they'll be pretty hard to spot."

"And they send data back to Atlantis via subspace?"

"Yes, but only through an encoded network. Basically a lot of dummies, really short messages and some fancy coding." She tapped the map's surface. "If anything bad happens within three light-years, we'll know about it thirty minutes later."

Ellis had nodded, lost in thought. "Not bad... Although if something did pop in your backyard, what would you do? Move the city again?"

Carter had given him a lost look. "That's the part we haven't worked out yet."

Series number: SGA-7

STARGATE ATLANTIS: CASUALTIES OF WAR

by Elizabeth Christensen
Price: £6.99 UK | $7.95 US | $9.95 Canada
ISBN-10: 1-905586-06-X
ISBN-13: 978-1-905586-06-6

It is a dark time for Atlantis. In the wake of the Asuran takeover, Colonel Sheppard is buckling under the strain of command. When his team discover Ancient technology which can defeat the Asuran menace, he is determined that Atlantis must possess it—at all costs. But the involvement of Atlantis heightens local suspicions and brings two peoples to the point of war. Elizabeth Weir believes only her negotiating skills can hope to prevent the carnage, but when her diplomatic mission is attacked—and two of Sheppard's team are lost—both Weir and Sheppard must question their decisions. And their abilities to command. As the first shots are fired, the Atlantis team must find a way to end the conflict—or live with the blood of innocents on their hands...

STARGATE ATLANTIS: BLOOD TIES

by Sonny Whitelaw & Elizabeth Christensen
Price: £6.99 UK | $7.95 US | $9.95 Canada
ISBN-10: 1-905586-08-6
ISBN-13: 978-1-905586-08-0

Series number: SGA-8

When a series of gruesome murders are uncovered around the world, the trail leads back to the SGC—and far beyond. Recalled to Stargate Command, Dr. Elizabeth Weir, Colonel John Sheppard, and Dr. Rodney McKay are shown shocking video footage—a Wraith attack, taking place on Earth. While McKay, Teyla, and Ronon investigate the disturbing possibility that humans may harbor Wraith DNA, Colonel Sheppard is teamed with SG-1's Dr. Daniel Jackson. Together, they follow the murderers' trail from Colorado Springs to the war-torn streets of Iraq, and there, uncover a terrifying truth... As an ancient cult prepares to unleash its deadly plot against humankind, Sheppard's survival depends on his questioning of everything believed about the Wraith...

STARGATE ATLANTIS: EXOGENESIS

by Sonny Whitelaw & Elizabeth Christensen
Price: £6.99 UK | $7.95 US | $9.95 Canada
ISBN-10: 1-905586-02-7
ISBN-13: 978-1-905586-02-8

When Dr. Carson Beckett disturbs the rest of two long-dead Ancients, he unleashes devastating consequences of global proportions. With the very existence of Lantea at risk, Colonel John Sheppard leads his team on a desperate search for the long lost Ancient device that could save Atlantis. While Teyla Emmagan and Dr. Elizabeth Weir battle the ecological meltdown consuming their world, Colonel Sheppard, Dr. Rodney McKay and Dr. Zelenka travel to a world created by the Ancients themselves. There they discover a human experiment that could mean their salvation. But the truth is never as simple as it seems, and the team's prejudices lead them to make a fatal error—an error that could slaughter thousands, including their own Dr. McKay.

STARGATE ATLANTIS: ENTANGLEMENT

by Martha Wells
Price: £6.99 UK | $7.95 US | $9.95 Canada
ISBN-10: 1-905586-03-5
ISBN-13: 978-1-905586-03-5

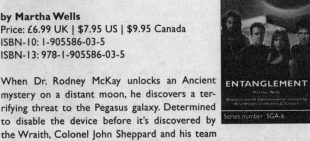

When Dr. Rodney McKay unlocks an Ancient mystery on a distant moon, he discovers a terrifying threat to the Pegasus galaxy. Determined to disable the device before it's discovered by the Wraith, Colonel John Sheppard and his team navigate the treacherous ruins of an Ancient outpost. But attempts to destroy the technology are complicated by the arrival of a stranger — a stranger who can't be trusted, a stranger who needs the Ancient device to return home. Cut off from backup, under attack from the Wraith, and with the future of the universe hanging in the balance, Sheppard's team must put aside their doubts and step into the unknown. However, when your mortal enemy is your only ally, betrayal is just a heartbeat away…

STARGATE ATLANTIS: THE CHOSEN

by Sonny Whitelaw & Elizabeth Christensen
Price: £6.99 UK | $7.95 US | $9.95 Canada
ISBN-10: 0-9547343-8-6
ISBN-13: 978-0-9547343-8-1

With Ancient technology scattered across the Pegasus galaxy, the Atlantis team is not surprised to find it in use on a world once defended by Dalera, an Ancient who was cast out of her society for falling in love with a human. But in the millennia since Dalera's departure much has changed. Her strict rules have been broken, leaving her people open to Wraith attack. Only a few of the Chosen remain to operate Ancient technology vital to their defense and tensions are running high. Revolution simmers close to the surface. When Major Sheppard and Rodney McKay are revealed as members of the Chosen, Daleran society convulses into chaos. Wanting to help resolve the crisis and yet refusing to prop up an autocratic regime, Sheppard is forced to act when Teyla and Lieutenant Ford are taken hostage by the rebels...

STARGATE ATLANTIS: HALCYON

by James Swallow
Price: £6.99 UK | $7.95 US | $9.95 Canada
ISBN-10: 1-905586-01-9
ISBN-13: 978-1-905586-01-1

In their ongoing quest for new allies, Atlantis's flagship team travel to Halcyon, a grim industrial world where the Wraith are no longer feared—they are hunted. Horrified by the brutality of Halcyon's warlike people, Lieutenant Colonel John Sheppard soon becomes caught in the political machinations of Halcyon's aristocracy. In a feudal society where strength means power, he realizes the nobles will stop at nothing to ensure victory over their rivals. Meanwhile, Dr. Rodney McKay enlists the aid of the ruler's daughter to investigate a powerful Ancient structure, but McKay's scientific brilliance has aroused the interest of the planet's most powerful man—a man with a problem he desperately needs McKay to solve. As Halcyon plunges into a catastrophe of its own making the team must join forces with the warlords—or die at the hands of their bitterest enemy...

Series number: SG1-9:

STARGATE SG-1: ROSWELL

by Sonny Whitelaw & Jennifer Fallon
Price: $7.95 US | $9.95 Canada | £6.99 UK
ISBN-10: 1-905586-04-3
ISBN-13: 978-1-905586-04-2

When a Stargate malfunction throws Colonel Cameron Mitchell, Dr. Daniel Jackson, and Colonel Sam Carter back in time, they only have minutes to live. But their rescue, by an unlikely duo — General Jack O'Neill and Vala Mal Doran — is only the beginning of their problems. Ordered to rescue an Asgard also marooned in 1947, SG-1 find themselves at the mercy of history. While Jack, Daniel, Sam and Teal'c become embroiled in the Roswell aliens conspiracy, Cam and Vala are stranded in another timeline, desperately searching for a way home. As the effects of their interference ripple through time, the consequences for the future are catastrophic. Trapped in the past, SG-1 can only watch as their world is overrun by a terrible invader…

STARGATE SG-1: RELATIVITY

Series number: SG1-10

by James Swallow
Price: $7.95 US | $9.95 Canada | £6.99 UK
ISBN-10: 1-905586-07-8
ISBN-13: 978-1-905586-07-3

When SG-1 encounter the Pack—a nomadic space-faring people who have fled Goa'uld domination for generations—it seems as though a trade of technologies will benefit both sides. But someone is determined to derail the deal. With the SGC under attack, and Vice President Kinsey breathing down their necks, it's up to Colonel Jack O'Neill and his team to uncover the saboteur and save the fledgling alliance. But unbeknownst to SG-1 there are far greater forces at work—a calculating revenge that spans decades, and a desperate gambit to prevent a cataclysm of epic proportions. When the identity of the saboteur is revealed, O'Neill is faced with a horrifying truth and is forced into an unlikely alliance in order to fight for Earth's future.

STARGATE SG-1: SURVIVAL OF THE FITTEST

by Sabine C. Bauer
Price: $7.95 US | $9.95 Canada | £6.99 UK
ISBN-10: 0-9547343-9-4
ISBN-13: 978-0-9547343-9-8

Colonel Frank Simmons has never been a friend to SG-1. Working for the shadowy government organisation, the NID, he has hatched a horrifying plan to create an army as devastatingly effective as that of any Goa'uld. And he will stop at nothing to fulfil his ruthless ambition, even if that means forfeiting the life of the SGC's Chief Medical Officer, Dr. Janet Fraiser. But Simmons underestimates the bond between Stargate Command's officers. When Fraiser, Major Samantha Carter and Teal'c disappear, Colonel Jack O'Neill and Dr. Daniel Jackson are forced to put aside personal differences to follow their trail into a world of savagery and death. In this complex story of revenge, sacrifice and betrayal, SG-1 must endure their greatest ordeal…

STARGATE SG-1: ALLIANCES

by Karen Miller
Price: $7.95 US | $9.95 Canada |
£6.99 UK
ISBN-10: 1-905586-00-0
ISBN-13: 978-1-905586-00-4

All SG-1 wanted was technology to save Earth from the Goa'uld … but the mission to Euronda was a terrible failure. Now the dogs of Washington are baying for Jack O'Neill's blood—and Senator Robert Kinsey is leading the pack. When Jacob Carter asks General Hammond for SG-1's participation in mission for the Tok'ra, it seems like the answer to O'Neill's dilemma. The secretive Tok'ra are running out of hosts. Jacob believes he's found the answer—but it means O'Neill and his team must risk their lives infiltrating a Goa'uld slave breeding farm to recruit humans willing to join the Tok'ra. It's a risky proposition … especially since the fallout from Euronda has strained the team's bond almost to breaking. If they can't find a way to put their differences behind them, they might not make it home alive…